The Sun on Their Backs

To Wendy

with best wishes from

Linda Anne Baker

The Sun on Their Backs

Linda Anne Baker

© Linda Anne Baker, 2015

Published by Seamless Publishing

Except for historical political figures, the characters in this novel are entirely fictional. Lundby is a fictional village, though a few landscapes have been respectfully borrowed and may be recognisable to some readers.

A CIP catalogue record for this book is available from the British Library.

ISBN 978-0-9932557-0-0

Book layout and cover design by Clare Brayshaw

Cover images © Goodwinx, Miramisska, Rrodrickbeiler
www.Dreamstime.com

Prepared and printed by:

York Publishing Services Ltd
64 Hallfield Road
Layerthorpe
York YO31 7ZQ

Tel: 01904 431213

Website: www.yps-publishing.co.uk

Dedication

For the grandfather I never knew,
William Leonard Baker, who died as a result
of a fall of coal in 1924.

For my beloved Mum,
Margaret Cowling 25.12.1922 – 3.11.2014

Acknowledgements

I owe a debt of gratitude to:

Sophie Hampton, for friendship, patience, encouragement, writerly suggestions and honest criticism.

Steve Brunt, former Business Development Manager at Northern College, Barnsley, and former Derbyshire miner, for his hospitality, time and account of the Battle of Orgreave and his own story of a career path after the strike.

Norman Strike for permission to use stories from his strike blog.

Miners and their families who shared their stories freely on the BBC website *On This Day*.

Tim Baxter and Stuart Morgan for police anecdotes.

Cathy Vicars for encouragement as reader of the first draft.

Rebecca Stirrup for encouragement and advice.

Mike Bird and the members of the Erstwhile Borders writing group in Leeds for friendship and faith in the story.

The Seven Quills writing group at Sheffield Hallam University for Wednesday workshops.

My husband for encouragement and support.

Other sources

Quotation from the poem: *Prayer Before Birth* by Louis MacNeice (1944)

The Enemy Within by Seamus Milne (Verso, 2004 third edition)

Marching to the Fault Line by Francis Beckett and David Hencke (Constable, London, 2009)

Strike By Name by Norman Strike (Bookmarks, 2009)

Barnsley Conference to mark 25 years since the end of the strike. (Northern College, June 2010)

Contents

Prologue

April 17th 2013
South Yorkshire

It's mid afternoon. The streets of a former mining village are filled with those who seek closure, those who are angry, those who are jubilant, with television crews, journalists and the simply curious. Spectators cheer as a Scottish piper approaches at the head of a procession in which a horse-drawn cart is carrying an effigy of Margaret Thatcher in an open coffin. Union banners and cardboard placards punch the air.

A girl filming a documentary pushes through the crowd, instructing camera to follow. She calls to an elderly man with a toddler in his arms and beckons him to the microphone. 'What do you say to people who think that a mock-funeral is disrespectful?' she asks. 'Isn't it time to forget?'

'Thatcher robbed us of everything,' the man says. 'There were no fresh jobs here after the pit closed.'

'What about the children? Surely they're too young to understand?'

The child makes a grab for the microphone.

'The strike's in their blood.' The man has to shout to be heard. 'This is my grandson. What future is there for youngsters? This village used to be a thriving community. It's nearly thirty years since the strike and yet... well look around you.'

'Do you think...' but voices are drowned by car horns, by cheering and applause, and the man and his grandson disappear into the throng.

The camera pans along a row of terraced houses where it's clear no one has lived for some time. Shop windows are boarded and fading graffiti defaces the doors and walls.

The girl and the cameraman follow the procession to the waste ground, past the remains of a demolished building where spikes of grass reclaim the earth between scattered bricks. Pall bearers off-load the make-shift coffin and construct a bonfire. Flames leap; the effigy burns, fireworks spew fountains of orange and blue; beer cans fizz in celebration amid banter, laughter and jeers. A boy jumps in front of the camera, waves then sticks out his tongue. Cheeks flush in the heat from the pyre.

At dusk the crew pack the film equipment into the van.

'Happy with that?' the cameraman asks.

'It's a good start,' she says.

'Did you say you were brought up in this area?'

'Further south. My Dad was a miner though.' She settles in the driver's seat, adjusts the rear view mirror. 'I was born just after the strike.'

The man laughs. 'I see,' he says, climbing in beside her.

'See what?'

'Not biased then?'

'Professional, I hope.'

'Who would have thought it? Our fearless director is a child of the strike. *Strike Babies, the movie*,' he says, adopting a phoney American accent. 'Good title, don't you think?'

'Idiot,' she says and cuffs his arm.

'So what *did* Daddy do in the strike then?'

'I'll introduce you. Think he's in need of company right now.'

She glances over her shoulder at the waste ground. The wind flips empty cans, flaps rogue sheets of newspaper, fanning the embers of the bonfire. Discarded carrier bags rise like white kites and float away over roof-tops.

The girl puts the van into gear and heads for the motorway.

Part One

When you do dance, I wish you
A wave o' th' sea that you might ever do
Nothing but that.

Shakespeare: A Winter's Tale

Chapter One

A Slaughtered Lamb

March 4th 1984

London

When she heard his key in the lock she froze for a second. Guy was early.

He strode into the kitchen, unravelling swathes of tissue paper from two bottles of claret. 'Can I smell smoke, Helen? You do know that lamb should be pink?'

She switched off the oven. 'I've made your favourite—

'Good,' he said, casting her a sideways glance as he opened a bottle. The cork popped. He sniffed it. 'Let that breathe while I take a shower. Jack and Celia will be here soon. Make sure there's a bottle of white chilling and put some music on will you?' He closed the kitchen door behind him. Of late Guy closed doors as if they were never meant to open again.

She slipped through the archway into the dining room, set the table with the wedding present cutlery and napkins, not much used since they'd lived in London.

Celia. Now there was a woman. Accomplished hostess, competent cook and a model MP's wife; Celia could pick a dahlia from the garden, add a twig of greenery and create an arrangement fit for the Chelsea flower show. Not a friend exactly but kind enough. Helen admired Celia's self-assurance, envied her the comfort in her own skin. Nothing worried Celia. She might pop a pound into a charity box but never question why a box was necessary in the first place. But then, wasn't class something you inherited and had little choice about? And Jack? He knew how to charm, had been something in the city before becoming an MP; still had irons in business fires. If Guy wanted to impress Jack, why hadn't he booked a restaurant?

She placed a basket of French bread on the table and lit a dinner candle.

Music. What would Guy's golden couple appreciate? Earlier she'd been listening to a radio programme devoted to Abba, foot tapping; a little dancing in the kitchen—as far as space would allow. *Dancing Queen*. Anything to distract from preparing for a dinner party. *Money, money, money.* Upwardly Mobile. Wasn't that the latest expression?

Guy wouldn't appreciate Abba.

Jazz? Blues? Classical then? Certain Beethoven couldn't offend she chose the Emperor Concerto, set it on the turntable and poured herself a glass of sherry from a decanter on the bookcase. Her eye was drawn to a dusty piece of rock used as a bookend, a lump of chalk, a worthless souvenir, a silly memento she'd meant to discard but found she couldn't. She remembered the day she'd collected it from an east coast beach. It was a wonder it hadn't disintegrated after so many years. She gazed at her reflection in the glass doors of the drinks cabinet. What did the little black dress say about her? That she had no idea what else to wear or she'd forgotten her true colours?

Guy had showered, changed into chinos and a cream shirt, his rolled cuffs revealing a gold Patek Phillipe watch which dazzled in candlelight. In his twenties Guy too had dazzled: dark hair, an easy smile, his sharkskin suits. Ten years on he was leaner, gaunt, taut as if he might snap. 'Not a peck on him,' her aunt would say.

He marched to the Hi Fi, removed the Beethoven, cradling the vinyl between his palms–he was always careful not to leave his prints–and replaced the strings of the Emperor with a Miles Davis album: the wail of a trumpet, the squeal of a saxophone.

'Friends to dinner, darling – informal,' he said. 'Not *Last night of the bloody Proms*. And please. Try not to interrupt the politics tonight.'

It was months since they'd discussed anything, let alone politics.

At seven, the doorbell rang.

'What a lovely apartment,' Celia said, peering from the hall into the galley kitchen. It boasted oak units, down lighting, integral dish washer and the latest black ceramic cooker. 'Open plan too. Very trendy.' The French windows in the lounge-diner led to a balcony with a peep of the river if you leaned out far enough. 'Bound to be a gold mine in the future.'

'An expedient buy,' Guy said. 'We needed to find somewhere quickly in the circumstances. Always meant to be temporary. Not quite in the same league as your Edwardian pile though.'

'You should come over to lunch, Helen.' Celia said. 'You look peaky. Stuck here all day on your own is doing you no good. It's not that far to Richmond. Not seen a glimpse of you, since New Year's Eve.'

Helen blushed. 'Sorry. We've been slow to invite anyone.'

'Thought your uncle must have kidnapped you,' Jack said, 'carried you off to Yorkshire.' He kissed Helen's cheek.

'The bugger would love that,' Guy said. 'Let me get you a drink.'

Guy had insisted he'd found the perfect apartment: small but convenient, and just thirty minutes' drive from his newly acquired constituency. Uncle Billy had been less than approving. 'You can buy two houses in the north for the price of a 'posh flat' in London,' he'd said. 'Anyway, isn't it the wrong time to move?'

'Flat? It's an apartment, Uncle Billy. Besides, you of all people should understand, you have to move with the job.'

'It certainly has everything. Everything but room to dance.'

Celia slipped out of a silver fur jacket. 'Your uncle sounds a card, Helen. Though I have to admit Guy's little flat cap speech on New Year's Eve did make me giggle. Quite the party piece.'

'It was meant to be a generic union man. Not Billy exactly,' Guy said, leading the way into the dining room and leaving Helen to hang up coats. 'My wife didn't get the joke.'

Helen was grateful Celia's jacket smelled of Chanel no 5 rather than dead fox. The generic union man explanation was Guy's defence when they'd arrived home from the party, when Helen said his slur had embarrassed her. A fake speech to *comrades*. He'd even costumed his monologue with a checked cap. It was without doubt a cruel parody of Uncle Billy and a poke at her upbringing. Uncle Billy had been a loyal union man, a man of principle. Hadn't Guy started out in politics with the same intentions? *To make a difference*? Not the same colour party admittedly, but Uncle Billy didn't deserve to be caricatured, lampooned.

'You must miss the family,' Celia called.

Yes she missed them. Uncle Billy's Dean Martin singing in the bathroom; the smell of his once-a-week dab of

Old Spice aftershave; his slow fox-trotting of an imaginary partner across the kitchen–a performance which never failed to make her laugh. She missed Tibby: her aunt's silly soft shoe shuffle on the vinyl floor between the cooker and the sink when she was preparing a meal. There was always dancing. What Helen didn't miss was Uncle Billy's habit of claiming the last word on a subject, any subject. The only characteristic he shared with Guy.

'Haven't seen much of them lately,' Helen said, delivering a platter of smoked salmon to the table.

The subject of politics unfolded early with talk of miners, pit closures and the prospect of strike. How could Guy expect her to have no opinion? Eventually, emboldened by a glass of wine, Helen set down her cutlery, having eaten little more than a few vegetables.

'I think the miners have a good case,' she said, 'Whole villages and towns could lose their livelihoods.' Guy bit his lip as he opened another bottle of claret; she noticed his hands trembled as he refilled Jack's glass.

'If miners are always moaning about how wretched the job is they should be happy to have a few pits closed, surely,' Celia said, glancing from Helen to Guy.

'What would you know about the working classes, Celia?' Jack said, rolling his eyes. 'The nearest you ever got to hard graft, my love, was grooming your pony.' Despite the knot in her stomach Helen laughed.

Guy reached across the table, patted Celia's hand. 'Don't listen, Celia. I'm with you. Miners chose the bloody job.' He scraped the lamb aside. 'See you've cremated the meat again, Helen.'

Jack winked at Celia. 'You didn't tell us you were married to a subversive, Guy. Helen's your very own *red under the bed*. Don't introduce her to the Blessed Margaret

5

or the Lady will have your bollocks on one of your miner's shovels.'

'Do miners still use shovels then?' Celia said, leaning into Jack.

'So we sacrifice thousands of decent families,' Helen said, 'to satisfy Mrs. Thatcher's thirst for union blood?'

Beneath the table Guy squeezed her hand, crushing her finger nails into the soft flesh of her palm. 'I seem to remember, darling,' he said, 'that when we married you were quite happy to be rescued from the sacred slagheaps.'

'Children, children,' Jack said, tapping a spoon on his wine glass. 'I sympathise, Helen. But it's a simple question of economics. The country can't afford to keep pits open that don't pay.'

'Economics?' Helen said. 'Are you sure it's not revenge?'

'Pure market forces. And don't worry. I'm used to my meat *brulée*, aren't I, Celia?' Jack cupped his wife's chin. 'Only teasing.'

'Then, I'm sorry,' Helen said. 'I think the whole thing stinks.'

Jack laughed. 'I love a firebrand.'

Guy tossed her hand aside. 'If they've got any sense the miners will see through Scargill, not follow him like bleating sheep.'

'Baa-aa. Lambs to the slaughter, eh?' Jack said, examining the piece of meat on his fork. 'I'll drink to that.' He grinned.

Celia yawned. 'Politics can be so boring. That black dress you're wearing is very flattering, Helen. I was in Selfridges today, spotted a gorgeous little *all in one*. Flying suits, they're calling them. All the rage. You're the right shape. No good for my bum, but they'd suit you. You're enviably thin. No dessert for me by the way.'

'Nor me,' Guy said, curling his lip. 'I've seen it.'

Jack shook his head. 'Nothing wrong with your bum, Celia. Or your dessert, Helen, I'm sure.' He patted his stomach. 'But not for me either, thank you.'

Guy pushed his chair from the table. 'What you should realise, my friends, is that nothing suits my wife.' After pouring generous measures of whisky into two tumblers, he opened the French doors. A blast of cold air snaked Helen's ankles.

The men withdrew to the balcony, carrying cigars and drinks. Searching for an ash tray, Guy returned briefly, but finding none to hand, he scooped up the chalk from the bookcase. 'This will do. It's got holes.'

'Like my socks eh, Celia?' Jack called.

Celia didn't reply. She was trailing Helen into the kitchen, completing her fashion report. Helen dropped the chocolate cheesecake into the bin.

★ ★ ★

It was after midnight. No sooner had the guests left and the deadlocks on the front door clicked, than Guy's farewell smile had faded.

Helen and Guy stood in the hall, Guy examining the makeshift ashtray, cradling it in one hand. The heating had cut out an hour ago and the apartment was chilly.

'Better start the dishwasher,' she said.

'Is that all you've got to say for yourself?'

Without warning he leapt forward, jabbing a finger into the top of her arm. 'Hypocritical bitch! You think you can humiliate me?' His face in her face, his breath reeking of red wine and single malt.

With one fist he knuckled her shoulder. Push, push, into the kitchen. 'I told you to keep out of the politics. But you had to have your say, didn't you? You're not a wife; you're a bloody liability.' Before she could answer he tossed the rock into the air. It rose and fell as if in slow motion, fracturing a floor tile as it landed and smashed.

Hoping a simple act of domestic routine might deter him, she turned from his ranting towards the dishwasher, but he spun her round.

'Don't you dare turn away from me,' he said, his eyes flashing, a gob of spittle at the corner of his lips.

She flinched, a second's anticipation before his slap buckled her knees and she fell against the fridge and onto the floor. 'Why do you do it for Christ's sake?' he shouted, then he slunk off to bed, kicking a kitchen stool out of his way as a parting gesture.

The French-doors had been left open: she could hear the hinges creaking. She watched a spider as it crawled through a joint in the black plinth below a base cupboard; it left one long hair-breadth leg exposed before drawing it after its body and into the dark.

She fingered her cheek. White dust, stale ash and the burnt stubs of four cigars littered the tiles. Her dress was soiled. She should get up. Get up. She clung to the stool, dragged herself to her feet, picked up the pieces of chalk. As if somehow the halves might fuse and reverse time she fitted them together –then dropped them into the bin where, contrary to the solid thud she expected, they soft landed on the cheesecake.

She stumbled to the sitting room, took refuge on the sofa, curling her legs beneath her like the spider and counting the hours struck by a doleful, distant Big Ben.

Nausea, uncontrollable shivering. More wretched than last time … the first time … after the New Year's Eve party. After the argument about Uncle Billy, when she'd told Guy to go to bed, he was drunk. She remembered the whisky spilling down his shirt when he slapped her.

She buried her face in a cushion.

Slap. Just a four letter word, a stinging blow from an open hand. But this was her husband's hand.

At seven a.m. she heard the pipes in the bathroom clanking. She held her breath. Wardrobe doors juddered. The front door banged. Windows rattled.

Guy had a meeting in Westminster.

When she'd showered she dressed in a sweater he'd bought her last birthday and a pair of denim jeans. There was a feeling she couldn't articulate, evident in her hunched reflection in the mirror. A smaller self, perhaps? She applied foundation to mask a blossoming bruise. What time would he be back? Maybe after the meeting. House business didn't start till eleven-thirty and he might return before then. What if he'd had time to find more drink? He might keep a bottle of vodka in his desk drawer, it left no evidence on his breath. She stroked the sleeves of her sweater. Guy always bought quality. Cashmere: as soft to the touch as a baby's blanket. She checked the time; she was late. She didn't want to let down a friend.

She packed an overnight bag then wrote a note which she left on Guy's pillow.

★ ★ ★

Exhaust fumes from buses and cabs tainted the air, leaving a carbon taste on Guy's tongue. Despite the aspirin breakfast burning his stomach, his headache had not eased. He would have to face Jack at the committee meeting this morning. Guy unfastened the top button of his overcoat, clutched the briefcase across his chest.

A wedding car passed him on the Embankment. It was empty but decked with a fluttering of white ribbons it trailed an air of optimism and excitement that offended him. He didn't need reminders of happy marriages, but he found them all the same: in cheers on the steps of Town Halls, in flower stalls and city-centre church bells and even in Jack and Celia's sickening displays of affection. He flung the briefcase onto a bench and flopped beside it, his gaze following the river as it slipped beneath the bridge.

He remembered his wedding day all too well, the scene had often replayed in his head recently: Helen's delayed entrance to the church, her faltering vows at the altar, her uncle's sarcasm and insults at the reception. Swaggering with the bravado supplied by a few pints of bitter, Billy had drawn Guy aside.

'I'm drowning my sorrows, young man. Can't believe my lovely niece has married into the opposition. Guy Bartholomew Eagleton? It has a ring to it, I'll give you that. But Bartholomew? You kept that quiet.'

'My mother's maiden name,' Guy said, glancing around to locate Helen. She was parading between tables, the way brides do, the lace too heavy to swish.

'No offence but you know you've no chance round here, don't you?' Billy said. 'Folks'd rather vote for a chimpanzee than a Tory. I'd try for a seat in the Home Counties if I were you.' Billy laughed—he always laughed at his own jokes—and Guy allowed the coughing which followed to subside before he answered.

'What seat? I'm only a candidate for a local council, like you, Billy. And I've no intention of living in Yorkshire. We'll be staying in Cheshire for the foreseeable future.'

Billy nodded. 'I know. I'm just pulling your leg. You're a sharp lad and you've got the gift of the gab. You've certainly charmed Helen. I think you could do it. Get into parliament, I mean.'

There was no chance of charming Billy.

Guy's eyes strayed to Billy's shoes–brand new shoes, probably with the price tag still on the sole–and then settled on his throat. The cravat needed tightening. 'That's a strange endorsement, Billy. I'm not sure whether to be flattered or insulted.'

'The power of oration is a gift, Guy,' Billy said, sidling closer then sucking on his pipe. 'Even though you talk tripe.' Guy's grip tightened on his champagne flute. Billy grinned, poking Guy's arm with the pipe stem. 'Your party will need somebody sharp, now we've kicked 'em out of office and got rid of Ted Heath.' Billy spluttered and his face suffused with colour; he coughed and thumped his chest. 'Dust! You know how it is.'

'Shite!' Guy said, out of the corner of his mouth.

'Maybe Guy. But "shite" you'll not easily shift!' And with a final nod of satisfaction Billy had shuffled away to join the toddlers on the dance floor.

Approaching the House, Guy noticed a flower seller on the corner. Just a teenager with almost colourless lips, her eyes circled in shades of purple, like the girls he passed in the cardboard box world of Kings Cross. Perhaps he should buy a bouquet on his way home, perhaps not. He couldn't allow his wife to undermine him and he shouldn't pander to her– though he'd vowed not to strike her again and he'd failed. Guilt and palpitation fought for equal attention and he tried to ignore both.

A few members had already taken their seats in the committee chamber by the time he arrived but he spotted Jack beckoning, indicating an adjacent chair. 'It was a lovely evening last night, Guy. We must return the compliment.'

'Thanks.' Guy took a sheaf of papers from his briefcase.

'Listen. I'm sorry about Helen's outburst. She was very contrite this morning; said to give you her apologies. Too much to drink.'

Jack frowned. 'I only saw her with the one glass. Why should she apologise? She's allowed an opinion. It's not as if the press are hounding back benchers' wives for quotes, is it?' Jack looked around. 'What we were discussing last night is a complicated issue. And anyway, it was a private conversation between friends. No harm done. We like Helen. And you were too hard on her.'

Guy loosened his tie, undid the top button of his shirt and poured himself a glass of water. When the committee chairman peered over half-rimmed spectacles like a headmaster viewing the day's playground culprits, Jack lowered his voice. 'Let's face it; there are a few moderates in our own ranks who are a little uncomfortable with—'

'*Wets!*' Guy spat.

The remaining seats had been taken. Jack scanned the agenda. 'Relax. I've been here a few years longer than you have. Learned to prioritise. Why should you worry? There's not a miner in sight in your constituency, so don't let this business gnaw your innards.'

Guy sat upright, manoeuvred the chair nearer to the table. 'Are you telling me that you're against the energy policy?'

'There are equally important issues but you're making this one almost personal. I've been concerned about you, Guy. I know it was bound to be a difficult time for you and Helen after—'

'When's the old sod going to get this meeting started?' Guy took a sip of water.

A hush settled. Jack whispered. 'Take it from me: You shouldn't allow Arthur Scargill to sneak into the bedroom. He's not worth it.'

Though Guy detested Scargill, he could never accuse the man of lacking passion. Unlike Helen. Guy poised his pen above the minutes of the last meeting, circled the date, cleared his throat.

The chairman called the meeting to order.

Chapter Two

Omelettes and Potato Cakes

March 1984

London

In Trafalgar Square a handful of tourists sat with their backs to the stone lions, feeding the pigeons. A lone young man in a parka waved a protest placard but no one paid him much attention. Perhaps in Mrs. Thatcher's Britain people were too busy looking over their shoulders and at their feet. And no one seemed to be showing much interest in the monument.

It was only when Helen had bumped her head on the low beams of the *Victory* in Portsmouth harbour and discovered the Admiral's stained naval uniform in the museum that the story of Nelson had taken on meaning and she'd begun to understand the power of old bloodshed. She wondered if politicians learned anything from history.

Dodging the pigeons, she lugged the overnight bag up the steps to the National Gallery, hoping Isaac hadn't given up on her.

She'd first met him by chance a year ago, on a bench in front of *Renoir's Umbrellas*. Just an old man resting aching legs, she'd assumed, until he'd smiled and explained it was his favourite painting. Later in the crowded café he'd called her over to share his table, and striking up a friendship they'd been meeting here ever since; always first at the Renoir and then, after discussing the merits of further masterpieces, they'd head downstairs for lunch. She hadn't mentioned him to Guy.

When he spotted her, Isaac waved his trilby. 'You made it after all. Remind me. Did we agree on Canaletto today?'

She nudged the bag along with her foot until they stood in front of the painting of *Palazzo Grimani*. 'Guy and I went to Venice on our first wedding anniversary,' she said.

Isaac nodded to the bag. 'And where are you schlepping off to today, young lady?'

'I thought I might take a break on my own for a couple of days. Guy's so busy. Last minute decision. He doesn't mind.'

'A trip to Yorkshire?'

'Maybe. I've not really had time to decide.'

'In that case, why don't you come home with me this afternoon? We could take a trip on the river. That's if you have time, of course. While you make up your mind. I'd enjoy your company. Stay to dinner. Nothing elaborate. Do you like omelettes?'

She glanced at her watch, wondering if Guy was still at the House. She had time. Time was all she had.

★ ★ ★

They travelled to Greenwich by tourist boat. Helen shuddered as they passed the Tower of London and Traitor's gate. The sheer brutality of abandoning prisoners till the tide came in. Drowning them slowly. A faint recurrence of earlier panic fluttered at her throat. Isaac took her hand, rubbed it between his palms.

'You're cold, Helen.' She had forgotten gloves and scarf. 'Shall we go inside?'

'No. It's fine. I prefer to sit on deck.' Waves whipped by a sharp breeze slapped the sides of the vessel. At least she could breathe here, hold her face to a pale sun while listening to the captain's commentary. After almost two years in London she still had so many places to explore.

'Not quite a substitute for the Grand Canal,' Isaac said. 'But will this do?'

'Perfectly.'

Escape. Every ripple on the river, every throb of diesel engine, carried her further from Westminster.

Isaac's home was an early Victorian townhouse near to the park. He told her he enjoyed the proximity to the river, loved to gaze on the skyline and to stand on the meridian. 'It makes me feel like – what do they say? – I'm where it's at!' He fumbled in his coat pocket for the key to a Downing Street style front door painted regency blue, the house itself reminiscent of a safe haven for some unfortunate but grateful orphan in a Dickensian novel.

Once inside, Isaac hung her jacket alongside his own on a bentwood coat stand, dropped his hat and keys onto the hall table. The sun filtering through a fanlight above the door illuminated a polished chequered floor.

Isaac sniffed. 'That's good. My cleaner has been.'

Behind the beeswax the smells were of burnt toast and mustiness.

Along a corridor between two reception rooms, an open door offered a glimpse of an obsolete gas cooker on bowed metal legs and a yellow 1950s Formica cabinet. The kitchen was clearly in some need of refurbishment. 'It's a large house for you to maintain, Isaac. Full of character and original features though.'

'I suppose I should find something smaller but I like it. Solid. Modern buildings don't impress me: those neo-Georgian estates popping up in the suburbs.'

'At least they have more soul than sixties' tower blocks,' she said, following him along the passageway. 'Whoever thought that people could be rehoused from terraced street communities into boxes?'

'Agreed. Though community is not always confined to the streets we live in.'

She followed him into a high-ceilinged dining room decorated with William Morris style wallpaper. Daylight and time had leached colour from the velvet curtains and they hung in folds of patchy green.

'As for design,' he said, 'in Germany we had the Bauhaus. Cubes. To me, soulless. Though I think evil is in men's deeds, not in their art.'

'Maybe sometimes in both,' she said. He laughed.

In the midst of this faded elegance she was surprised to see Isaac lighting a coal-effect gas fire, though a rush of warm air and flame brought welcome instant heat.

'Necessity,' he said, tapping the modern fender as if reading her mind. 'Some things you can't fight. My arthritis is one of them.' Beneath the window, a tubular radiator ticked and clanked as it woke to its purpose.

There were family photographs on the mantelpiece and she tried to match faces to names he'd mentioned over recent months, in his stories of his life in 1930's Berlin.

'Even now,' he said, 'it's hard to believe they're gone.' He picked up a silver filigree frame from the side-board. Helen recognised a younger Isaac with a protective arm around a dark haired woman. The couple appeared to be sharing a joke. 'Miriam, my wife. About 1960,' he said. 'I was still practising as a lawyer then. Did I tell you my sons are in charge of the business now?'

He'd told her several times. 'I think you did.'

He ran a finger around Miriam's face. 'My Soul Mate.'

'She was pretty.'

'I'll put on some music, shall I?' he said. 'Hitler admired Wagner apparently. I don't bear a grudge against Wagner, but I've always preferred Rachmaninov.'

When he refused Helen's offer of help in the kitchen she settled in a fireside chair. A recording of Rachmaninov's second piano concerto crackled to life from the sitting room across the hall; crockery rattled, a kettle whistled.

The music lulled her into dozing but she woke with a start when Isaac bustled into the room with a tray of steaming soup. 'Here we are,' he said, placing bowls on the table. As if playing piano keys, he flexed his fingers to the trills of high notes.

'Oh, to be so talented,' he said.

'Do you play, Isaac?'

'No. But Miriam did. I sold the piano six years ago, after she died. The empty stool was a painful reminder.'

'When I was small Uncle Billy played. I used to sing while my aunt turned the sheet music. I knew all the words to songs from the shows.' Uncle Billy had called her his Little Songbird. 'The piano was an old, tinny contraption and eventually he chopped it up for firewood, but for a while it lay in the back garden with the front panel removed, and when Uncle Billy was out at work I danced on the strings.'

'I can imagine,' Isaac said. He drew a chair away from the table, tapped the seat. 'Chicken soup,' he said. 'A panacea for all ills – at least according to my grandmother.'

Helen took her place at the table. 'I love this piece. Haven't heard it for ages.'

Isaac flapped a linen napkin across her knee. 'A composer expressing his inner turmoil through beautiful melodies. Strange that such a genius should be wracked with self-doubt.'

The soup was thick and comforting, her first meal of the day since they'd decided to forego lunch in the gallery café. 'Tell me more about Miriam,' she said between sips.

'Some couples marry, settle for routine, but a Soul Mate is different.'

Helen wondered if Miriam had embellished the linen with its neat feather stitching and French knots, maybe at a time when a family would gather around a wireless set listening eagerly for news yet dreading the consequences. 'Do you really believe some people are made for each other?'

'Perhaps'

'You're an old romantic, Isaac! Look at the divorce rates.'

'And you're too young to be cynical.'

'Not that young. I'm thirty one.'

'A very old lady then.'

'When were you married?'

'1936. We fled from Berlin the same year, the rallies of Hitler and his speeches echoing behind us. Our families in Germany ignored the warnings, didn't imagine the unthinkable until it was too late. All murdered in Auschwitz. Our sons were born here in London. But you must have heard this story already. I forget when I repeat myself.'

'I never tire of listening,' she said.

The Rachmaninov rose to a crescendo.

After a dinner of omelettes, salad and latkes, Isaac set out china cups and poured coffee from a stainless steel percolator which spluttered on the sideboard, infusing the room with a strong aroma that reminded Helen of Sunday mornings in a happier past. The metal was scratched, brownish in patches and had lost its shine.

The old man seemed lost in thought. 'But let's talk about you,' he said suddenly. 'I've known you for months but you're still something of a mystery.'

Billy and Tibbys' hearth had glowed with real flames: unpredictable landscapes that flared cobalt blue if a pocket of coal gas was unleashed, or collapsed into a sea of ash. As a child she'd spent hours watching, imagining castles and fire-breathing dragons in underground caves. Artificial coals flickered with unnerving regularity. They held no stories or places to hide.

'Sometimes you... how shall I say?' Isaac said. 'You bring down the blinds.'

'I think you mean shutters.'

'You admit it then?'

She laughed. He often caught her out this way. 'I admit nothing.'

'But you are... guarded. Is that the word? Tell me why you're afraid to go home.'

He offered a cheeseboard and fruit. She thanked him but shook her head. 'I'm not afraid. It's just that ... Guy and I had a tiff. He supports the Government's case for pit closures. And I was defending the miners.'

'Understandable.'

'So it's good for us to have a little space for a few days.'

How could he understand what it was like to fear the person you slept with?

'Forgive me if I'm too bold,' he said. 'Age. I omit the niceties and try, as my grandsons say, to cut to the chase.' He chuckled, left the room, returned immediately with another photograph.

'Ah,' she said. 'The famous grandsons, Max and Solly.' The children were a welcome diversion.

'*Infamous* grandsons,' he said, pondering over the picture as if remembering some jape of the boys that he himself had indulged, or at least long since forgiven. 'Young men already. Fourteen and sixteen.' Had Isaac forgotten what he was cutting to the chase about? 'But we were talking about your husband,' he said. 'And I think he struck you. Am I right?' He stood the photograph on the table. 'Don't look so surprised. A swollen cheek, red eyes, your voice a little shaky. And you're carrying an overnight bag. Not exactly a *Poirot* mystery. Is this the first time?'

She hesitated. 'It was an accident.'

'I see.' Isaac swished the curtains along a brass pole as thick as a fist, cutting out the glare from a street lamp. 'Dusk. Too late to be wandering about the capital or running off to catch trains. I think you should stay here, at least for tonight.'

She agreed, thanked him, surprised at how easily she accepted his hospitality. Relief was palpable. She wondered if he noticed.

'Have there been other *accidents*?'

'It wasn't always like this,' she said, blinking away tears. 'Things changed after we came to London.'

'You expect politicians to beat their wives?'

She flinched. 'Of course not. He didn't intend—'

'What did he intend?'

'He seems so weighed down with responsibility.' She twisted her wedding ring. 'Guy grew up surrounded by farmers and understood country matters. He insisted the colour of your politics wasn't important in local issues. The crucial thing was what you achieved for your community. I admired that.'

'And that's why you married him? His devotion to community?'

'He only became a local councillor after we were married.'

Guy would think she'd fled to Yorkshire. He couldn't find her here. 'He was very charming,' she said. 'Different from... just different from other young men I'd known.'

'And what did your family think?' Isaac held out the coffee pot.

'Isaac, would you mind if I phone my uncle? I usually call once a week. If I don't, he'll phone the apartment. He'll worry.'

'Of course. I'll clear the table. The telephone's in the hall.' He took the tray from the sideboard and began loading it.

The voice of a television newscaster rose and fell to a background mumble, mingling with Tibby's soft mewling at Bevan, Billy's dog. Helen pictured the mongrel on her aunt's lap, looking as if he ruled the world when his ears were tickled. She'd been eager for the comfort of a familiar voice, but was tempted to hang up when Billy began ranting about the government stockpiling coal, the commitment to go nuclear and Margaret Thatcher's intentions for confrontation. It was as if he'd been waiting for Helen to call, rehearsing his speech.

'On this subject Scargill's right, Helen, though I might not like the man's style. What does Guy think?'

'He thinks it would be a mistake to take on Margaret Thatcher.' What did Billy expect a loyal supporter of the PM to think?

A sharp knocking startled her – probably Billy's knuckles rapping the telephone table. 'A mistake? Helen, somebody has to fight the woman.'

'I'm not saying I agree with Guy.'

Isaac had left the kitchen door open. He was washing up, his hands flapping in oversized rubber gloves.

'Do you think there'll be public sympathy?' she said. 'A lot of people believe trade unions have too much power,'

'That's what the government's banking on. Thatcher's out to smash unions in general and ours in particular.' Wasn't that what Helen had told Guy? 'Damn it. Tell Guy from me,' Billy said, 'it can't be right to have tons of coal underground and buy it from other countries.'

Billy's wheeze worsened as his exasperation grew. Sometimes she would hold the telephone at arm's length, dip in and out of his speeches and still understand the gist.

'... difficult for you to have an opinion,' he said. 'Whatever you... I might not see eye to eye... party politics...'

She waved to Isaac. He nodded and smiled. Billy continued. 'See Guy in the cabinet one day. Hope not while this damn woman...' He stopped.

The only cabinet Guy was into, housed vodka, whisky and assorted liqueurs.

'What's happened to your feminist principles?' Billy said. 'I thought you'd want to take me up on the woman Prime Minister topic. Or have you sold out completely?'

'Are you hankering for an argument?' she said. 'I was hardly a Pankhurst.'

Sold out, burned out. Maybe both.

Billy coughed. At least he'd ditched the pipe. 'I haven't seen you for months, Missy. I need a spot of sparring practice.'

'This time I'm on your side, Uncle Billy, but I'm too tired to argue.'

Isaac was drying crockery, then stacking it, clearly trying not to make a sound.

'Are you not well?' Billy asked. She lied, said she'd had a virus.

'Oh, and, just before you go, Helen, thought you'd want to know that Pavel Kowaleski's in the thick of it.'

'Pavel?'

'Yes. They've voted him local strike coordinator. Tib wants a word before you go.'

Tibby updated Helen on village news, said she was dragging Billy to a Latin American dance evening, away from constant news bulletins.

'Bye, Tibby.'

A click. A dialling tone.

Isaac led her across the hall into the sitting room. 'Would you like an aspirin for your virus?' Helen blushed. 'I didn't mean to eavesdrop, Helen. But Tibby? You talk to the cat?'

'Tibby's my aunt.'

'Ah yes. I remember. An unusual name.' He set the needle back to the beginning of the record and switched on Tiffany table lamps which cast a pinkish glow over the cream walls.

She settled on an ancient leather sofa, cushions sinking and sighing beneath her. 'I couldn't pronounce *Aunty Bea* when I was small so she became *Tibby.*'

'So tragic for a child to lose parents,' Isaac said, flopping into an armchair opposite Helen. 'Your father. A mining accident, you said?'

'A fall of coal. When I was two. My mother died of pneumonia soon after. Dad was Billy's younger brother and had no children of his own. Other kids had Mums and Dads. I had a Tibby and an Uncle Billy. I was always loved. Never felt deprived, you know.'

'On the contrary. I expect they doted on you. So you don't remember your parents?'

'Not really. I have their wedding photograph. What I remember is... night terrors and Tibby taking me into her bed.'

'And I heard you mention Pavel. An Eastern European name.' Isaac narrowed his eyes, raising his chin as if peeping from beneath a blindfold, like Helen had as a child cheating at Blind Man's Bluff.

'His parents were Polish. He's an old friend I haven't seen for years. Uncle Billy bumps into him occasionally. When I was a teenager, Uncle Billy and I were always embroiled in heated discussion. Political stuff mainly. I'd often slope away to listen to the Beatles to annoy him. Leave him lecturing an empty space.'

'With my sons it was always Elvis.' Isaac curled his top lip, sang. 'Uh Uh Uh.' He laughed. 'I digress. Continue – this friend – Pavel.'

'I resented being told what to believe, accused Uncle Billy of *outdated ideologies*.' She rolled her eyes. 'Thought I knew it all.'

'As teenagers do.'

'I passed the rhetoric onto Pavel. *Uncle Billy thinks* – and so on.'

'I see. A contrary young woman, then. And the poor boy listened?'

She laughed. 'He must have. Uncle Billy tells me he's a union official.'

'Tsk, tsk. So your friend becomes an activist and now there's a strike. The trouble you've caused.'

She opened her mouth to protest but caught the twinkle in his eye.

The low light, the music and the antique furnishings lent an old film quality to the room as if it were suspended in time. Isaac folded his hands over his knees, gazed into the middle distance. 'Miriam loved this music too. It was used as the theme for the film, *Brief Encounter.*'

'About a love affair that came to nothing.'

Isaac nodded. 'There's an ancient sect, Kaballah Jews. They believe that Soul Mates are two parts of the same soul, male and female. Two sides of the same coin. They say that Soul Mates are destined to find each other, though it can take several lifetimes.'

'Really?' she said, brushing her hands over her jeans as if sweeping away crumbs.

He shrugged. 'You may or may not believe it. Miriam did, though I think it more likely we met by good fortune. A gift. I fear I didn't deserve her. I was guilty of neglect on occasion, paying too much attention to business matters.'

'One life only, Isaac. No point in relying on the possibility of another to sort out our problems and failures.'

'Perhaps. But you don't have to spend your one life with a man whose only gift is a slap in the face.'

* * *

Guy opened the door to darkness. The bedroom curtains were open. He switched on the table lamp, tossed the bouquets of irises onto the bed, called her name. Helen liked irises and he'd bought bunches of both white and blue. Elongated petals peeped above the cellophane wrapping, one flower unfurled like an open mouth with tongues of purple and, at its throat, deep ochre.

He found the note on the pillow. She was not sure how long she'd be away, it said. She was sorry. He folded it, tore it in half. He checked her clothes. She hadn't taken many. If she'd caught a train that morning she'd have arrived in Yorkshire by now. Where else would she run? Billy Farrimond should never know what had happened. Guy's hands trembled. He picked up the phone from the bedside table, dialled. No answer.

His footsteps echoing on the wooden floor added to the apartment's hollow modernity: fashionable but empty at heart. It had been a mistake to move here. The wrong time entirely. In the kitchen, he rubbed the sole of his shoe over the cracked floor tile, opened the fridge door, shut it. He dropped an Ella Fitzgerald tape into a cassette player, paced the kitchen, then the hall and the kitchen again.

Finally settling in the sitting room he switched on the television and stretched out on the sofa watching an interview with Scargill. He flicked through the channels. There was a fourth now but the only mind-numbing programme he could find was a darts show with a quizmaster who reminded him of Billy. He watched for a couple of minutes then threw the handset onto the coffee table. It skittered across the glass top and dropped onto the rug.

At around nine o'clock Jack rang and told him he would be visiting his constituency for three days and suggested they fix a return dinner date. Guy told him that Helen had gone to her family in Yorkshire. Her aunt was unwell.

'By the way have you seen the evening news?' Jack asked. 'Corton Wood pit's out on strike tomorrow. I reckon you were right. The Prime Minister will probably have the troops out.' Guy said he hoped so. Jack said he was joking. They arranged to meet for a drink the following week.

Guy's memory of the dinner party was a blur. He took a bottle from the brown paper carrier he'd stowed in the back of the cloaks cupboard and poured himself a whisky which he downed in one; he poured another. Perhaps she wouldn't tell Billy. Didn't Helen need her uncle to believe her life was perfect? Since she'd let the old bugger down with her choice of husband she needed Billy to believe it had been worthwhile. There was no knowing what Billy might do to discredit a Tory.

The whisky warmed Guy's stomach. He poured a third and began to feel confident that she'd soon limp home shame-faced.

He phoned at five minute intervals until Billy answered.

'We've been out, Guy. She's not here. I had a gut feeling something was wrong when she rang earlier. You'd better find her and sort it or –'

'A tiff, Billy. She's sulking that's all. Probably with our friends in Richmond.'

'I'm telling you, you'd better –'

Guy hung up. 'Or what?' He kicked the hall table. 'Patronising git.'

Back in the bedroom he gathered the bouquets, inhaled their scent, crushing the stems at the thought of the old man's criticism. The cellophane crumpled. He flung the flowers across the room. They hit the window pane, fell to the sill. Where the hell was she?

His vision blurred as he blotted tears with the heel of his hand.

★ ★ ★

After listening to the late news, Isaac switched off the radio. 'So it seems the strike will go ahead and your Polish man – *your friend* – will be leading the battle.'

'Hardly leading,' she said, unable to imagine Pavel a militant. She stifled a yawn and Isaac pulled himself up with the arm of his chair, offered his hand.

'Come. You're tired. I've asked too many questions.'

The guestroom was furnished with a double bed, a corner washbasin and a winged fireside chair on which she folded her clothes. A poster of Darth Vader attached to the wall above the headboard, sagged, hanging loose from strips of sellotape which had lifted the pattern from the flocked wallpaper. Beside the wardrobe several boxed games with dog-eared corners were stacked between the legs of a table football stand, and a pile of comics on the bedside table proved at least three years out of date. Though Isaac often talked about his beloved grandsons, they had certainly not slept here for some time.

Fearing the poster might land on her head in the night, she stood on the bed, patting the sellotape to the wall. Exhausted yet unable to sleep, she snuggled beneath a duvet with a washed-out Star Wars cover, imagining Max and Solly in this room. Had they listened well to their grandfather's stories? Bar Mitzvah boys would be steeped in their history from an early age, understand roots. Her feet discovered a hot water bottle that Isaac must have supplied while she'd dozed earlier.

Did the boys squabble? She couldn't imagine they'd appreciate the flowery wallpaper.

She pulled the duvet to her chin. Old squabbles. There'd been so many. Debates about the rules of the games they'd played. Whether Monopoly or politics, it was always the same. Uncle Billy. So predictable. The peace offerings that had followed: white chocolate bars he'd bought on his way home from work, extra pocket money, a bottle of fizzy pop.

She remembered the film, *Brief Encounter*. That last long summer, before she'd left home, a series of black and white movie classics had featured at the local cinema – before it lost its red velvet grandeur to graffiti, bingo and eventual closure.

She remembered sharing a plush double seat with Pavel Kowaleski. There had never been an argument about him.

Uncle Billy might not recognise her now. He would say his once outspoken niece had been crushed, that his Little Songbird had been gagged. And he might say, 'Told you so, Missy.'

Chapter Three

Room to Dance

East Yorkshire

August 1971

On a trip to the east coast it was unusual to leave jackets on the coach, even in August, but today was an exception. Pavel had led her to a strip of beach where scallops of lacy tide met the chalk cliffs; there was little evidence of the resident breeze. It was a relatively remote spot. Only the shouting of distant day-trippers, the squawking of a few greedy seagulls and an occasional speed boat skimming and bouncing across the bay threatened their seclusion.

In preparation for the Christmas ball her uncle was organising, Helen decided to teach Pavel to waltz. There was plenty of space and nobody would notice. At home Uncle Billy would have interfered, offered his unwelcome expertise.

In her early teens, at the weekly ballroom dance in the church hall, Billy had taught her the waltz, the quickstep, foxtrot and tango, whisking her across a chalky floor to the sounds of Victor Sylvester seventy eights. He said he'd taught her all the steps she'd need to know.

A band of turquoise was dissolving on the horizon. 'It's too hot to dance,' Pavel said.

'One – your right foot. Two – left foot. Now together. Simple.'

Though an uneven beach was a hindrance and they sank in swells and troughs and tripped over boulders, they soon quickened, ploughing a furrow. Pavel held her at arm's length allowing room for his head to follow the progress of his feet.

He stopped. 'Hang on. Aren't we supposed to turn? We're heading straight for the sea.'

'There'll be time for turning. You'll be perfect by Christmas.'

Christmas. Four months away. Four months apart, he said. Why couldn't she find a course nearer? Because she'd applied to college before she met him and it was too late to change. He raced her back to their towels.

Pavel lay on his back, eyes closed while Helen trickled warm dry sand through her fingers and onto his chest 'You don't fool me,' she said, poking his cheek till his eyes flickered.

His lips wobbled. He opened one eye. 'I'm asleep. Whacked from all that dancing.'

'You promised me an ice cream.' She nibbled his ear and he jumped to his feet and chased her in circles. When she allowed him to catch her he carried her into the sea and dropped her.

'You've wet my hair,' she said. 'You'll pay for this, Kowaleski!'

They splashed each other for a few minutes then ran up the beach. Pavel shook the sand from his towel and used it to dry her hair which hung about her face like strings of seaweed. She took a comb and small mirror from her bag. 'Don't think you can get out of the ice-cream.'

'Never satisfied are you?' he said, draping his towel over her head. 'I bring you to the Riviera and you still moan. Okay. The Yorkshire Riviera. But I got you away from the crowds, didn't I?'

She threw the towel at his chest. 'Your crowd. How many members of the Miners' Institute are there? I can't believe how many coaches we needed to get here.'

'And we all paid our weekly dues for this one day out. Poor sods.'

A few yards along the beach Pavel found a child's abandoned plastic bucket and shovelling with his hands he filled it, patted and flipped it, until he'd forged a perfect sand castle. He surrounded it with pebbles and pink cockle shells then topped with a feather he found up on the rocks. 'Cormorant, I think,' he said.

'A castle needs a flag to have class.' Pavel swiped the castle with the side of his foot until only the feather remained.

She rolled on her side and he settled beside her, fingertips beneath the strap of her swimsuit. She could feel his breath on her neck, inhale the scent of him: Imperial Leather, salt.

'What are you reading?' he asked.

'1984. George Orwell. I'll loan it to you when I've finished.'

'Will I like it?'

'You won't know if you don't read it, will you?' she said, brushing his hand from her shoulder.

The sun dried her, but when fronds of surf licked her toes, she donned her jeans and tee shirt. 'We'd better move, Pavel, or we'll drown.' She tousled his hair, yanked the pillow of folded jeans from behind his head, then left him to dress and pack the beach bag while she wandered off, picking up lumps of chalk at the foot of the cliffs. She rolled each one between her palms, poked fingers into the holes, then discarded them one by one, listening to them clink and splinter as they collided.

In stormy weather the cliffs crumbled, leaving cavernous gaps in the landscape. A sign warned of the danger of rock falls, and she'd once read that a few miles further north, a thousand years before, Vikings had invaded the North Country through a breach in the coastline's natural defences. It was hard to imagine a violent assault in such an idyllic place. How long did it take the sea to pound rocks into sand, to chomp chalk layers into white lumps and spit them out like gigantic broken teeth? If she and Pavel came here when they were old, the tides would still be marking time. How many lovers might an ocean witness: lovers building sandcastles and making promises they might not keep?

'I like this one,' she said, finding one she thought a good size to sit on a windowsill. 'I'm keeping it.'

'And I suppose I'll have to carry it?' He was holding her beach bag open.

'Naturally.' And then, to appease him, 'It will remind me of you.'

'Come on. Suppose I'd better buy you an ice cream or I'll never hear the last of it!' They headed back towards the crowds.

'I'll come home as often as possible, Pavel, and you can visit me some weekends. You could get Jakub to bring you on his motor bike.'

'What? Come to see you with my little brother in tow?'

He stooped to kiss her and they walked on, barefoot, Pavel clasping her waist with one hand, carrying the beach bag with the other while Helen carried a tapestry bag across her shoulder and swung her sandals from one finger.

Nearer the funfair and harbour, the crowds had retreated from the incoming tide and the fringe of beach that remained was cramped with day-trippers, discarded sandwiches and collapsing sand castles.

When they stumbled across a gang of lads huddled around a transistor radio, Helen recognised Pavel's workmates from the morning's coach journey. The group had been quiet then, no doubt still half asleep from a drinking session the night before.

A skinny young man with long hair lay propped up on one elbow. She recognised him. Coker. He'd been in her class at school.

He tossed the hair out of his eyes. 'Eh up. Look who's here. If it's not the two love birds! Get anything, Pav?'

Pavel stopped. 'Shut it, Coker!' The lads laughed.

'Tetchy, eh?' Coker said. 'What's up, get some sand in it?'

'Nice bag, Pav!' one of Coker's mates shouted.

Helen put a hand on her hip. 'Why don't you get back to your Beano?'

Coker flicked sand at her feet. 'Ooh, hark at her. You've got a right one there, mate. She'll bite your balls off.' The gang sniggered.

'Don't rise to it,' Pavel told her.

Coker turned up the volume on the radio, looking Helen up and down as he sang along to the Rolling Stones, *'Satisfaction.'* Pavel drew her away and hurried her along. Sensing Coker's stare boring holes in her back, she turned.

'A filthy look,' Coker shouted. 'I'm scared!'

The lads wolf-whistled. Pavel groaned. 'I told you, Helen. Leave it!'

Several yards down the beach the sniggers still rang in her ears. 'How do you put up with mindless hooligans every day?' she said.

Pavel shrugged. 'They're harmless; just fooling around. I'll have to put up with worse on Monday. They're jealous – and drunk, most of them.'

By the sea wall the sand lay in soft peaks like hot meringues scorching her heels, and she was relieved to reach the steps to the promenade. While she dusted the sand from her feet Pavel held her by the elbow, steadying her.

At a kiosk between an amusement arcade and a hot dog stand, he bought the promised ice cream and they shared it, sitting on the wall, legs dangling over the sea, ducking from the gulls that swooped for food and scavenged in open litter bins. She licked her fingers. Pavel took off his sunglasses, shut his eyes. A patch of freckles blossomed on the bridge of his nose; the sun was highlighting his sandy coloured hair. How could someone who so loved the outdoors spend eight hours a day below ground?

Across the promenade, a miniature railway rattled with wagons, bells and waving toddlers. It reminded her of the latest mining recruitment ad, a snippet of film that presented the journey into a pit like a fairground attraction. Cheerful, clean working men in shiny helmets seated in a truck that disappeared down a tiled tunnel. She'd seen it last week on television and Tibby said it was showing at the cinema between features. But it didn't show the men's return, faces covered in coal dust with only the whites of their eyes shining; coughing up grey phlegm like Uncle Billy.

She stroked Pavel's face. 'You're like a pit pony.'

'What? There *are* no pit ponies.'

'You're let out on high days and holidays to kick your heels and breathe fresh air. You'll be tethered up and led back down into your black hole on Monday.'

'It's a job.'

'I know your dad's a miner but he didn't have much choice did he; a refugee in the war? I thought he'd expect you to aim higher.'

Pavel swivelled on the wall, his back to the sea. 'When they escaped from Poland, my parents had nothing but the clothes they stood in. I suppose that makes you settle for anything that puts food on the table. They don't talk about what happened and I don't ask.'

She'd met Pavel's parents once. His father hadn't spoken, seemed a surly man. She sidled closer. 'I think...'

'Don't think!'

She lowered herself from the wall, faced him. 'Listen. Did you know that, when Jewish refugees came here last century, mothers used to take soup to the school railings at playtimes, so their sons would be well nourished, ready to learn? Uncle Billy told me.'

'And their daughters? Did they starve?'

'I'm serious. The point is they realised that while possessions and property could be stolen, education could be their passport to a future wherever they settled. A lot of first generation kids went on to be doctors, lawyers, chemists...'

He glanced along the promenade as if checking his workmates weren't following. 'What are you trying to say? My mother should have given me more soup?'

'I'm saying they valued education.'

'Education didn't help when Adolph marched into town did it? You and your ideals.'

'There's nothing wrong with aspiration, Pavel.'

He shook his head. 'Somebody's got to do my job so don't sneer at it.' He pressed his hand to his heart. 'My country needs me,' he said, drawing her close with his feet.

She rested one hand on his chest, his heart beating against her palm. 'It's dangerous.'

'Nothing could be as dangerous as you! Watch out.' He moved her aside gently and jumped from the wall.

They ambled through the funfair, until they reached the waltzers. The speed of the ride whipped her hair into her eyes, lured her closer. Hadn't she always been the fascinated child, the dare-devil too near the edge of a station platform when an express train tore through? On the dodgems teenagers were bumping into each other. Sparks flashed, burned like tiny stars then seemed to evaporate. A siren sounded, dodgems slowed and the drivers jumped out. Young couples staggered away kissing, laughing, clutching sore arms and each other, but were quickly replaced in a fresh scramble. The clamour drowned Pavel's voice.

He tugged her sleeve, nodded towards the Ferris wheel. She shook her head. Talk of leaving home, leaving Pavel, had saddened her, as if she'd aged in one afternoon and could sense her childhood spinning out of reach. And for a moment, something else. An ominous feeling. It glanced from her like a tap from a beach ball, the mood lifting before she could define it.

'Cheer up,' he said. 'It might never happen.'

But somehow she knew it would.

At the harbour they lingered, watching a trawler dock, the catch hauled ashore in crates of ice. A few fish were gasping for air, gills dilating.

'Being a fisherman. Now that's what I call real danger,' Pavel said at last. 'Out in all weathers, facing gale force winds and colossal waves. They're a tough lot.'

'I wonder how many would choose to do something different, if they could,' she said.

'It's the life they know. Brought up to follow their dads. But there's always a choice. This is your Uncle Billy's land of equality and opportunity isn't it?'

'It is if you have qualifications, Pavel.'

Three children climbed on the wall, peering at the boats below until their mother shouted and they scrambled down and shot off along the pier.

'How many children shall we have?' he said.

'Has nobody told you? Babies are no longer obligatory.' She thumped his stomach and ran on ahead, laughing.

'Hey. That hurt,' he shouted, but she knew he'd chase after her.

Dusk was settling when the coach prepared to set off on the homeward journey. Helen rested her head on Pavel's shoulder, hoping to sleep. Coker made a drunken entrance, tripping up the coach steps and stumbling into the driver before settling behind Helen and Pavel and squeezing his face into the gap between the seats.

'Sleeping together already, Pav? You'd better watch out for her Uncle Billy; he's on coach behind.' Coker stood up, swaying slightly. 'Billy Farrimond'll chuck you out of fuckin' union if you get his precious niece up duff.'

A shout from the back of the coach startled Helen. 'Shut it, Coker! Watch your language!'

Pavel whispered. 'That's Roly Beresford with his wife, Kath. Watch out.'

'Aye, Roly,' Coker said. 'And we all know you'd have been up for a bit of action yourself if your missus wasn't with you. What about Doreen from canteen then, eh?'

An expectant hush followed as Roly marched down the coach, swooped and grabbed Coker by his shirt front. 'I'm warning you.'

'Okay. Okay. It were only a joke,' Coker said.

'Last chance. Now shut it or I'll put you off the bus! Understand?'

'Yes. Cool it, Roly.' Their noses were almost touching.

Roly pushed Coker into his seat. 'Now think on!'

'Who's Doreen?' his wife shouted as the coach swerved round a corner. Roly lurched unsteadily, muttering oaths and protesting innocence.

Pavel's gaze fixed on the window; Helen looked where he looked. It was dark, difficult to make out the scenery. 'Serves Coker right,' she muttered to Pavel's reflection.

Once the lads had fallen asleep – brought on by the drone of the engine and an alcoholic stupor – the homeward journey proved uneventful. Even so, when the gang woke she had to endure their crude rugby songs for the final few miles and Coker was still singing when the coach arrived back at the Miners' Institute. He must have taught them the songs. He'd once been a Grammar school boy in the Under Sixteens. She remembered him well.

Pavel hurried her across the road towards a side street and when she glanced over her shoulder, Coker was stumbling off the coach, hindering everyone else's departure.

'I think you'd be wise to stay away from him,' she said. 'He's a bad influence. You're better than those idiots.'

'No I'm not. They're mates,' he said, slipping an arm around her shoulders.

When she was fifteen, Coker had asked her out, followed her home from school pestering her for a date until she'd told him to *drop dead!*

'First time I've met Coker,' she said. 'Hope it's the last.'

Pavel dropped his hand to her waist. 'He's off to Spain on a package tour soon.'

'Let's hope they keep him there.'

As they crossed the park, a breeze flipped a storm of fish and chip trays around their feet. 'I didn't see your Uncle Billy today,' Pavel said.

'He didn't go on the trip. Don't listen to Coker. Uncle Billy likes you.'

Pavel kissed the top of her head. 'After the last union meeting, he told me they were sponsoring one of the lads to Ruskin College, Oxford. He says I should at least apply for a local day release course.'

'You should. You know I think you could be anything you wanted.'

A squally shower followed the breeze. They crept up the garden path, seeking shelter beneath the eaves: below the weak light of an outdoor lamp Uncle Billy always left switched on for her.

'I won't ask you to come in, Pavel. It's late. They'll be listening out for me. You'd better go home. You'll be soaked.'

'Your hair smells of seaweed,' he said.

'And whose fault is that?'

'I love seaweed.'

Rain had washed his hair forward into a flat, boyish fringe. She combed it aside with her fingers.

'So will you marry me?' he said.

'I might – if you'd stop asking every five minutes.'

'Okay.' He bowed his head.

She skipped up the path. 'And don't sulk. Good night, Pavel.'

'Hey,' he shouted after her. 'What about this rock? It's heavier than a sack of coal.' She ran back, snatched the bag.

'Love you,' he whispered. She ran inside and upstairs to her bedroom where she watched him from the window as he jogged away. She was moved by the sight of his hunched shoulders, his collar raised in useless defence against what had become a relentless downpour. Uncle Billy was snoring in the next room. She dropped the lump of chalk onto the window sill. It was heavy. A boulder. Pavel had carried it without complaint. She couldn't imagine meeting anyone else so generous, unselfish. But he *was* easy to tease.

The room was stuffy. The heat of the day, trapped behind sealed windows, hung in an oppressive layer beneath the ceiling. She undressed in the dark. Her nightdress, usually under her pillow, was missing. Tibby must have washed it. Helen was too tired to find another.

Naked, she climbed into bed, wishing Pavel had not had to leave, imagining his arms around her. Fresh sheets smelled of soap powder and newly mown lawn and were crisp and cool against her skin. She was eighteen. Time to stop teasing.

Chapter Four

Mermaids

March 6th 1984

London

In Greenwich Park Helen and Isaac sat on a bench watching a swarm of small children navigating tricycles around the legs of doting mothers and grandparents. Isaac chuckled when a toddler's failed attempt to kick a football resulted in the boy landing on his back on the grass, legs in the air.

A young woman with a pram, stopped to rest beside them. The baby began to grizzle. The mother sighed, rocked the handle; pram springs squeaked. Helen asked if she could 'take a peek' and without waiting for an answer she peered under the hood. The baby wore a blue bonnet; couldn't have been more than a few weeks old. A scratch and a streak of blood smeared his cheek, presumably from a clumsy attempt to chew his fists. When Helen made soothing noises the young woman eased her aside, and mumbling that the baby was hungry, wheeled the pram away.

Isaac frowned. 'She seemed nervous, as if you might steal him.'

Perhaps the woman could smell more than the baby's need. 'I shouldn't have interfered,' Helen said, plunging her hands deep into her jacket pockets.

She walked a stride ahead of Isaac. Had he too sensed her ache to touch, to stroke the baby's face, to tuck the child's hands inside the blue cotton mittens on the pram pillow? She should have told him about her own baby then, but the moment passed.

After drinking coffee at a table outside the café they headed towards the park exit pausing at the top of the hill to view the college, museum and river. She loved the symmetry of Georgian buildings, their proportions and grandeur, but on the north bank of the Thames, an expanding sprawl of office blocks punctured the skyline.

'It's a...wonderful sight... isn't it?' Isaac said, a little out of breath from the climb.

Daffodils nodded; camellias and rhododendron were already in bud. Spring arrived earlier here – flowers were always weeks behind in Yorkshire – though seasons sometimes resisted being too easily described: March winds in August, April showers in October. On the steep path to the observatory she'd noticed a young oak with last year's parched leaves clinging to its slender branches. Sometimes it seemed there were no seasons at all, the sky just one long grey canvas occasionally shot with a little colour. Everything faded quickly.

'I've decided,' she said. 'I'll collect my bag and go back to the apartment this afternoon. I should talk to Guy.'

'If you go back – ' but she was quickening her pace.

★ ★ ★

Guy had stayed in bed for most of the day, yesterday's clothes lying in a crumpled heap on the bedroom floor. He'd thought he could take a day off and not be missed. He'd swallowed the strong prescription painkillers he'd wheedled from his GP by complaining about imaginary back pain, and washed them down with a bottle of tonic. Then, as an afterthought, a slug of vodka, straight from the bottle.

He tidied the bedroom, clearing Helen's perfumes into a drawer, her dressing gown into the laundry basket; he changed the bedding. He gathered the flowers from the windowsill and squashed them into the bin. After striding around the apartment plumping cushions, clearing glasses into the dish washer and scrubbing the kitchen surfaces, he threw his briefcase into the cloaks cupboard along with the day's post; checked there were no official documents lying around. No parliamentary crests, no identification.

He showered and dressed in jeans and an open-necked shirt, ran a comb through his hair. He had shaved. His face was smooth. He looked into the mirror. His pupils were enlarged. Did these women so profligate with their bodies bother to look? Over the last few months he'd compartmentalised the players in his life: the father he avoided, the mother he listened to, the constituents he patronised, the shallow friendships in the political networks that he clung to. All were separate particles, satellites to his world. It had been easy at first, keeping up appearances. The drink helped. Even Helen had aided and abetted with simpering attempts at support. The other women he'd craved had nothing to do with his wife. He'd tried to blot out the image of her, of how things used to be. Hide her away. A china doll in a box. If only he didn't need her.

The doorbell rang. Though it was only mid-afternoon, he'd drawn curtains, lit table lamps, lowered blinds. He looked at his watch. He waited. It rang again and then a third time. He was satisfied it wasn't Helen – she would have her key and he was certain from her note she wouldn't be home yet, and even if she did return, wasn't this a justifiable pay back? She'd left him. A frisson of danger. He trembled.

He opened the door. He'd used this particular agency several times in the past year, usually in a central hotel, never at home — but had not met this girl. She offered her hand and he took it; introduced himself as John and invited her across the threshold.

★ ★ ★

Helen caught the train to Waterloo. The grey-haired man opposite folded his newspaper and scowled over half-frame reading glasses when he noticed she was trying to peek at the photographs on the front page. She managed to read the strike headlines.

Next to her a little girl was combing the white-blonde hair of a fashion doll. 'I can make it grow to her waist,' the girl said. 'Watch this.' With a few gentle tugs, the girl stretched the hair down the doll's back.

'She's like a mermaid,' Helen said.

A black cab dropped her outside the apartment. Guy wouldn't be back from the House yet and she wondered if there was anything in the freezer she could defrost in time for dinner. She unlocked the door, dropped her bag and kicked off her shoes. The windowless hall had always been gloomy, relying on open doors to steal light from adjacent rooms. Except for the master bedroom at the end of the hall, the doors were wide open, yet the apartment seemed shuttered, claustrophobic. She heard a woman's voice. Maybe from the television.

In the sitting room she discovered a leather coat draped across the sofa, a pair of black stilettos on the rug, a dusting of white powder on the coffee table. She caught a scent of a cloying perfume she couldn't identify. The voice came from the bedroom. It rose and fell, a whine. A girlish voice. She retraced her steps into the hall, listening at the bedroom door before flinging it open.

A girl with straight mermaid hair was sitting astride Guy, her back obstructing Helen's view of his face. The duvet was on the floor, beside a heap of crumpled clothes. When the girl turned, Helen backed out and along the corridor, scrabbling for shoes and bag.

★ ★ ★

At King's Cross she bought a single ticket to Doncaster, then, at a platform kiosk, a carton of bitter black coffee and a magazine. As she kicked the overnight bag to a bench the coffee splashed and scalded her fingers.

The train was so long that the driver's cabin nosed beyond the station. Carriages were locked and the train empty except for a liveried steward collecting debris and a chef in white jacket and blue checked trousers who was chattering to a waiter setting tables in the dining car.

Passengers gathered in huddles and pairs: an old man with his wife in a wheelchair, two lovers kissing, a young woman perching on an upended suitcase, three men with briefcases and a little girl practising a tap dancing sequence, swinging her arms forward and backwards: *shuffle, ball change*. Helen tucked the coffee beneath the bench and opened the magazine.

Two boys about six and ten were shoving each other and laughing until the younger boy drew a plastic pterodactyl out of a Natural History Museum bag and began to whirl around, flying the dinosaur at arm's length, dipping and diving like a fighter plane, spitting out machine gun fire as he passed Helen. *Nee-iaow, tatter tatter tat*.

Why had she and Guy not discussed children before they were married? She reached for the carton but knocked it over. *Nee-iaow*. Coffee puddled around her shoes.

William would have been nearly two years old now.

She'd never forget the pitying look on the consultant's face when he told her that, at twenty six weeks, though survival was possible, this baby's lungs and heart were not strong enough for him to live for more than a few hours. Her son's hand was not big enough to curl around her little finger.

The dancing girl was pirouetting, a long red Sunday-best coat impeding the length of her strides, a halo of fine hair floating around her head.

Surely there was no doubt about the apartment girl's occupation. The coat, undeniable cocaine, the air weighted with perfume. Not an affair. That would have demanded affection.

The mother of the dinosaur child caught the boy by the hand, reining him in as the engine fired up, throbbing imminent departure. The magazine was open at a fashion page: at the jumpsuits that Celia had been so fond of. Helen threw the empty coffee carton and the magazine into a bin.

A flurry of movement; passengers scrambled aboard, heaving holdalls and suitcases onto overhead racks. In front of Helen in the queue the girl in the red coat was chanting. '*Mind the gap, mind the gap*. What does that mean, Mummy? *Mind the gap*.'

Helen's limbs were suddenly heavy, unwieldy; her head fuzzy. Images blurred. Why had Guy refused to talk about their loss? Could there ever be a way back from this? She waited for a moment in the connecting space between two carriages, in the turbulent in-between area where metal plates slid and clunked. *Mind the gap*. She wondered whether she should stay there – in a vacuum.

The guard passed, asked if she was ill, advised her there were still plenty of seats even if she hadn't made a reservation. She found a vacant seat but struggled to lift the bag onto the rack until a young man at the other side of the table sprang to her assistance. He smiled. She thanked him. Glancing through the window to avoid his scrutiny, she found a reflection she barely recognised as her own. She wished she had something to read, remembered the magazine. A steward announced that dinner would be served in first class. The mention of food was nauseating.

The young man disembarked at Peterborough. Maybe it had been merely the smattering of freckles that had made him seem familiar. Free from his distraction, she dozed, drifting in and out of feverish dreams which featured faceless mannequins dancing in the dark.

Chapter Five

The Home Coming

March 7th

Lundby South Yorkshire

A shaft of light squeezing through a gap in the curtains woke her. She threw back the covers and tiptoed to the window where she gazed across a field to the site of former woodland and marshes. As a child she'd fished for frogs and newts here, carried her floundering catch home in jam-jars like fairground prizes; jars that dangled from handles fashioned from bits of string which Uncle Billy unearthed from his garden shed. When he'd examined the specimens and congratulated her on her cleverness, she'd squelched through mud in black wellingtons that chafed her calves, returning the clammy creatures to their rightful wilderness.

The present landscape was a wasteland of old bedsteads, discarded fridges and broken bikes. Oak, elm and silver birch had been uprooted to make way for a planned housing development which, after excavations and council deliberations, had never been built. The ground was too waterlogged, Tibby said. Any child could have told them. The bulldozers of hasty and negligent developers had destroyed a natural wetland and no one had made any attempt to prevent it.

At least Helen's bedroom hadn't changed much. She could almost imagine she was still seventeen, when she'd frequently woken to thick ice-crystals on the window on a winter's morning, but now there was a radiator on the wall and a floral bedcover which matched the curtains. The same furniture presided, comfortable and outdated, and her feet sank into a deep sheepskin rug.

On the dressing table a collection of kitsch rabbit ornaments languished on ceramic toadstools: Bugs Bunny teeth and blue spotted waistcoats. She'd collected them in her early teens. This bedroom belonged to a young Helen Farrimond.

If she opened the window and leaned out, she could just spot the spoil heap on the sky line, the rope way halted now by the strike; the steady stream of rectangular buckets suspended above a no-man's land of unwanted pit-rubble that Uncle Billy said had become a sought after commodity in past strikes. He'd confessed to boyhood illicit coal picking in the General Strike.

Billy still carried the childhood scars on his wrists from a pit-tip escapade when he was ten years old, when his friends − like him, in holey jumpers and boots lined with newspaper − had dared him to ride the rope way. It was a dangerous rite of passage, a road to early death, but he'd agreed to it. Fortunately when he fell, he'd suffered only a broken arm, an emergency operation and his mother's tongue lashing. Tibby complained that Billy showcased his scars regularly after a few too many beers at the Miners' Institute.

Tibby's spare dressing gown hung from the wardrobe door and Helen slipped it on and crept across the landing to the bathroom. A deep old-fashioned porcelain bath would hold enough hot water to cover her entirely, allow her to luxuriate for a while in steam and bubbles.

She lay on her back submerging her head, seeking distance and calm until she could no longer hold her breath. There was a tap on the door and Tibby bustled in carrying fresh towels. Why had they never fixed the lock?

'Now you can tell me what happened?' Tibby crouched by the side of the bath. 'You have a swollen cheek.'

'Can you pass the towel please? I'm cold.'

'After you rang the other night, Guy phoned. He thought you were here. Where were you calling from?'

'A friend's.'

'Billy says you'll tell us when you're ready but – '

'There's nothing to tell. I bumped into the door as I was rushing out to catch the train.' She stepped out of the bath. Soap bubbles floated from her and she blew on them, scattering them like dandelion clocks. She watched them settle on Tibby's hair.

'Helen. Are you listening? What is the matter with you?' Tibby wrapped the bath towel around Helen's chest, tucking the ends beneath her arms like she had when Helen had been a child, lifting her down from the kitchen sink after scrubbing ingrained dirt from her knees. The results of long summer day's playing in open fields were difficult to wash away. Sometimes Helen had complained that Tibby rubbed too hard or that she was tugging when she combed her hair.

Helen sighed. 'It was an accident, Tibby. Wouldn't I tell you if – '

'I'm not sure if you would tell me. If Guy – '

'It's nothing. Please, Tibby. Don't say anything to Uncle Billy. He'll believe the worst.'

Tibby took up a smaller towel and rubbed Helen's hair. 'This is not just a flying visit, is it? You look awful, love.'

'Maybe it's delayed reaction.'

'To what? The baby? Almost two years delay? Whose reaction? Yours or Guy's? We've never had secrets have we?'

'I can't tell you what I don't know myself, Tibby.' Helen pulled the head towel over her face, dabbed her eyes.

Tibby hugged her. 'This will always be your home.'

When Tibby's footsteps on the stairs faded, Helen perched on the edge of the tub. She could hear the radio playing in the kitchen, Billy at the front door whistling Bevan the dog in from the garden. Doors opened and shut; the telephone rang; the last of the bath water gurgled down the plug hole. She dreaded going down to breakfast.

She cleared a porthole in the steamed up mirror and examined her face: the face of a liar. A prickling throat, stinging sinuses, a furry coating on her tongue.

On her arrival the night before, she'd told them it was an impromptu visit and that Guy was away on House business. They must have known it was a lie but hadn't contradicted. Uncle Billy had been watching *News at Ten*. He'd said she looked 'done in,' but mostly he'd talked about the strike.

'We can't let it happen. I don't believe it'll be just twenty pits they'll close,' he'd said, almost before she'd taken off her coat.

'Give the poor girl time to get through the door, Billy,' Tibby said.

Helen was glad that Uncle Billy was retired and wouldn't have to suffer from strike action. In his heyday he'd been a strong union official and was still a local councillor, so it was not surprising he was so preoccupied with the events of the last weeks. But she wished he didn't make a habit of pointing his finger when he gave one of his speeches. She hated that: pointing fingers, clenched fists. They led to hands that lashed out and slapped your face or jabbed your arm. Though he would never hurt her, it disturbed her just the same. She'd had a headache since dozing on the train.

Billy switched off the set. 'Makes your blood boil. I told Pavel only yesterday. I said to him, "If Scargill doesn't call a ballot..." ' He stopped. She'd been rubbing her temples as he spoke. 'Have you got a headache, love?' he said. 'It'll be the travelling or the virus you told me about.' She'd accepted the two aspirins Tibby had offered and had gone to bed.

After breakfast Helen expected interrogation, but Billy was reading the newspaper editorial. He looked up. 'Good morning, love. Have you slept well?' Not a hint of inquisition.

She nibbled a piece of toast. 'Is that all you're eating,' he said. It was difficult to eat when someone slapped the appetite for life out of you, but she lied again, told them she'd eaten a sandwich from the buffet car the night before. No mention of the bathroom incident. Perhaps now her face had cooled the swelling was no longer noticeable.

Bevan squatted beneath the table pawing Helen's legs and when she asked if she could take him for a walk, Tibby rummaged in a cupboard to find a lead, insisting that Helen wear a scarf.

'And you're too thin,' she said, fastening a length of paisley cotton beneath Helen's chin.

'I'll look like the Queen,' Helen said.

'She's calling you a corgi, Bevan,' Billy said and the dog barked approval.

Once outside she snatched the scarf from her head, allowing it to hang loose around her neck.

At the limestone crags on the edge of the old village she settled on a flat rock, seeking peace in the familiar landscape of ancient farmland. The stream still meandered through the meadow below but across the valley the former patchwork of fields had been transformed into an ugly prairie. The hedgerows which for centuries had

53

marked field boundaries and provided habitats for local wildlife had been ripped out.

When she was a child there'd been a small open-air swimming pool nestling between the brook and the rocks. A lido: a grand name for something so small that a strong swimmer could complete a whole length with just a few strokes of front crawl. It had disappeared; there was no sign that it had ever existed. Indoor baths took pride of place in the centre of the village now: new facilities that Uncle Billy's council had funded.

'Much more convenient, all year availability and a constant temperature,' he'd said, offended by her disappointment. Did she enjoy freezing to death? Did she not approve of progress? She'd told him that all she could remember of the old pool was the sun on her back.

She was lost suddenly. There was so little recognisable and today she'd needed to find everything as she'd left it. The scarf fluttered across her face and into her eyes. She lowered herself onto the rocks, drew the dog closer. Bevan licked her cheek, whimpered and buried his head in her lap.

Even in a bitter March wind it was easy to recall old summers. She imagined voices echoing up the hillside, bare feet slapping on concrete slabs, a diver springing from the low board. She could smell the chlorine, so strong sometimes that it had stolen her breath. This was where she'd first met Pavel just before her eighteenth birthday. The pool had always been too cold, seemed colder in a heat wave. She'd been dangling her legs in the deep-end when he'd surfaced at her feet, clambered out and settled beside her. She'd thought him endearing: water dripping from the end of his nose and his hair flattened.

Bevan's brown eyes searched her face for reassurance and she kissed his snout. She was shivering with a flesh-creeping feeling that, from experience, she knew warned of more than a common cold. Her forehead burned. She clambered over the rocks and led the dog to the top of the hill to the war memorial, where she sheltered on a stone bench reading recognisable family names carved on an obelisk. K for Knight and Knowles. No Kowaleskis.

She wondered how Pavel would cope with the strike responsibilities lately thrust upon him, and how her husband in London – with an empty apartment, a job that hung from his shoulders like an oversized cape, and with maybe more than one call-girl draining his soul – might cope with anything at all.

★ ★ ★

It was a chilly evening. Guy let himself into the apartment, turned up the heating and marched to the drinks cabinet. Normally when he arrived, Helen was cooking dinner, playing records if he was not too late: usually some God awful pop band but occasionally the classics. She vacillated between Elgar and the Eurhythmics. Always contrary and unpredictable. Her outburst the other night was typical. One minute, the dutiful wife applauding his constituency acceptance speech, and the next, ranting like an activist from the Socialist Worker Party. She'd called herself *apolitical* when he'd first met her and he'd been stupid to believe her. And now? It was little wonder he became so frustrated that he sought solace elsewhere.

He poured himself a drink. Where had she slept for two nights? A phone call couldn't annoy Billy any more than the last time he'd spoken to him. He picked up the phone on the hall table.

Tibby answered. Helen was having an early night, she said. 'What's going on, Guy?'

'I told Billy. We had a silly row.'

'She had a mark.'

So Helen hadn't told them. What did Tibby know?

'She says she bumped into the door on her way out,' Tibby said as if it were a question.

'I don't know anything about that. I left the apartment before her.'

'If you did this –'

'Why on earth should you think that? I need to speak to her, Tibby.'

'She's asleep. I'll not wake her.'

'Then I'll phone tomorrow.'

'I've never seen her like this, Guy. So preoccupied. Unsettled. I think you should leave her be for a while. We'll take care of her.'

Take care? Billy would think he'd won her back. Erode her loyalty. 'Ask her to phone me, please.'

'I can't promise anything.'

'Well, at least tell her I phoned – '

The dialling tone interrupted. Guy drained his glass. He had no knowledge of any marks. Had she walked into the door? She was always daydreaming. Maybe it had nothing to do with him. A slap couldn't have... What was she up to? So what if he'd hit her? She deserved it. He should be able to count on her loyalty.

Sweat dripped from his brow. He removed his tie. His heart beat fast. There was a tightness in his chest. He tried to breathe slowly but his rage was sudden; gave no warning. He threw his empty glass against the wall. It shattered. He leaned on the hall table, swept a hand across it, clearing it of the lamp and the phone.

★ ★ ★

Derbyshire
Late March

It was Pavel's turn to drive and there were three other pickets in his car besides his mate Roly. He parked the Allegro on the lane and the five men got out and walked towards the pit gates where a small police presence waited, chatting, yawning. Pavel glanced at the winding gear above the fitters and welders' workshops, and the brick built management offices at the far end of the yard where faces of women peered from windows.

The five pickets joined a number of local miners already out on strike then Pavel spotted Coker: hands buried in anorak pockets, laughing, holding court. Pavel would have to keep an eye on him. Coker would do anything for trouble; thrived on it.

Pavel had no doubts about the strike being just but wondered if Billy Farrimond might be right when he said that Scargill didn't have the necessary negotiating skills. That worried him. Pavel had a strong regard for Billy, though he knew there was a joke among the lads that, if you left a gap for breath in a conversation, Billy would fill it with a speech.

He would not forget that it was Billy and Roly who'd encouraged him into union business – the branch committee at first – back in the days he'd rather not remember: days when it was all he could do to get out of bed in the morning. In a small way the union had restored purpose to his life. And now he was a father he had a greater reason to forge a future.

Roly insisted that Pavel argued well, that he had a calming influence on the men and that, in any case, his English was better than the other contenders for the position of strike coordinator. 'We've found summat you're good at, Pav,' he'd said, jabbing a friendly punch at his shoulder.

Helen Farrimond had once had similar faith. It was ironic that her uncle, with such strong union loyalties, seemed to have little belief in the chances of the strike being a success. 'Scargill's a dogma man,' he'd said, which was rich coming from Billy. Much as Pavel liked him, hadn't the old dog indoctrinated his niece so much that she'd married into the opposition? Though it would be unfair to blame Billy entirely. After all, it wasn't Billy Farrimond who'd driven the girl out of town.

Roly nodded in the direction of the police group and taking a cue, Pavel wandered over to the sergeant in charge. 'I need just five minutes. I'll put our case and be gone.'

'Two minutes is all you'll get,' the sergeant said, pulling himself up to his full height. The same officer had been quite chatty the week before. He'd seemed sympathetic, said his brother was a miner. What had changed?

'Go on, Pav,' Roly said.

The pickets were closing ranks to block the entrance to the pit yard. Then the bus transporting men for the two o'clock shift turned off the main road and crawled to a halt in front of the human barrier, almost nudging the pickets' chests. Pavel, with Roly behind him, climbed on board. Though his heart was racing, he felt Roly's hand on his shoulder and was grateful for the support.

He nodded to the driver who was leaning on the steering wheel and chewing gum as if none of it was his business. He heard Roly speak to him. 'It's your job at risk an'all, Guv.'

Pavel steadied himself with one hand on the front seat and waved his newspaper with the other. 'Just a minute of your time, lads. It's all I ask.' He scanned blank faces, donkey jackets, woollen hats. There was a subdued atmosphere, a few bitten lips. 'I'm Pavel Kowaleski and this is my mate, Roly. We're from Lundby Edge Colliery in South Yorkshire.' He let go of the seat. His hand felt clammy. He'd been gripping hard. He tapped the tabloid headline. 'Look at this. *Railway Workers Support Striking Miners!*' He waited for the words to have impact. 'They're supporting us to help save your jobs! Don't throw it in their faces. You don't turn your backs on your mates in this job.'

Only a few miners at the back were looking at him, albeit sheepishly. The others were staring at their feet or straight ahead, anywhere but at his face. 'We've got wives and kids to feed like you have,' Pavel went on. 'We've got rents and mortgages and electricity bills to pay. We're all making sacrifices. We're fighting for the industry. Don't let Thatcher win.'

There was a general mumbling then the growl of a single voice, 'That woman should be shot, I'll grant you.'

'If you think that, mate, don't do her work for her. It's in your own interests to come out on strike.'

'What about my apprenticeship?' It was a young lad. Pavel would have to avoid being side-tracked.

The mumbling grew. He threw his newspaper to the man in the front seat who was fiddling with the winder on a watch, as if the union interruption was an everyday occurrence. Pavel straightened his shoulders, raising the palms of his empty hands. 'Look. Is it asking too much? If you don't stand up to Macgregor and Thatcher, it won't be twenty thousand jobs that are lost. In the end nearly every man in this industry will be on the dole.'

He tried to catch the eyes of individuals, hoping for at least one convert. 'Come out with the Yorkshire lads for a swift victory.'

A thin faced man in a red checked jacket had his head in his newspaper, but looked up. 'Tell Scargill to give us a bloody ballot. Has anybody told him we're supposed to be a democracy?'

The driver revved the engine and looked over his shoulder, as if suddenly interested. 'Keep your gob shut, Ozzie and give yer arse a chance,' he said. 'Bleeding Democracy? Don't start on that old chestnut. Let the bugger finish and we'll all get to work.'

'I'm not here to talk about Arthur Scargill,' Pavel said, 'though he's right. There's no other way. History proves it. It worked in '72, didn't it? Because we were united. Don't let Thatcher destroy our communities.'

'She won't have to. Arthur bloody Scargill will do that for her,' the man Pavel now recognised as Ozzie shouted. 'If your pit's dead it's dead. Be realistic.'

Pavel felt his colour rising. 'My pit's not dead, Ozzie. It's not even on the hit-list. I'm on strike for all of us.' He hadn't meant to sound like a bountiful do-gooder. 'Corton Wood's nowhere near worked out yet. They've just spent a load of money on it…' He was being drawn into the conspiracy theory that he knew might be counter-productive. *Stick to the saving jobs argument*, Roly had advised. There was no time for all the issues. At least a few of these men would have voted for Thatcher in '79. Pavel was well aware that Arthur's brand of socialism was not universally popular with some of the older union members.

Others were joining in now, including a man who looked near to retirement age. 'My bloody wife'll murder me if I don't bring home bacon. That's the truth.'

'Give over, Bunny,' somebody called. 'From what I've heard, your wife's had more than her fair share of meat and two veg.'

Miners on the back seat sniggered. 'Hey, Bunny, we can vouch for that. Chas 'ere says he kept your bed warm regular when you were on nights.' Bunny waved two fingers. A cheer. Laughter.

Pavel stifled a smile. He'd need to shout to regain control and his throat was dry. Through the back window he could see the sergeant approaching.

'Listen. This Government's paid off the police force with hefty wage rises and it wants its money's worth. Thatcher will be getting coppers to do her dirty work. She took on Macgregor to sell out the steel industry didn't she? And now she's put him in charge of the Coal Board to carve us up.' He swallowed hard, hoping he wouldn't cough. 'I'm asking you to think again. Think about your wives and kids. Do you want 'em to have a future?' He pointed at the young lad. 'And I want us to save your apprenticeship as well, pal.' The lad nodded.

Pavel glanced over his shoulder. The police officer had climbed on board and was shoving past Roly. 'Okay, that's it, mate. They've listened to you long enough. It's time to come off.'

'Thanks for listening,' Pavel said, and raising his hand in acknowledgement, he followed the officer and jumped down from the bus. Roly followed. The picket line parted in the middle, the men moved aside and two constables opened the gates. Grim faced, the sergeant waved the driver through into the pit yard.

Roly patted Pavel's back. 'Well done.'

The remaining pickets gathered into small groups, chatting for a few minutes before wandering away.

Pavel had no sense of a job well done, only a deep unease. He wondered if some of the workers might have followed them off the bus, joined the strike, if Roly had been coordinator.

'They'll think on tonight, Pav,' Roly said. 'There'll be some of them join us next week, you'll see.'

Pavel rubbed his hands together, tried to look cheerful. 'Hope so.'

'Power to the People!' Coker shouted, fisting a salute as he headed back to a waiting car. Pavel rolled his eyes. Coker didn't give a shit about anybody but himself, let alone the People.

'Come on,' Roly said. 'Don't bother with that silly sod. He's been watching too much telly. We've done our bit. If we leave now we'll be home in time for you to get to school gates and collect that little lad of yours.'

Chapter Six

Camping Trip

September 1971
Lundby, South Yorkshire

By nine a.m. Pavel had already spent two hours by the Earl's lake. He had a permit. He read the sign that told him fishing here was a concession that a former Lord had bestowed on his miners sixty years before, when the family had not only owned the land but also the rights to the coal beneath it. He tossed bread crusts into the water, watching a pair of mallards paddling towards him from nearby reeds.

Out of bed at first light, he'd cycled through the woods to be assured of catching any tench that might rise on an early September morning. There were two other men on the bank when he'd arrived and they'd responded to his wave with nods and a quiet, 'How do.' This was not a place where men shared idle chit-chat. They might help each other to handle a landing net or weigh a pike, even whisper to each other briefly, but the need for silence was understood. The same men might meet in a pub later, yell across a bar – but not across a fishing lake.

A bee buzzing with late summer laziness landed on Pavel's open lunch box. In his hurry he'd only had time to pack a few jam sandwiches. From the woods he heard the low coopee-coo of a woodpigeon and the squawk of a distant pheasant. The sense of peace was so overpowering and perfect that Pavel was content to sit, to think, to watch the lake shifting in the wake of a coot or from the whirlpool of a roach.

Helen was collecting her textbooks from a bookshop in town. He'd offered to help but she'd told him he'd be a distraction. Did she think he would complain again at her leaving? He had to admit she needed more space than he'd given her, like a butterfly he might hold for too long, feeling its wing tips beating against his cupped hands. He cast the line out over the muddy fringes of the water then wound it forward a fraction until the reel clicked.

Close to the bank a pond skater landed. Pavel studied it. It had no weight, looked fragile. Yet there must be strength in its spindly legs, standing so tall on water. There was so much teeming life beneath this filmy surface. So much you missed if you didn't look. Sometimes he thought people skimmed through their days, caught up in trivial tasks. No depth. Not like Helen. She was right to nag him. He could achieve more. On days like this though, a simple life appealed: solitary contemplation. Freedom.

The roar of a motorbike shattered the peace and Pavel groaned when he realised it was Jakub. Not a fisherman, it wouldn't occur to his brother to switch off the engine before he reached the lake.

One of the anglers threw down his rod. 'Hell's teeth, Pav. Can't you do summat about that lad? Bloody nuisance. No chance of a bite with him around.' The man waved Jakub away. 'Oy. Evel Knievel. Sling your hook.'

Pavel sighed as Jakub, still astride the bike, manoeuvred it towards him with his feet. 'What do you want, Jakub? Couldn't it wait?'

'Remember Stan's dad who runs the Scouts?' Answering a question with a question was a sign Jakub was on a mission. 'He says he could get us a couple of tents next weekend if I let him know today. We could go to Derbyshire.'

Pavel gazed at his fishing float. 'We? Two tents? What are you up to?'

'If you brought Helen, I could ask Maria. You know she's from a good Catholic family so there's no chance her dad would let her come with me, not without a minder.'

'Can't blame him.'

'It could be a laugh, the four of us. Maria knows Helen. I can tell her dad we've got one tent for the girls and another for the lads.'

Pavel shook his head. 'So you want me to baby-sit.'

'I thought you might be glad of an opportunity to – be alone with Helen.'

Pavel yanked the rod back, wound in the line for more bait, lowering the rod onto the metal rest beside him. 'Alone? With you there? And what about transport? You're not thinking of taking your bike are you?'

'Thought the old man might let us have car for one night if you were in charge. You've passed your test.'

Pavel groaned. He didn't relish a weekend with the whinging Maria, but on the other hand... 'Go on then. But you can ask Dad yourself. And if Helen says no, I'm not coming either. Find another mug.'

Jakub grinned. 'Thanks, Pav. Owe you one.' He signed thumbs-up, revved the bike and skidded off down a track between the trees.

Pavel glanced sheepishly at the two fishermen. 'Sorry, lads. He's a bugger, my brother.'

The man fishing nearest to him nodded. 'Aye. Last I heard he'd been seen scrambling through some lass's bedroom window. Like a rat up a drainpipe. Thinks he's Casanova. You better keep him away from my daughter any road! I'll hold you responsible, Pavel. Now, let's have some hush.'

A dragonfly hovered, flashed blue and green and shot off across the lake.

Pavel had never been able to deny his younger brother anything. As brothers they looked alike but Pavel wondered how they could be so different. They shared a bedroom, shared their plans. Jakub wanted to travel. There was no chance of a girl like Helen Farrimond tying Jakub down too soon, he'd said. Pavel wished Jakub would show more responsibility. Maybe it was time to have a strong word with him. As if he'd listen.

Pavel fished for the rest of the day, occasionally laying down his rod, resting his head on his rucksack and napping.

At dusk he cycled home and discovered that Jakub had persuaded their dad to let them borrow the car and that both girls had agreed to a weekend's camping. Jakub's ability to charm never failed to amaze.

★ ★ ★

Derbyshire dales

They climbed the hill above the campsite, stopping to rest on an outcrop of limestone and take in the view. 'I think I could stay here,' Pavel said, with a sudden uncharacteristic dread of returning to the pit on Monday morning.

Shades of green deepened then paled beneath wedges of shifting sunlight. His eyes panned the fields, village, stone farm buildings, a cluster of cottages around the church, the Kinder Scout peak. He'd climbed it once, in his last year in school, in Army and Navy store boots which he'd paid for with his wages from a paper round.

On the campsite below he could see his father's old Morris 1000. With ninety-five thousand miles on the clock, it had spluttered, steamed and smoked onto the field as they'd arrived, convincing Pavel there'd be no jaunts around the dales this weekend. They'd have to stay put. He didn't intend to be the one accused of finishing off the jalopy.

'Don't you think we should have helped with the shopping?' Helen said.

Since they'd only packed a few tins and packets – beans, peas, rice pudding and cornflakes – Maria and Jakub had agreed to find a local shop where they might buy milk and fresh bread.

'No. It's Jake's plan to con Maria into thinking he has a domesticated side. He says it never fails with women.'

'Think you'll find me harder to please.'

'Got that message. Still, I'll cook breakfast tomorrow.' He jumped down from the rock and began to gather the last of the summer daisies, splitting their stems and threading them into a chain. 'Did I mention I'm starting the engineering course next week?'

'No. That's great.'

He wound the daisy strings around his wrist and gazed into the distance, wondering if he dared to mention...

'You've gone quiet,' she said.

He turned to face her. 'Been thinking. Not now. I mean, after your course. We could get married.' He untangled the daisy chain and lowered it over her fringe like a medieval coronet. 'I know – you told me to stop asking.'

'Down on your knees,' she said. He fell onto his knees and she pushed him over, laughing. 'You'll have to do the traditional thing. Ask Uncle Billy's permission.'

'He can't wait to get rid of you,' Pavel said, scrambling to his feet. 'He'll probably pay me to take you off his hands.'

She punched his arm and ran down the hillside, scattering sheep. 'I can't stop,' she shouted, her feet slithering in tennis shoes.

Pavel chased her to the campsite till he caught her, held her. 'I promise to look after you.'

'I'll hold you to that,' she said.

After a makeshift dinner of tinned mince and instant mashed potato, Pavel took photos using his new instamatic camera, then suggested a trip to the pub.

It was a traditional stone hostelry with wooden settles and open fireplaces filled with dried flowers for the summer. Personalised tankards hung from a beam above the bar and hand pumps were decorated with horses, beagle hounds and huntsmen. Despite being underage Jakub had ordered their drinks.

'Interesting pictures,' Pavel said.

Jakub was leaning on the bar, chin on his fist, eyeing the barmaid. 'Huh?'

'On the pumps. Interesting pumps.'

The two girls had settled on a bench in a corner and Pavel delivered orange juices to them, marvelling at how nobody ever questioned Jakub, requested ID. When he returned to the bar to collect the beer, Jakub had progressed to flirting.

'Behave yourself,' Pavel said. 'Don't upset Maria.'

The barmaid wiped her hands on a bar towel and sashayed through the back of the pub to the tap room. Pavel followed Jakub's gaze: the mini skirt, legs as long as –

'So are we swapping tents tonight then?' Jakub said.

Pavel took a swig of beer, wiped the froth from his top lip as he considered the implications. 'They've set their sleeping bags out in their own tent. You'd better remember what you promised Maria's dad.'

'Bugger that.'

'Helen feels responsible for Maria and I'm responsible for you.'

'Oh come on, Pav. You're a bloody kill-joy sometimes. Are you telling me you've not – '

'I'm telling you nothing. Mind your own business.'

Jakub slipped a small packet into the back pocket of Pavel's jeans then glanced over his shoulder at the girls. 'I bought a pack of three. There's a spare.' Pavel peered into his drink, cheeks flushed. Jakub nudged him. 'Listen. You and Helen go to campsite first. I'll wait half an hour, then bring Maria back. Whichever tent you're in will tell me how the land lies. Okay?'

Pavel laughed, picked up his glass. 'You've got it all worked out haven't you?'

'Don't invent problems. Shouldn't it be you leading me astray? Call yourself a big brother.'

Pavel spluttered into the beer.

There were mostly old regulars in the pub: farmers scowling over jars of real ale, men with walking sticks chewing over the price of sheep, beer, and the problems of cottages sold to posh weekenders. When Pavel said hello, the locals responded with sharp nods.

After a couple of hours chatting about sport, music and the recent high jinks of miners they knew, there was a lull in the conversation and Pavel blurted out that he and Helen were engaged. Maria squealed like a seven year old at Christmas and congratulated them. Jakub put his head in his hands. Helen begged Jakub to keep the news to himself and scolded Pavel. 'You shouldn't have blabbed to Jakub. It'll be all over the pit by Tuesday.'

According to instruction, at ten o'clock Pavel suggested he and Helen return to the campsite and Jakub said that he and Maria would stay for another drink.

Miles from the city, the sky was clear of light pollution. Pavel stopped by the church, scrambled onto a wall. He hauled Helen up beside him and pointed out the Plough and Cassiopeia and told her about giant stars and dwarf stars and pulsar discovery and how much he loved her – to test if she was still paying attention.

'You know so much,' she said. He'd anticipated a lecture on the fore-shortening of his school life but she kissed his neck. He lifted her from the wall and they walked on.

The only light on the camp-site came from a handful of dim hurricane lamps, luminous dots scattered across the field where a few tents had been pitched at random. Pavel had remembered to bring a torch and he swept the beam from side to side across the grass, stumbling over guy ropes until he found his tent. He pulled Helen inside and propped up the torch against a rucksack. Their giant shadows were cast on the green stained canvas walls that smelled of mildew and old age.

'Have you two planned this?' she said.

'Jakub wants to swap places.'

'Not your idea then?'

'No, course not. If you don't want to…' They sat down on the sleeping bags.

'Ouch,' she said, pulling something from beneath her, 'What's this?'

It was Jakub's shoe. The rest of his belongings were strewn across the groundsheet as if he'd held his rucksack upside down and shaken out its contents.

'Sit here,' Pavel said. 'My bed's tidier.'

She moved closer, suggesting he switch off the torch to conserve the battery. 'People might see our shadows.'

'People are inside tents. What don't you want them to see?' He switched off the torch, kissed her, lowering her onto his sleeping bag. He felt his world shrink suddenly to this one cosy pocket of space and time. No Uncle Billy around now. She kissed his ear lobe. 'Oh God,' he said, 'You know that drives me insane.'

He unfastened her blouse, his fingers fumbling from button to button in the dark. His lips swept across the top of her breasts.

There was a sudden tugging at the guy ropes and the tent flap opened. Helen rolled away.

'Psst! Pav! It's me. Can I come in? We've had a row. Maria's crying. She's asking for Helen.'

'Bloody hell, Jakub. You pick your moments. Can't you tell her you're sorry? Sort it.' Pavel switched on the torch.

Helen fastened her buttons and patted around on hands and knees till she found her shoes. Pavel took her hand. 'Don't go.'

'I'd better calm her down,' she said. 'See you in the morning.' She crept out of the tent and Jakub crawled in.

'I'll put it right tomorrow, Pav, honest,' Jakub said.

Pavel groaned. 'Too damn right you will. I'm in bloody pain here!'

The air was sharp with promised autumn and Pavel's breath formed clouds in the torchlight. He undressed, shivered, moaned that it was cold and snuggled down into his sleeping bag, zipping the sides up to his neck.

Jakub switched off the torch. 'From what I saw you were warm enough a few minutes back.'

'Shut it.'

A baby was wailing in a nearby tent, a mother soothing. Owls hooted from the woods, male and female calling and answering. A car boot clicked, a billycan rattled. Sound travelled easily at this time of night. A girl was whimpering.

'Oh, no,' Jakub said. 'That's Maria snivelling.'

He promised, Helen. My dad will kill him when he finds out.

Then Helen's voice, calm, apologetic. 'Shh. I'd no intention of spending the night with him, Maria.'

Jakub sniggered. 'Your girlfriend tells porkies.'

'Go to sleep. You've caused enough trouble.'

'Said I'm sorry. I'll make it up to you.'

Pavel grunted and turned over. He lay awake for what seemed like hours. Would he ever find an opportunity to be alone with Helen?

He woke early but there was no sign of his brother. Jakub's sleeping bag was empty, his belongings tidied away. Eager to keep his promise to cook breakfast, Pavel crawled out of the tent, blinking and bleary eyed. The grass, wet with overnight dew, soaked through his jeans leaving wet patches over his knees. He unlocked the boot, finding an old primus – also on loan from the scout master – a carton of eggs and a pack of bacon. He lit the stove and switched on his portable radio.

The smell of frying brought the girls from their tent and the three of them rummaged in the provision box for cutlery and sauce bottles. Maria questioned Pavel on Jakub's whereabouts but Pavel shrugged. 'Anyone's guess.' Then the conversation turned to Led Zeppelin, T. Rex and the demise of the Beatles.

After breakfast Pavel spotted Jakub marching across the field towards them, carrying a bunch of Michaelmas daisies. 'He's back,' he said.

Jakub ran the last few yards to Maria, hung his head. 'Got these for you. Sorry. I was – a bit presumptuous.' Pavel marvelled. Four syllables. Impressive.

No one asked where the flowers came from, but since it was Sunday and there were no shops open, he assumed that Jakub had either picked them from a local garden or robbed the graveyard.

The gift appeared to impress Maria and the couple wandered off hand in hand across the dale. Pavel boiled the kettle, washed up the breakfast dishes and Helen dried. They packed the plates and cups back into the box then sat on plastic bags on the grass. Helen picked up a book.

'I'm supposed to have read this before I start the course.'

He had not forgotten that Helen would be leaving for college within the week and he knew that Jakub's long walk with his girlfriend was more a peace offering to his annoyed brother than a romantic gesture to Maria. Jakub was offering opportunity.

'Care to dance?' he said, pulling Helen to her feet before she could answer. She dropped the book. 'I'm still practising what you taught me. One, two three,' he said, treading on her toes and steering her towards the tent.

Chapter Seven

Band Concert

April 1984

Lundby, South Yorkshire

Semolina and boiled cabbage. Uncle Billy had said institutions reeked of the stuff. Since he was old enough to remember when the General Infirmary had been the workhouse, and when the old people's home had been a pub, Helen had asked if he feared boiled cabbage and semolina were his future. He'd laughed, told her not to be cheeky. He made no secret of his delight at his niece's return.

She sat in the headmaster's study, noting a whiff of optimism about the school where she had once been a pupil. This morning when she'd walked into the entrance hall, floor to ceiling artwork had lifted her spirits: collages of frogs leaping from lily pads and paintings of butterflies, symmetrical wings of orange and black. They breathed warmth and colour into what had once been a labyrinth of bleak, post-war corridors. Moreover, there was the prospect of a job.

'The school needs somebody urgently for temporary cover,' Billy had told her. 'Why don't you offer? Take your mind off – whatever it's on.' He was Chair of Governors of the school. The job information, he'd said, was hot off the board's press.

Thankfully there was no application form to complete for just a few weeks' supply teaching, just the usual registration and insurance numbers which she'd found on a scrap of paper in the back of her purse. The headmaster, Mr Read, had shown no interest in why she'd left London.

The rattle of a tea trolley outside the staff room and the sound of children singing, offered an unexpected sense of homecoming, like the soft hug of old slippers on tired feet. Suddenly she was hungry. Even the smell of cheese pie, baked beans and mashed potato whetted her appetite, raising hope of an invitation to lunch.

'Your uncle tells me you've been teaching in Cheshire, Helen?'

'Yes. Eight years in a village school, but I haven't worked for the last two.'

She had not told Tibby or Billy any details of Guy's behaviour. After several weeks spent brooding over preceding months, Helen suspected the girl in the apartment was unlikely to be Guy's sole infidelity. And if Tibby had any suspicions, she hadn't voiced them again, nor had Billy pried into her motives for wanting to stay on in Lundby. Not yet.

The sore throat and shivers she'd experienced the day after her return had culminated in sickness, exhaustion and a week in bed. A lost week. Mostly she'd slept. She recalled Tibby changing sheets around her, delirium, a visit from the local GP. When she was well enough to sit up and eat breakfast from a tray, she was confronted by an extravagant bouquet of white lilies on her dressing table. They dominated the bedroom, the air laden with their scent while the rabbit ornaments were filmed with a dusting of orange pollen. A small card attached to a wire stem read: *from Guy with love. I hope you're feeling better. Speak soon.* Tibby told her she had been fielding nightly phone calls.

Through an open window in Mr Read's office, Helen heard children chanting skipping rhymes and her eyes were drawn to a simple arrangement of pink tulips in an earthenware jar on his desk. It was a school standard–issue pot, the sort of rough unglazed clay that begged to be touched. He was turning the vase idly as he spoke and she noticed the petals speckled with dirt as if they'd been picked from a grass verge and splashed by passing traffic.

'A gift from the garden of a generous Top Infant,' he said. 'I'm not sure that parental permission was involved. A bouquet wrapped in waxed bread paper, would you believe?'

'A lovely thought.'

'Yes but I wonder what he's after. Sorry, that was cynical.'

The deathly sickliness of the lilies in her room had been so oppressive that she'd asked Tibby to take them downstairs. She understood cynicism.

Mr Read explained that a final year student who'd been on teaching practice was due to leave and that the class teacher was unexpectedly in need of back surgery and unlikely to return before September. 'But nothing's certain so I can't offer a contract. I don't think we've ever had a past pupil return to teach here but the job's yours week by week if you want it.'

Helen thanked him and accepted, realising the implication: she couldn't return to Guy immediately even if she wanted.

'Start after Easter then,' Mr Read said. 'And welcome back.' A bell rang to mark the end of playtime. 'I'll show you round and you can meet the children.' She smoothed the skirt of the crisp navy suit that she thought made her look prim but which Tibby had persuaded her to buy.

The week after she'd arrived, Billy had handed her a sealed envelope. 'An overnight bag won't keep you clothed for a fortnight let alone a term if you find a job.' When she opened it she'd found three hundred pounds. He'd insisted it was a gift but the chance to repay him had given her a good reason to find temporary work. She had only a small amount in personal savings and was reluctant to use the marital joint account, and, in any case, she hadn't made contributions to that for two years.

She followed the headmaster into the corridor. For her once child-sized feet, the route between classrooms and the school hall had seemed endless. Now she realised it was no distance at all. She could hear dinner staff chattering, a radio, the rattle of crockery, doors banging and children giggling in the toilet block by the cloakroom.

Displayed, on a board alongside a Monet poster – a brooding view of London with the Houses of Parliament in the background – she noticed a collection of paintings: children's attempts at impressionism. But any brief yearning for the capital soon evaporated when Mr Read ushered her into the midst of a lively group of nine year olds. She clutched her handbag as if it contained everything most precious to her, though it held only a small pack of tissues, her purse and Uncle Billy's biro.

The headmaster explained to the children that she would be teaching them after the Easter holiday and the student teacher assured her that there was already a topic on the locality planned for the summer term.

'Mrs Eagleton grew up in Lundby, children. She'll know all about its history and geography,' Mr Read said. Right now the only history she remembered was her own.

A freckle faced boy raised his hand. 'We're having an Easter egg hunt this afternoon. Will you be coming?'

Mr. Read shook his head. 'No she won't, Jake. She'll be spending the rest of the day browsing through class work and finding her way around our school resources – after she's had lunch of course. Cheese pie today I think.'

'Thank you for asking,' she said.

She stayed in the school for the rest of the day exploring library books, photocopiers and the latest BBC computer which alarmed her. So much had changed since she'd last taught and she hoped she wouldn't make a fool of herself. It didn't take long to become outdated.

When she arrived home she found Uncle Billy glued to the television news but he gave her a hug on hearing she'd accepted the job, though his conversation soon turned to his favourite topic.

'They've announced there'll be no ballot,' he said, when she'd settled beside him on the sofa. He lowered the volume on the television. 'Thirteen votes against, eight for and three abstentions. I think the union's making a mistake, don't you? A ballot *about* a ballot?'

Tibby was standing behind the sofa. She placed her hands on Helen's shoulders. 'Guy phoned again this afternoon, love. I didn't say where you were.'

'And we know whose side he'll be on, don't we?' Billy said. He'd started on a crossword now and was fumbling beneath cushions trying to locate his missing pen.

'I don't think that's going to help the situation, Billy.' Tibby rolled her eyes and went into the kitchen.

He shrugged. 'I saw Pavel Kowaleski today. Did I tell you he was strike coordinator?'

Helen nodded, handed him the biro. 'You told me weeks ago.'

'He agrees with Arthur Scargill. Legally they don't have to call a ballot. You can be sure the Government will beat them over the head with that decision… where did you find this pen?'

'How is he?'

'Pavel? He's fine.'

'You didn't mention me to him, did you?'

'I did. I told him you were staying with us and he said he'd heard. You might have his son in your class. He must be about nine.'

'I may have met him. Does Pavel know that Guy's – ?'

'He's known for some time. I told him.'

She wondered how often the two men had spoken of her. 'I suppose he thinks I'm a traitor.'

Billy looked up from the crossword. 'He's got enough on his plate without worrying about you or your husband.'

The rebuke stung. After all, Billy had initiated the Pavel conversation. She took a tissue from her handbag.

'Sorry,' he said, 'Didn't mean to snap. Pavel did say, "Remember me to her."'

Tibby came in from the kitchen, laid out sandwiches and iced fingers on the coffee table and handed Helen a plate. 'I'm getting involved in the women's support group, fund raising for the strikers: organising events, soup kitchen, jumble sales, collections in town. That sort of thing. I thought you might like to help, Helen.'

Billy groaned, threw down the newspaper. 'Are you mad, woman? She's the wife of a Tory MP. What would people make of that?'

'No one will know, will they?' Helen said.

'Surely they wouldn't make a connection,' Tibby said. 'Guy wasn't an MP when she married him, and I've never told anybody – even if you have. I don't think Pavel would snitch.'

Billy coughed, dropped his biro. 'If some of the lads find out, there could be bad feeling, that's all.'

Helen finished the tea, rolled up Billy's newspaper and tapped it on his head. 'But am I not the niece of a well-respected councillor? You're my cover.'

'Anybody would think MI5 were watching her,' Tibby said.

Billy snatched the newspaper from Helen and flicked the pages back into shape. 'And what makes you think they're not?' After muttering about how he hated people messing up his paper, he resumed the crossword.

'There's a band concert on Sunday evening. I'd be glad of help with refreshments,' Tibby said. 'So what do you think, Helen?'

'I'd like that.'

Billy shook his head then bit into a ham sandwich.

★ ★ ★

Colliery band concerts had been a frequent part of her early life and she remembered accompanying Billy to competitions and galas, concerts and processional marches across the region. Wherever there was a banner, there was Billy. Though Helen enjoyed brass, she'd only learned to play a descant recorder and a tambourine.

The concert hall at the Miners' Institute would be packed with fans, Billy said. Tickets were free to the miners and their families, so it would be more a morale boosting exercise than fund raiser. As they needed to help prepare the venue, Billy and Tibby left home early: refreshments to deliver, the stage to clear of equipment from the dance the night before, and raffle prizes to display.

Attendance at the event worried Helen more than the visit to her old school. It was years since she had been in the Institute and she was unsure who'd be there, who might remember her. She dressed in blue jeans and a new white embroidered shirt, applied make-up to boost her confidence.

She found Uncle Billy waiting in the porch to sign her in as a non-member guest.

The entrance door opened onto a side view of the stage. Musicians were adjusting folding chairs, tuning their instruments in discordant bursts, in short riffs and recognisable melodies. They were wearing green and gold uniforms that Billy said had been purchased, fortunately, just before the strike. Some members of the band were striking miners, others born into brass families and had inherited their instruments, pit jobs and musical culture. Girls were admitted to the band now, though Helen doubted they'd gain permission to play pool or snooker in the games room.

Formica tables and low chairs were ranged around the concert hall. All seats were occupied and the room was beginning to fog with smoke that caught the back of her throat. The snippets of conversation she heard on her way to the kitchen, mainly concerned the strike.

'Don't know how we'll manage.'

'Let's hope it's not for long. We've had to cancel our holiday.'

'Isn't that Billy Farrimond's niece? What's she doing here?'

She squeezed between tables, lowering her eyes, as if she had TORY WIFE tattooed across her forehead. She hung her coat behind the kitchen door and asked Tibby what she should do first.

Tibby was setting out cups and saucers. 'You look lovely, Helen. Good to see you making an effort. You've got your colour back. You'll find tea and coffee in the carrier bag. The water in the urn's almost boiling.'

Helen dropped tea bags into an earthenware pot that looked too heavy to lift, poured milk into jugs and spooned cheap instant coffee into cups while Tibby arranged shortbread biscuits onto mis-matched plates. Preparations were halted to listen to Billy's introductory speech and subsequent applause.

As the lights in the hall dimmed, a hush settled and the band began to play the *William Tell Overture*. Helen switched off the water heater to silence its bubbling and laughed at the sight of children bobbing on chairs as if on horseback.

The second piece was a change of tempo. Tibby looked puzzled. 'It sounds familiar. It's sad, but a lovely melody. Do you recognise it, Helen?'

'We played it at William's funeral,' she said. 'Ravel's Pavane: a tune for a dead child.' It sounded more tragic played by a brass band.

'I'm sorry. I should have realised,' Tibby said. She opened the kitchen door wide, switched off the lights. 'Come here. Look. There's Pavel by the window with his wife, Cheryl. He has his back to us. That's Jake between them.'

Even in the half-light Helen recognised Pavel's bowed head, his hair short, straight. Pop stars and footballers might be sporting frizzy perms, but not him. Perhaps his shoulders were a fraction broader. She caught his profile as he turned and hugged Jake. She'd wondered if Pavel might attend the concert but she hadn't expected to be so stirred by seeing him.

The Ravel ended to restrained applause. There was a lump in her throat. Tibby touched her hand. 'Are you all right, love?'

'I'm fine.'

The band launched into a brisk Rodetsky march. Jake was clapping, stamping to the beat, Pavel's wife glancing around the room.

Tibby whispered. 'His wife looks common, don't you think?'

Helen had a shadowy view of a girl in a jacket with padded shoulders, hair clipped to one side, blonde curls cascading over one ear. 'He must love her. He married her.'

'Got her pregnant and had no reason not to.'

'They have a lovely son.'

It had been a mistake to come here. If Helen escaped now, would Tibby believe she'd been struck by a sudden migraine? Negotiating a route between packed tables would not make for a quick exit.

'Your uncle says the boy's the only reason he stays with her,' Tibby said. 'There's no way that girl will sacrifice her nights out, or her shoe money for the strike. She's a flighty piece.'

There were shouts, cheers and whistles on the final note of a Strauss waltz. 'Gossip, Tibby. I don't want to hear any more about Pavel – or his wife.'

Muttering, Tibby switched on the lights and rummaged in a cupboard. When she heard Billy announce a short interval, Helen rolled up the kitchen hatch and the audience headed either towards the bar in the next room or to the coffee counter.

First in the queue was Jake followed by Pavel then Cheryl who slouched with her back against the counter, scanning the hall. Pavel was near enough to touch.

'Hello, Jake,' Helen said. 'Enjoying the concert?'

'Yeah. Great. My dad bought me a trumpet. Could I have orange juice please?'

'So are you hoping to play in the band when you're older?'

'If I'm good enough. I'm having lessons at school. I have to practise every night though, don't I, Dad?' Tibby poured the juice.

'You'll be good enough if you work hard,' Pavel said.

Helen stirred tea bags. Her hand trembled. She looked up. 'What can I get for you, Pavel?'

'Hello, Helen,' he said, picking at coins in his palm. 'This is Mrs. Eagleton, Cheryl. She's going to be Jake's teacher. What would you like?'

'Jake told me. I'll have coffee thanks,' Cheryl said, offering Helen a weak smile. 'And his father never makes him practise, Mrs Eagleton. That's my job. Pavel's too soft.' Jake grinned. Cheryl teetered away on her high heels, Jake behind slurping orange juice through a straw.

'I'll have tea, please,' Pavel said. 'It's good to see you again, Helen. How many years has it been?'

'I've not been counting,' Helen said, catching exchanged glances between Tibby and Pavel.

'Are you staying long?' he asked.

'Probably till the end of July.' Their eyes met. He held her gaze for a second longer than she expected and the milk she was pouring overflowed into his saucer. She grabbed kitchen paper and mopped it.

'Don't worry about it,' he said. 'How much do I owe you?'

She was about to reply but Billy interrupted, slapping the counter. 'Sorry to push in.' He nodded at Pavel. 'I can see you're flustered, Helen. But can you serve the pensioners quickly or there'll be all hell let loose.' Billy had invited the occupants of a local nursing home and a succession of wheelchairs and carers were blocking the aisle.

'Yes. If you send them back to their tables I'll take the tea out to them,' she said. Beneath the counter was a crockery cupboard and she rummaged for longer than she needed gathering more cups and trays.

Tibby had been wiping up the earlier milk spillage and was refilling a teapot at the boiler. 'There's no charge for refreshments tonight, Pavel. Didn't Helen tell you?'

'Think she's forgotten me.'

How could he expect a meaningful conversation – with a sea of faces watching, with Jake and his trumpet chatter, with Cheryl glowering and Billy's demands? Now Jake had returned, nagging for an ice cream.

'Yes, you can have one,' Pavel said. 'Thanks Tibby.' Still gathering fresh cups, Helen peeped above the counter, watched him – tea slopping into his saucer – as he led his son to the far side of the room where ices were on sale from a cool box.

By the time she spotted Coker, the queue had dwindled. There was a slight touch of premature grey at his temples but the smirk was the same. It defined him.

'Well, this is a blast from the past,' he said. Tibby banged the teapot on the counter and Coker retreated as a fountain of hot liquid shot in his direction.

'This is my niece.'

'I know who she is, Mrs F,' he said, looking Helen up and down. 'Slumming it here aren't you? Does Cheryl know you're back?'

'As if you didn't tell her,' Tibby said, narrowing her eyes.

Coker winked. 'Why would I? I only came to say hello to her ladyship here. I'm off to the bar for a pint. Expect we'll be seeing more of you then.' He grinned, helped himself to biscuits and swaggered away.

A few minutes later Helen noticed he'd made himself comfortable on Jake's empty seat, drinking beer, nudging Cheryl as if sharing a joke. The pair glanced towards the hatch. When Jake and Pavel returned with ice creams and the lights dimmed for the second time, Coker crept to a table nearer the stage.

The concert ended with a standing ovation, foot stamping and shouts of 'Encore.' Billy gave a thank you speech, though his exhortation to support the strike seemed unnecessary. As the audience left, Jake swayed towards the hatch balancing a tower of dirty crockery which tumbled onto the counter. Pavel followed, catching two cups as they rolled off the edge.

'Phew,' Jake said. 'That was close. Goodnight, Mrs Eagleton.'

'Goodnight, Jake. Thank you – for collecting the cups.'

'See you around then, Helen,' Pavel said.

She took the cups from him. 'Expect so.'

'Do you want me to collect any more cups, Dad?' Pavel gave her a sheepish half-smile and steered Jake away.

Tibby sidled up to Helen. 'Someone must have told Cheryl who you are. Did you see her face?'

'An ex-girlfriend in town? Hardly significant.'

'In this village they have long memories.'

'Was she local? I don't remember her. She's pretty.'

'A brassy piece.' Tibby giggled at the pun. 'You wouldn't remember her, Helen. She's three years younger than you.'

The musicians were packing instruments into cases and acknowledging members of the audience with waves, nods and *how-dos* as they left. Some had already disappeared through swing doors to the post-concert bar. Pavel had stopped to talk to Billy by the exit.

'I heard Pavel call you Tibby, not Bea like the others,' Helen said. 'Isn't that a bit familiar?'

Tibby raised her eyebrows. 'It was you who insisted Pavel should call me Tibby. Remember? I don't mind. Do you?'

'Yes. I think I do. Is that childish?'

'Yes. And it's a pity you were so prickly with him. Brusque.'

'I wasn't brusque.' Pavel and Billy were laughing. 'Was I?'

'I've met cuddlier hedgehogs,' Tibby said, and left the kitchen to check for further abandoned crockery. The kitchen offered Helen a good view of the hall.

Pavel shook Billy's hand and left.

'Damn,' she said.

Chapter Eight

Chicken wire

April 1984

Lundby, South Yorkshire

Pavel's habit of leaning against the kitchen cupboards and not sitting at the breakfast table irritated his wife. She'd told him it made her edgy: the way he tapped his fingers on the side of his mug as if he were waiting for something to happen or someone to knock on the door to whisk him away to more important matters.

A recent row had resulted in his retreat to the spare bedroom; the arrangement suited him. There was as much chance of communication and cooperation between him and Cheryl as the NUM and the Government. And now there was Helen. He'd suffered a battery of questions about her as soon as Jake had gone to bed after last night's band concert. Pavel was certain Coker had planted the poison. It was usually him.

From Pavel's position by the sink he could see Jake poking a carrot through the wire mesh on the rabbit hutch. It was the single mouldy carrot he'd found in the bottom of the vegetable rack. Bags of dried rabbit feed from the pet shop were too expensive, Cheryl said.

'But what if he dies, Mum, without proper food?'

'Ask your dad. He's the one on strike.'

'Don't worry. We'll get Harvey what he needs. But it won't hurt to find some natural stuff,' Pavel had told him.

'I think he'd like dandelion. There's plenty about at this time of year. Give him the carrot now and I'll call at the pet shop later.'

Cheryl emptied the dregs of the cornflakes into her bowl. The shopping was now Pavel's responsibility and he'd forgotten to buy a new packet. She hated the crumby bits at the bottom of the box. She threw the spoon into the dish and dropped two slices of bread into the toaster.

'For goodness sake, Pavel, sit down. If it makes you feel better, I'll apologise to Jake before I go to work.'

Pavel sat on the stool opposite and she stared at him.

'What is it now?' he said.

'It's you...it's as if... as if you're not here. Oh I don't know. '

'I'm always here.'

He'd tried to give her everything she wanted. He glanced around the kitchen at the pine units, the split level appliances, the beige ceramic tiles with Dutch windmills dotted at random intervals, the frilly café curtains he hated. All her choices. He'd fitted the kitchen himself between shifts, and bloody hard work it had been. The microwave was an addition, bought just before the strike.

'You know what I mean,' she said.

The toast popped. 'How can I know when you say you don't know yourself? The toast's done, by the way.'

'Don't get clever with me, Pavel, trying to avoid the issue.' He did know exactly what she meant, and he knew that she knew that he knew. It was why he preferred to lean against the cupboards looking out of the window and why he'd now take his time buttering a piece of toast.

'So, your old girlfriend's back?'

He bit the inside of his mouth, groaned and swallowed. 'Not this again. How have I ever given you reason to doubt my commitment to this family?'

'I've just said how.'

'You're making something out of nothing.' He licked the lesion forming in his cheek, realising too late that this would lend him a less than serious appearance.

'Coker says you were engaged. Take that look off your face.'

'What look? I just bit my...' Not a good time to explain why his tongue was in his cheek. 'I was only twenty for God's sake.'

'Did you sleep with her?'

'It was way before I met you.'

'Stumbled into me, you mean. Drunk. You never said you'd been engaged.'

His neck burned. The curse of honesty. He collected the plates, filled the bowl in the sink with hot water, adding the last squirt of washing-up liquid. He glanced through the window, hoping Jake wouldn't hear the bickering.

'I suppose you picked me up on the rebound,' she said. He sighed, shook his head. The way he remembered it, Cheryl had picked him up.

If he focused on the window pane he could see her reflection, the pert pretty features he'd once found attractive. Wouldn't most men find her desirable? So what was wrong with him?

Since her parents had retired to Skegness, Cheryl had been quick to retaliate after an argument, whisking Jake away for weekend visits to the seaside. Even so, something might be salvaged if he'd put down the dishcloth and kiss her, tell her he loved her. He couldn't.

He waved to Jake. How weird was that? Helen. Jake's teacher. And all Cheryl was concerned about was whether he'd slept with her, not whether he'd loved the girl. He remembered being young and inexperienced but it had involved love.

The stalemate was not Cheryl's fault. Pavel's entirely. He'd used her. Shameful. He should have known better. He had to take responsibility. His wife deserved better. A psychiatrist might say Pavel's snatched pre-marital affair with Cheryl had been the last outpourings of grief and anger. A primal scream. Pavel remembered Coker's ribald sarcasm. 'Three rounds and a knock out, was it, Pavel?' As if an unplanned pregnancy was something to snigger about.

Pavel had not made it to Jake's birth: baby two weeks early and father two miles underground at the time. But he knew as soon as he saw the tiny fists, the waxy, bloody screwed-up face, that something had been restored; that the world was somehow back in kilter. He'd made a promise right then to whatever it was that settled on his shoulders – maybe his conscience, (not God, he'd discarded that notion by then) – that he would protect this scrap of life to the end of his own. He'd remembered a poem Helen had once read to him. Some Irish poet, she'd said.

I am not yet born,
Let not the blood sucking bat or the rat… come near me.

Only the two lines Pavel remembered. They'd sprung to mind in that instant, when he picked up his son. Though he'd never profess to understand poetry, these words at least took on meaning. For the first couple of years of marriage he'd been content enough, so wrapped up was he in fatherhood – in spite of the failings of his own father as a role model.

Cheryl dropped an empty milk jug into the washing-up water, startling him. 'If you wash that plate any longer the pattern will disappear.'

'What?'

'We should have bought a dishwasher.'

Maybe he was too old and embittered for romantic notions, but seeing Helen again had stirred something in him, if only a memory of some emotion he'd forgotten. He picked up the tea towel, dried the plates. There was a word he was searching for: one you didn't hear much down a pit, except if somebody was acting the goat, singing love songs in the baths – one or two of the older blokes fancied they were Frank Sinatra.

A word.

Tenderness?

That was it.

'I can't think what you had in common with her,' Cheryl said. 'Coker says she was a snob. Did you fancy her because she was Billy Farrimond's niece? Thought you could get into his union good books and her knickers at the same time?'

He threw the tea towel onto the draining board. 'For crying out loud. It's history. She's married. I'm married. No need to be crude. And I'll thank Coker to keep his nose out. Wait till I see him. Sodding trouble maker!'

'What's she doing here anyway?'

'How the hell should I know?'

Cheryl grabbed her handbag from the kitchen worktop. 'One of us has to go to work so I suppose it had better be me. Make sure Jake has his packed lunch and his PE kit. I don't want Mrs *whatever she's called*, picking on him.' She slammed the door.

Most wives supported the strike. Why not Cheryl? 'She doesn't start teaching till after Easter,' he said, under his breath.

From the window Pavel watched her as she clip-clopped down the garden path then tiptoed across the lawn. She was well practised at keeping her stilettos out of the mud. She kissed her son's cheek. Jake had unlatched the chicken wire cover, taken the rabbit from the hutch and was cuddling it. 'See you later, sweetheart,' she said. Pavel never doubted her devotion to Jake.

With her full time office job, they depended on her wages. Strike pay and picket money wouldn't keep the rabbit fed, let alone the family. Cheryl enjoyed work, whatever she might insist to the contrary. Wouldn't the office of a haulage company bring in plenty of drivers for her to flirt with? Who could blame her? He couldn't remember the last time he'd touched her let alone... Tenderness was a good word. Yes, he'd forgotten it.

Would his son grow up believing that this was how married couples lived? Or would Jake begin to recognise something else? The stench of his dad's cowardice? He opened the kitchen window. 'Come in, Jake. It's time for school.'

★ ★ ★

It was Roly's turn to drive. Pavel read out the union instructions and directions to the colliery where they were due to picket. Earlier that morning he'd jotted the details onto the back of the band concert programme he'd found folded in his jeans' pocket.

'Just off the M1 then,' Roly said. 'Same place as before.' How long would it take to get these men out?

'Good concert was it, last night?' Gus asked.

Pavel nodded. 'Yeah. Jake enjoyed it.' His stomach always churned before a picket line, though it was difficult to feel calm and in control of the group when he was supervising from the back seat of the car, crushed between the two younger lads, Gus and Swannie; especially since Coker, last to climb in, was sitting in the front passenger seat with his legs stretched, lording it as usual.

Attempting to free his arms, Pavel leaned forward as far as the seat belt would allow. From the faint scent of *Mr. Sheen* he was sure Roly had been valeting, but stubborn undertones of stale ash mingled with Coker's cheap pungent after-shave made a nauseating cocktail. At least Coker wouldn't be able to afford poncy scents soon, though why on a picket-line he would want to smell like a Boots perfume counter beggared belief.

A combination of Radio One DJ chatter, corny jokes and pop music, lifted Pavel's spirits, distracting him from thoughts of confrontation.

'*Relax. Dum, dum, dum...* I like this,' Coker said, tapping his fingers on the dashboard and singing a tuneless accompaniment to *Frankie goes to Hollywood*. Coker had the seat so far back that Swannie's legs were almost beneath his chin.

'Can't you pull forward a bit, Coker? Gus is squashed,' Pavel said. Gus wouldn't complain. There was a pecking order in the group with the younger lads on the end, and Pavel thought it would have been more fitting if he – as coordinator and therefore senior by definition – had taken the seat in the front, next to Roly. The psychology of his role was still new to him and he wished he'd realised the subtlety of the seating arrangements earlier. Coker ignored the request to move and continued his drumming, making twanging air-guitar riffs between choruses.

'Hey, Pav,' he said when the track ended. 'Talking of *when you want to come*, expect you'll be getting some action with the old girlfriend back in town!' Groans from the lads drowned the click of Pavel's seat-belt, allowing him opportunity to grip Coker in a headlock.

'You dirty –.'

'Whoa,' Gus shouted as he and Swannie hauled Pavel back.

Roly glanced over his shoulder. 'What the hell are you up to, Pavel? I'm trying to drive. And you Coker, bloody idiot, what're you playing at? That would look great, wouldn't it? Cops arrest pickets for beating the shit out of each other.'

Gus laughed but stopped suddenly when no one else did and cleared his throat. The car veered to the right as Roly glanced over his shoulder again, steering unwittingly towards the middle lane. 'What's going on, Pavel? It's not like you to retaliate at this daft bugger. What's up with you?'

A speeding Mercedes overtook them, horn registering a near miss. Gus took a slow intake of breath then whistled. The car wobbled in the down draft, swerving to the left as Roly tucked in behind a lorry and turned off the radio as he slowed.

'You know what this idiot's like,' Pavel said. 'Bloody insinuations. The girl's been around five minutes and he's making out there's summat going on. Feeding Cheryl garbage, a complete pack of lies.'

Coker peeled the foil from a packet of chewing gum and stuffed it into the open ash tray. 'Can't you take a joke?'

'Back off, Pav, and you Coker,' Roly said. 'Or I'll put you both out on bleeding hard shoulder!'

It was a different scene from their last assignment, already more cops than pickets. Before the bus could enter the pit yard, Pavel's men were impeded by a police cordon which funnelled them into groups, corralling them.

'Scabs, scabs, scabs!' The pickets roared and stamped their feet, insults overlapping in bizarre syncopation as each group joined in.

'We're not getting anywhere near,' Roly shouted.

Swannie had been trying to dodge around the police cordon. 'They've had a change of tactics, Pav. Hopeless.' A new phase. It didn't bode well.

The bus carrying the workers for the afternoon shift inched through the picket line then picked up speed. Some of the working miners on board had covered their heads. A jeer went up and the crowd surged.

'You've some need to put your bleedin' heads down!' Swannie shouted, managing at last to break through the barrier, give chase to the bus and thump his fists on the wing. 'Scabs,' he screamed, but grabbed from behind by two officers, he was thrown aside. Pavel caught his arm and dragged him into the midst of the Lundby men.

'Easy, Swannie. Stay out of trouble.'

It was over. No minds changed today. No gains. The police relaxed their barriers and the men mingled freely. Kicking idly at a few loose stones at the kerb-edge, Gus and Swannie commiserated with another group of Lundby miners and arrangements were made for a game of darts back at the Institute. Pickets stood around for a while then drifted away to their second-hand cars parked in the lane. Others, locals, slouched off on foot, heads down, hands in empty pockets.

'A waste of petrol,' Coker said, as if it were his car they were using.

The five men piled back into the Toyota and Roly made a tight three-point turn, tyres squeaking, the screech of the fan belt begging for attention. The car drew quizzical looks from a group of officers who were eying departures.

Pavel gave a sharp salute and nodded. 'Clocking faces for future reference, no doubt,' he said.

A few miles north, Roly stopped at a motorway services, parked at the fuel pumps. Coker yawned, stretched and Swannie and Gus said they fancied a coffee. They tipped out their pockets to see how much change they could muster and Pavel donated thirty pence to make up the deficit.

'Bring a flask next time,' Roly said.

'I'll come with you,' Coker said, suddenly chirpy. 'I need a pee.' He scrambled out of the car and the two lads followed him towards the food service area.

Pavel could smell chips. He hadn't been inside the main building but he knew the form: a greasy spoon cafe, toilets, a newsagent's, a small one-armed bandit enclosure and four back-to-back telephone booths. He leaned against Roly's car, watching the lads' progress across parking bays: Coker tapping bonnets as they wove between stationary cars. By the hedge on the fringes of the service area, Pavel glimpsed two coppers in a police car, one of them speaking on a radio. Had the lads been followed? Or was he paranoid? 'I bet Thatcher loves this,' he said. 'Divide and rule. This lack of unity sickens me. Why can't some men see the trap? We're all facing the same future.'

Roly unscrewed the petrol cap. 'Stop brooding. It does no good.'

'I'm not brooding.'

'Well for Chrissake's don't get depressed now. One thing's certain: if there are jobs left at the end of this, we won't have men on that sodding bus to thank for it, will we?'

The total on the pump increased and Roly squeezed the trigger on the fuel gun, stopping and starting until the digits landed on five pounds exactly. Pavel suspected the note his mate took from his back pocket would be his last that week.

'Precision, Roly.'

'You never know what skills we'll have by time we get back to work. Take shopping. Take cornflakes in fact. Did you know you can buy 'em loose, cheaper than a box?' Roly shook the end of the nozzle, hooked it back on the pump. 'I can spot a bargain. Wife says I'm a brilliant cook.'

Pavel laughed. 'Congratulations. Cooking cornflakes. Handy skill that is.'

Cornflakes. Pavel had forgotten to buy them, and the washing up liquid, but he had remembered the rabbit food. Cheryl had stocked the chest freezer in the garage before the strike but he'd forgotten to take out the pork chops he was supposed to defrost for tea.

'How's your daughter doing with her A levels, Roly?' Pavel said when Roly returned from the pay kiosk. He'd been meaning to ask but, like the shopping list, it had slipped his mind.

Roly had bought a bar of chocolate. He snapped it and handed Pavel half. 'Jenny? Works hard.'

'Not like me then?'

'I've not forgotten the trouble I had keeping you focussed on your studies. So don't lose the plot now. There's no room for sympathy for men who can't get their backsides out on strike.'

'Sympathy? Who said owt about sympathy?'

'I know you. You never did understand the principle of being cruel to be kind. If you had to put down a rabid dog you'd be dithering, looking for a doggie treat to soften the blow. You'd be bitten to death while you made up your mind.'

Nibbling on the chocolate Pavel spotted Coker swaggering across the car park, hands in pockets, Gus at a distance carrying a coffee carton. Swannie brought up the rear.

'Coker's whistling,' Roly said.' That usually means he's up to summat.'

Pavel held open the car door. 'Your turn to be squashed, Coker.'

Coker stopped at the boot. 'Pulling rank are we, Pavel? I'll wait for other two to get in first,' he said, and grinned. 'Hey. Had a chat with your girl friend last night at band concert. Didn't she marry some Toff? Is *he* staying at Billy's an' all? Could stand us a pint. Mind you – ' Pavel's fists clenched.

'Don't start that again,' Roly said. 'Give it a rest.' Pavel's lips twitched. Coker adjusted a wing mirror, took a comb from his pocket and slicked it through his hair.

'Gerroff, man,' Roly said. 'Might be last motor I ever own.'

'Spit it out, Coker,' Pavel said. 'What are you trying to say?'

'Been thinking,' Coker said, tapping his comb on Pavel's chest. 'You could sell your story to the *News of the World*. Raise a bit of cash for the cause.' He slipped the comb into his back pocket, outlined an imaginary banner above Pavel's head. 'I can see the headline now: *Flying Picket Shags Tory Wife.*'

A rush of blood shut Pavel's eyes for a second, his heart missed a beat. His fists, which had been hanging awkwardly and twitching at his sides, reacted without instruction, lashing out, punching Coker's chin. A dull thud. Coker staggered, his arms rotating like a stricken helicopter. He pitched, his head thumped on the boot and he collapsed onto the garage forecourt.

'I told you, Coker, *watch my car*,' Roly said, patting the bodywork before inspecting Coker's injuries. 'Christ, Pav. I think you've broken his jaw.'

Pavel's fingers throbbed; he blew on them.

Gus and Swannie were sprinting back, coffee dripping from Gus's sleeve as he dropped the carton, showering Pavel's trainers. The heat seeped through, warming his toes.

'Bloody Hell!' Gus said, crashing into the petrol pump. Pavel blushed and Swannie glanced at the police car. Roly grabbed tissues from the glove compartment, soaked them with cold water at the tap by the kiosk, and applied them to Coker's jaw which was already swelling.

'Cops must be inside, thank God,' Gus said, helping Coker to his feet.

'At least you can stand, Coker,' Swannie said. 'Mind you, your knees are doing a fair Elvis impression.'

Roly tossed the keys to Pavel. 'Here. You drive. Keep your hands under control. And get us to casualty. Quick.'

With the fan-belt squealing Pavel clung onto the steering wheel, focusing on the HGVs ahead and keeping an eye on the rear view mirror for police cars in likely pursuit. Somebody must have witnessed the fracas. There was always somebody out to score points. It was easy for anybody passing to see what the lads' business had been. Even if they'd floated football scarves through the window, which Gus had suggested, it wouldn't have fooled anybody.

It was not like this in westerns. Pavel's hands trembled and his knuckles were stiffening. You didn't see Clint Eastwood nursing scuffed knuckles. And what had happened to that Hollywood sharp crack, bone on bone? He hadn't heard it. Only a thud. Maybe it was a good sign.

Nobody had any money for the parking machine.

'Sod it,' Roly said. 'Least of our worries. Pavel can explain if anybody comes. He got us into this mess.' The two younger lads pulled Coker from the car and held him puppet-like as Roly slammed the door; the four men lumbered towards the hospital entrance.

Swannie's lanky legs and sideways gait always reminded Pavel of an animal but he'd never decided which one. Now as Swannie loped towards the infirmary, it came to him. A baby giraffe. That was it. Gus and Swannie – what were they, nineteen and twenty? They had the bounce of youthful optimism. They would stick with strike action because it wouldn't occur to them not to. So far, it was as if they were gallivanting off on day trips from primary school. All that was missing was their duffle bags, sandwiches and a couple of cardboard discs with their names on, pinned to their jumpers. Pavel smiled. Self assurance oozed from their pores – along with a hefty helping of testosterone. Had he ever had their certainty?

Thank goodness Roly had taken charge of the situation. The shortest of the quartet, he had a powerful upper-body strength, the kind you associated with a rock climber, a gymnast on a pummel horse or a monkey swinging through trees. Why hadn't Roly taken the coordinator job instead of lobbying for Pavel?

Outside the hospital door, a group of male patients in dressing gowns and bedroom slippers clutched packets of cigarettes and hung onto mobile drip-stands. Heads turned and eyes followed Coker into the building. A picket hit by a picket would be a new take on the strike for the nurses. Pavel closed his eyes, sinking further into his seat, not sure whether he should laugh or cry.

What the hell was Helen Farrimond up to, involved in events that should be of no concern to her? Did she not realise what trouble somebody like Coker might stir up if he knew about her husband's job? Somebody should warn her and Pavel would – if he ever got to speak to her again.

He tugged the neck of his tee shirt, wound down the window, then climbed out of the driver's seat and sat on the bonnet, waiting, wondering. He had a sudden urge to smoke. Though he hadn't craved nicotine for years he regretted not asking Roly for a fag at the service station. It might have curbed his temper. A temper he'd never been known for. He would be now. And to think that Coker's wife had pleaded with him only that morning at the school gates.

'You know what a hot head my husband is, Pavel. I do worry. I'm counting on you to watch out for him.'

What would she think now?

The dressing gown brigade had stubbed out and disappeared, probably followed his mates inside. How could he ever have believed Coker was a mate? Pavel scanned the car park for the attendant.

Eventually the hospital's revolving door spat out the four men who marched towards him in single file. He climbed into the driver's seat, revved the engine. On the end of the line Coker cupped his chin.

'It's okay,' Swannie said, 'It's just badly bruised.'

'Well, don't sound so disappointed,' Roly said as he manoeuvred Coker onto the back seat, steering him by his collar. 'Not as damaged as his bloody ego. Get in, Coker, you daft bugger.'

It was a fifteen minute journey from the hospital to Lundby and Pavel drove as fast as he dared – keeping one eye on the mirror, still convinced a police car might give chase.

They dropped Coker off first – Pavel stayed in the car, a lump in his throat when he spotted a child's tricycle on Coker's garden path – then Gus and Swannie who lived on a nearby street.

He parked outside his own house. 'I'm sorry, Roly.'

'We're all under a lot of strain. But you, Pavel, losing your rag? You've always taken the flack from Coker, laughed it off.'

'The bastard has been asking for it.'

'This old girlfriend thing's hit a nerve, hasn't it? I know there's nowt going on. But I do remember her, Pavel. I remember your engagement party. You were smitten once. There's bound to be some banter.'

'*Smitten?*' Pavel said. 'Good word. You're right, there's nothing going on. But I'm not letting Coker say one filthy thing about her. I'm damned if I'll ignore his slanderous shit.'

'It sounds to me like you still have feelings for the lass. You'd not be uptight otherwise.'

A burning neck, Pavel's affliction. 'The *lass* – as you call her – has a name: Helen.'

'I know what her name is, clever bugger, and I know you fell right into Coker's trap today. Now he'll think he's hit on summat and he'll not forget. I'll grant he's a goading bastard, but my advice is to stay away from Helen and ignore him.'

Pavel climbed out of the car and bent down to the open window as Roly slid across into the driver's seat. 'I'm not looking for trouble, Roly. All I know is that she's staying with Billy and teaching Jake's class for a term. Last night I spoke to her for the first time in years – and, if you must know, she cold-shouldered me.'

'So that's what pissed you off.' Roly laughed. 'Truth is: you and Cheryl have never been much of a match. But Billy's niece is temptation you can't afford. Don't get distracted.'

'Thanks for the advice, Uncle Roly.' Pavel tapped the roof of the car. 'Now bugger off.' Roly grinned, wound up the window and drove away.

The house was empty. Since Pavel had arranged for his mother to pick up Jake from school and Cheryl had not yet returned from work, Pavel collected his car keys from the kitchen drawer and drove off to find his son. He'd worry about frozen chops later.

Mrs Kowaleski lived alone now and was always glad of Jake's company. By the time Pavel arrived, she had already provided her grandson with a meal and a bag of lettuce for the rabbit. 'Jake's been no trouble,' she said.

Pavel nodded. 'Wish I could say the same for your son.' Her expression clouded. He patted her cheek. 'It doesn't matter, Mum. Just a joke.' Her face lit when she smiled. Her eyes were like his brother's, though the blue had paled with age or perhaps from war-time experiences never discussed.

She took hold of his shoulders. 'Sit down. I'll make tea.'

How long would it take for Cheryl to discover what he'd done to Coker? He should phone her, explain about the chops. Explain? That he'd been delayed, distracted by a fight over his ex fiancée?

Pavel picked up a photograph from the mantelpiece. It was the picture he'd taken of his younger brother years before, sitting outside the old scout tent in Derbyshire.

'Come on then, our kid. How would *you* sort out this bloody mess?

Chapter Nine

Fog

March 1972

Lundby, South Yorkshire

It was one thing sharing a bedroom with your brother but quite another tolerating his debris and his tendency to trash your belongings. Lying on the floor was a heap of slim-fit shirts – plain, checked, striped, flowered, some of them Pavel's – which Jakub had been trying on and casting aside in a hurry.

'How will she be able to resist?' Pavel said, assuming a girl was involved. He was lying on the bed, feigning interest in a book, but peering over it, observing. 'Where does this one live?'

Jakub splashed aftershave over his cheeks and inspected his face in the mirror. 'Sheffield. I'll tidy the gear up later, promise. I'm pressed for time.' Having settled on a navy polo-neck sweater from his own chest of drawers, Jakub combed his hair for a second time, brushed his shoulders and dashed downstairs.

Pavel tossed the book aside and followed. 'You must be keen, taking her out on a Thursday.' Friday night was lads' night, Saturdays ring-fenced for girlfriends.

Shoes on, laces fastened, Jakub dashed into the sitting room where he tossed each cushion in turn from the sofa onto the coffee table, scattering magazines. The wallet was on the mantelpiece. 'Is this what you're looking for?' Pavel asked, handing it over then plumping up the cushions and arranging them symmetrically, as if they were on display in a furniture showroom – the way he and his mother preferred.

'Thanks,' Jakub said. 'There's a film she wants to see, on at the *Wicker Arches*. I'm due to pick her up soon.'

'Not on your bike, surely?' Pavel ran into the doorway, blocking Jakub's exit. 'Have you seen this fog?'

Having fended off his brother's rib tickling Pavel was left clutching his chest as Jakub squeezed past him to don biking leathers and helmet. 'It's half-past seven already, Pav. I'll be late,' he said, fastening his chin strap. 'Stop worrying. It's only ten minutes down the M1.'

'You're mad. Wait. I'll ask Dad if I can have the car. I'll drive you.'

Jakub opened the front door. 'Didn't he mention it went in for service? Garage kept it. That dodgy radiator's finally packed in.'

'Damn. I'll find a bus timetable then. We've got one somewhere.'

'Don't bother. Tell Mum I won't be late. Don't want her trying to stop me either. See you, our kid.'

Outside the fog curled around lampposts and shrouded parked cars, leaving its breath on their windows. In black leathers, Jakub was camouflaged, the glow from his bike lights just visible. The Norton revved, then roared away until Pavel heard only a fading engine throb. He shut the door, leaned against it, listening. No sound of passing traffic.

It had been a gloomy afternoon; the sort of day that defied the season and yet, when he'd finished his shift at two, Pavel had marched across the pit yard whistling, a spring in his step even in boots. Relieved another strike was over, he could continue to save. (That new bloke

Scargill knew what he was about, picketing the Coke plant. Swift end to trouble. The union could do with him at national level.)

With Billy promising to pay for the wedding, in two years Pavel might have a reasonable deposit for a house.

Helen was due to phone tomorrow. If only his dad would agree to have a telephone installed, speaking to her would be easier. But that wasn't likely and, in any case, young Robbie would be out of a job if he did. Robbie. *The Go Between.* Cheeky little lad, riding his bike round the phone box. No dad. Just needed a bit of attention. It didn't take much effort to make a difference to a kid's life. He liked Robbie; reminded him of Jakub at the same age.

The fog had clung like lichen to the trees on either side of the lane, painting trunks an eerie silver-green. Spiky branches, like the bony fingers of a cartoon Grim Reaper, bowed over the road, almost brushing his hair. There was no sign of new life yet. It was more like November than early March.

Finding nothing on television that interested him, he opened the front door again. Was it his imagination or were the lampposts even less visible? His mother came along the hallway. It was an absent-minded habit she had: throwing a tea towel across her shoulder when she'd finished drying dishes. She'd forget it was there. It usually made him laugh. Not tonight.

'What is it, Pavel?'

'Just looking at this fog.'

She squeezed around him, looked out. 'Where's Jakub?'

★ ★ ★

Chester

There was no one there, not even Robbie to take the call. Helen always phoned on Friday evening. Robbie invariably played near the phone box, riding around on his second hand *Chopper*. If Pavel was a minute late, or if she phoned a few minutes early, it was always Robbie who picked up the receiver. 'He's coming now,' he'd say and then she'd hear him yell down the street, instructing Pavel to hurry. She suspected Pavel arrived late deliberately to let the boy answer. She loved the way Pavel handled kids.

There was a queue, as usual, at the telephone on the campus. She'd often had to arrive at six-thirty to be sure of securing the phone-box by seven, but students could become fractious if they saw anyone hogging the box, waiting for prearranged calls. It was seven-twenty. A long haired girl in a mini skirt had been tapping her clogs for some time, arms folded. 'Are you going to be much longer?'

'No. I'm sorry,' Helen said, heaving open the door. 'You can have it now.'

The girl pushed past her. 'About time.'

East of the Pennines was usually colder, so Robbie might not play out tonight. At his age, he shouldn't be out in the dark at all. It was typical of Pavel to take Robbie under his wing. He'd even managed to get hold of a second hand cub uniform so that the boy could join the local pack. The child's mother wouldn't have bothered.

This was the first time their phone arrangements had failed in the five months since she'd embarked on her college course. Clogs girl tossed her hair and turned her back on Helen, tucking the receiver beneath her chin as she fed money into the coin box. Along the road from the college was a public kiosk which Helen had noticed was often empty, so she ran, fumbling for her purse in the tapestry bag she'd slung across her shoulder.

'Come on, Pavel. What's wrong?' she said, the repeated ring tone jangling her nerves.

Finally Robbie answered. He'd not seen Pavel today, he said, but told her he'd spotted a police car at the house the night before.

'You shouldn't be out this late, Robbie. Go home and when you do see Pavel, tell him I rang.'

With no coins left, she decided to phone home reversing the charges. They wouldn't mind. She should ring them more often than Sunday afternoons. Uncle Billy might be out at the Institute on Friday night, but Tibby would be there, watching television or baking an apple pie for the weekend.

'I'm having trouble getting hold of Pavel, Tibby. I always ring at seven but he's not there tonight for some reason. It's not like him to let me down.'

'Speak to your uncle, love.' Something was wrong. From muffled voices, she guessed Tibby had her hand over the receiver.

Eventually, Billy spoke. 'You'll need to come home tomorrow if you can, Helen.'

'What's happened? Is it Pavel?'

'It's Jakub. We only found out tonight. There's been an accident. His motorbike.'

In the background Helen heard the brass strains of the *Coronation Street* theme and Tibby's whispered: 'Tell her, love.'

'Jakub's... not made it,' Billy said.

★ ★ ★

Lundby

The leaden legged pall bearers hefted his brother onto their shoulders and carried him slowly through the Lych gate and down the path towards the church. Heels clicked on stone flags. There were black shoes in front of him and behind, and his own so polished they were almost reflective: glassy as the seam of anthracite he'd been working on the week before.

That morning Pavel had dried the dishes. Domestic chores were what you did when you wanted to forget or use up the time you didn't want to inhabit. Cleaning shoes, dusting, drinking tea. Helen's boots were black and polished too, the tops covered by a long grey patterned coat he disliked. Her feet following his feet. She was holding his hand. When he wriggled his fingers and freed himself she gripped his arm. He walked faster then slowed, false footing her. He followed the coffin, his eyes fixed on the sharply pressed trousers of the six men carrying Jakub, their neat turn-ups. He heard his name spoken as he passed through the church-yard. He didn't look up.

The wind had tipped over vases on nearby gravestones, scattering shrivelled daffodils and irises like Jerusalem palms before Jakub's procession. *Ho, bloody, sannah.*

There was a strong scent of flowers in the church. Wreaths of white lilies and spray chrysanthemums lay on the coffin. Jakub would have laughed at suits and wreaths. Ceremony and protocol had never failed to make him laugh. Pavel remembered how the peaked cap had always been in Jakub's pocket until they'd reached the school drive, how his jumper had hung below his blazer and the loose knot in his tie had never quite touched the unfastened top button on his shirt.

The organ was playing. Pavel followed the twelve feet down the aisle, noting their imprints on the crimson velvet carpet that looked regal, too new and costly to bear all these people. Jakub would have hated this music. He loved T Rex and the Stones. Feet were for tapping and jiving, kick-starting motor bikes and scoring goals. And the hypocrisy of this religious fiasco with its false promises of life ever after. He would have sniggered.

Somebody read from the Bible. Corinthians. The words droned: something about love. Jakub read science fiction; said he was an atheist. Pavel recognised his mother's soft weeping and from somewhere behind him, a miner's intermittent black-lung cough hacked without apology into the Vicar's lame attempts at comfort. He could hear sniffing and muttered responses to the Vicar's prayers: pious mumbling for people who only came here on the usual three occasions and rarely on a Sunday.

There were mourners outside, Helen said, and the church was spilling over. Spilling over! Coal spilled over tubs in the pit. Tea spilled constantly from tea-pots when somebody died. *My cup runneth over.* Tears were like eternal waterfalls. Oil spilled from tankers and blood spilled over the motorway from bodies crushed by unstoppable lorries. At times like these, the curate had told Pavel, God's love spilled over.

Coffins reminded him of giant pencil boxes. He and Jakub had fought over a pencil case once. It was wooden and shiny with a sliding lid they both wanted to play with. Pavel had soon given in. He wanted to break open the coffin, shake his brother and wake him. But this lid was nailed down. The brass plaque engraved with Jakub's name glistened beneath the altar candlelight. He couldn't believe that he would never speak to Jakub or wrestle with him or argue with him, or laugh with him again – never. Pavel's heart skipped a beat; his breathing was shallow, stopping, starting, choking like his dad's old car.

She was holding his hand again, squeezing it now, like a child. Love was for believers. Love was for fools. His tears had dried up and his eyes were as raw as the wind he heard howling mercilessly in the church porch when the organ stopped playing. It rattled the latch. *Let me in. Let me out.*

Billy's voice. A eulogy of platitudes. The Vicar. A trite tribute to a lad he didn't know. *Bullshit spilled over.*

Pavel should have, could have stopped Jakub. If he'd only delayed him by five minutes the lorry would have passed. All that was left was a bloody buckled motorbike and a broken body. The police said Jakub died instantly. Helen said he wouldn't have known anything about it. What did she know? He wished she'd stop this hand patting and stroking.

More music, weak singing, more sniffling and stirring. He looked up. The pallbearers were heaving his brother onto their shoulders. The coffin wobbled, the flowers slipped. With faltering steps the men carried Jakub's wooden box through the church door and past the yew tree, four hundred year old branches spreading a canopy over the grave stones they'd watched over for so long. Their branches cut out the light on this part of the path, casting shadows. Branches familiar with nodding at the dead, sheltering the weeping.

Stumbling over uneven flag stones, the pall bearers slid the coffin onto the brass rails of the hearse. It was only then that Pavel recognised them: the six ashen-faced young men were Jakub's friends from the pit, not much more than eighteen. Their job: to take his kid brother away to burn. Two of them put their arms around each others' shoulders, locked for a moment, stubbly cheek on cheek. Another wiped his eyes on the cuff of his shirt. They would have to lift Jakub again at the crematorium. The silent glide of brocade curtains fooled nobody. They would have to release their mate into the flames, knowing he'd be reduced to nothing but white dust. Black dust, white dust. No difference. It suffocated you just the same. A belch of smoke would be Jakub's epitaph.

Pavel had told Billy Farrimond he couldn't carry the coffin. Perhaps when it was his own turn to burn, Pavel's smoke would be yellow. Fingers over closed eye lids could obliterate sunlight. Cold fingers soothed the soreness that had dogged his eyes like coal grit for days, kept him awake night after night.

The funeral director shut the hearse doors. Pavel told Helen to go on ahead with his parents. She didn't argue.

The graveyard sloped away from the church to the bottom of a wooded ravine. This was the heart of the old village he'd learned about in school, the one recorded in the Domesday Book; the farming village that lay here before the all-conquering Normans built the church and left behind their herringbone stone work, their subdued surfs and ennobled landlords. Before mines were dug and model villages were built for workers and refugees from jackboots and famine. Why was he here, why was anybody here but to dig out a short paltry existence? Digging the land, digging for coal, digging graves.

Helen called his name. He walked away from the church and the lych gate, away from the mourners and his parents and away from her. He heard the cars drive off and footsteps fade: sounds replaced by the stream gushing in the valley below and his heels on the wooden bridge.

The iron hand rail was cold, coated in rust. He sat down, took off his shoes and socks, lowered himself into the freezing water which bubbled below his knees, tumbling past him over shifting pebbles.

'In pastures green, He leadeth me, the quiet waters by.'

He stood there for as long as he could endure the current cutting into his calf muscles and the stones on the river bed slicing into the soles of his feet, one hand shielding his eyes from the sun. He cursed his father for indifference, his brother for recklessness. There was no point in regaling God. No God listened. Pavel howled into a gust of a bitter easterly wind and it bore his cries away over woodland.

A pheasant squawked from the undergrowth and in a flash of colour, it flapped into the trees above him. He hauled himself back onto the bridge.

His feet were tinged with purple. He took the socks from his shoes and stuffed them into the pockets of his jacket, wrung out the water from the bottoms of his trousers, forced his numbed toes back into the leather. White foam frothed at the water's edge and he followed the stream for a few yards, shoes squelching in the mud.

He climbed the bank and walked back to the churchyard stopping only to kick his toecaps against crumbling headstones. Dates had faded, names had disappeared. Ancient forgotten souls. All of them fooled. He kicked until his feet throbbed.

The cortege had left.

★ ★ ★

How strange Helen thought these young miners had looked in their Sunday best suits, nodding their respects and condolences.

It was her uncle who'd given the eulogy and the mood was lifted when he'd mentioned Jakub's alleged romantic escapades and some of his pit pranks. Billy Farrimond had the lad to a tee, everyone said. When they sang the hymn, she'd put her arm around Pavel's waist but he looked down, both hands gripping the order of service. He'd not attempted to sing.

The vicar had talked of celebrating Jakub's life not mourning. He'd said that death was God's intended mystery. It tested our faith like nothing else. The family should take comfort in Jakub's joy in life; he had not suffered. Finally a lad from the colliery band had played a plaintive solo on a flugal horn. Everywhere she looked there was sniffing and handkerchiefs dabbing. Except for Pavel. He'd had no tears.

The Miners' Institute provided a buffet. No one ate much but Helen busied herself, helping Mrs Kowaleski, passing plates of sandwiches, distributing solace in cups of tea. Pavel sat with his father in a corner and spoke to no one. Two men, suddenly and inexplicably alike, brooding, silent and broken. She noticed the bottom of Pavel's trousers wet and muddy. Where had he been?

'I'll keep an eye on him, Helen,' Roly said. 'I'll make sure he keeps up with his college course. And he's got you. You won't be gone forever.'

'I don't seem to be much help at the moment.'

Pavel was smoking, though she'd never seen this before, and his eyes seemed focused on the hollow centres of smoke rings he'd created, as if mesmerised by the wispy circles that hung above him. He waited until their blue edges faded, then inhaled and repeated the process. Since his legs were crossed, his trousers had shortened at the ankle and she noticed he wore no socks. Though only a few yards separated her from him, she sensed his determination to ignore her; he'd distanced himself. In a pit of his own making.

Chapter Ten

Nature Lesson

May 1984

Lundby South Yorkshire

The familiar routines of playtimes, assemblies and school dinners punctuated Helen's days with heartbeat regularity and welcome distraction.

Morning has broken like the first morning. Blackbird has spoken like the first bird.

Today lunch hour offered a chance to read Isaac's letter which had arrived just as she was leaving for school. Ashamed at not contacting him sooner, she had written at some length, disclosing the truth of the London events. Isaac must have replied by return post.

Greenwich

May 1984.

Dear Helen,

I was delighted to receive your letter. I have missed our chats and meanderings in the gallery. Since I have been unwell – angina the consultant insists – my city jaunts have been curtailed and for weeks I have walked no further than my own garden, though pleasant enough at this time of year now the azaleas are blossoming. My elder son has planted geraniums in the window boxes and marigolds and lobelia in terracotta pots, though I told him my rule was no bedding plants until the first of June. One curse of old age is no longer wielding any authority over your offspring.

I was shocked by your husband's infidelity and not a little dismayed by the way in which you discovered it. Thank you, by the way, for confiding in me about the loss of your son. It explains so much and yet is no excuse for Guy's behaviour.

I must admit I am mystified by your indecision. Though I am a great supporter of marriage, I see no happiness for you with Guy, despite the ten years you were together and your shared loss. Why do you feel you must be loyal when he is not? His parliamentary career? Or are you in love with him still? You don't mention contrition on his part. I am left to wonder what power this man has over you. Does this sound harsh?

I understand your reticence to speak freely with your aunt and uncle but I think, Helen, that they deserve honesty. I am sure they suspect more that you suppose. My advice is to tell them what you told me. The temporary teaching appointment is a splendid idea. I know you will enjoy it as you have often spoken of your wish to return to education.

I have no news other than the creaking heart. My sons call regularly and, since my diligent cleaning lady lives only a few streets away, she has taken on the cooking and delivery of my weekday dinners. The woman has become a well-intentioned bully. I tell her I hate rice pudding but she insists it's good for me. Suddenly she is my grandmother, though unlike Grandma it seems she has a repertoire of a single dessert! When I tactfully suggested a little variety she added prunes. Do I seem ungrateful?

In the meantime, be assured of my support and friendship. I hope that you will visit London soon.

Yours sincerely,

Isaac

PS. The recipe for your aunt Tibby's special bread and butter pudding would be more than welcome next time you write.

Isaac's footnote made her smile. She couldn't analyse why she was so indecisive about Guy. She was coasting, living in the moment. It was as if she had stepped through a portal from a surreal, barren world, stepped over a threshold but couldn't close the door behind her. She folded the letter into the envelope and tucked it into her handbag.

Beyond the staffroom window the playing field teemed with footballs, hoops and children tumbling down a grassy bank and spilling onto the football pitch. Hill rolling was a tradition she'd enjoyed when she was nine years old, especially when the grass was newly mown and the smell as ripe and delicious as Uncle Billy's June strawberries. It was as instinctive for children as running or playing *catch*, as much a childhood rite as climbing a tree or walking on a wall. Didn't the old wish they'd taken more risks when they were young? She had a desire to kick off her shoes, join in the games. Though hill rolling was now forbidden on the grounds of health and safety, the chatting dinner supervisors seemed oblivious to the high jinks on the field. It was easier to pretend she too hadn't noticed. Let the children have their five minutes of fun in the sunshine.

The headmaster arrived in the staffroom armed with a sandwich box and a copy of the Times Educational Supplement. He settled beside Helen, expressing surprise there was a father joining the afternoon's outing. When Helen had sent out a letter to parents seeking volunteers to help supervise a nature walk, Pavel had been first to offer assistance.

'Mr Kowaleski will be useful on a woodland expedition,' Mr Read said. 'He's knowledgeable about the local flora and fauna. I've met him out walking over the common with Jake on Sundays.'

'He spent his childhood running around the pit woods with an Observer *I spy* book,' Helen said, adding, 'so I've been told.'

Mr Read seemed curious. 'Do you know him well, then?'

She fumbled with the fastener on her handbag. 'Knew him when I was a teenager. School. Youth club. That sort of thing.'

'We don't get many dads on trips, do we? Good of him to offer.'

The teaching assistant, Kath, rescued Helen. 'It's the strike. These miners have time on their hands. Like my Roly. He's supposed to be cleaning the house today. Keep them busy, I say.'

Mr Read swallowed the remains of his sandwich and laughed. 'You'd be formidable on the picket line, Kath.'

'And that's where I'll be in the school holidays,' Kath said.

Helen made for the staffroom door with Kath following. There were resources still to prepare for the afternoon's excursion.

★ ★ ★

'...And Pavel punched Coker so hard they had to take him to hospital,' Kath said.

Helen had collected handfuls of pencils and crayons from the pots on the children's tables, wrapped them in elastic bands and stowed them in carrier bags, one for each group. Kath emerged from the stock cupboard armed with a heap of clipboards so high that they left only the top of her head visible.

'And was Coker alright?' Helen said, though her only concern was that Pavel might be accused of assault.

Kath dropped the boards onto Helen's desk. 'Badly bruised, and not just his jaw. He'll be hell bent on revenge, Roly says. So you need to be careful. Don't give him ammunition.'

'What has it got to do with me?'

'Well, Roly said I shouldn't tell you, but... the trouble centred on you. Coker was making insinuations and Pavel lost his temper.'

'How could it be about me? I saw Pavel once, before Easter. We hardly spoke. What insinuations?'

'Pavel's marriage is shaky, Helen, and Roly thinks you could make matters worse.'

'Do you think we've got enough drawing paper?'

'What Roly meant was that it wouldn't take much to turn Pavel's head and – well, you're both married,' Kath said, tapping a ream of A4. 'There's plenty of paper.'

'I don't need reminding I'm married, Kath. Is that everything? I mean for the walk?'

Kath clipped worksheets to the boards. 'I'm sorry. It happened last month, but I thought you should know, especially as Pavel's coming with us this afternoon. He's waiting outside in the corridor by the way.'

Helen swallowed, tucked her hair behind her ear. 'If it makes you feel any better, I'll put him at the back of the class, out of moral danger.'

Kath blushed.

Once Helen had arranged the parent helpers along the children's line with Kath between, the chattering crocodile marched off through the streets of council and colliery houses that made up the school's catchment area in a maze of post-war red brick and pebble dash. 'Would you mind being on the end, Mr Kowaleski? Keep the stragglers from falling behind?' Helen asked. The other parents would notice any first name familiarity.

'Yes, Miss,' he said.

Cherry blossom trees were growing in Uncle Billy's street: in the gardens of houses purchased by former council tenants taking advantage of Mrs Thatcher's 'right to buy'. It was a pity that the first woman Prime Minister was less enthusiastic about safeguarding jobs to help new owner-occupiers pay their mortgages, Billy had said. How many would fall foul of repayments if the strike was prolonged?

Guy had talked of the benefits of individualism. Home ownership for all was his party's aspiration. But one-upmanship was perhaps the most basic of human frailties, even for those who voted Labour, and Uncle Billy had been the first in the village to buy his council house.

'Try not to walk on the cracks,' she heard one of the girls say. 'It's bad luck.'

Waxy pink petals dotted the pavements like confetti. How many cracks had Helen trodden on over the years? The sun had come out. It warmed the top of her head and she closed her eyes, inhaling garden scents.

Remembering too late that it was Friday, she led them on a short cut through the market place. But she needn't have worried about shopping crowds. There were only a couple of fruit and vegetable stalls today, another selling cheap clothing and a fourth with canvas suitcases, imitation leather handbags and plastic belts suspended from wire coat hangers. She stopped to check everyone was following, including Pavel.

They passed through streets where litter rolled like tumbleweed and fish and chip cartons claimed the gutters, until they reached the lane that led to the common and the pit woods beyond, the path cutting between canopies of wild parsley, banks of ox-eye daisies, bluebells and beds of bracken.

Lundby was an island surrounded by wilderness. The woods and common land formed a link between generations of forgotten childhoods. Village heritage was mixed: farms and spoil heap – though children were more interested now in Spectrum ZX computers and Space Invaders than nature study or their own history. Still, she was hopeful of capturing their attention, engaging their senses.

Organising the class into groups, she took skipping ropes from a plastic bag and asked the children to lay them on the ground in circles. They were quickly engrossed in searching for as many living things as they could find, ticking off wild flowers and insects from identification sheets fastened to their clipboards. Pavel dropped to his knees to help with Jake's group, drawing attention to small plants and tiny creatures, upturning stones and logs to reveal a minutia of life within the rope's circumference.

'This is ace,' she heard Jake say.

Once she'd walked here with Pavel. She remembered how he'd identified a bird by its song long before he saw it and named a host of wild flowers. He'd pointed out speedwell, cowslips and wild orchids; told her he'd spent his early years playing in the pit woods with nothing in his pockets but a bird book and an egg sandwich wrapped in greaseproof paper. It was with Pavel that she'd heard her first woodpecker, a cuckoo and the song of a yellow hammer – recognisable by its repeated chirruping of '*a little bit of bread and no cheese,*' he'd said.

On another occasion he'd found a trembling wood pigeon beneath a bush, picked it up gently – taking off his sweater to wrap around it. He'd carried it home, placed it in a cardboard box and tried to feed it, though after a couple of days it had died and he'd buried it in the garden.

A child calling her name interrupted her thoughts. 'What's this insect, Mrs Eagleton? It's not on the sheet.'

'You could ask Jake's dad,' she said.

When the class had finished filling in the charts, Pavel led them to a sawn log, reminding them how to identify its age by the rings in the trunk. He taught them how to differentiate cow parsley from deadly hemlock by the stems and leaves, and warned them of the poisonous fronds in bracken.

'If you let the kids off the leash to find sticks, I reckon they'll enjoy poking around in leaf mould as much as anything,' he told Helen, when the children's questions were exhausted. 'I'm sure they won't run away.' She was less sure but let them anyway.

Pavel joined in the search, finding long twigs beneath hazel trees. The groups had disintegrated now, lost in the stirring up of peat and insects and listening to Pavel's explanation of how rotting vegetation fed the next generation of plants and how ancient trees buried below them had formed the layers of coal miles beneath their feet.

'That's what brought most of your grandparents here,' he said. 'Dead animals formed oil, vegetation formed coal. So the next time your mums and dads fill up with petrol just think: they might be putting a dinosaur in their tank.' This brought a round of laughter and more questions. Might last week's gallons have contained a Stegosaurus or Triceratops? If it had been any other parent, Helen might have felt diminished, side-lined by his sudden stardom, but instead, she stood at a distance, observing, admiring... until she became aware of Kath observing her.

When rain began a horizontal sweep, they gathered the children together for the return march and Pavel reclaimed his position on the end of the line.

'You wouldn't believe how quickly a day can change, would you?' Kath said.

Delayed by sheltering for a few minutes inside the market hall, they arrived at school after the end of day bell, when children from other classes were already spilling through the school gates.

After thanking the helpers, Helen supervised the children out of the cloakroom. A small group of boys were lingering by the pegs, swapping football stickers, swinging pump bags and miming shots at imaginary goal posts. Jake reminded Helen there was a PE club at half-past three and she directed the remaining gymnasts, including Jake, to the hall.

'Could my dad take a look my art work while I'm gone?' Jake asked, handing Pavel his book bag and lunch box.

'I'm sure Mrs Eagleton has too much to do,' Pavel said.

Jake ran after the other boys. 'Well you told me to ask, Dad.'

She headed back to the classroom, calling over her shoulder. 'You can come in anytime, Mr. Kowaleski.'

'I don't want to impose,' he said, following.

'The school has an *open door policy*. I'm not offering a personal favour.'

Pavel shut the door behind him. His hair was wet. He'd stroked it forward with his fingers and he hung his head as if suitably admonished. Suddenly mindful of her last brusque encounter with him at the band concert, Helen drew paper towels from a dispenser by the classroom sink. 'You'd better use these. You're soaked.'

He rubbed them across his head, around his face and the back of his neck then fingered a rough parting in his hair. 'Thanks. But wasn't that one?'

'One what?'

'A personal favour.'

'No. I just don't want you dripping over my classroom.'

Kath appeared in the doorway. 'Pavel's looking at Jake's work,' Helen explained. 'I'll see you tomorrow, Kath. Nine o' clock at the bus stop.'

'Don't stay too late,' Kath said. 'It's Friday. And remember to wear old clothes. No cashmere sweater like last time or you'll be no help. I'll tell Roly I saw you, Pavel.'

'What did she mean?' Pavel said when Kath had left.

'The support group is collecting in Sheffield tomorrow.'

'No. What did she mean about telling Roly?'

'Give me your coat and I'll dry it,' she said, dragging a convector heater from the stock cupboard. Pavel wriggled out of his jacket and she hung it on the back of a chair, plugged in the heater. 'I'd better clear up. We left a mess. The cleaners get cranky if it's not tidy.'

Pavel offered to help but she directed him to one of Jake's paintings on the pin board: a landscape of splodgy brushstrokes which was nonetheless recognisable as the local limestone crags.

'Pity there's no lido anymore,' he said. He circled the classroom slowly studying the work on the walls, taking in all of it, not just the art: the graphs and pie charts, science diagrams and map work; the children's attempts at poetry composition about the strike. She had considered sending the poems to Mrs Thatcher.

Pavel laughed. 'Kids always use corny rhymes, don't they?' he said, but then spent some time reading them all, silent.

'Children understand more than most adults realise,' she said, recalling the day she'd overheard Jake telling a friend that he'd been kept awake by his parents' arguing.

There were faint odours of pencil sharpening, wax crayon shavings, singeing dust from the heater and rising steam from Pavel's jacket. From beneath the desks she retrieved the debris of the morning: a collection of stray pencils, a crumpled paper hanky which she picked up between finger and thumb, and a grey balled-up sock left behind after PE. She wondered which boy had not noticed he was wearing only one sock.

'It's probably Jake's,' Pavel said.

'You are allowed to ask about Jake's work,' she said, dropping the tissue in the bin.

'I thought I had to wait till parents' evening.'

'But you're here now,' she said. Maybe if she could get the appointment over she wouldn't have to face his wife across her desk at a later date. 'He's a bright boy. Doing well. Maths and English well above average.' Pavel's gaze was fixed on her; she lost her thread. 'He... he has that cheeky charm of your brother's.'

Pavel smiled. 'I spoil him.'

'I can see you dote on him.'

'He knows I'm a soft touch.'

What right did she have to say that this kind of devotion was dangerous? That Jake would be happier with one stable parent than a warring couple. What did she know about parenting? 'I'll find his art folder for you,' she said.

From the stock cupboard she viewed Pavel through the gap between the door and the frame. She brought out the folders and spread them on a table. Several slid to the floor. 'I'll find Jake's observation drawings. They're in here somewhere.'

He helped to pick up the folders, stacking and arranging them into alphabetical order.

She held Jake's pencil drawings of fruits and flowers at arms' length in turn, viewing them from different angles.

'Can we talk?' he said.

'Jake has a great eye for detail, don't you think?'

'Gets that from me.'

She showed Pavel Jake's pastel picture of cross-sections of red and green peppers. 'I like this one in particular,' she said. 'Good enough to frame. Look how he's caught the light.'

'In fact, Helen, I've noticed quite a lot.'

'I thought you didn't want to take up my time.'

'I don't blame you for being angry,' he said.

'Angry? Why would I be angry?'

'For the way I treated you.'

'It's not important. I'm married now.'

'Married and angry then. In my experience it's the same thing.' He laughed. She picked out an abstract painting. 'I've always wanted to apologise,' he said.

'Forget it, Pavel. I have. It was twelve years ago.'

'You told me you hadn't been counting how long since – '

'Good aren't they?' she said, moving onto Jake's watercolour of a bowl of snowdrops.

'Only... I've noticed your husband's not with you.' She gathered the pictures to file them away but he picked up the folder, held it to his chest. 'I'm a nosy bugger aren't I?' he said.

'Yes, you are.'

'It's just that I can't help wondering why you've come back, unexpected. Billy and Tibby are really pleased though. I know they miss you.'

She looked at her watch. It was nearly four. The gym club would end at four-thirty and unless he stayed until then, Pavel would have to walk home and back to school within half an hour.

'Sorry, I'm keeping you from your work. Outstaying my welcome,' he said. 'Thanks for letting me see Jake's work. It's great. Though to be honest, I came to warn you, Helen. I don't think you should take risks.'

'In Sheffield? We'll only be rattling tins. I'm not throwing myself in front of police horses,' she said.

'I didn't mean tomorrow. Look. I know you're married to a Tory MP. Billy told me. The rest of the lads are in the dark. What will your husband think about his wife supporting striking miners? Don't jeopardise your marriage for us.'

For us? Her mouth fell open. It was too late to consider risk. The risk was not in her support for striking miners. Risk was here, staring her in the face, raking up memories. 'Do you think I don't know the implications?' she said. 'But thanks for your concern.'

There was a small patch reddening above his collar. She remembered it. He brushed his hand across his chin and around the back of his neck, scratched his head.

'I'd always planned a spring visit,' she said. 'As you pointed out, Tibby and Billy miss me. I miss them too. Then the temporary job turned up.' It was suddenly hot. She opened a window, tidied her desk.

'I see,' Pavel said. 'So he's happy to let you stay?'

'Who?'

'Your husband.'

'It's only until the end of July.'

'Right.'

'I was at a loose end and he's very busy with – '

'It's hot in here,' he said. 'It's that heater. Cooler outside though. The windows are steaming up.' He gestured to the door. 'I've got to be back here for half past four. Hardly be worth leaving if I don't set off now. It's stopped raining.'

'Don't forget your coat.' She slipped it from the chair back. 'It's a bit drier. I could make you a coffee if you wanted to wait.'

'Best not.' He took his damp jacket from her. 'I enjoyed it. The walk, I mean. Thanks for letting me...'

'You're welcome.' She followed him to the door. 'There is one thing I wanted to ask, Pavel.' She searched for a topic. 'How's your mother?'

'She's fine. I expect you heard about my dad?'

'Yes, I'm sorry. Uncle Billy mentioned some years ago that he'd died,' she said, 'but no details.' It had been one of those rare occasions when Billy and Tibby had visited. Helen had quickly changed the subject when Guy had entered the sitting room.

Pavel picked up an atlas from a shelf, flicked through it. 'So you don't know that my dad died from an overdose? Coroner judged it most likely accidental. Dad was suffering with back pain.' Uncle Billy would have told her if she had not dismissed his chatter as conversation about her old boyfriend, conversation intended to annoy Guy.

'I was glad of the verdict for Mum's sake,' Pavel said. 'But I have my doubts. He was always depressive. All that distance he put between us. No wonder Jakub and me... we formed such a strong bond. We didn't really have a dad in any normal sense. We relied on each other.'

She recalled the man with never a word of encouragement for either of his sons or much to say to anyone for that matter.

Pavel replaced the book and glanced through the window. 'Mum eventually told me Dad had killed a man in the war. Sounds lame. Isn't that what wars are about? Killing? Legalised murder? Apparently it haunted him. After Jakub died he felt he was being punished, that it was his fault: divine retribution.' His voice faltered. Pavel wiped the cuff of one sleeve across his cheek. 'An overdose of pain-killers. Senseless. Jake was a year old when it happened. Just when there was somebody to live for.'

'I'm so sorry,' she said, lifting a hand to touch his shoulder but using it to sweep her hair behind an ear.

'Maybe if we'd made more demands on him when we were kids,' he said, recovering, 'climbed on him, wrestled him, forced him into a game of cricket or a bedtime story. Nagged for attention. Instead we accepted the way he was. I have no intention of making the same mistake with Jake.'

'Don't blame yourself. Your dad must have been in a personal hell. Maybe when he saw how you were as a father with Jake, he realised what he'd missed. Better to accept it was an accident.' There was a moment's silence.

A cleaner opened the door, interrupting the conversation by steering a bucket of water into the room with a floor mop. 'Do you mind if I make a start?'

'No, come in. Mr Kowaleski's just leaving,' she said. 'What about Robbie? Is he still here? Not still pedalling his bike round phone boxes, is he?' Above Pavel's forehead a little tuft of hair had defied his finger combing, forming a spiky crest.

'His mother moved to Birmingham to be near her sister,' Pavel said. 'I had a letter from him a while back. He said he was joining the police force.'

'Your fault then. When you persuaded him to join the cubs you gave him a taste for uniforms.'

He smiled. 'You could be right.' The cleaner slapped the mop behind Pavel's feet.

'And how's the picketing going?' Helen said. The cleaner frowned.

Pavel shrugged. 'The action's shifting to Orgreave, to stop coke getting through to Scunthorpe steel works. Mass picketing.'

'Be careful then.'

The cleaner rolled his eyes, leaned on his mop. 'If you ask me, they should lock Maggie and Scargill in a room together. Let 'em thrash it out. Throw away the key. We wouldn't miss either of 'em.'

'Cue for me to leave,' Pavel said, 'Thanks for the chat. By the way. I notice you've lost your Yorkshire accent, Helen. Proper southerner now.' He grinned, and attempting to stride over the wet floor in a hasty exit, he tripped over the bucket.

The cleaner leaned on the mop. 'Who does he think he is? Some of these parents take liberties, don't they? As if you haven't got enough to do, without striking miners wasting your time.'

Dismayed by the size of the pile of marking, she sat at her desk, realising that she hadn't dealt with the worksheets from the afternoon's walk. The mop flapped around her feet.

'You've got your work cut out there,' the cleaner said.

'I'm finding it hard to concentrate. Sticky weather.'

'That heater won't have helped. You look flushed.'

She considered explaining about the wet coat but his smirk dissuaded her and she opened a maths book instead, took up a pen, chewing the end, contemplating Mr Kowaleski senior and the nature of his death. Pavel had entrusted her with such confidential information. As if they were still close. As if …

The gym club children arrived in the cloakroom; she

heard their shouts, jokes and plans for the weekend as they changed out of their PE kits and collected their coats.

Outside a downpour doused the flower beds, lashing the playground, gushing from a crack in the guttering and cascading down the window. Pavel was waiting in the rain, his hair flattened again. Even the spiky tuft had given in to the weight of the deluge. She had delayed him. There had not been time for him to go home and return. He could have borrowed her umbrella; she should have thought to offer it.

A few yards from Pavel, another waiting father had pulled his anorak hood over his forehead and was glowering into puddles. Coker. Both men looked in her direction as she shut the window. Pavel smiled.

It was a school rule to close the classroom blinds at the end of the day. She lowered them slowly one by one, glancing at Pavel from each window in turn as the wooden batons hit the sills.

Chapter Eleven

The Visitor

June 1972

Chester

With first year teaching practice and exams over, there were only weeks left till the end of the summer term. Helen intended to return to Lundby, find a casual job to increase the wedding savings and devote the rest of her time to Pavel. Even fishing with him – if it helped. His mood swings had made her afraid for his safety, though she had not mentioned this to Tibby or her uncle. She waited by the college car park, twisting the sapphire engagement ring around her finger. Today Pavel was due to visit her for the first time.

The Friday phone calls had come to an end when he'd told her he was to start working afternoon shifts from two till ten. Uncle Billy had once worked shifts, but *afternoons* then came around every third week. Maybe things had changed.

Though male visitors were not allowed to stay overnight in the women's halls of residence, there were always men students willing to house a visitor – let them sleep on their floors for the price of a pint in the college bar – so she had hoped Pavel would stay for the weekend. But he'd insisted he could only manage a day visit and she was so grateful for any opportunity to see him, she'd sought no explanation.

In Pavel's last letter, he'd estimated leaving home around seven a.m. By her calculation the journey would take three hours but it was eleven and she'd been waiting for an hour already. Brief letters had been their only contact since Jakub's funeral: notes, a few lines. She'd recognised his mother's handwriting on the envelopes and wondered if they would have been posted at all if not for Mrs Kowaleski's diligence.

The old Morris 1000 pulled into the car park half an hour later. She ran forward to hug him. 'I was worried; thought you'd got lost. How long did it take?'

'About three hours. I didn't stop. I came over the Snake Pass. Great views. It's really clear today.' He looked at his watch. 'I left home later than planned. Sorry.' She was encouraged he'd noticed the countryside, even if he hadn't yet looked at her.

'You're here now. That's all that matters. I thought I could show you around the city.'

'Fine. The weather's too good to stay inside.'

After hiking around the Roman walls – stopping to oblige tourists by taking their family photographs and giving directions to two Americans sporting kilts – they strolled through the park by the river. Peonies, rhododendron and azaleas were in bloom, scents scorched by a fierce mid-day sun. When they finally reached the water's edge they rested on a bench, watching tourists and children waving from pleasure cruisers. Helen had packed a lunch of sandwiches, buns, cheese and fruit but Pavel ate little, choosing to feed the bread to quarrelsome ducks that waddled ashore at the first sight of a picnic.

'Jakub would have loved this,' she said, daring at last to mention the name that hovered like a spectre between them.

'I can't believe he's gone,' Pavel said. 'I expect him to tap me on the shoulder, confront me with some daft idea. There was always a plan.' He took a bun from its case and crumbled it, sprinkling it on the path. 'My dad's hardly spoken since the funeral. But Mum tries to keep things as normal as possible. Daily routines: washing, shopping... even bakes buns sometimes.'

A large drake nudged its beak around his feet and stole the last sandwich from the lunch box. Pavel laughed. 'Cheeky blighter,' he said. 'Still it would have been wasted. I'm sorry. I'm not that hungry. You went to a lot of trouble.'

'Don't worry. If the duck hadn't grabbed it, my friends would have. College food's pretty boring.'

'Lovely place though. You're lucky.'

'Suppose so. But I'm looking forward to —'

'Let's walk on,' he said.

She lead him along the medieval balconies of the shopping centre, expecting him to be impressed by the quaintness of the buildings, to show an interest in the city's history, but he seemed indifferent and dismissed her suggestion to visit the cathedral.

'It would be cool and peaceful there,' she said.

'I've had enough of churches for one year thanks.'

Conversation dwindled until their awkwardness was so tangible that she wondered if it was visible to the strangers they passed. 'We'll head back then, shall we?' she said.

He shrugged, 'I can't stay long.'

Her first floor study was unremarkable in its layout — student bare essentials: a sink, wardrobe, single bed, small rug over a tiled floor, a bookcase and a desk beneath the window. But what made it distinct from its neighbours was the view of the playing fields. The Welsh hills glinted purple and green in the distance, a picturesque backdrop to rugby matches that were cheered on by scarf-waving supporters from rival colleges. Friends sometimes dropped by for coffee on Saturday afternoons, teasing Helen that the view was wasted on a girl whose interest was elsewhere.

There were photographs of the Derbyshire camping trip displayed on her bookcase alongside the chalk Pavel had carried from the beach almost a year before. He studied the pictures for a moment then picked up the rock.

'Don't get it on your clothes,' she said. 'Covers you in dust. As bad as coal.' She'd noticed a faint black line beneath his eyes. 'Speaking of which... looks like you've got eye liner on.' She licked her finger. 'Here, let me –'

'Leave it,' he said, shrinking from her and sitting on the edge of the bed. He dropped the rock beside him, wiped a thumb across his eye lids. 'Sometimes you can't get rid of it.'

A red Dansette record player filled one corner of her desk and a collection of LPs lined the window ledge. She chose a Beach Boys' album he'd once said was his favourite.

'This machine is so out of date,' she said. 'P'raps we should buy a new one – together. What do you think? A stereo player with speakers and a perspex lid.'

Pavel replaced the rock on the bookcase. The chalk had left a white patch on the bedspread. He washed his hands in the sink, scrutinising his face in the mirror.

What's wrong?' she said 'You've hardly said a word.' She wondered if the harmonies of the ballad were too poignant, if they raked up emotions. 'Shall I switch it off?'

'Not on my account. It's their best album.' He sat at her desk watching the rugby until the referee ended the match with three long blasts on his whistle. 'You could sell tickets to spectate from here,' he said.

'All these rugby men and I only want to see you, eh?' She laughed. 'Shall I make coffee?'

He glanced at his watch. 'I have to go. You know how my mother worries. I was lucky Dad agreed to let me borrow the car at all.' He turned from the window, fixing his gaze on the rug. 'You should enjoy your time here, Helen. I don't want you to miss out on anything because of me.'

'Miss out on what?'

'Opportunities. Fun. Parties, dances. Don't students have parties? You like dancing. Bet there are discos on campus.'

'What do you mean?'

'Look. You must realise. Things have changed. There'll be no magical recovery, Helen. Good old Pavel, back in the fold. It won't happen. I don't want you to wait. Don't waste your time.'

'Waste my time? We're engaged. You wanted the wedding as soon as —'

'I was stupid, childish. I'm older now. It feels like a thousand years older.' He rubbed his forehead, groaned. 'This is difficult.'

'Say it. It's the oldest cliché. You don't want to hurt me? I'll leave college if that's what you want.'

'No. It's not what I want.'

'Have you found somebody else?' Her voiced cracked, she swallowed.

Pavel shook his head. 'No. But you will.'

'Second oldest,' she said. 'Next you'll say you want us to be good friends.' He slipped his jacket from the back of the chair, made for the door. 'You're not walking out on me, Pavel. Not like this.' Her face burned. Tears stung. 'I'm happy to wait. It's my choice.'

'I'm making it mine. The problem with you Helen is that you can't stand to be thwarted. You're spoiled. Always have been. You live in a fantasy world. Happy ever after. I blame Billy. Anything Helen Farrimond wants –.'

'That's not fair. If you're trying to make me hate you, to let you off the hook –.'

'I'm trying to be truthful: I don't think we should see each other again.' He made for the door.

She followed, held on to the hem of his jacket. 'I can't believe you mean this; that you'd do this to me.'

'For God's sake, Helen, don't beg. I'm not the person you knew or need. I don't have your aspirations, your books or your highbrow intentions. I'm sorry.'

She dropped to her knees, clutched his legs. 'Stay. We can –'

'Get up. I don't want to see you like this.' He opened the door. 'Let go of me, Helen. Please.'

She released him, pulled herself to her feet by the door handle. She was queasy. She wrenched the ring from her finger.

'Keep it,' he said.

'Don't insult me.'

He took the ring and dropped it into the breast pocket of his shirt. She thought he would lose it; it would be of no consequence to him if he did.

'I'll find my own way to the car park,' he said.

From the window she watched as he followed the last of the rugby players to leave the field. He didn't look back.

★ ★ ★

On the top of the Pennines he stopped, peered into the valley where a reservoir sparkled in the late afternoon sun. This was not how he'd intended the day to unfold: as if they were second-rate actors in some bloody awful film. But he could no longer have responsibility for Helen, for her happiness to depend on his. He couldn't remember what he'd said, what she'd said, only that he'd intended to be kinder. He'd tried to rehearse a speech but it was all crap.

If he chose, he could run down the hillside, wade in until the water covered his waist then his chest, his neck, his mouth. Fill his lungs. Was it possible to drown if you could swim? Would instinct take over? What if you filled your pockets with stones? Could you stop the nightmare of screeching brakes, a blood-soaked shattered body, a mangled bike?

If he had any sense of responsibility, any compassion, he should go back to her but he couldn't. He was sick of responsibility, sick to the stomach.

He returned to the car and drove on towards Sheffield.

It was after seven when he arrived home. He tossed the car keys onto the kitchen table. His father glanced up from his evening newspaper, lost in his mindless evening ritual of drinking tea – tea so rarely finished that every mug they owned was tannin stained. By the look of the milky skin on its surface, it must be cold. Pavel was tempted to snatch the mug, smash it against the wall, watch the liquid drip down the trellis patterned wallpaper that his mother frequently cleaned with her scrubbing brush hands. Tempted to scream at his dad: *Feel something, say something. Your son is dead*.

Always busy. Busy mother. Filling the silence with the scratching of scouring powder on the draining board, her hands chapped and rough as sand paper. Busy washing dishes; everything submerged. Everything below the surface: their paltry lives, a meaningless marriage.

His mother stood at the sink, wringing out a dish cloth. 'Oh you're back, Pavel. How is Helen?'

'It's finished.'

She dried her hands on a tea towel, slung it across her shoulder; wrapped her thin arms around him. 'She will be upset. Poor girl. But if it's what you wanted...'

'It is.' He rubbed his eyes with his fists. 'God, I need a drink. Don't wait up for me. I've got a key.'

He walked two hundred yards to the pub on the corner where he found Coker drinking at the bar. The room was dimly lit, but a spotlight over the snooker table revealed a huddle of lads he knew from the pit. Cues clicked, arrows landed dull thuds against a dartboard and some indistinct voice regaled him through a cloud of blue smoke. He nodded towards the group. Coker patted his shoulder, drew him towards a bar stool. Touching, patting. Not what he wanted.

'Pavel mate, let me get you a drink. My God, you look bloody terrible.'

'A pint thanks. I've had a shit day.'

The barman slammed two beers on the counter. They sloshed over beer mats and bar towels. 'You've had a belly full already, Coker. I don't want any trouble. Police were in here earlier. Tip-off about drugs.'

Pavel downed the beer in one.

'Blimey,' Coker said and ordered a refill.

'I've finished with her,' Pavel said.

Coker applauded slowly. 'About bloody time. Good man. She'll get over it. Right little raver that one. She'll find somebody else, no problem.'

'Watch yourselves,' the bar man said, serving another two pints. Coker nudged Pavel's arm.

'Heh. Did you hear that, Pavel? Drugs? Around here? Never.'

Pavel shook his head, drank. Billy Farrimond would have something to say about drugs. If it were pit lads involved, he'd want it sorted. He had something to say about everything. Like his niece. What would he say about her? About what Pavel had done?

Coker shouted to the barman. 'We're just having a few drinks and a chat, aren't we, Pav? That's all. No trouble. He's had a bad day. He's dumped his snotty bird at last.'

Pavel hauled himself up onto a high stool, elbows squelching on a beer-soaked bar towel. He ought to stop Coker's comments about Helen.

Coker slurred. 'Here, have a chaser.' He handed Pavel a whisky. Pavel turned to see if anyone he knew was watching but the last customer had sloped off into a corner and was tipping out a box of dominoes onto a baize table.

'Here,' Coker said. 'This might numb the pain.' Coker pushed a screwed up tissue parcel into Pavel's hand.

Pavel opened it, took out a pill and held it for a moment between his finger and thumb then tucked it into his jeans pocket.

'Vitamins,' Coker said, 'from a friend of mine. Do you the world of good.'

More beer. More whisky chasers. Pavel laughed, cried. Coker hauled him from the bar stool by his lapels. 'Lean on me. I'll get you home.'

They staggered along the pavement, into garden walls, into parked cars. Pavel felt a sharp pain in his heel as he lost his footing on the kerb and tumbled into the road. Coker hooked him beneath his arms, dragged Pavel to his feet. 'Come on, you pillock.' He searched Pavel's jacket pockets. 'Where's your key?' He found it, unlocked the back door. The kitchen was in darkness. Pavel patted the wall to find the light switch. Coker's knee in his back propelled him onto a kitchen chair. Coker laughed. 'Bloody idiot. You'll never learn.'

Pavel slid to the floor with neither strength nor will to get up.

★ ★ ★

At six o' clock on Monday morning Pavel waited, orange overalls and helmet on, a *snap tin and Dudley*★ hanging from his belt. His stomach lurched as the metal screen shut with a clank and the cage descended. He felt his feet in the air for a fraction of a second as it plummeted, his body suspended, weightless. Then his stomach sinking. He was aware of Roly standing behind him, his steadying hand on his shoulder but took no comfort from it.

At the bottom of the shaft, men spilled into the tunnel and Pavel was swept along in the tide of swaying bodies marching to the paddy truck. It would take them to the coal face. Then they would walk. March. Miles of boots. Trudging. He was silent, shoulders hunched, concentrating on each foot forward.

Clumsy, coal-crusted boots, led him step by weary step. His legs were heavy. He didn't control them.

Roly laughed, shouted: 'Here we are again, boys. The tunnel of love.'

Someone sang *Monday, Monday,* men behind fooling, attempting the harmonies of the Mamas and Papas. Pavel's chest tightened. In spite of a draught, sweat beaded his

★ *Lunch box and water bottle*

142

brow. He found a grimy handkerchief in his pocket and mopped his face. Soon it would be hot. Hot as hell.

Monday, Tuesday, Wednesday, Thursday, Friday. Every day was a tunnel, a hell-hole from which he envisaged no return.

Chapter Twelve

Well Meaning Friends

June 1973

Lundby South Yorkshire

A woman's frantic voice called from an upstairs window as Roly rapped at the door and rattled the tarnished letter box. 'Wait, please.' Patches of blue paint showed through the flaking red on the front door, making the house look as shabby and uncared for as Pavel himself. Pavel's mother tried her best to keep the semblance of a home life, but since Jakub's death, it must have been difficult for the woman to cajole her miserable husband out of bed every morning, without the burden of her one remaining son proving hell bent on self-destruction. The death of a child was unimaginable; Roly wanted to be at home with his wife and daughters

He didn't know Mr Kowaleski's Christian name, nor his wife's. 'Leski,' as Pavel's dad was known in the pit, was considered a different species from his once cheerful sons. Leski was a man more muttered about than conversed with.

Roly got back in his Ford Escort and waited.

Why he cared about Pavel he wasn't sure, except that the lad had always possessed a generosity, honesty, a wisdom beyond his years, which seemed to be slipping away. Pavel's smile had been replaced by a morose, hollow look and the vagueness in his eyes exaggerated by a rim of coal dust never quite washed away. If Pavel didn't follow the rest of the shift to the pit head baths, Roly was certain he wouldn't wash at all. He was freefalling into a black hole, as if the hole they worked in wasn't dark enough.

Roly doted on his daughters; eight and six, doing well at school. His wife Kath was a loving woman and they'd worked hard to provide a comfortable home and a holiday once a year. He couldn't complain. Approaching forty, he'd say he was content. So why was he here when he should have been at home in bed? God knows, he was tired. Only got home at 6.30 from a night shift. If he'd wanted to help anybody this morning, it should have been Kath, who'd be tearing about getting the girls ready for school, hanging out washing, preparing a lamb stew before she left for work. The least he could do was offer his own family a lift, not get entangled with Kowaleski problems.

He sounded his horn and tapped the dash board. 'Come on, Pavel. I haven't got all bloody day.'

The door opened. Pavel's mother peeped out, ran a hand through her unkempt hair. Roly could just see the shoulder of her quilted dressing gown, the same one she'd worn the day he'd called to offer his condolences. Surely her husband or son could see she needed a new one. Did the family not have birthdays? There was such a look of desperation in the woman's eyes he wondered if he should ask Kath to call on her. Have a chat.

'He'll be there in a minute, Mr Beresford. I have been trying to get him out of bed for the last hour. He knows you are here. Thank you.' Roly nodded.

A clipped Polish accent gave her a respectful formality. She'd never picked up the local dialect and Roly thought she sounded humbled, grateful. He waited. She'd left the door ajar. Was she trying to convince him that Pavel was on his way at last, or was it a plea? *He's coming. Give him another chance.*

Roly drummed his fingers on the steering wheel, adjusted the wing mirror and dashboard switches, tuning into Radio 1 for Pavel's benefit – not that Pavel would notice. Did he listen to anything anymore? Poor woman. Bloody husband. Feckless, time wasting son. Roly would hang around a bit longer for her sake.

Five minutes later Pavel emerged, a brown cord jacket dangling from one hand. It brushed the kerb, the sleeves trailing in the gutter. His eyes scanned the pavement with a furtive look that reminded Roly of a tramp searching for discarded fags. And surely he was wearing last night's clothes? Which hedge had he crawled under in that pair of filthy jeans?

Roly opened the passenger door. 'Get in, quick.' Pavel climbed in the car. 'Fasten your seat belt. Hurry up.' Pavel fumbled with the buckle, a hint of a tremor in his pale long-fingered hands. Roly set off at speed, gripping the wheel, his stomach in a knot. If his own hands were free he would shake the stupid lad till his teeth rattled.

Pavel turned the radio down. When he spoke his voice was soft, monotone. He sounded exhausted. 'I thought you were on nights, Roly.'

Roly jerked his foot on the accelerator. 'I am.'

'What're you doing here then? You should be in bed.'

A car horn sounded. Roly waved two fingers, called the driver *a prat*. 'Good of you to notice. I should be in bed, you're right, Pavel. And why am I here? I'm getting you to college, idiot. I'll remind you shall I? Your exams are next week.'

'I know that. I slept in.'

'Slept in? Like you did last Tuesday when you couldn't force your arse out of bed? What time did you get in last night?'

'Can't remember.'

'And why? Summat Coker gave you, was it? Summat to keep you up all night? You daft bugger.'

'I'm sorry, Roly. I'm letting you down, I know that.'

Roly cursed at the bus in front and overtook it, averting his eyes from the road for a second to glance at his passenger. Pavel stroked and picked at shadowy stubble.

'Not bothered to shave then?' Roly said.

'No time.'

'You're letting yourself down. You're letting your brother down an' all. Do you think he'd want to see you like this?' Roly swerved to avoid a lorry.

'That's below the belt, Roly.'

Screeching to a halt, Roly wound down the window and shook his fist at a school boy jay walker, who in return shouted obscenities at the windscreen.

'Gobby little bugger! Wait till I see your mother.'

'Do you know his – ?'

'Shut up, Pavel. Below the belt, did you say?' He set off again, more slowly this time. 'I'll tell you about belts. My dad would have taken his belt off to me if I'd even so much as thought about shirking duty. You get a chance like this and you're throwing it away.'

'I'll try harder. It's just that –'

'Just that what? You've lost your brother. I know that's tough. Like it was tough for my mam when she lost three brothers in the trenches. And bloody awful for my sister when her husband was killed in the D-day landings. Married two months. Blown into so many bits there was nothing to bury. Shit all of it, Pavel.'

From the corner of his eye, Roly noticed Pavel was biting his knuckles.

'Some people cope better than others,' Pavel said.

Roly shook his head. 'Don't give me that hippy shite. You can cope as well as the next man if you try. You can pull yourself together or you can go under – with the help of Coker and his *little friends.'*

Neither spoke again until they drew up outside the local *Tech*. It was ten past nine. Pavel climbed out of the car. 'Thanks,' he said and walked up the steps to the college.

Roly waited. Pavel stopped at the double doors of the red-brick building, raising a hand in feeble salute. Roly nodded, looked in his rear view mirror, allowed a stream of corporation buses to overtake then set off home. He wished he could believe that the lad would try. One last look over his shoulder assured him Pavel had at least entered the building, though what he'd be capable of when he sat at a desk was anybody's guess.

The breakfast dishes in the sink were evidence of the family's early morning scurry to leave for school on time. After Roly had washed up and tidied the kitchen, he went upstairs, closed the curtains and climbed into bed, setting the alarm for three that afternoon. Five hours sleep would be enough and then he'd pick Pavel up from the college, drag him to the doctor's surgery and be down the pit again by ten that night. He punched the pillow and pulled the sheet over his head. He hated this shift.

If Pavel needed drugs, then Roly would make sure they were the prescribed variety and he'd give Coker a visit an' all. Time somebody sorted out that dealing little scumbag.

★ ★ ★

Chester June 1973

It was a first floor flat in an imposing Victorian terraced house near to the college. There was no television, no phone. In the sitting room an antique mustiness pervaded, masked slightly by the smell of lavender which reminded

Helen of the old library in Lundby. Wrapped in a cardigan she sat on a brown utility sofa, one hand flicking a small tear in the fabric, reading a book. Neither the frayed rug nor the peeling lino around its edges provided any sense of comfort. Even in June the room seemed chilly: you opened the sash windows to let warmth in and stale air out.

A cloud of dust rose as Jane, her roommate, flopped beside her. 'You're twenty, Helen. If you're not careful you'll be here when you're fifty, decked out in cobwebs like Miss Havisham.'

'I've told you. I don't like dancing,' Helen said, and wondered what Tibby and Uncle Billy would think if they heard.

It was Jane who had persuaded Helen into student work in the holidays and Helen had not been back to Lundby since – though Billy and Tibby's concerns had brought them on three visits, and their disappointment at her Christmas absence had been painful. In the first post-Pavel summer, the two girls had found waitress jobs in Scarborough, where by day they'd served coffee at a corporation café and, in the evenings, scampi and chips in baskets at the Spa ballroom. The seaside provided fresh air and escape. She couldn't face Lundby or the possibility of bumping into Pavel.

Aware of her roommate's intended lecture – there had been plenty over the year – she turned an unread page. Jane handed her a carrier. 'You have no choice now but to come out with us tonight.' Inside the bag was a blue floral dress. Helen stroked the cotton lawn. She could see her fingers through it. The flatmates had all chipped in. 'We all agreed it would suit you. A year in mourning is long enough.'

★ ★ ★

The night club was split-level, tables raised around a sunken dance floor, a wooden balustrade separating the drinkers from the dancers. A row of young men in blazers and suits leered over the rail at the girls dancing – those wearing jeans had been turned away at the door. Low lighting and a glitter ball reminded Helen of the seaside ballroom; the same swirl of suffused colour dappling faces. She sat on a banquette wishing she had not been persuaded into several drinks in a pub earlier. She felt dizzy. Her foot tapped awkwardly to the music. She'd forgotten how loud discos were.

A dark haired young man stood in front of the table, shouting over an Elton John record. 'Have your friends deserted you?' She recognised him from a group in the pre-disco pub and had noticed his crowd gathered on the balcony.

'They're dancing. I'm looking after the bags.'

'Some friends. Tell them to dance around their handbags like everyone else. I'm Guy, by the way.' He slid along the bench until he sat next to her.

'Helen.'

'I've not seen you here before.'

'My first time. I'm at the college.'

'Don't they let you out much?'

She smiled. 'Not often.'

He was good looking: a shock of dark hair, brown eyes. A strong jawline. The music changed. John Lennon's *Imagine*. A slow dance. The girls were wandering back to the table.

'Come on, you're about to be let off prefect duties,' he said.

Persuaded by her friends to try something new, Helen had been drinking bottled schooners of sherry in the pub. She was dizzier now she was on her feet. He took her hand, drew her onto the dance floor, held her close. There was a scent of aftershave against her cheek, a sweet scent she didn't recognise. His embrace and the music reminded her of Pavel holding her at their engagement party. The tempo turned to disco. The air was close, bodies touching, sweating; the sprung floor sagging beneath the weight of the dancers. Guy released her, loosened his broad purple tie, unfastened the top button of his white shirt which glowed mauve in the disco lighting. She swayed and he caught her, asked if he could buy her a drink.

'Actually, I have one already,' she said, pointing to the table where her flatmates were watching.

'Let me buy you another. There's a second bar,' he said. 'Quieter. Cooler. We won't have to shout.'

She collected her bag from the girls' table. 'Don't leave without me,' she told them then allowed Guy to steer her across the dance floor, through swing doors at the end of the room.

Fluorescent lighting in the half-empty bar, dazzled her and she shielded her eyes. He led her to a corner, to a table littered with glasses, beckoning to a barmaid who promptly collected the empties, wiping sticky patches from the beaten copper top.

'Thank you,' he said.

'You're welcome, Guy,' the girl said. Clearly he was known. His interest flattered Helen; she found his courtesy reassuring.

It was cool beneath the open window, perspiration chilled on her back. She could hear the traffic in the streets below. She shivered.

'You're cold,' he said. 'I'm sorry. I should have thought.' He draped his jacket around her shoulders. 'I'm glad I didn't leave it in the cloakroom now. What will you have to drink?'

'I'm not sure I should have anything.'

'Let me choose. '

She nodded, not wanting to offend.

'Don't go away,' he said.

When he returned from the bar he placed two gin and tonics on the table. Hadn't Uncle Billy warned her not to mix her drinks? Helen had never seen a man drink gin and tonic. The most genteel drink for a Lundby man was a half of mild as opposed to the usual pint of bitter. He had elegant fingers, smooth skin, nails carefully manicured. And his shoes: soft black leather: highly polished yet creased, pliable like Tibby's best kid gloves. She took in his clean-shaven face. When she reached for her glass he took her fingers in his, stroked her hand.

'So who is Helen?' he said. 'I'll tell you about me first if it makes you feel safer.' He told her he lived ten miles away in a Cheshire village, had left Oxford two years before with a first in Economics and Politics and worked for a chemical company. 'Where we make acid rain if nothing else,' he said. 'Dad's the MD, so I want to move on, avoid the nepotism trap. He's a forceful man. We don't always agree.'

She told him she was from Yorkshire, that her uncle was a miner. He laughed.

'No chance of your uncle wangling you a job then.'

'My uncle wangles most things. He's a union man.'

'Really? What? A Commie?'

'Uncle Billy? Hardly.'

'And here was I thinking how pretty you looked in blue.'

'Uncle Billy and I don't always agree either.'

Guy showered her with compliments until the cynicism she'd nursed so carefully over the last year evaporated.

'Come out with me tomorrow,' he said. 'We could drive into the countryside. Maybe have a pub lunch.'

'I'm not sure.'

He led her back onto the dance floor. Strobe lighting confused her, caught her off balance; bodies flickered in a haze of smoke and the hiss and mist of Co2. An unreal scene unfolded, a dream-like bacchanal. She leaned into him. Over his shoulder she caught a glimpse of a man who resembled Pavel: the short sandy hair, a young man towering above the girl he danced with.'

'Who are you looking at?' Guy asked, following her gaze.

'Thought I recognised somebody,' she said.

Flashing lights stopped. The DJ played the Beatles: *PS I Love You*. Guy told her this was always the last record. Regulars drifted from the dance-floor.

'I'll have to go, Guy. The others are waiting,' she said, disoriented, desperate for air. When the house lights went up, Helen saw the girls had collected their coats and Jane was waving Helen's shawl to attract her attention.

'What about lunch?' he said. She had to decide quickly. It was only a meal. No harm in that. He kissed her lightly on the cheek, told her he'd pick her up at noon the next day. She gave him directions to the flat, said goodnight and joined the girls at the exit.

'About time too,' Jane said. 'The taxi's waiting. For a minute we thought lover-boy was coming home with us.'

When she climbed into bed the room was spinning and she clung onto the mattress as if she were falling backwards down a well. At the top she could see several Guys reaching for her.

She woke early, her mouth parched. After coffee and hangover remedies, the flatmates picked over the evening's events, teasing Helen about how easily she'd given away their address; how quickly her resolve had crumbled. Helen's tongue was furry, her head ached, her stomach churned. What had she agreed to last night?

Guy arrived punctually, parking a racing green open-topped MG outside the flat. Helen and Jane watched from the window. 'Forget miners, Helen,' Jane said. 'You've bagged yourself a class act.'

Chapter Thirteen

Cornered

May 1984

South Yorkshire

It was the sort of rain that made her long to draw curtains, light fires, curl up on a hearth rug. There'd been no easing of the downpour that had drenched Pavel and Coker while they'd waited for their sons to leave the gym club. Consumed by marking and distracted by thoughts of Pavel, Helen was still at her desk at six o' clock and it was only when the caretaker, rattling keys, informed her he was locking up that Helen grabbed her umbrella and left school.

She needed time to digest everything Pavel had said. His apology for one. Had she seen too much in his concern? Had he always been there beneath the surface, picking away at her relationship with Guy? Pavel. Her head was awash with him. She'd even written, 'Well done, Pavel,' on Jake's maths book and had to search the drawer to find correction fluid.

At the end of the school drive she was surprised to find Uncle Billy waiting in his Ford Escort, headlights on, engine running, windscreen wipers on frantic. He wound down the window. 'Come on, love. Get in. You're late. I thought you'd like a lift.'

'Thoughtful of you, Uncle Billy. Appreciate it.' She climbed in beside him. The interior smelled damp; the windows had steamed up. Billy switched on the blowers. She kissed his cheek. 'Thanks.'

Uncle Billy was like slippers and a cosy dressing gown, or a ragged teddy bear not to be parted with, even though threadbare and reeking of dust. A comfort blanket; familiarity; safety. And yet he'd never offered to collect her from school before. He blushed at the kiss, muttered about the weather, crunching gears as he set off.

'Something wrong?' she asked

'Nothing that a service won't fix,' he said.

After tea Billy sat in his armchair like a brass Buddha, his hands clasped on his ample belly: a post-retirement paunch that strained the buttons of his shirt. He appeared to be watching a soap opera that Tibby enjoyed, but the absence of his usual critical commentary suggested his thoughts were elsewhere. Bevan lay with his head on his master's foot, snoring.

As the credits rolled Billy rose from his armchair disturbing the dog, turned off the television and stood with his back to it. Bevan barked and jumped into the vacated seat. 'Guy rang today, Helen.' Billy's eyes darted to Tibby and he held up his hands. 'I know, I know. Don't shoot the messenger.'

'What did he want?' Helen asked.

'I suppose he wanted to speak to his wife,' Billy said, shifting his weight from one foot to the other. 'He phoned to say he's coming up by train tomorrow.'

Helen groaned. Guy had phoned her several times over the past weeks: insincere checks on her well-being and requests for her return date, but had never threatened to visit. 'Did you know about this, Tibby?'

Tibby shrugged. 'First I've heard. I was out shopping this afternoon. I would have deterred him.'

Billy examined his finger nails. 'I might not like his politics, Helen, but he wants to sort things out and he has a point. You've been here two months and done nothing about him. He has rights.'

She shook her head. 'Rights to what?' Why was it her fault?

'You should have told him to phone back when Helen was home,' Tibby said.

'But that's the whole point,' Billy said. 'Helen's spoken to him before. Nothing is ever resolved.'

'Maybe it was resolved when she left,' Tibby said.

'Unless you know something I don't, Helen hasn't yet told us what his crimes are. Personally I believe supporting Thatcher's a capital offence, but that doesn't explain Helen running away, does it? Ten years is a long time.'

'I told you, Uncle Billy. It's a trial separation.'

'You didn't mention any trial. You arrived here looking like a lost waif. Couldn't get a word out of you.' As Helen remembered it, she couldn't get a word in. 'And though it's lovely to have you back –'

'You encouraged me to stay, and to find a job. Why are you on Guy's side all of a sudden?'

'I'm not. You stay as long as you like, love. But do the right thing. If you want to divorce Guy I'll support you. But we can't have him phoning here every –'

'Point taken. I'll sort it.'

Billy scowled. 'If you don't want him, be honest. No man deserves to be fooled around – even Guy.'

Helen caught exchanged glances between Tibby and Billy. Was there something else she should know? 'Okay. I heard you the first time,' she said. 'But I'm not letting the women down tomorrow. I'm collecting in Sheffield.'

'And I'm going into the kitchen to iron,' Tibby said, red-faced. 'I'll leave you to it.'

'I told Guy you'd be out till teatime,' Billy said. 'I didn't tell him what you'd be doing. He's coming up in the afternoon; booking into a hotel in Doncaster for the night.'

'I don't give a damn if he knows what I'm doing.'

'Apparently he's buying you a meal somewhere. Course, what he actually said was he'd be taking you to *dinner*.' Dinner to Billy was at half past two in the afternoon. When a man came in from the day shift.

'It won't look good to anyone who knows I'm in the support group,' she said, 'me going out for a posh meal. I hope nobody sees us.'

'If it's that Nouvelle Queen stuff, you'd better have a sandwich before you leave.'

Billy stood up, steadied himself on the mantelpiece.

Was it pride, shame or embarrassment that prevented her from telling Tibby and Billy the truth? If she'd informed Billy about Guy's behaviour, he'd have driven her to a solicitor himself, probably called in the police.

Billy headed for the hallway, returned wearing a Mac and a checked trilby, a small feather peeping from its brim. 'Anyway, it shouldn't matter who sees you, Missy. I told you to keep out of strike matters, but as usual you didn't listen. I'm off now, to a finance committee meeting at the Institute.'

'Finance on Friday night?' Tibby shouted from the kitchen.

'And Pavel said if I was around he'd like a word. It was good to see him helping you today, Helen. Saw him when you passed on your walk. Glad you're speaking again. Mind, I heard a rumour that he had a bust up with –'

'*Aarrgh.*' Helen ran her fingers through her hair. 'You're infuriating sometimes.'

'Now what did I do wrong?'

158

Tibby opened the front door, 'Bye Billy.'

'Nearly forgot. Guy told me he'd send a taxi to collect you at seven. I suppose you don't have to go with him, love, if you —'

'Thanks Uncle Billy. Bit late now.'

Billy mumbled about being late and left.

★ ★ ★

The city of seven hills had witnessed its share of unrest: two years before, steel workers had taken strike action over the threat of redundancies and factory closures. Helen expected the women from the support group would receive solidarity, encouragement, empathy. Sheffield knew how it felt to have its industry bled. The phoenix was the emblem of the most famous steel company but there would be no rising of mines from the ashes if the government had its way.

Helen and Kath found a corner opposite the railway station where they could catch visitors as well as locals. A second group set off towards the City Hall, a third to the Town Hall and a fourth to Fargate: the usual location for collections, campaigning and petition signing. Buses spewed shoppers onto the pavements, engines roared, diesel fumes caught the back of her throat. She imagined Jack and Celia stepping through the station arches, arriving from London, bumping into her, finding her collecting. Or even Guy's parents. Defiance was intoxicating. She seethed with indignation at Guy's presumption that he could turn up uninvited.

Wartime thrift had left Tibby with a hatred of throwing anything away and she'd supplied Helen with an old quilted anorak from her dog walking collection. It hung over Helen's jeans almost to her knees. Kath had tied a cardboard '*Victory to the Miners*' poster to a nearby lamppost and as the morning passed, people donated a few coins to the bucket or dropped a can or packet into a food box.

A woman in heels clicked by, swinging carrier bags: Cole Brothers, Atkinson's, Marks and Spencer. It's disgusting,' the woman said. 'Begging in the streets. Tell the lazy buggers to get back to work.' She kicked the cardboard poster that had slipped to the foot of the lamppost. 'They're lucky to be employed at all.'

Collecting was not as easy as Helen had expected. When a tramp shuffled across the road towards them she dragged the grocery box close and rescued the money bucket. There was no way she would let him touch either. His filthy grey gabardine was tied with a tangled string and there were pads of newspaper strapped with duct tape to his shoes. The smell of him hit her nostrils from yards away. He held up a ten pence piece. 'Here you are, love,' he said, dropping it into the bucket. 'My Granddad was a miner.'

'It's surprising where you find generosity,' Kath said.

★ ★ ★

Lipstick, eye pencil, mascara and two shots of Tibby's Christmas gin; the tools Helen employed to bolster her courage. She wore a red dress topped off with a black wool jacket, convincing herself that an outfit Guy had not seen before would assert her independence, not attract him exactly but maybe throw him off guard – though she remembered he liked her in red.

The taxi arrived promptly at seven. Since Tibby was engrossed in a Saturday night *Morecambe and Wise* repeat, and Billy pottering in the greenhouse, Helen slipped through the front door unnoticed, only to find that it was not the driver who held the cab door open for her. It was Guy. Typical of him to make an arrangement then break it. Undermine her. Not even a minute into a reunion and he'd gained the upper hand with surprise tactics. She clutched her handbag.

'Hello, darling,' he said, slipping onto the back seat beside her. The taxi driver glanced over his shoulder, probably as surprised as Helen at the 'darling'. He wouldn't have heard the term used much around this neighbourhood.

'I didn't need an escort, Guy,' she said.

'We're not going to Doncaster. I've booked the Old Smithy Restaurant in Bickley.' He stroked her hand as if there'd been no rift.

How did he know about the restaurant? It had only been open a year and she'd heard there was a sixth month waiting list for a booking. At least with the prices charged there'd be no miners, or anyone else who might know her.

The taxi sped along country lanes that led out of the village and past the colliery, past the woods where she'd walked with her class and Pavel. Though Bickley was only four miles away it might as well have been a hundred. There was a cultural divide, a chasm of difference. It had become a smart village for transient professionals: middle class accountants and marketing directors passing through in a CV building tour of duty in Yorkshire.

Every minute seemed an eternity. At every sharp bend Helen clung to her seat to avoid brushing shoulders with Guy. She averted her eyes, staring through the window, aware that he was watching her, burning holes in her resolve.

When they arrived Guy paid the driver and told him to keep the change. Perhaps she should have brought the collecting bucket, asked Guy for a donation.

A solicitous maître d' in a suit and bow tie greeted them, ushered them to high stools by the bar where Guy ordered her a gin and tonic – without asking what Helen preferred – and himself an orange juice. The restaurant was busy and a raucous male-only party huddled in one corner, drinking champagne. The tiny dining area explained the waiting list, but she had no intention of asking Guy how he'd managed to secure a table.

'My agent's mother lives in Doncaster,' he said. 'She told him about it. So I rang on the off chance of a cancellation. I was lucky.'

How did he know what she was thinking? 'You don't have to explain.'

'You thought I'd pulled strings.'

'You usually do.'

'I know you don't think much of me right now.'

'What do you expect?'

Guy gazed into his orange juice but didn't drink. 'I've made mistakes, Helen. I'm sorry.'

Pavel had also apologised. What was it with these men? One had beaten her with false promises, the other with slaps and infidelity.

A young waitress and waiter uncovered silver tureens at a nearby table. Enormous lids covering tiny pieces of beef. The spectacle was faintly ridiculous. What a palaver for a lump of meat. Helen stifled a giggle. The girl looked familiar. Then she recognised her: Jenny Beresford, Roly and Kath's daughter, working here while studying for her A levels.

The head waiter showed Helen and Guy to a table for two in a window bay, not quite big enough for them to be seated comfortably. They squeezed into their seats, causing a single red rose in a china vase to wobble and a sepia photograph of the Smithy, taken a hundred years before, to clatter face down onto the window ledge. 'They should have taken out this ledge, made more room,' Helen said, refusing to be impressed by the restaurant's reputation, regardless of its silver tureens and opulent drapes. She glanced around then back to Guy.

'A red dress always suited you,' he said.

A portly middle aged couple settled at the next table. Guy ordered a bottle of Sauvignon Blanc and a bottle of Perrier and the maître d' lit a candle in a crystal candlestick. Guy studied the menu. The wine waiter uncorked the bottle, wrapped a napkin around it and attempted to pour a drop into Guy's glass. 'No, no. I'd like my wife to taste the wine.'

'I'm sure it will be fine,' Helen said. 'Just pour it. Wine protocol is so pretentious, don't you think?' The waiter filled her glass and settled the bottle into a bucket of ice. 'Cheers, Guy,' she said. 'Not having any?'

'No, I've not had a drink for weeks.'

'Have you given up the hooker as well?' Helen caught the eye of the woman at the next table. The couple's silence indicated they'd been married for years and, having long since run out of their own conversation, were intent on listening to everyone else's.

'Can't we just enjoy tonight?' Guy said. 'I wanted it to be perfect.'

'We can't pretend nothing happened. I thought we were here to talk.'

He poured himself a glass of water. Bubbles sparkled in the candlelight. Helen drained her wine glass. Guy refilled it.

This would cost him a fortune. She perused the menu: the price of a meal at the Smithy would keep a miner for a week. Guy wouldn't understand the irony or morality of that. She would choose the most expensive dish; he deserved to pay dearly.

The smell of fish lingered above floral displays and customer perfumes. The restaurant was feted for sea food, though a note attached to the menu announced that lobster was unavailable. Helen ordered sea bass. Guy ordered veal. The waiter returned carrying a fish knife and fork.

'Pity the lobster's off,' she said. The waiter muttered apology.

'Helen,' Guy said, scowling. 'Try to be polite at least.'

Guy had ordered fois gras for his first course, Helen baked mushrooms. 'Bon appétit,' the waiter said, backing off. She offered him a sickly smile.

'Don't patronise him,' Guy said.

'Why are you whispering?'

Guy glanced around; spread a morsel of pâté onto a finger of melba toast.

'Poor bloody goose!' she said. 'Did you know they were force fed till their tiny livers burst?'

'Just eat, Helen. And don't swear.'

'And did you know that we export veal cows to France to be slaughtered and then they send them back?' She ran a finger across her throat. 'Kaput. They go off on the cross channel ferry with the rest of the holiday makers and come back hung drawn and quartered. Butchered at the hands of the French.'

'What's your point?'

'I'm just saying. You should always be aware of the wider issues.'

'If you say so.' He fidgeted, adjusted the position of his chair.

'And did you know –'

He lowered his voice. 'Helen. Just listen. I want you to come back.'

'Why?'

'I want things the way they were... before.' he said.

No mention of the word love. 'Really?'

'There's a chance I'll be promoted. A junior post. That's the rumour.'

She finished the second glass of wine, enjoying the boldness it gave her. The loose tongue. 'Which department? Trade and Industry?' she laughed. 'There'll be no industry left after your boss has finished.'

'If that's what you think, all the more reason to support me. I can work from within. Not everybody is wholly Thatcherite.'

Helen sniggered. 'But you are, Guy.' She helped herself to a third glass.

'There'll be a change of leadership one day.'

'A change of heart? I thought the Blessed Margaret was your ideal woman. Personally, I think she's been around too long already.' She took another swig of Sauvignon Blanc. Then another. She knew the woman at the next table was still listening, had noticed her leaning towards the conversation. Helen spoke loudly. 'I've thought long and hard about our future, Guy.'

Guy fidgeted with the cutlery, knocking a knife onto the floor. The head waiter leapt forward, retrieved it, clicking his fingers at Jenny Beresford who replaced it.

'Hi Jenny,' Helen said. 'How's your dad? Been picketing today?'

Jenny smiled then scuttled through the swing doors into the kitchen. Helen finished her wine. 'I like these large glasses, don't you?' she said, pouring another. 'No messing, no sedate sipping with these.'

'Yes. I think we get the picture.'

His eyes were brown. Pavel's were blue. Either way, eyes were disconcerting. She took another drink. 'So, why the prostitute? Was she the first, or the last? Or didn't you count?'

The woman at the next table coughed. Guy had begun to pour himself a Perrier but stopped, glared as if in a freeze-frame, as if he didn't recognise Helen. Did she recognise herself?

'Helen, please.'

'And what about the baby? You couldn't even discuss William. Do you know what that did to me?'

His face flushed. 'I let you down. I wasn't ready to be a father. I had such a bad relationship with my own, I couldn't hack the responsibility. Blamed myself when –'

'My ex-fiancé had no relationship with his father but he's a great dad.'

'You've seen him again then?'

She hesitated, 'A few times – his son's in my class.'

'Come home, Helen. Back to London. Come with me to the hotel tonight and we'll collect your things from Lundby in the morning.'

Helen banged the empty bottle onto the table. Guy placed it in the bucket, neck down.

When she stared at the sea bass, it stared back. She hated fish eyes. She chopped the head off, scraped it to the side of her plate. She stabbed the fish, forked the flesh away from its spine, lifted the back bone by the tail and dangled it in front of her face, peering at Guy through the skeleton. The smell was overpowering.

'What did the hooker do that I didn't?' she said.

'Helen! That's enough! We'd better leave.' Guy pushed his chair from the table. 'Get your coat. I'll pay.'

After mumbling an apology to the couple at the next table, Guy paid the bill and ordered a taxi. At the open door, he gave Helen a push and she slipped from the doorstep and out onto the pavement. 'Not even a bloody pudding,' she said.

It was a cloudless evening; a half-light hung over empty streets. The arched entrance to a former coaching house yawned: dark, hollow. Above her stars blurred, beneath her, paving slabs shifted. Helen shivered. She missed being held. 'I'm cold,' she said.

'You're cold because you're drunk,' Guy said. 'Your jacket's in your hand. Put it on for God's sake. I'll get you to Lundby, then take the taxi back to the hotel. There's no point in trying to have a sensible conversation with you tonight.' She tugged his arm but he turned away.

The more she tried to forget the eyes of the sea bass, the more she saw them, tasted its headless body. It was probably off. She'd never come to this restaurant again. 'Anyway, I can't come back to London with you. My job's till the end of July.'

'And when will you know – if you're coming back at all, I mean?'

'Don't know. You still haven't explained...'

He groaned and walked to the pavement edge.

All she'd wanted was an explanation. But she couldn't stomach the memory of a mermaid in her bed. She couldn't stomach anything. Guy tapped one foot on the kerb.

Beneath the yellow sodium glare of the street lamp, his blue jacket morphed into an angry purple. His fists were clenched, twitchy. She took a deep breath, glad when the taxi drew up but afraid of what the motion of the car might do to the curdling contents of her stomach. When the driver opened the door for her, she collapsed onto the back seat, losing a stiletto. The driver retrieved it from the gutter and fitted it over the shoeless foot she wiggled at him, like a helpless toddler waiting for a wellington boot.

'Here you are Cinders,' the driver said. 'Had a good night?' She wound down the window. The taxi made a U turn and sped off towards Lundby.

Down the lane, there were a handful of pickets outside the pit. 'They're out late,' the driver said, 'You have to feel sorry for the poor sods.'

'They're stopping shcabs,' she said.

The driver laughed.

'I can't believe you said *scabs*,' Guy said.

The word seemed to annoy him, so she said it again, and again. She liked the sound of it. 'Scabs. Scabs. Scabs.' She fumbled in her bag for a packet of mints. It was definitely Guy's shirt that was doing it: making her nauseous. Stripes, like a humbug. Just as well there were no mints.

The taxi pulled up outside the house and Guy jumped out to open the car door, ever the gentleman: *Gentleman Cheater; Gentleman Wife Beater; Humbug*. She wished she had a coat. She wished she had a bucket. He made no attempt to kiss her goodnight. His words hissed through clenched teeth. She'd heard that tone before.

'I'll phone you,' he said. 'When I've recovered from your rudeness.'

She waved to him weakly then, when the taxi reached the end of the street, she threw up in the front garden. She took a tissue from her bag, spat, wiped her lips. She would have to admit to Uncle Billy that nothing was sorted after all.

A little revenge was all she'd wanted but Guy was sailing off in a taxi, sarcastic as ever, claiming the moral high ground.

The pool of vomit glistened. One thing was certain: she would never again let anyone force her to drink a whole bottle of white wine, especially with fish.

Chapter Fourteen

A Slow Fox Trot

October 1973

Cheshire

A row of sycamores screened the house from the road while rolling lawns offered distance from its neighbours. From the guest bedroom Helen watched an elderly gardener raking leaves. The man scooped them between gloved hands and tossed them onto a bonfire he'd lit by the perimeter wall. The fire snapped twigs and sprayed embers over his boots as it battled with the damp and mist of an autumn morning.

Uncle Billy had a garden; Guy's parents had grounds.

She tied the belt on her dressing gown. Chintzy, that's how she would describe the bedroom to Tibby: roses on the wallpaper, curtains to match, a parquet floor covered with Chinese rugs, a silky eiderdown, a primrose coloured vanity basin plumbed into a corner. The furniture was dated but not shabby. Heirloom old.

As Guy had collected her on Thursday evening she'd had to send a letter of excuse to her college tutor – but not without guilt. Uncle Billy had insisted education was a privilege, not to waste a single opportunity, but Guy had laughed when she'd protested that she couldn't miss a Friday seminar. And Guy could be persuasive.

There was a tap on the door. She opened it.

'I've brought you tea. Can I come in?' Guy carried in a tray, set it on the bedside table. 'I've remembered. No sugar and not too strong. Did you sleep well?'

'Certainly did. I've never slept in such a big bed. It's so comfortable.'

He smoothed the rumpled sheet, patted it and she climbed back in, still wearing the dressing gown. 'A bed too big for one,' he said, handing her a cup. There were roses on the china too.

His mother called from the foot of the stairs. 'Guy, will you come down? I need you for a minute.'

'Don't be too long. Mum's given me orders to get you to the hairdressers in good time.' He gazed at Helen, as if reluctant to leave.

'If you stand there much longer I'll never be ready. What are you thinking?'

'I'm a lucky man.'

A charity ball was to be held in a nearby hotel and Helen had been invited as Guy's guest, courtesy of his parents. A 'County' affair. Her red ball gown hung from the top of the wardrobe door. In the swirl of the wood grain Helen had imagined a face like the one on an old wardrobe in the spare room at home, which had frightened her as a child. Since the Eagleton wardrobe face was uglier and seemed to have horns, she'd covered it with the dress. She sipped the tea, contemplating the glamour and shine of taffeta. The dress was a snug fit, flattered her figure, but she worried that it showed too much cleavage. Guy had insisted on buying it, preferring the red to the navy version which would have been Helen's choice.

When she'd finished the tea, she washed, dressed in trousers and tunic top. The front door was open and as she came downstairs she could hear Mrs. Eagleton's voice from the drive. 'Look after Helen. Remember. Hairdressers for ten-thirty! Your father will be flying into Manchester about eleven. Plenty of cold meat and salad in the fridge. I've left him a note in case you're not back.' Guy stowed golf clubs in the boot of his mother's car then joined Helen on the doorstep.

Helen looped her arm through Guy's and waved as the sports car swept down the gravel drive, through wrought iron gates and away into the Cheshire countryside. 'Come on,' Guy said. 'You heard what my mother said and you haven't had breakfast yet.'

Having plied her with toast, eggs and orange juice, Guy snatched the keys to his father's Range Rover and drove Helen to a hair salon in the nearby village.

'I'll be back for you about eleven thirty,' he said. 'Don't forget. Ringlets. They'll look fabulous with that dress.'

★ ★ ★

Lundby

It was the end of Pavel's first week back at work. In the underground heat the helmet stuck to his forehead and he rubbed his fingers across his brow, adjusted the face mask, cleared his throat of dust as the cutter screeched and sheared black rock from the face. In the darkness with only a dim light from his helmet, he could barely distinguish Roly in the driving seat of the machine; there was no chance of speaking to him in this racket. The vibration made Pavel's teeth chatter which seemed at odds with the sweltering temperature.

Roly switched off the machine and jumped down. Day shift over the men set off to cover the two miles back to the cage.

Coker asked if Pavel would be at the Institute later. 'Buy you a pint.' Roly squeezed Pavel's shoulder: Roly's reminder that Coker was a bad influence.

'I thought you were seeing your girlfriend,' Pavel said.

'Cheryl? Yeah. But I'm not giving up mates am I?' Coker said. 'There's music on in concert room and she's bringing a friend.'

Pavel had no plans. 'I'll see how I feel.'

The daily grit that clung to Pavel's skin generally disappeared with hot water and a scrub with a block of soap in the pithead baths. Except for the eyes, where it stuck to the inner lids as if it had been pencilled on.

Tears made inroads into the dust on his cheeks, but the shadowy demons of grief that had plagued him for the last seven months were harder to shift. They squeezed the air out of his lungs, strangled and suffocated more than the job itself. Working underground added to their weight, their power. They fed in the dark. No light, no air. Twice he'd been brought to the surface. Panic attacks, the doctor said, and he'd prescribed medication; signed him off for twelve weeks. It had helped. But when Pavel thought of his father, withdrawn and impossible to reach, he feared for his own future. He would have to fight back. Pills from the doctor had loosened the demons' hold but he had to help himself.

He'd made progress, had ditched Coker's alternative remedies and was managing to work now without constant fear that the cage would crash, girders collapse, tunnels cave in, that gas would poison him. Though these were real and ever present possibilities, no one could work with fear or, worse still, with the fear of fear. The doctor had suggested a different occupation might speed recovery, but Pavel intended willpower and guts to beat the crap out of this God-awful disease. Leaving the pits had to be his choice, not the decision of the doctor or the devil.

At the top of the shaft the cage juddered to a halt, discharging its cargo of men, helmets and battery packs.

'I'll see you tonight, Pav,' Coker shouted.

★ ★ ★

Cheshire

After locking the Range Rover, Guy wandered along the street towards the hair salon, past the antiques shop, the saddlers and the Copper Kettle tea room. At the window of the 'bespoke gentleman's outfitters', he gazed at his reflection, smoothing back his hair.

'Stop that bloody twitching,' his father had shouted. Guy was ten. That's when it had begun, a nervous habit he'd grow out of, the doctor said. And he had. But it hadn't stopped his father trying to beat it out of him. On one occasion his dad had slapped Guy's face at the dinner table, almost knocking him from his chair. His mother had tried to intervene but his father was stronger.

Guy had struggled through enforced music lessons for which he had no aptitude, through rugby coaching which he hated and extra lessons in maths and English for the Common Entrance exam. At boarding school he'd attempted an aspirin overdose but had been sick before it could take effect. Later, his father considered anything less than Oxford as failure and Guy had studied till he thought his head would burst.

On a stag weekend last May, after an afternoon at the races in York, Guy and a few former university friends embarked on a pub crawl inside the city walls. At eleven-thirty the group had returned to their hotel, making their way to a dungeon bar for a nightcap. Guy spotted his father in a corner, with a girl in a short red dress. A girl he recognised by her ringlets. A girl from the office. So engrossed was the man in pawing her, he didn't notice his son. Guy had feigned sickness, retired to his room and, skipping breakfast next morning, he'd caught an early train home.

Mr Captain of industry. The man for whom there had been no compromise, no weaknesses allowed, nothing less than perfection. Guy wondered what his father would make of Helen: a working-class girl. Not quite what he'd expect. What goes round... He couldn't wait to introduce her. Perfect symmetry.

Eleven thirty. Right on cue. He heard the jingle of a door bell and Helen appeared. She twirled on the pavement, tossing the sculpted curls that cascaded onto her neck. 'What do you think?'

He flicked the ringlets. 'Love it. Like an eighteenth century courtesan.' Guy laughed, opened the car door. 'It's beautiful. Come on, harlot. I'm taking you out for lunch

* * *

Lundby

From the concert room bar, Pavel watched Billy Farrimond slow fox-trotting his wife around the dance floor. *Slow, slow, quick, quick, slow.* A trio of pit-surface workers had a regular slot at the Institute playing drums, guitar and piano on Friday nights. He knew them well. They never altered their far-away expressions. Neither had they changed their sequence of tunes in at least twelve years. They'd played the same programme of 'Golden Oldies' at Pavel's engagement party. In spite of Helen's coaching Pavel had trodden on her feet, so she'd danced the last waltz with her uncle. It always amazed Pavel how gruff old miners, more used to pit boots than patent dance shoes, transformed into Fred Astaires at the first hint of a dance band.

The pianist whispered *one two three,* then struck up a halting version of *the anniversary waltz,* heralding the interval, raffle and a game of bingo.

When the music stopped Billy escorted Tibby to a table and joined Pavel at the bar. 'And how is Mr Kowaleski this fine evening?' Billy bought himself a pint and his wife a gin and orange.

'Much better, thanks.' Pavel drained his glass. 'Though I shouldn't have too much of this poison.'

'Won't offer you any then.'

Pavel hesitated. 'I've been meaning to ask you... about Helen? How is she?'

Billy took a clutch of coins from his trouser pocket, picked out the exact change for the barman. 'Well enough, I think. Busy studying. We haven't seen much of her these last months. She phones.'

Pavel stared into his glass. 'I thought I was doing the right thing. I was in no fit state to –'

'You don't have to explain, Pavel. But I appreciate you asking. Take good care of yourself. Glad to hear you're on the mend.' Billy placed his hand on Pavel's arm. 'Better go,' he said. 'They'll be after me in a minute. I'm due to draw the raffle.'

★ ★ ★

Cheshire

When the conductor announced a slow foxtrot Guy steered Helen onto the dance floor, a firm hand in the small of her back.

'I've met so many people,' she said. 'My head's spinning with names. I'll never remember them all.'

'You don't have to. Most of my father's friends are bores. Dad can't take his eyes off you though. And neither can I.'

'Thank you.'

'For what?'

'Inviting me. I hope I didn't let you down.'

'How could you? You're worth ten of everyone here.' He steered her into a turn.

'I'm impressed you can dance. Most men trample on my toes,' she said, though the only young man she'd danced with before was Pavel.

'Had to learn at boarding school. With hapless fellow schoolboys as partners. I was the lucky one. Always chosen to take the lead.'

'So,' she said, 'there are a host of damaged young men out there somewhere, dancing backwards?'

'More than a few dance backwards, Helen. Still – that's boarding school for you.' They both laughed and she blushed.

'I like to see you smile,' he said. 'Did the miner make you happy?'

She looked away. 'Sometimes.'

'But he made you cry more. And now I've mentioned him you've stopped smiling.'

'Why did you mention him?'

Guy held her close, so close he was squeezing the breath from her. 'I wish you'd forget him.'

'Forget who?' Guy relaxed his hold and nuzzled her neck

The last waltz. *One, two, three.* Guy was as intoxicating as the fruit punch he'd introduced her to. Her head swam, the room circled twice with each step, the band a blur of royal blue jackets, the female singer a haze of sequins.

Taxis arrived at 2 a.m. Guy sat beside Helen on the back seat, stroking her arm. His father squeezed alongside them, his knee brushing Helen's, leaving his mother to hop into the front seat. 'My son has been keeping you all to himself,' Guy's father said.

Mrs Eagleton turned. 'Let the girl sleep, darling, before you interrogate her.'

'I'm returning her to college after breakfast,' Guy said. 'She has essays to catch up on.' Helen moved closer to Guy, wrapping her stole around her shoulders. 'Don't you think Helen resembles the girl from accounts, Dad? The girl with the ringlets. Can't remember her name.'

'Don't know who you mean.'

'She's nowhere near as pretty or as intelligent as you, Helen. Is she, Dad? And from what I hear she has awful taste in men.'

★ ★ ★

Lundby

Beneath a fug of smoke Coker elbowed his way to the bar with Cheryl and her friend behind him. He ordered another pint for Pavel. 'You know Cheryl and Susan don't you?' he said, handing the girls glasses of cheap champagne perry garnished with cherries on sticks. Pavel nodded. Cheryl sucked the cherry, making doe-eyes at Pavel over the glass.

After the bingo a volunteer DJ played rock hits and Cheryl pulled Susan onto the dance floor, dropping her handbag and gyrating to the music with her arms in the air. The red dress hardly covered Cheryl's knickers. So like Coker to choose such a girl, though Pavel had to admit she was pretty. But then who was he to judge? Judgement was not his strength. He'd scraped through his first year exams and that was only thanks to Roly's efforts.

Cheryl waved. Pavel looked away. He had no intention of encouraging her, nor would he be falling for Coker's cheap attempts to fix him up with her friend. He finished the drink. 'Right, mate. I'm curbing the booze. I'm off.'

'Still on tablets?' Coker asked.

Pavel zipped up his jacket. Not Coker's pills at least. 'Not for much longer, I hope. See you Monday.'

★ ★ ★

Cheshire

Back in the guest bedroom, Helen hung the taffeta dress over the wardrobe door before the devil could cast his eye over her nakedness. She'd discarded her underwear on the floor, and she crawled into bed, too drowsy and tipsy to remove make-up or find her nightdress. She switched out the light and sank back into the feather pillows. She didn't hear Guy until he was by the bed. 'Helen,' he whispered. She fumbled for the lamp, sat up, pulling her knees to her chest, the sheet to her chin.

'Guy, what are you doing? I was almost asleep.' Guy was waving a bottle of champagne and two long stemmed glasses which he set down on the bedside table. The cork hit the ceiling, champagne fizzed onto the quilt. Helen giggled.

His bowtie was undone, it dangled over the front of his white dress shirt, over shiny pearl buttons. 'Cheers,' he said. 'You were a great success tonight.' He handed her the glass.

'A success? You make me sound like an actress after a debut performance.' She drank. He stroked her shoulder then tipped the remains of his drink into her empty glass. Unfastening the top buttons of his shirt he leaned over, kissed her. She stroked a finger down his breast bone as Guy pulled the shirt over his head. The rest of his clothes he threw across the bedroom floor and collapsed onto the mattress beside her. The headboard clattered against the wall.

'Shh. Your parents will hear.'

'I don't care. I'm in love with you, Miss Farrimond.'

Guy held her close. She hadn't expected this tonight, or ever again: the power of being desired. He rolled her onto her back. He smelled of wine and aftershave and when he kissed her she tasted the Cuban cigar his father had handed him after dinner.

There was a small chandelier suspended above her. It seemed out of place among the chintzy covers and curtains. Showy for a bedroom. She expected it to shimmer in the half-light, to reflect pink, green and indigo; but it cast grey blotchy shadows across the ceiling.

The rhythmic tap tapping of the headboard would surely wake his parents. She wondered why she'd never noticed the chandelier before.

Chapter Fifteen

Champagne and a Plastic Bottle

August 1974
South Yorkshire

A storm in the early hours had woken Billy, thunder rumbling, lightning flashing. Was it a portent? When calm returned, he had lain awake for what seemed hours listening to Tibby's purring snores – she could sleep through a Luftwaffe raid. He was worried about the day's arrangements: about taxis, the weather, the speech he'd been writing and re-writing for weeks. And he was worried about Pavel Kowaleski.

Now the air was refreshed and sunshine streamed through the open window, warming Billy's back as he stood in front of the mirror.

'It's a beautiful day,' Tibby said.

Billy flicked the tails on his morning suit. 'Whose idea was this ridiculous outfit? I've already got a perfectly good jacket. Like new.'

'Stop moaning and stand still.' Tibby took up a clothes brush. 'Your best suit is ten years old.'

'Exactly. And as for giving her away. It doesn't feel right.'

'Thought you'd be proud to play *father of the bride*. You need to look the part.'

'I am proud. And chuffed the wedding's local at least. But the Helen we once knew didn't much care for convention, certainly would have resisted being *given away.*'

'She's grown up. Mellowed. Chosen tradition over teenage rebellion.'

'I wonder just what she has chosen.'

'Billy! She leaves for the church in an hour. Forget politics.' Tibby brushed his shoulders. 'It's a wedding, a happy occasion. You can see Guy loves her. He's smart, attentive...'

'Full of bull —'

'That's enough. She's not interested in politics — in spite of your best efforts.'

It was in Guy's eyes, not in his politics: insincerity. Surely Helen could see beyond money, beyond status? How could she be so gullible, fall for such glib patter: the *darling* stuff? Oh the bugger was clever, talked well. It was not his politics that made Billy dislike Guy. It was a gut feeling. 'I suppose after they've signed the register,' Billy said, 'I'll have to walk down the aisle with his mother on my arm. Labour and Tory: a pair of political bookends.'

'I expect you to be civil.' When Tibby had finished the grooming, she took a pink rose from a box on the dressing table and pinned it to Billy's lapel. 'Helen has to make her own decisions. You can't protect her forever.'

'I've tried to guide, not control her.'

'I know you've done your best — we both have. But sometimes it's... backfired, affected her judgement.'

'So you agree she's making a mistake?'

'I didn't say that. Please, love. Look happy today even if you're not.'

'I'll be charm personified,' Billy said. Tibby smiled, seeming unaware of his sarcasm. He caught her hand, kissed it. 'If only everyone was as good natured as you are, Tib.' He grinned, drew her into a bear hug.

She shook him off, straightening his cravat. 'Don't squash the button hole.'

'I still think I should tell Helen what Pavel said.'

'Don't you dare. There's no point in stirring things up. Pavel will be fine. Stop fretting about him.' She adjusted her hat. 'I'd better go and help dress the bride.'

Billy leaned into the mirror, checked the closeness of his shave, looked himself in the eye. Last night's conversation at the Institute dogged his thoughts. Pavel had asked for Helen's address. He was well now, he'd said, and there were things he needed to tell her; if he could just write to her.

Depression. Billy had witnessed plenty of it after the war, though nobody called it depression then, preferring the term *nervous breakdown*. Sorrow was always in the eyes. You could see a man's soul in his eyes – or lack of soul. On this occasion Billy had seen only regret.

'I'm sorry, Pavel. I don't think that would be a good idea. She's getting married tomorrow. Twelve o'clock at the Parish Church. I've just come from the rehearsal.' The colour drained from Pavel's face. 'Don't you remember? I told you about that accountant chap she was seeing. Unfortunately he's the groom. And what's worse – I have to give her away; hand her over to a bloody Tory.'

★ ★ ★

As he passed the stone cottages on the hill down to the church, Pavel inhaled the scent of sweet peas which clung to trellised walls in bursts of pink and purple. Bees, spoiled for choice of nectar, stirred the lavender beds, borders of lupins, gladioli and red hot pokers. He'd always loved the sense of the old village here, the landscape unscarred by winding wheels and rope ways. It was a lovely day for a wedding his mother had said, though he found the grass in the churchyard wet after the storm. He slipped, steadied himself on the headstone. Wet grass soaked the knees of his jeans when he knelt.

He had brought a bunch of carnations and a plastic lemonade bottle filled with water. He removed the dead flowers from the grave, baulking at the sudden stench of decayed vegetation. He tipped the putrefying liquid from the vase onto the grass, refilled it with fresh water from the bottle and arranged the carnations in the stem holder.

His mother had insisted on interring Jakub's ashes, creating a place of pilgrimage and memorial. Such was her dedication that she'd tended the grave weekly, though she was always alone; neither Pavel nor his father had felt able to go with her. But his mother had suffered a summer virus recently, and an absence of a month was long enough for the grave to look neglected – grass climbing the stonework, bouquets crumbling to dust. A twinge of guilt surfaced: not only had Pavel not supported his mother but he'd come here under false pretences.

He ran his fingers over the black letters carved into white marble.

'Our beloved son and brother, Jakub'

And beneath it, in Polish:

'Tu Spoczywa w Pokoju'

'Here Rest in Peace'

It was quarter to twelve. 'She's getting married, Jakie boy. Miss you, kid.' He swallowed a knot of emotion, tugged at the long grass at the base of the headstone.

Several guests had already entered the church: couples he'd watched as they parked shiny cars. Mercedes, Daimlers, a single red Porsche. Men in tail coats, women in frothy hats, familiar aunts in flowery frocks – Tibby's side of the family – a couple of cousins, three of Helen's former school friends (wobbling on platform heels and clutching straw boaters). No one seemed to have noticed Pavel kneeling by the gravestone, not even Tibby. The groom, he guessed, was already inside the church. It was better not to see him, not to be swayed by Billy's bias. The church bells pealed a cascade of changes. All on tape now his mother had told him. Just a quick *press play* and pretend. A sham.

The bride would be here soon. He gathered the dead stalks, dropped them onto the compost heap, picked up the empty bottle and strolled over to a yew tree which overshadowed the graveyard. Its girth, he hoped, was sufficient to conceal him. From here he had a view of the lych-gate and the path leading to the porch. The knotted bark dug into his spine as he leaned against it. Awed by the tree's size, he considered what it had witnessed in its long history. How deep were its roots? Were they strangling foundations, eating into the graves? Burrowing beneath the aisle?

Above ground, below ground. Her world, his world. Upstairs, downstairs. Irreconcilable. Worlds apart.

When a car door slammed he started, turned, pressed his chest to the tree. He squashed the bottle between his feet, freeing his fingers to grip ropes of bark, inadvertently snapping hammocks of spider thread. The plastic bottle cracked and buckled. A spider, at least, could rebuild its web.

The bridesmaids arrived. As he didn't recognise them he guessed they were Helen's college friends, the friends he should have met two years before. Pretty, preening in pink satin, they too passed him without a glance.

A white limousine glided to the gate; ribbons fluttered. Billy helped Helen from the car and she hopped and leaned on him, releasing the heel of her shoe from her hem. Pavel heard a tinkle of laughter as Billy remarked that top hats were for magicians.

He tried to take a mental photograph – his mother would want a description. Helen's dress: ivory, he supposed you'd call it. A medieval style – like the folk singer they'd once seen in concert at the City Hall. Lace. At least he'd tell his mother it was lace. She'd like that. A headband of roses, a matching posy. He tried to catch the scent.

His chest tightened, a knot in his throat. Recalling the doctor's advice, he inhaled deeply, edging further round the tree as she passed. He saw her stop in front of the lych-gate to smooth the gown with one hand. He drew in his head when he thought she glanced in his direction, but was certain she hadn't spotted him. He was tempted to call out, at least wish her good luck, but, suddenly ashamed of his role as peeping Tom and of his intrusion into this precious moment between niece and uncle, Pavel wished the tree could open, swallow him for the fool he was.

She walked on. He rested his forehead against the bark, waited until he heard the church organ strike up the introductory chords of the wedding march, then thumped the tree with the plastic bottle. *Shit, shit, shit.* Kicking the bottle ahead of him, he ran out of the churchyard.

There was a pub at the top of the hill.

★ ★ ★

After the photographs in the grounds of the hotel and a five course dinner, the guests separated onto opposite sides of the dance floor. The speeches had been short, uneventful: good taste and champagne had prevailed.

'We have to go, darling,' Guy's mother said. 'Dad's off to Germany tomorrow and we have an early start.' Guy thought it typical that his father couldn't even keep a weekend clear in his diary for his only son's wedding. His mother had tolerated Helen's uncle with a measure of bemusement; she and Billy had even shared a joke. But Guy's father wore his disdain as plainly as his buttonhole. He couldn't even wait another hour to wave the bride and groom off on their honeymoon.

The master of ceremonies invited the bridal couple to take the floor for the first dance.

'So what's it like being Mrs Eagleton?' Guy asked. He took Helen's hand, twirled her round.

She laughed. 'Ask me again in ten years' time.'

'Your Uncle Billy has been on his best behaviour. Not a single political jibe in his speech. No doubt he'll regale me at the bar hustings later.'

'You're a good match for him, Guy. I'm sure he likes you really.'

'I'd settle for respect. But Tibby's a gem. Don't understand how she puts up with him.'

The sooner he and his wife could leave the better.

★ ★ ★

A deep head on the beer was expected as standard. Pavel drew a face on the froth with his finger and drank. He hadn't returned home after closing time at the pub; he'd sat on the rocks above the swimming pool eating a bag of chips. After staring into the distance for hours he eventually found his way to the Institute.

'Now then, Pavel. Not at the posh wedding with Billy?' Coker said, an arm around Pavel's shoulders. 'I hear the ex-girlfriend's married into money.'

'Wouldn't know,' Pavel said. 'None of my business.'

'You're well rid of her ladyship.' Coker slammed his beer on the bar. 'And who's paying for that little shindig?

Can't be Billy can it? I've heard they've gone to Bickley Hall. I don't know anybody who could afford a reception there, do you? Stands to reason his lot must have paid.'

'I've no idea. I don't really care,' Pavel finished the drink and held out the empty glass for a refill. 'Where's Cheryl?'

'Dumped her. Too clingy. I'm going with her mate, Susan.'

One more drink and Pavel would leave.

Coker nudged him. 'Don't tell me you hadn't noticed Cheryl making a play for you? You could be in there, Pav, if you don't mind picking up my cast offs. Why don't you? It must have been a while since −'

'I'm not interested.'

It was a long time since he'd had so much to drink. No sign of Roly. No one to stop him. On this occasion he'd every right to get pissed.

The two girls arrived together. 'Still friends are they?' Pavel said.

'Inseparable. Probably compare notes. I suppose I could take them both on. Now that would be a challenge.'

Pavel shook his head. 'Always the gentleman, aren't you Coker?'

As the band struggled through its repertoire, Pavel bought drinks for both girls and the four of them found a vacant table.

A strange hush settled over the concert room and eyes turned towards the entrance. Through dimmed lights and the usual fog of smoke, Pavel spotted Billy Farrimond in the doorway, amid cheers and laughter. Billy was decked out in a morning suit, Tibby beside him in the flowery dress and feathered hat Pavel had seen earlier.

'Where's your topper, Billy?' Coker shouted.

The guitarist wolf-whistled into the microphone. 'Ladies and gentlemen, a round of applause for Lord Farrimond.'

Another cheer. Billy swayed to the bar, one hand on his hip, the other extending a regal wave to his audience.

'I say, old man,' the drummer called. 'Where's the chauffeur tonight? Watch you don't sit on the wrong end of your shooting stick.'

Coker bawled over Pavel's head. 'That'll do no damage. He's too tight arsed!'

Billy bowed, picked up his beer.

On the pretext of buying crisps for Cheryl and Susan, Pavel joined him at the bar. 'Had a good day then? Reception over already?'

'Hello, Pavel,' Tibby said. 'Would you believe this man? No sooner had the bride and groom left for the honeymoon than he says, "Come on. I've got time for a last decent pint at the Institute." So we had to get a taxi.'

'No head on it, see' Billy said. 'Warm and twice the price!' Tibby rolled her eyes and carried her drink to a nearby table.

'I saw you in the churchyard,' Billy said. 'Fortunately Helen didn't.'

'I promised Mum I'd take flowers to Jakub's grave and –'

'Come off it.'

Pavel glanced around, tugged his collar. 'I'm sorry. Thanks for not telling her.'

Billy untied the cravat, stuffed it into his trouser pocket. 'No need to apologise. I suppose it's my fault. I shouldn't have told you about the wedding. Or maybe I should have told you sooner. But it was a short engagement. If it's any consolation, I wish I could have changed her mind. I think she's making a mistake.'

'I hope you're wrong.'

'It's done. But what about you? How much have you had to drink, Pavel? You smell like a bank holiday bar towel. Steady on, lad.'

When Coker left with Susan, Pavel was stranded with Cheryl, the table a jungle of half-empty tumblers, pint glasses and pink stained cocktail sticks. She was pretty in a fashion. Blonde hair, blue eyes, pert features. Not his type. But what was his type? They finished their drinks. It was quarter to eleven: too late to leave a girl on her own. 'Come on,' he said. 'I'd better walk you home.'

The route took them on a short cut through council garages on the perimeter of the housing estate where Cheryl lived with her parents. She hung onto his arm as he swayed a little.

'Did you once go out with Billy Farrimond's niece?'

He kicked gravel from the path into a garage door. 'Ages ago.'

'She got married today. A posh do, Coker said.'

'So I heard.'

'You know that I've fancied you for ages?'

'I'm flattered.' Pavel laughed, though was startled when she grabbed his lapels and hauled him into a narrow gap between two garages. It was a shadowy place used by day for children's games of Hide and Seek and at night – according to pit gossip – a scene of free love, a source of scandal. She pressed him against a wall of corrugated iron, banging his head. The garage shook with a hollow rumble like a wobble board. He giggled. Then with one knee between his legs, one hand through his hair and the other unbuttoning his shirt, Cheryl kissed him, forcing her tongue between his teeth. A surge of lust surprised him, overwhelmed him. He kissed her in return, slid his arms around her. Besides, he didn't want to offend.

★ ★ ★

Helen couldn't sleep. She had lowered the window blind. The spotlight above Guy's head caught the facets on his platinum wedding band and it glistened as he stroked her hand. Her ring matched his. She had chosen them along with the bridal dress, though most decisions had been made by Guy's mother. Mrs Eagleton wanted the best and was prepared to pay for it, including a honeymoon in California as a wedding gift.

The flight would last a further eight hours before the plane landed in San Francisco but the rattle of cabin trolleys and constant steward interruptions deprived Helen of sleep. She was too tired to read, too troubled to chat with Guy.

When she closed her eyes an image haunted her: Pavel dodging out of sight behind a tree. Alerted by Billy's nervous hesitation outside the church, his glance beyond her shoulder, she'd turned for just a second. But by then she had already sensed Pavel's presence, spotted the fresh white carnations on Jakub's grave. There had been only dead pinks in the vase the night before, on the evening of the rehearsal when she'd wished she'd brought fresh flowers, though an explanation to Guy would have proved awkward.

Then this morning at the church door she'd stopped. 'It's not too late to change your mind,' Billy said. They waited until she regained composure, until the chief bridesmaid, Jane, arrived on the porch steps announcing that Guy was anxious: Helen was late.

Guy squeezed her hand. 'Are you alright, darling?'
 She smiled. 'Tired.'
From beneath the seat he pulled out a blanket, wrapped it around her, tucking in the edges like a fussing parent with a small child. He unfastened his seat belt, took a flight bag from the overhead locker, found an eye mask. He slipped the elastic over her head, tapping the mask into place on the bridge of her nose. 'Try to rest.'

What was Pavel up to? Why couldn't he send a card like everyone else, a conventional greeting: wedding bells, hearts, champagne flutes? A message that said, '*all the best,*' something banal yet appropriate. What did he want? After two years of no contact, not even a note, he'd turned up to spoil her day. She couldn't believe it was a coincidence, that he'd just brought flowers for Jakub and been caught out by a random wedding.

She released Guy's hand, patted the mask. It was wet on the inside but, she hoped, absorbent enough to soak up tears.

Husband: the title that had once caused a flutter of excitement now created a tremble of panic. She tried to breathe deeply, waiting for sleep and oblivion.

Part Two

*"The legal seal that seals documents is not able to
utter a word in witness. It is better to mark your heart
with the seal of justice and truth."*

His Holiness the 6th Dalai Lama (c1700)

Chapter Sixteen

Ten o'Clock Horses

June 18th 1984

Lundby

Pavel sighed, leaned on the counter watching Helen, his fingers fumbling with the last two eggs he'd salvaged from an almost empty fridge. The house rule was that you brought your own egg to accompany the bacon and watered down beans and tinned tomatoes: a soup kitchen fry up before picketing. Sustenance before the battle. But Pavel hadn't realised until that morning that Helen was on the support group breakfast rota at the Institute. This was dedication from a girl who'd be teaching thirty kids in two hours time. She was frying and toasting while her aunt served at the counter, pouring tea into mugs.

Thoughts of Helen kept him awake at night.

He was aware of his mates juvenile sniggering from the table in the corner of the makeshift canteen. The others had been served apart from Gus who was in front of him in the queue.

'No favouritism, Miss. He's trying it on, bringing two eggs,' Swannie shouted. Then he heard Roly's voice, incapable of a whisper.

'Don't start that again! Remember what he did to Coker.'

Over the spit-spat of bacon and the drone of a cooker hood Pavel didn't think Helen would notice the banter.

He turned towards the men, flagging two fingers, and Swannie mimed a punch on the chin and a cut to the throat. 'Brilliant that smack, Pav. Never forget it! Neither will Coker.'

'Lay off him,' Roly said, waving a piece of fried bread. 'His wife's away in Skegness. He's been scraping out his fridge.'

Helen delivered Gus's breakfast and took the eggs from Pavel. Her fingers brushed his. 'You're the last one,' she said. He smiled. She would smell of fried bread all day. Same girl, but different. Not older exactly, maybe wearier. Not as feisty as he remembered. He didn't believe her baloney about needing to spend time with Tibby and Billy. It didn't make sense, but it was impossible to speak to her with this gang around, scrutinising his every move; difficult to speak to her at all unless he found another excuse to visit Jake's classroom. He was running out of excuses.

Gus picked up his breakfast and sloped away to join Roly and Swannie.

The dregs of tea spluttered into Pavel's mug. 'Where are you picketing today, Pavel?' Tibby said, refilling the pot with hot water.

'Orgreave again. Well we can't get into Nottinghamshire can we? It's shut.'

'I bet you're sick of the sight of that coke plant. Stay out of trouble. I can't stand much more of my husband cursing at the television. And he's on your side.'

'We've got season tickets to Orgreave, haven't we, Pav?' Swannie said as he delivered his empty plate to the counter and slapped Pavel on the back. 'Coke lorries still get through.'

Roly had said that Scargill was basing his tactics on the Saltley coke plant: Birmingham in the '72 strike. Action there had brought success: the lorry drivers had refused to cross the picket lines, the police had shut the gates and the government had capitulated. 'And Scargill became King Coal!' Roly said. Pavel remembered that strike well. It had ended just before Jakub's accident. Strange to think he'd been engaged to Helen then. But this time Scargill hadn't taken account of Thatcher and her henchmen. Maggie was never likely to capitulate.

'It's ironic,' Tibby said, shoving the mug of tea towards him. 'If you could get into Nottingham, half these pickets would be there; not massing at Orgreave like sitting ducks. There'd be less trouble.'

Swannie, at the counter for a tea refill, nudged Pavel. 'I hadn't thought of that, had you? You might have something there, Mrs F.'

Even when she was wearing Mr Men oven mitts Pavel couldn't take his eyes from Helen. As she delivered his breakfast he rubbed his hands. 'Thanks. That looks great.'

'Did you say Orgreave?' She lowered the plate onto the counter. 'Be careful won't you?' Their eyes met.

'I will. I promise.' He picked up the plate. 'Ouch. Fff–Bugger.' He passed it from hand to hand until she took it from him with the oven mitt.

'Pavel. I meant: be careful, the plate's hot.'

'You were spot on, Roly,' Swannie shouted. 'You said he'd get his fingers burnt.'

★ ★ ★

Orgreave
South Yorkshire

The policeman directing the group to a parking space told Pavel that crowds had been arriving since seven. Coaches carrying pickets. Coaches carrying coppers. 'Like a bloody gala,' Swannie said.

Pavel took off his tee shirt and lay on the grass. Though it was only eight-thirty, the strength in the sun threatened a midday scorcher. Roly had brought sun cream at Kath's insistence and shared it with the others. Pavel squirted a blob on his nose, smeared it across his face, rubbed it in. 'I like this weather but I don't want to end up like a beetroot.'

'You're fair skinned like our Jen,' Roly said. 'You have to be careful. Sun can do a lot of damage.'

'You two are like a couple of old women,' Gus said, hands on hips.

Pavel wrestled him to the ground, stuffing a handful of grass down the back of his younger mate's jeans. They rolled around laughing till Pavel sat up, suddenly uneasy. Fine lying around enjoying the sunshine, but there was something amiss. You could taste it. An atmosphere building. Not silence – there was chatter, banter, even a few picnics. He couldn't say what it was. Like holding a breath: as poignant as the stillness men experienced before a roof collapse.

Gus bit his thumb, watching the build up of police vans and pickets on the other side of the field. And there were horses.

'*The Ten o' Clock Horses*,' Gus said. 'When I was a kid my mum warned me if I stayed up too late, the *Ten o' Clock Horses* would come and get me. I was terrified. I dashed upstairs and dived under blankets. No messing.'

Galloping horses. A primeval fear. 'Horses make me nervous,' Pavel admitted.

'You're talking bollocks,' Swannie said. 'Mamby pambies.'

Pavel stood up. On either side of the road leading up to the coke plant the police were splitting the pickets into two groups. And cameras were setting up. He remembered what Tibby Farrimond had said: *sitting ducks*. 'I think they've herded us in for a showdown,' he said.

Roly laughed. 'It's been *ShowTime* every time here.'

'You'd think it was a bloody rock festival,' Swannie said. 'From the makers of *Woodstock '69* we bring you, *Orgeave '84*.'

Roly nodded and folded his arms. 'Have you read that book, *1984*? About a totalitarian state where they have *Thought Police*. Torture folk.'

'I've read it,' Pavel said.

'He were right then,' Gus said, nodding towards the police ranks. 'Look at 'em, Thatcher's army.'

Roly shook his head. 'I can't get over the way they waved us in. Wonder they didn't hand us a parking permit.'

'Yeah, or stamp your hand in case you leave, but want to come back later, like disco night at *Top Rank*.' Swannie said, then bit into a Mars Bar.

Pavel pulled a face. 'You've just had breakfast, how can you be filling your face with chocolate already?'

'I only had one egg, Pavel – unlike you.' Swannie licked the remaining chocolate from his fingers and ripped the ring pull from a can of Coke. The froth fizzed over his trainers. He guzzled the whole can, then used it as a makeshift cricket ball, practising his bowling action towards the police ranks, but not throwing.'

'Did I tell you my granddad went to school with Freddie Truman?' Gus said, removing bits of grass from his underpants.

'Everybody's dad or granddad went to school with Freddie Truman round here,' Swannie said, 'Apart from Pavel's dad in Poland. He were batting against Gestapo in his street.'

A familiar voice shouted from behind. They turned.

'Keep that can for later, Swannie. Useful ammo.' It was Coker, hands in pockets, grinning.

Roly groaned. 'Eh up, it's bleedin' Rambo. Where did you come from?'

'Got a lift with Sparky and his mates. Reckoned it were safer than Kowaleski's company. I saw you two silly buggers rolling about.' He nodded towards Pavel. 'Sunday school outing is it?'

The two men hadn't spoken since the day of the punch-up and Pavel had no intention of rising to Coker's bait. Coker picked up a stone, slid it into his jeans pocket and waved both arms at the swelling police ranks. 'Bring it on, you bastards.' He stared at Pavel. 'No slacking! No bricking it, eh?'He sniggered and swaggered away.

'Who does he think he is?' Roly said. 'He'll be bricking it alright. Let's hope he's arrested. It's overdue.'

'You didn't hit him hard enough, Pav,' Swannie said.

On the flatter part of the field Pavel could see two men tapping a ball between them. Right foot to right foot. Left to left. He recognised them as Derbyshire miners they'd met on picket lines several times. Nodding acquaintances. The four mates marched over, Gus in front mimicking the Police, arms swinging, chest out. Left, right, left, right. Then Pavel negotiated a kick about, fashioning goal posts from tee shirts discarded in the heat. When several pickets joined in, including a welsh miner in a rugby shirt, they played five aside.

After ten minutes Pavel stopped, one foot pinning the ball to the spot. He pointed. A convoy of lorries, lead by a line of police vehicles, had arrived to collect coke. The objective to stop the lorries entering the plant had not been forgotten, merely put on hold for an hour as they'd been distracted by the weather and the mucking about between mates.

The police massed forwards. The pushing started, the banter ended. Men were sprinting to the picket line. 'Right, come on,' Pavel said. 'We'd better get down there.'

They pulled on their tee shirts as they ran. At first it was the usual scrum, heads down, pushing as hard as they could. Pavel could feel Gus' back leaning against him like he'd leant against the car when it had broken down in March and they'd pushed it to their first picket line. That seemed an age ago. Back then they'd chatted with the local police, had a laugh with them, knocked a bobby's helmet off as a prank. Not now.

Shove, push. Someone slipped.

'Man down,' Roly shouted.

There was a constant fear of a crush or a trampling. Police and pickets alike eased off and a young lad further up the line got to his feet. Pavel had seen him selling the *Socialist Worker*. Last time they'd ribbed the youngster about peddling the paper at the back of the crowd, not doing his bit; not putting his money where his political mouth was. By Pavel's estimate he couldn't be more than five years older than Jake.

The shoving resumed, and in the background, the police taunts, goading, insulting. 'Come on, you yellow bastards. Have a go!' a copper shouted.

The pushing strengthened. An officer laughed. 'We hate spades but we hate miners more.'

Then another cry from the back of the police lines. 'Come on, lads; get your backs into it. Keep my overtime pay coming, yellow wankers.' The laughing policemen. Pavel would put every fibre of his body into it.

Swannie was next to him. 'Christ almighty, look what's happening. Riot squads.'

The air changed suddenly, like a down draft coming through a tunnel in the pit after a distant explosion, anger fuelling mounting resentment, contempt seething on both sides. A melee of fists. He could see an officer being led away, the side of his head bleeding, and he heard the police commander shouting in the distance. Though he couldn't make out what he said, Pavel was certain it would wreak havoc. The first two rows of uniforms had been replaced by a different group in full riot gear. A beating of truncheons on shields began: a bloodcurdling call to arms. A rush of blood to the communal head and then the response from a significant few: stones hurled from the back of the picket lines.

Pavel turned, spotted Coker among the culprits and yelled, 'What the fuck? Stop throwing, Coker.' It made no difference. Spitting. Hissing. The sun shimmering on perspex shields made the image unreal, dreamlike, a flickering vision of brutality that made Pavel sick to his stomach and fearful for the lives of his friends.

'Bloody Zulu film,' Roly shouted, but nobody laughed.

The helmets and shields pressed forward into the miners' lines, into their faces, truncheons raining down on anyone who didn't clear the way. Pavel saw the Socialist Worker lad knocked aside with one blow to his head. He heard him scream as he fell rolling in the dirt and he ran to help him, but stumbled over Gus who'd been clubbed on the back and sent sprawling. 'Get out of here,' Pavel shouted, and the lad limped off down the field.

Gus was on his knees and had taken another hit, this time to his arm. Pavel screamed into the waves of uniforms. 'Stop, you mad bastards.' He looked around for Roly, grabbed Gus by his tee shirt, dragging him from a pulse of truncheon blows. 'Where's Roly?' Gus shook his head, dropped onto the ground, vomited.

A helicopter hovered, low, close; dogs barked; men spun away. Pickets were dispersing but in the confusion

Pavel couldn't find Roly. Though he'd experienced dark moods before, never purple fury. His temples throbbed. Where was Roly? He charged down the field to find him – running into the police. A baton thumped his back. He turned on the copper responsible, kicked him to the ground, wrestled the shield from him, threw it aside 'Come on, you bastard, how clever are you without that?'

He seized the man by the lapels and snarled into his face but the officer caught Pavel's brow with the truncheon then cried out as Pavel knuckled his ribs and groin. The truncheon fell. A second officer floored Pavel with a blow to the thigh and dragged his colleague to safety. Pavel got to his feet, hobbled to the edge of the field, escaping police reinforcements. There were plenty of pickets taking his place to distract them. He took off his filthy tee shirt and used it to wipe the sweat from his chest, armpits, blood from his brow. Gus sat with his head between his knees.

Smoke from burning plastic drifted across the grass: a picket had set fire to the captured shield. He brandished it like a flaming trophy then tossed it back towards the police.

Then Pavel saw what he'd dreaded most: the horses. As the riot squad retreated, they were replaced by a cavalry charge, the thunder of hooves and snorting nostrils. He imagined he smelled the horses' sweat, felt their hot breath on his neck. He watched the charge, shaking with awe. It was as if he were watching a film playing out on a giant screen.

More stones: a canopy of missiles.

Once the pickets were shifted, the riders regrouped and returned to the other end of the field. But they'd come again. *The Ten o' Clock Horses*! His breathing was shallow, heady, and the fear Gus had described took hold of him. The horses were claiming the child in him. Had they trampled Roly into the dust?

The lorries passed into the coke plant. More police support vans arrived. Then Pavel spotted a familiar shape running towards him: Roly grimacing, his hand gripping one shoulder. He fell on his knees and examined Pavel's cut brow. 'Are you okay? Hey. Good time for another Great Train Robbery. Every bleedin' copper in the country is 'ere! You might need a stitch in that.'

'Been trying to find you, Roly.' Pavel glanced at Gus who was throwing up again on the grass, and realised that in his panic to find Roly, he'd offered the youngest lad no support. 'You okay, Gus?'

Gus sat up, a trickle of fresh blood on his cheek. 'I'm alright. I dived. The bastard only clipped me.' He pointed across the field to where the police were hefting wriggling pickets into white vans. 'Swannie's been arrested though. They're sending out snatch squads, grabbin' anybody.'

Pavel could still feel the effects of punching in his fists: the imprint of another man's body, the crack in the ribs behind the uniform, the fleshy give in the copper's groin.

'They've got Coker an' all,' Roly said. 'Saw him dragged off after he threw bricks. Bloody idiot!'

Gus nodded. 'No justification for this bloodbath though, is there? I can't believe it.'

Pavel had been lucky to escape. He pulled his knees up and rested his forehead against them. His heart raced. His jeans were smeared with blood; his thigh throbbed like a constant kicking.

'We'll all be bloody black and blue tomorrow,' Roly said.

Pavel looked up. 'Democracy? Right to strike? Okay, we gave almost as good as we got, but this shouldn't have happened, should it?'

Roly rested his hand on Pavel's shoulder. 'It's what they call the *full force of the state*. They're working men like us,' he said, pointing after the riot squad who'd retreated after the lorries had passed through. 'And you'll see. Tomorrow they'll say they were only doing their job.'

'They were. Maggie's work. Now they're earning their pay rise,' Pavel said, wiping tears from his cheeks with a forearm. An image came to his mind of soldiers in trenches, men without choice. He understood the need to struggle, to fight for freedom, but now more than anything he felt a rush of shame at the futility of violence, the pure sin of ripping out another man's throat for any cause. For the first time in his life he'd experienced hatred. How much worse had it been for their fathers and grandfathers on the real killing fields of two great wars? *Great*: a misnomer by anybody's definition.

'Come on, Pavel,' Roly said. 'Get a grip. It's only a bloody strike.'

Pavel's mouth fell open at Roly's understatement. Gus laughed. 'Just the end of our way o' life, that's all.'

But Pavel couldn't laugh. He recognised the resurgence of grief, the weight in the pit of a churning stomach, the welling sense of loss that he'd thought he'd suppressed.

Gus told them there was a supermarket at the top of the road. They could buy more drinks, patch up wounds. 'We'll have to come back,' he said. 'The lorries will be out full o' coke later.'

Across the field Pawel saw that more vans had arrived delivering police, armed and equipped. These were well fed, well trained troops. The infantry had succeeded, backed up by the bleeding cavalry. And the lads? They were in jeans and tee shirts.

Roly jumped to his feet. 'Are we up to it?'

'Well I am,' Gus said.

'Course I am,' Pavel said, suddenly longing to be at home with Jake.

'Well,' said Roly, 'I could do with a sandwich and a sausage roll first.'

There were growing numbers of pickets and police spewing onto the field. As some miners left, either too weary or injured, more were arriving to take their place. Wherever he looked a new group gathered: placards waving, 'Coal not Dole,' 'Victory to the Miners.'

Barking dogs. Growling handlers. Steaming horses. Vans and coaches. Cars. Ambulances. Sirens. Radios clicking. Shouting. Spitting. Miners from every age group and from every area of the country by the sound of their accents; each new man angered by stories of the morning's events and enraged by the knowledge that thirty-five lorries had entered the coke plant. And, no doubt, each police officer fresh to his shift, embittered by stories of wounded colleagues. Pavel feared more injuries increased the odds on a fatality.

Shields and helmets stretched across the roads around the site and he counted rows of police four deep behind each riot shield. The troops had regrouped, refreshed, ready to attack. They stretched at least three hundred yards back from the front line. He watched as the lorries loaded with coke made a successful exit. The stone throwing resumed.

'Look at that lot,' Roly said, pointing to a small group of men lobbing bricks. They stood out from the rest. Why? How? Not dirty enough? 'They're not miners,' he said. 'They're dressed like miners but they're bloody not. I wonder how much they get paid.'

Pavel knew what Roly meant. Jeans, trainers, tee shirts. They all knew there'd been stooges planted to look like miners, create a bad impression. Cameras lapping it up.

Horses and riders charged again, galloping straight at them. Some veered off, chased pickets from the field, through the terraced streets of Orgreave village. Women screamed, ran inside, slammed doors. Pickets, followed by horsemen down ginnels between houses, cursed and bled.

A picket from the Derbyshire football gang ran past, sprinting towards the railway bridge, shouting. 'Run for it, lads, before they trample you to death.'

'If he's running, we'd better start,' Roly said. 'I can't keep up wi' him. He ran London marathon in April. Come on. Call it a day.'

Smoke rose from a car on fire outside a garage. Debris everywhere. They ran across the bridge, police abuse echoing behind them. 'Cowards, yellow bastards.'

Arthur Scargill was yelling through a megaphone, exhorting miners to continue, not be beaten, but the three men ran on. They jumped into Roly's car. One dent in the boot. Just the width of a truncheon. Unlucky. But not as unlucky as the poor bugger whose car was alight.

The car crawled up the motorway, held up by slow vans and coaches, pickets returning in droves to their respective villages. The road resembled a bank holiday traffic jam after a seaside trip. Roly switched on the radio. Reports of picket violence. Lies and half truths.

'My dad wanted me to learn a trade in the army, not work in a pit,' Gus said.

'Sent into battle either way then,' Roly said. 'Your dad knew the pit was a shit-hole.'

'Would you let Jake work down pit, Pav?' Gus asked.

'I'd like him to get an education; I want him to have choices.'

Roly laughed. 'And we're just asking for the choice to work. Okay it's a shit-hole, but it's our shit-hole.'

'And after this, Pavel? What will you do?' Gus said. 'Still thinking of a degree?'

'Dead right I am. Especially after this.' Before the strike began, Pavel had been considering taking up a part-time university course, sponsored by the union. 'I was looking at *Politics and Industrial Relations*,' he said. There was spontaneous laughter.

Roly slowed almost to a standstill allowing a police van to pull in in front of him and enter the slip road to leave the motorway. The driver raised his hand in thanks. Gus giggled.

'The world's gone bloody mad,' Pavel said.

Chapter Seventeen

Consequences

June 18ᵗʰ 1984

Lundby

Playground battle lines had been drawn: police, strikers, a small group pretending to throw stones and three girls galloping around on make-believe horses.

'It's not fair. I wanted to be a copper but Darren said I had to be a picket.' A six year old's face crumpled as he pointed to the child who was the source of his misery: Darren, top infant, Coker's son. Helen pulled the weeping boy to his feet, wrapped a reassuring arm around his shoulder while another infant picket resisted arrest by kicking Darren Coker's shins.

'Gerroff, you pig!'

'You're nicked!' Darren said.

A second whistle. 'Come here, all of you.'

The boys gathered around Helen, jostling for position. A sneer, a tongue stuck out, an elbow in a rib. She shook her head 'This isn't a good game, is it?' What should she suggest they play? Cowboys and Indians? Daleks? Either way, the outcome would be extermination.

'My dad's a picket,' Darren said.

'But he wouldn't want you to fight at school would he?'

Darren scowled. Knowing his father, she understood the boy's uncertainty. 'My dad says if somebody hits you, you have to hit back harder.'

Coker would. 'Not at school, Darren.' Darren's bottom lip trembled and he contemplated his feet. And this was only playground duty? Pavel was at Orgreave. Children in Belfast drew pictures of soldiers, guns, bodies spurting felt tip blood. She feared the long term consequences of a prolonged strike on the children, though her main concern was Pavel's safety.

When playtime ended Junior Coker joined in his class line mumbling threats at the boys in front.

Earlier she had opened the doors and windows to encourage a current of air through the classroom; it was too hot to teach, too humid for the children to concentrate on maths. And though cooking breakfast in the soup kitchen was a convenient – if not altogether honest – way of meeting Pavel, the five a.m. start to the day was taking effect, draining her energy.

It was PE at eleven. She had planned a dance drama lesson on a battle theme to the accompaniment of *Ride of the Valkyries*, hoping that the children could explore their aggression safely. 'The challenge is, children, to mime conflict without actually touching the enemy,' she told them. But when two boys discovered a basket of sponge balls at the back of the hall and lobbed them at the opposing forces, she realised the project had been too ambitious.

Worried about Roly, Kath brought a radio to the staffroom to hear the lunchtime news, but reports of pitched battles and injuries sent Helen back to her classroom, cutting her break short. At four o' clock she collected the books for marking and left school an hour earlier than usual.

The sun was fierce for late afternoon and she found Uncle Billy in the garden wearing a straw trilby and assembling new furniture: four folding chairs, a plastic table and a parasol.

'Very Mediterranean, Uncle Billy.'

He was trying to fix the parasol at a suitable height. 'You're early,' he said. 'I suppose you've heard. I've just got back from the Institute. The lads were checking in, taking a roll call.' He shook the parasol. 'Here, sit underneath so I can test it.'

The chair wobbled as she sat down; she dropped the basket, spilling the children's exercise books onto the paving slabs – slabs that Tibby called *a patio* – and the parasol collapsed over Helen's head.

'Are you all right in there?' Billy said, lifting one spoke, and burrowing his head into the dark. 'Seems Coker's been arrested and that young lad, Swannie.' Billy opened the parasol again. It clicked into position and he stood back in admiration.

'Did you see Pavel and Roly?' Helen asked.

'Certainly did. Savagery. There's no other way to describe it.'

'Was Pavel hurt?'

'Dried blood on his head. I think he had stitches. Pavel, Roly and the young lad, Gus, arrived just as I was leaving. Thought I was best out of it.'

'I should see if there's anything I can do.'

'What can you do? Think you're Florence Nightingale? Don't get involved. Why you have to be in the women's group at all is beyond me. The strike's not your fight.'

'I want to help.'

'Be sure you're helping for the right reasons.' He patted the trilby onto the back of his head, drew a handkerchief from his pocket and mopped his brow.

Tibby brought out a jug of orange juice and tumblers. Helen scooped up the books; Billy disappeared into the greenhouse. 'Tea will be on the table for six,' Tibby called after him. She examined the parasol. 'He managed it then?'

Billy popped his head around the greenhouse door. 'Told you. Piece o' cake. Make tea quarter past six, then we can watch the headlines first. The lads said Arthur Scargill took a clobbering.'

Sunshine eased the task of marking books – and the wait for the news. At the sound of the titles, Helen perched on the arm of Billy's chair, hugging a cushion and burying her face as the footage of Orgreave rolled onto the screen. Billy shook his head. 'Thatcher will want blood after this.' He switched off the set. 'I've seen enough.'

Tibby had set out salad and crusty bread on the garden table. 'There are strawberries and cream for afters,' she told Helen. 'Your favourite.'

'Don't stare at your plate, Helen,' Billy said. 'Eat for goodness sake.'

Helen nibbled a piece of bread, sliced a tomato. 'I've lost my appetite,' she said, laying down her knife and fork. 'I'm going to find out what's happened.'

Tibby looked from Billy to Helen. 'Go where?'

'I told you what happened. There's no point going to the Institute,' Billy said. 'They'll be home by now.'

'I'm going to see Pavel.'

Tibby groaned. 'You can't do that. What will his wife say?'

'She's not there. Jake's not in school this week. He's on holiday with his mother at his grandparents.'

'All the more reason.'

'Pavel's a friend.'

'It's not right.'

'It's 1984, Tibby. Men and women are allowed to be friends. You told me not to be so frosty towards him.'

'I didn't mean you should visit him when his wife's away.'

'You needn't worry, Helen' Billy said, squirting salad cream onto his lettuce. 'He's still in one piece.'

Helen pushed her chair from the table. 'I need to see for myself. I'll be back before you know it. Promise. Save me a bowl of strawberries.'

Billy pointed his fork. 'If you're not back by seven, you can say goodbye to strawberries.'

'It's only round the corner. Take me five minutes.'

'I won't bet on it.'

Helen ran upstairs to the bathroom. The window was open and she could hear the continued discussion.

'You should stop her, Billy,' Tibby said.

'Since when have I been able to stop her doing anything? Anyway. You told me back in March when she came home. Play the long game, you said.'

Even as Helen combed her hair, swept blusher across the apples of her cheeks and applied lipstick, she convinced herself this would be a swift visit, innocent, with no ulterior motive but to check on a friend. She bolted through the front door with a final call, 'Won't be long.'

It was a five minute walk. She opened the gate, stopped on the path, appraising Pavel's red brick ex-colliery house for the first time: its neatness, replacement windows, leaded lights. She tip-toed to the white front door, past the sitting room window, avoided peering in, but caught her reflection in the brass letter box. Clearly somebody had been polishing. She glanced around the garden.

Ceramic flower pots sat empty. Picket money wouldn't have paid for the luxury of bedding plants this year but there was a trimmed privet hedge, a well manicured lawn, colourful shrubs. A deep blue hydrangea nestled beneath the front window and two clumps of peonies, one red, one pink, waved from a corner of the garden. The house had a country cottage feel, in contrast to its neighbour where the garden was nothing more than a mud patch with a wreck of a car propped up on a pile of bricks.

Ignoring the doorbell, she tapped on the door and was surprised when Roly opened it. His eyes widened, then his eyebrows met. Pavel appeared at Roly's shoulder. She bit her lip. 'Helen?' he said. 'What are you doing here?'

She blushed; she shouldn't have come. 'I just wanted to find out how you were – all of you. I saw the news.'

Roly folded his arms. 'I suppose we'll live.' He puffed out his chest, blocking the doorway.

'I won't disturb you then…,' she said. 'If you're busy.'

'Come in,' Pavel said, opening the door wider. 'We've not been home long. Roly's just about to leave, aren't you?' She squeezed around Roly and followed Pavel across the hall into the kitchen. Roly trailed behind her. It seemed he'd changed his mind about leaving.

'What happened to your eye?' she said, peering at Pavel's stitches.

Roly grunted. 'What do you think? Got in the way of a truncheon like rest of him.'

'I'm okay,' Pavel said. 'There's worse than me. Roly took a beating.'

'Only a knock to my shoulder,' Roly said, tapping one foot. 'I could give you a lift home, Helen – now you know we've survived.'

She hesitated. Pavel looked from her to Roly. 'I was just going to offer her a drink.'

'Thanks. A coffee would be nice,' she said. Pavel's brow was swollen. 'I can't stay long. If I'm not back by seven, Billy says he'll eat my share of the strawberries.' She laughed, Roly scowled. She glanced at her watch. 'It's quarter to now.'

Roly nodded. 'I'd better be off then. Kath will be worried. We'll catch up tomorrow, Pav, at the post mortem. Don't forget what I told you.' He closed the hall door. A second's silence. The front door banged. Roly had left.

'What did he tell you?'

Pavel shrugged. 'Search me.' He switched on the kettle, sniffed at his tee shirt. 'Sorry. This stinks.' He pulled the shirt over his head, threw it on the floor in front of the washing machine. 'I wasn't expecting visitors.'

She was tempted to pick it up, offer to wash it. It would dry quickly. There was still enough heat in the evening. 'I was just passing so I thought...'

'I'll run upstairs for a clean shirt while you make us a drink,' he said. He turned, opened the cupboard, took out two mugs and a jar of instant coffee. When Helen saw Pavel's back aflame, she gasped.

He shut the cupboard door. 'What?'

'You can't see the marks.' She dragged a stool from beneath the table, placed it in front of the sink.

'I can feel them,' he said. 'Don't fuss. I'm fine.'

But she was already running the tap. 'Sit here. You need something cold. Have you got a clean towel?'

'Second drawer down.'

Despite his protestations he settled on the stool, leaned over the sink. She soaked a tea towel in cold water, laid it across his back. His sharp intake of breath touched her. 'Sorry,' she said. 'You'll feel worse tomorrow.'

'You're a great comfort.'

The heat from his back soaked through the towel, warmed her fingers. 'This should take the sting out,' she said. She lifted the towel to survey the damage again, then ran a fingertip along his raised skin. His back arched. 'Does that hurt?'

'It hurts.'

'How could anyone do this?'

Her actions were instinctive, like a kiss to a scrape on a toddler's knee: she brushed his back lightly with her lips, dropped the towel. Pavel leapt from the stool, spun around. 'Christ, Helen. What are you doing?'

She flinched, backed away. 'I'm so sorry. What a stupid thing to do.' She pushed her hair behind her ears, her face as inflamed as Pavel's back.

He laughed, took a step towards her, stroked her cheek. 'Come here.' He held her shoulders, drew her to him. It was good to have his arms around her, the hug of an old friend. His face was in her hair. 'You smell of fried bread,' he said.

She knew she should have showered. She broke free. 'I'm sorry.'

'Stop apologising.' He lifted her chin, kissed her. Her knees wobbled a little, her head whirled with the enormity of what she had done: what would Tibby and Uncle Billy say? And what about Jake? She should leave now. She stepped away. 'Frozen peas!' she said.

'What?'

'Frozen peas! That's what we need for your eye.'

'Do we? Right. I think there are some over there.' He waved across the kitchen.

She opened the door of the freezer. 'We're in luck. You have one bag. Nothing else.'

'Great. That will solve everything.'

She pressed the peas to his brow. He placed his hand over hers. She slid her hand from beneath his. 'I have to go.'

'Do you?'

'I'll leave you to find a clean shirt.'

She left him in the kitchen, scuttled to the front door.

At the garden gate she stopped. *Find a clean shirt*? She had dismissed him, patronised him, spoken to him like a pupil. She glanced along the street. There was nobody around. Nobody to judge, nobody to dissuade. He'd kissed her, reminded her of everything she'd lost, everything she still wanted. She turned back to the front door.

★ ★ ★

At the bottom of the stairs Pavel stopped at the sound of tapping on the front door. It had to be her. He hesitated. Should he let her in? What further torture would she inflict? He opened it. 'Yes?' he said, shifting the peas from his brow to his hairline. Nothing more could surprise him. The whole day was as skewed as a Picasso painting, surreal whichever way you looked at it.

'Can I come in?'

He raised an eyebrow, winced. 'Not for long. I need a shower.' He stumped into the kitchen, she followed. He leaned against the work top which dug into his back. He straightened. Muscles throbbed. 'Now what?'

'You were making coffee,' she said, '… only, you didn't.'

He fumbled to find the kettle switch behind him. He tried to scowl but it hurt. 'Anything else?' She stood by the door into the hall with her hands in the pockets of her skirt. Buttons, all the way up: skirt and matching blouse. That's what she was: all buttons and bloody attitude.

So much to undo.

She wore her hair shorter than ten years ago; she'd shoved it behind her ears again which irritated him. 'Well?' he said.

She edged towards him across the kitchen, peered at his brow. 'I think the swelling's gone down.'

'You think so?' Not according to the unmistakable ache in his groin. He rubbed his chin, avoided looking at her, focussing on a fly that had landed on the sink. 'Anything else?'

'I think the kettle's boiling.'

'Switches itself off.' He waited. He cast her a sideways glance. She was twisting the top button of her blouse, biting her lip.

'I didn't want you to think I'd run out on you,' she said.

'You did run out on me.'

'So where were we? Before, I mean.'

'You were teaching me the benefits of refrigeration.'

'Think those peas will start defrosting soon.'

'They've already defrosted. My last bag. Wasted, thanks to you.'

She was now so close that her nose was almost touching his. She placed her fingers over his lips. 'Nothing's wasted.' She brushed her cheek against his, nibbled his ear.

'Bloody hell,' he said. He threw his arms around her, swept her across the kitchen, as if in an ungainly dance, unwittingly treading on her toes. They tripped and stumbled, crashed into the hall door.

A tangle of limbs, laughter, an unbuckled belt, clothing in disarray. 'You and your bloody buttons,' he said.

★ ★ ★

They lay beneath a white lace bedspread. Everything in the spare bedroom was white: sheets, voile curtains, paintwork. Cheryl's idea of chic decor, a colourless place Pavel considered his camp. Stark, cold. It housed his clothes, books and nothing more. But now it had morphed into a bubble of soothing warmth. He lay on his back, watching dust particles as they glistened and spun in veiled light. Helen brought colour into this blanched space, her cheeks pink, flushed. Her breasts pressed against his chest: her skin on his.

He rolled onto his side, gazed at her in disbelief. The bloodiest day of his life now the sweetest. A sense of well-being washed over him, drowning any thoughts of responsibility, blotting out the horror of the day's events, side-tracking guilt. He noticed a bluish white scar on her belly and traced a finger along it. 'You're beautiful,' he said and she eased him onto his back, snuggled beneath his outstretched arm, one hand on his chest.

'You know what you forgot,' she said.

'Don't say it.' God forbid she'd spoil the moment with talk of precautions. 'What?'

'The coffee you promised. I'm thirsty.'

He laughed. 'Unbelievable.' He lifted her left hand, examined the ring on her third finger, a giant of a diamond. 'I still have it,' he said.

'Have what?'

'The engagement ring. It's in my drawer, in my old wallet.' He was light headed; the adrenaline that had fired him all day ebbed. His legs almost gave way as he crossed the room; found the ring. He brought it back to the bed, handed it to her.

'It still sparkles,' she said. 'Didn't think I'd see this again. I loved it.' Then she jammed it onto his little finger where it stuck on his knuckle.

What had happened to him? Memory forced an unwelcome inroad into his conscience. He'd never considered himself a violent man. Nor a man who stole wives. And what had happened to Helen? She'd become guarded, tense, a flippant jokiness masking something he couldn't quite fathom. It must be his fault, his rejection all those years ago. If he could keep her, he would. Keep her safe. 'I wish...' He squeezed the inner corners of his eyes. God he was tired.

★ ★ ★

They lay on their sides drinking each other in, saying nothing. She lay her head on his chest, listening to the regular thud of his heartbeat. His breathing grew deeper and the beating slowed. She kissed his forehead, tasted him.

His eyes flickered, closed. She stroked his arm. He slept. She slipped out of bed, found her underwear on the floor, wriggled into it, crept downstairs to the kitchen and, retrieving her skirt and blouse, she dressed. She picked up Pavel's jeans and the smeared tee shirt from the floor and folded them. What had he been through?

She glanced around the kitchen. So engrossed was she with Pavel, she hadn't noticed before how tidy and well presented it was. Oak cupboards, cleared work surfaces, café curtains on brass rods, matching cushions on the kitchen stools. Cheryl's pride and joy? And what was Pavel to his wife? A meal ticket? In that moment Tibby's rumours became fact: Cheryl was not worthy of him. Helen tucked the stool under the table, placed the unused mugs into the cupboard.

Through the kitchen window, she spotted a rabbit in a hutch in the corner of the garden and thought about Jake, wished he were her own son. There was a Peace Rose growing next to the hutch, yellow-pink heads wilting under the weight of the day's heat. From a butchers' block on the work top she snatched a pair of kitchen scissors, unlocked the back door, dashed across the garden and sheared off the largest bloom.

She crept upstairs, placed the rose on the pillow beside Pavel and his folded jeans and tee shirt at the foot of the bed. It was then she noticed a book case along one wall. They were all there: books she'd recommended to him so many years ago. Second hand books: Shakespeare, Dickens, Hardy, Austen, and newer paperbacks: Huxley, Orwell, Asimov, Lawrence and others she hadn't read. Travel books, politics, history. Moved by the certainty he'd read every one of them, she ran a finger along the peeling spines, resisting the desire to return to Pavel's bed.

She slipped through the front door, locked it behind her, posting the key through the letter box. The street was empty and she sprinted home as quickly as she could, hoping this would explain her flushed cheeks and breathlessness.

As she peeked around the sitting room door the clock on the mantelpiece chimed half past nine. Uncle Billy was watching the television, the back of his head just visible above the arm chair.

'You've lost your strawberries,' he said.

Chapter Eighteen

Identity

June 18th 1984

Orgreave South Yorkshire

Handcuffed, dragged across the field, kneed into the back of a waiting police van. The copper patted Coker's pockets, removed his wallet and cigarette lighter, shoved him onto a bench seat.

'Name?'

'Coker.'

'Good. Got the right man then.'

He'd expected to be disbelieved, for the copper to look at the coke plant and accuse him of taking the piss.

Pull the other one, my name's Arthur Scargill.

But why was he the only one in this van?

The doors banged, locked. He'd thought Swannie at least would have been here. He'd seen him nicked at about the same time. They'd been next to each other on the field. And plenty of other blokes had been snatched, arms twisted. Men kicked away from the action.

The van moved off. Surprisingly relieved to be out of the yelling, pushing, screaming, Coker relaxed. No doubt they'd take him to the local station, book him for affray, stick him in a cell, maybe offer him a crap meal then let him out. A welcome end to this pointless picketing. If he went back to it after arrest he risked jail. Never worth it, though he'd miss the picket money. It bought the odd pint. After buying cans of beer from the supermarket, he'd probably be short of a bus fare, and he'd lost his lift with the lads. He smiled, wondering if it might be to her Majesty's pleasure to have her boys drop him off at home. *Thank you, Maam.* But then, she wasn't the woman in charge nowadays, was she?

The van travelled further than he expected before it slowed and stopped. Then the sound of heavy traffic, the drone of lorries, engines changing pitch as they approached and passed at speed, convinced him that wherever he was, it was no police station forecourt.

The back doors opened. 'Okay, Coker,' the driver said. 'Your luck's in. Seems somebody wants a word. Out.' Coker jumped down. They'd stopped on the hard shoulder of the motorway. Sunlight blasted his eyes. A pain in his head. He squinted. His tee shirt stuck to his back and he wriggled to free it. Exhaust fumes clogged his nostrils. Dizzy, Coker stumbled into the side of the van and the copper grabbed him by the handcuffs, yanked him forward. From the signpost ahead, he realised he was on the southbound carriageway of the M1.

A few yards in front, a dark blue Volvo waited with the engine running, the front nearside door open. The copper released the cuffs, shoved Coker's head down, man-handling him into the passenger seat. Coker's wallet was thrown onto his lap and the door slammed, almost trapping his fingers. The copper tapped the window. Coker found the electric button to open it. Smart car this.

'No Houdini stuff, Coker. I'm watching.'

'What? Run off into three lanes of traffic? Yeah, okay, mate.'

Coker looked the Volvo driver up and down, smirked. This stooge was slightly built, easy to take on if need be. And the hair? Longer than regulation, too *shampoo and conditioner,* more golf club than Miners' Institute. And the clothes too clean and tidy for a fake picket, too casual for CID. Pristine jeans, navy polo shirt. 'You don't get shoes like them from Stylo,' Coker said.

The man's forearms rested on the steering wheel, limp wrists, hands dangling. A gold watch caught the light. A blue enamelled ring with a weird insignia decorated the little finger of his left hand alongside a broad wedding ring.

Volvo Man looked straight ahead. 'Right, Coker. Let's sort this and you can go home to your wife. You have got one haven't you? Susan? And three kids?'

Bastard.

'Am I arrested or what?'

The man's lips twitched, not quite a smile. 'Depends, Coker. I need a few details about your Polish friend. Picket Coordinator.' Coker tried to place the accent. Definitely south of Watford Gap. He offered Coker an open packet of *B and H.* Coker took a fag and reached into his pocket for his lighter, remembering too late that it had been confiscated. Volvo Man threw the packet on to the dashboard.

'Can I have a light?' Coker said. 'Your mate's got mine.'

The driver nodded at the dash where a lighter lay on top of an O.S. map of Sheffield, the folds tight, flat, the cover glossy. Coker picked up the lighter, tapped it on the map.

'Don't tell me. You need a guide to the Delights of the North. I can show you a good strip club in Rotherham.'

The driver drummed his finger tips on the steering wheel. Not a flicker of appreciation. Coker lit the fag and inhaled. 'My Polish mate? Pavel? His mother's Polish. Don't think he speaks a word. What you suggesting? Eastern bloc connections? That's a laugh.'

The man grinned. 'I see. Flat cap, sausage and chips man, is he, like the rest of you?'

Coker swapped the cigarette to his left hand, flexed the fingers of his right. Patronising git. 'Why would you think he's a mate of mine?' Coker guessed Volvo Man couldn't be much older than himself, maybe younger, thirty two at most. He didn't like the way the pig sneered when he looked at him, a smell under his nose. Coker sniffed his own arm pit realising the smell was entirely his. It was bloody hot.

'He married your ex girlfriend didn't he? And I understand he almost broke your jaw a few weeks ago.'

Coker laughed. 'Seems like you know everything already, Mr...?' This was ridiculous. If it wasn't June, Coker would think it was an April fool's prank.

The man lit a cigarette, lowered the window a fraction and blew the smoke out of the car. At least not into his prisoner's face, like on telly. 'I've heard the argument was about a woman,' he said. 'An old girlfriend? What's her name?'

'Helen Eagleton? Yeah, I was just arsin' around but he got stroppy. I reckoned he still fancied her and he took exception.'

'And does he? Fancy her?'

'I thought you knew everything. Ask him yourself. Why don't you tap his phone?'

'What makes you think we haven't?'

Coker drew on the cigarette. Ash fell on his jeans. What did this smug bastard want?

'You miners like to gossip, don't you? Love a juicy titbit. Does it surprise you to hear you've been discussed, you and Pavel? Picket lines and Institute bar tittle-tattle? All this time you lads have on your hands. '

'Bloody hell. There's guys back there fighting for their jobs and you... sewer rats, scuttling around in other people's shit.' Coker grabbed the door handle. 'Think I'd rather be arrested. More honesty in it.' Volvo Man, Polo Shirt Man, Faceless Wonder.

The man laughed. 'Very noble but hear the deal first: we pay you to keep tabs on Mr Kowaleski and Mrs Eagleton. Forty quid a week until he's no longer of interest to us. No arrest and no picketing. Don't tell me you're enjoying this strike, it's getting out of hand, isn't it? No fun in getting trampled to death, is there? And you know you're losing. You can't win. For every one of you, there are plenty more like me.' He nodded over his shoulder at the police van. 'And I don't mean PC Plod.'

Coker finished the cigarette, flicked the tab end through the window. The man stubbed his own in the ashtray. 'We'll finish off you and your union mates. We're almost there. It's laughable. You turn up at our beck and call; lie on your backs for us to trample on. Touching really.'

Coker clenched both fists. *Don't rise to this bastard's bait.*

'Duty, Coker. It's our raison d'être. You know this has little to do with pit closures.'

Coker looked through the windscreen. Lorries, more lorries. Men with jobs. The car swayed slightly in the wake. The smell of burning rubber. Blurred images hovered over the tarmac in waves of heat haze. What the hell was Pavel Kowaleski involved in? 'So are you trying to tell me that Pavel's a subversive?'

The man threw his head back, laughed. A flash of a silver filling. Just a bloke, a bloke who went to the dentist, not somebody Coker should fear. It might be worth having a go at him, then making a dash for it up the motorway banking. No point. They'd know where he lived.

Volvo man stopped laughing, took a deep breath, sighed. 'Pathetic. You still don't get it do you, Coker? You miners are all fucking subversives!'

'So why are you so interested in Pav? He's not even a communist like some of 'em. He's a lad trying to save a bloody pit. Wouldn't you be better off following Arthur Scargill and his comrades?' Coker knew that went without saying. Arthur would know his phone had been tapped for years.

The man wrote a number on a card. Coker reached for another cigarette. His hand trembled as he lit it. 'Can't you piss off and concentrate on the IRA?'

'Do you know who Mrs Eagleton is?'

Coker smirked. 'Yeah. She's the niece of a Labour councillor, ex NUM man; and she's a teacher. That's all I know. Unless you tell me different. I know she married a Toff.'

Volvo Man glanced in the rear view mirror. 'She's the wife of Guy Eagleton, Tory MP. A rising star. If his wife's screwing miners, we need to know about it. So does he.'

'Bloody 'ell. Nice one Pav.' Coker always knew that girl was up her own backside, snotty cow. But there was nothing more he could tell, or wanted to tell this bastard. 'I don't think anything's going on. She's in Women's Support Group which I suppose is bad enough for her husband, but Pavel's what you'd call principled. He doesn't mess around with married women. Not even his own at the moment – so I've heard.'

'Still friendly with his wife are you? No loyalty to Mr. Kowaleski then?' Coker said nothing. Who the hell had been talking? 'All we want is an eye kept on him. In a community like yours, they can smell an outsider from a mile away. We glean an earful of gossip in a tap room bar but when we hang around, it becomes... problematic. We're rumbled. Dangerous among the savage classes.'

Coker laughed. 'Piss off!'

'You, on the other hand, can keep tabs. And phone tapping? Half your phones are cut off anyway. You should try paying your bills.'

'Right gob-shite aren't you? So how do I explain not being arrested?'

'You don't. You let people think you were. We arrange a letter, invite you to court. You spend a day loafing around Sheffield, go home after and tell your mates you got off with a fine.'

Coker sighed. He didn't like this. He'd had problems with Pavel and he despised the ex girlfriend. Stirring things up for them was one thing, a bit of fun, but being a grass was another.

Coker opened the window, breathed in. A tang of traffic fumes laced his tongue. He needed to think. But for the time being he'd agree to what the wanker wanted – just to get away. 'What do I do?'

The man handed him the card. 'Telephone when you have something.'

'You can add cost of calls to my fees, chum. So her husband knows about you, does he?'

'We'll make sure you get paid.'

Volvo man turned, signalled to the driver behind. The police van moved off, accelerating down the hard shoulder and into the stream of traffic.

Coker rubbed his chin. 'What do I call you?'

'I'll drop you off myself. Rest assured we'll be in touch, if we don't hear from you.'

The man drove north to a motorway roundabout about two miles from Lundby. He stopped. 'No point in taking you further, is there?' he said.' You wouldn't want to be seen with me. You can walk from here.'

Coker got out, jabbed two fingers at the rear view mirror as the car hugged the roundabout then picked up speed down the M18 slip road. 'Slimy bastard.'

He wondered if Volvo Man would fork north or south on the M1. He set off walking, wiping his brow on the back of his hand. He couldn't remember a hotter June.

The walk allowed him to mull over the conversation, recall details, piece together implications. He had a headache. The idea that Pavel might be involved in anything other than an honest fight for pits stretched imagination, but on the other hand, the idiot deserved trouble if he was getting mixed up with that bitch again. Pavel must have known all along her husband was a Tory MP; Billy Farrimond would have told him for sure. Billy! Just like Roly. The pair of them, always looking out for their little pal. Pavel Kowaleski: everybody's fucking favourite.

And her? He'd like to get one over on Ms Farrimond. He'd asked her out once, when he was fifteen. No money, daft thing to do. She'd been in his maths set at school and he'd beaten her in every exam. Being turned down was one thing but being looked at like she'd looked at him that day was another. 'Drop dead,' she'd said. Top Set. The teacher had suggested Coker could study maths at university if he'd wanted. But he'd had to leave school before his O levels. His dad told him to get his *bloody arse down the pit like he'd had to*, and start *paying his way*. No bleedin' justice. Now here she was, stuck up little cow, sucking up to the lads, riding out her class guilt trip on the backs of their cause. Holier than thou little tart. Just a working class traitor with a secret which, in the long run, might be worth more than the forty quid this lot were offering. He'd like to do more to Helen Eagleton than grass on her.

His wife, Susan, believed his tale of unjust arrest. *Poor love: done nothing more than peaceful picketing.*

Coker had his tea, bathed his youngest son, read the *Three Little Pigs* and put his own *three little kids* to bed.

'*I'll huff and I'll puff!*'

Nobody would blow Coker's fuckin' 'ouse down.

Kids asleep, Susan told him he'd earned himself a pint at the Institute. She'd collected the family allowance that morning.

But he didn't go to the pub. Coker decided to visit Pavel. It would be easier to pick up on the dirty details by speaking to him. Much as it would choke him, Coker would apologise for past aggravation. Pavel was always up for a peaceful outcome. Even now, as picket coordinator, he'd never encourage violence. Silly bugger. Always been too trusting. He wondered if today's events had cured Pavel of principles. He'd call on him; see if he'd been on the wrong end of a baton like everybody else. Good excuse.

He tapped on the back door. No reply. Pavel's car was on the drive. A dint in the bonnet. A truncheon blow at the last picket line. Coker looked through the kitchen window. Stuff on the floor: jeans and what looked like women's clothes, pink. His imagination running riot? On the other hand, everybody knew Cheryl was away with Jake. He leaned against the wall. Well, well, well. It had been a long day, but he could wait.

Kowaleski was a damned hypocrite; thumping a mate for insinuating he was screwing his ex and now caught in the act. Coker heard the key turn in the back door. He dashed across the garden, squeezed behind the shed, keeping a view of the lawn. It was her, he was right. Pair of scissors in her hand. Nicking a rose. He heard her mewling at the rabbit. Soft voice. Bloody posh. What the hell was this MP's wife up to, getting Pavel into? She went back into the house.

Coker hauled himself out into the garden, grazing an elbow on the shed. He lingered down the side of the house, peeping around the corner to glimpse the front door. A soft click, a flap of letter box. He saw her leave – in her little pink blouse and skirt.

He wished he'd stayed by the kitchen window, he might have watched her getting dressed. What else might he have seen if he'd been earlier? She opened the front gate, sprinted to the end of the street. She turned the corner and ran in the direction of Billy Farrimond's. Citizen Billy. A man of integrity. Forthright. Upstanding.

Would he know what his delightful niece was up to in her spare time? Dirty secrets. Dirty truths.

Coker followed her from a distance, until he reached the telephone box. He took the card from his pocket.

It was then he realised the copper had kept his lighter

Chapter Nineteen

White Shirts

June 19ᵗʰ 1984

South Yorkshire

Sunlight woke him; his eyes, heavy lidded, flickered open. Pavel had a headache. He stared at the ceiling until memories of the night before dawned then he rolled across the pillows as if to recapture her. Rose petals brushed his cheek, invading his sinuses with sweetness and pollen, worsening the thudding in his head. A thorn pricked his nose.

The clock on the bedside table beeped seven, awakening his need for a shower and the clean clothes that were at least twelve hours overdue. He groaned at the ache in his back, stroked the stubble on his cheek, scratching his chin on the sapphire ring which was stuck on his knuckle. By the look of the swelling he'd need cold water and soap to remove it. Despite not a drop of alcohol passing his lips yesterday, he had a headache to match a New Year hangover.

He stumbled downstairs and found the telephone directory, fumbling under E for Eagleton before remembering that what he needed was Billy Farrimond's number. He knew it well enough. He dialled.

Pavel had forgotten what sex could be like – he glanced at himself in the hall mirror, – when you ached for one woman. He examined his chin, stuck out his tongue.

A furry tongue, bloodshot eyes, a stubbly chin. Very attractive. Would Helen want him now? He'd only ever ached for her.

He sat on the floor in the hall, reluctant to perch on the telephone seat that Cheryl thought was a necessity, along with the hostess trolley and the hat stand. When had he ever worn a bloody hat?

The phone rang four times before Helen answered. 'Can't you come back?' he said.

'I've got to leave for school in half an hour.'

'By the way,' he said, 'it will take me ages to get this ring off. It's completely stuck.'

Like her. She had stuck to him, skin on skin. Even after a shower he would be saturated in her scent. 'There's a meeting tonight, in a pub a few miles away. The landlord's sympathetic, lets us have a room. It shouldn't take long. Then we'll head into the country if you like.' He'd filled up the car with petrol two days before but thought he'd have enough money to buy her a drink.

'I can hear Tibby in the bathroom,' she whispered. 'Got to go.' She agreed to meet him at six that evening.

Since there was nothing in the fridge he decided to skip breakfast; the Institute kitchen would be open at noon. He placed the rose in a milk jug, fed the rabbit, tidied the house. There'd be no mass showdowns today. Everybody would need a rest. There were blokes with worse injuries than Pavel and he needed to check the men would be fit for the next round, though he didn't much relish speaking to Roly who would question what time Helen left last night – if he hadn't already compared notes with Billy. The two men meant well, but he wished sometimes they would butt out, let him crash headlong into his own disasters. He hadn't felt as alive as this for years. The memory of Helen in his arms was worth any subsequent grief.

Television and tabloids called it *The Battle of Orgreave*, and everyone at the Institute had their own version, each account more brutal and shocking than the man's before. Numbers were argued about, adjusted according to differing news reports which were broadcast on a black and white television in the games room. Rumours of ten thousand pickets to eight and a half thousand police were a fair estimate, Roly said. Swannie told them he'd almost been relieved when the police had carted him off to the station, especially since they'd treated him reasonably well and fed him. Gus looked pale, Roly was sore but not complaining, and nobody had seen Coker since he'd been dragged to a police van.

'And what's the *plat du jour* then, love?' Roly said to the volunteer wife behind the kitchen counter.

'Here we go. Roly's been reading his daughter's school books again,' Gus said.

The meal was soggy fishcake, chips and peas.

As the last scraps were served Coker arrived. Swannie cheered. 'Where did they send you then, Coker, Devil's Island? Nobody saw you for dust.'

'Police station, like rest of you. Kept me in a cell all afternoon.'

The woman behind the counter dolloped mushy peas onto his plate. 'Ah, poor lamb.'

'Not a mark on you,' Roly said. 'Typical, Coker. If you fell in pig shit we know what you'd come up smelling of.'

Roses. Pavel smiled. Coker slapped Pavel's back. 'Hell's teeth, Coker. Leave it out.'

'Sorry, mate. Didn't realise you'd taken a battering.'

It was the first banter the pair had shared since April and Pavel was glad of it. Maybe yesterday's events had mellowed Coker, caused him to re-evaluate who his friends were. As picket coordinator Pavel needed unity.

Bad form to bear a grudge. 'If we meet here for breakfast tomorrow, I'll let you know what the plans are for the next picket.'

Gus groaned. 'Not bloody Orgreave again, I hope.'

'I'll come to the meeting with you if you like, Pav,' Coker said. 'Join you for a drink.'

'Some other time. I'll be coming straight home after. Promised to visit my mum.' Even to Pavel it sounded a lame excuse and Roly snorted from behind a newspaper.

★ ★ ★

Pavel had agreed to pick Helen up from the bus stop on the fringe of the village where she would be inconspicuous. He could then turn off into a back road, take in the countryside, avoid familiar faces.

She slid into the passenger seat. He wore a short sleeved white shirt he had bought last summer but had never worn. He'd had to take it out of the packet, unpin it. The collar chafed his neck as he glanced over his shoulder into the traffic. 'Okay?' he said.

'Uncle Billy's not asked questions but Tibby is quiet, not saying much.'

'Are you sure you're not imagining it?' He squeezed her knee. Implications, consequences already. There was a touch of anxiety, a pinch of fear somewhere in the pit of his stomach.

Earlier Jake had phoned, full of stories about trips to the beach, arcades and candyfloss. Pavel hated the emptiness of the house without him. Hearing Jake's voice had reminded him of the folly of an affair. But he couldn't dwell on that now. He lowered his foot onto the accelerator.

After a few miles he stopped the car in a lay-by, kissed her. There could be only four days together. Cheryl and

Jake would arrive home on Saturday. The physical longing for Helen was unbearable.

'You look smart,' she said, and sniffed his collar. 'You smell fresh and new.' He wished he'd washed and ironed the shirt before he'd worn it. At a crossroads he shot a red light and she told him to keep his eyes on the road, his hands on the steering wheel. He wanted to hold her.

In the pub car park two crows were scavenging on fish and chip debris, beaks tearing at a piece of batter, pecking each other in between, claws tangled in newspaper wrappers. As Pavel pulled into the parking bay, the birds flew off dropping a beak-pocked chip onto the bonnet of his car.

'Not the most salubrious part of town is it?' she said.

'You're not in London now, Miss. The pub's been refurbished though. Victorian style. Plush.' He kissed her again. 'I don't think the meeting will last long. I'll leave you the keys. You can listen to the radio if you're bored.'

The porch smelt of toilets and beer. The sound of a juke box and electronic pinging from a space invader assailed him as he opened the door. The tap room was on the left. He pushed open a door to the right, entering a lounge bar where a glow from amber wall lights jaundiced the crimson seating and green carpet. Pavel scanned faces through a mirror behind the optics. The place was busy for a Tuesday night and he wondered if there might be a quiz later. The landlord nodded acknowledgement. 'They're through the back.'

Carrying an orange juice, Pavel opened a swing door to a room usually hired out for parties. Inside heads were bent, absorbed in conversation. Coordinators from across the town were holding an inquest into the battle of Orgreave with the vocabulary he'd become accustomed to: bastards, traitors, scabs, pigs. Eventually, a union official entered to a ripple of applause and conversation subsided as the man climbed onto a platform and shifted the knot in his tie.

'I don't need to tell you that yesterday was a disgrace, a miscarriage of justice but it does nothing but strengthen our resolve to continue. Democracy is in danger, not just our jobs.' A general mumble of agreement.

Pavel stood by the door listening, the buzz of voices from the lounge bar in the background and the bass beat of rock music thumping from the tap room juke box. Shadows crossed the frosted glass door beside him.

The official glanced over his shoulder. 'We need to be vigilant. There were men on that picket line that didn't belong to us. War rules apply: beware of careless talk.'

Pavel smiled at the Churchillian references. The clichés were out in force: warnings about careless talk when it was clear the police knew the miners' every move? Picket locations were given out in codes. He wondered why they bothered when the police were always at the pit gates before them.

A hush had descended on the neighbouring lounge bar and conversation was replaced by a rumble of shifting furniture. Women squealed, a man's voice shouted. 'Get out; get the fuck out.' Silence from the juke box; someone leaned against the door. It swung open then closed. Open then closed again. Something hit the door panel. Pavel ducked as splinters of glass showered him and he felt a sudden sting in his neck. He pulled out a shard, wiped away a trickle of blood. Unsure of an escape route he froze then spotted union delegates slithering out through a back door.

Before he had time to follow, police officers wielding truncheons burst into the room. 'Out, you bastards. Out.'

Seizing arms, legs, heads, they flung the picket coordinators into the lounge, jostling, elbowing. Pavel landed on the floor at the foot of the bar; the carpet sodden with beer. A stool toppled onto him. The police were ripping up seats; velvet hung in ribbons where the banquettes were slashed; stuffing like candy floss was strewn across the carpet. Tables were upturned, legs smashed with truncheons. The landlord, his hands clasped above his head, wept, helpless; his wife screamed. 'Stop it, you animals! You'll pay for this.'

The burly sergeant overseeing the operation leaned on the counter, grinned at the landlady. 'We're on overtime, love, we can afford it! You should be choosy who you let in.'

Pavel had no thoughts of retaliation, he feared only for Helen. A white-sleeved arm tried to grip him in a head lock but Pavel spun away, jumped over broken furniture, crashed through the porch, bumping into men pouring from the tap room and into the car park. The regulars ran in every direction, no one prepared to be on the end of a truncheon attack. No TV cameras to record events, no official record. He could hear Helen calling to him. She had started the engine and he raced towards her.

She opened the driver's door and Pavel jumped in. Gears crunched, tyres screeched. He drove for miles, faster than he should have, faster than he normally would. He drove until he was south of Sheffield and into Derbyshire.

The evening was balmy, the sun paling, lowering in the west but radiating enough heat to have enticed people away from their televisions and out for car trips into the countryside.

Pavel stopped at a Peak District pub where a beer garden was crowded with young families, children scrambling on a climbing frame, pop bottles and leaking straws abandoned on picnic tables. Jake would like it here. Jake. This place reminded Pavel once more that he was a father.

Inside the pub beneath low beams, they found the lounge bar empty. Horse brasses and warming pans festooned the walls, and logs had been stacked for the summer inside a fireplace that bore black marks, doubtless from years of tongues of smoke licking the stonework. Leaded windows let in limited sunshine; the smell of chopped timber and a dim red glow from a reproduction oil lamp, reminded Pavel of Christmas – and Christmas reminded him of Jake.

Pavel bought a half of beer for himself and a glass of white wine for Helen. 'Are you okay?' she said, taking his hand across a sticky table top.

He shook his head. 'If you were attacked in your own home by thugs and vandals, who would you call?'

'I know,' she said,' It's hard to believe. I watched them arrive and couldn't warn you.'

'The bloody Met, that's who's responsible. The great Metropolitan Police Force. White shirts. They think they're above the law and that we're scum. Even the local police can't stand them. And Thatcher talks about the *enemy within*. Ha. At the beginning of the strike I was naïve, convinced I was only fighting for a job. Now I'm not so sure.'

'We should ring the newspapers, television.'

Pavel laughed. 'Which papers? Television? I don't trust anybody. You watched the coverage of Orgreave yesterday: a mass of stones thrown at the police and then the baton charge. I was there! It was the other way round, Helen. There were a few idiots on our side chucking stones before that, but the massive hail of missiles they showed came *after* the police attack. A response to it. So who decided to show it that way round? Who is in charge of this country?'

She looked tearful. 'I had no idea what was going on. When I go to London I'll make sure –'

'Go to London? When?'

'On Friday. Just for the weekend. The women are collecting. It's been organised through the teacher's union. I'm staying with a friend but I'll be meeting Guy on Saturday night. I promised.'

He nodded. 'You were with him a few weeks ago, weren't you? Roly's daughter saw you in the restaurant.'

'Did she tell you I was drunk, made a fool of myself?'

Roly had told Pavel, to warn him off Helen: told him her husband had come to claim her.

'Just said she saw you.'

'I didn't sleep with him if that's what you think.'

'Hey, I wasn't suggesting that. But it's none of my business is it? You're married to him.'

She blinked, recoiled as if he'd punched her. He didn't know why he'd said it. Maybe it was fear, guilt. 'I'm sorry.'

She put down her glass. 'How could you say that, Pavel? Do you think I would have slept with you if I wanted Guy? I've never had a one night stand in my life. I've left Guy.' She stood up. 'I think we should go.'

He reached across the table, clasped her hand. 'Sit down. I'm sorry. I didn't mean it like that.' How had he meant it? 'I guessed you'd separated.'

'Would it make it easier for you if I went back to him? Are you having regrets?'

'No. I'm just clumsy with words.' He freed her hand, carried his stool around the table to sit beside her. 'Sorry.' Why had she left Guy? Surely not because of his support for Thatcher? Something else. Why had she married him? 'On your wedding day I watched you from the churchyard.'

She had taken a tissue from her handbag; she blew her nose. 'I saw you. Why didn't you speak to me?'

'Because I might have asked you not to go ahead. Can you imagine? Like a film. What would you have done, if I had?'

'I thought I loved Guy.'

'Thought?'

'The kind of devotion I'd had for you scared me. Guy was kind, wanted to look after me'

Pavel looked into his drink. 'And did he?'

'It's my fault,' she said. 'The way things have turned out. I think Guy always knew he was second best.'

'And how have things turned out?'

If Helen had deprived her husband of devotion, then Pavel had also denied Cheryl; she too must have felt second best. He searched for words to define what had been special about his relationship with Helen. Abandonment? Connection? Neither marriage had ever stood a chance. And now? The stomach churning was the same but they weren't kids anymore. He finished his drink. 'I'm an idiot.'

'When I see Guy on Saturday, I'll tell him what happened tonight. He should know what his masters condone. I can't believe he'd agree with these tactics.'

Pavel leaned back on his stool, hugged one knee. 'Have you forgotten who his masters are? Or mistress? But you're not running from his politics are you?'

'I've not exactly been a model MP's wife.' She scratched a fingernail at Pavel's shirt front. 'Specks of blood on your shirt. Soak it in salt water when you get home.'

For a short time last night she'd been the girl he remembered. Now she was evasive, defensive. Something else must account for the change, something deeper than his ending of their relationship.

'Whatever's happened you should stop blaming yourself, Helen. You sound beaten, defeated. You were fiery and opinionated when I first knew you.'

'The fire left the belly with a baby, fighting for its life.'

He placed his arm around her waist. 'I said the wrong thing again. I'm sorry. Billy told me about –'

'William,' she said

He glanced around the bar, realising that they were drawing curious stares from customers who'd arrived since the start of the conversation.

'Come on,' he said. 'It's time I took you home.'

'You've not mentioned Cheryl, how you feel about her.'

'We'll talk about this later.'

They drove in silence. Pavel stopped the car outside the Farrimond house, braking slowly, quietly. It was almost dark, curtains were closed.

'I had planned for us to go back to my house,' he said. 'I've been thinking about it all day.'

'I'd better not.'

She opened the door but he pulled her back, kissed her cheek, sweeping her hair aside with his lips. 'Can we meet tomorrow night?'

'PTA meeting.'

'Thursday then? Meet me at the market entrance at 7.30. We'll walk in the woods while it's still light. Nobody's desperate for firewood in this weather.'

'Okay. I'm not sure what I'll tell Billy and Tibby though.' She stepped out of the car, ran into the house.

Why had everything changed since this morning? He'd put Helen in danger tonight: physical and political danger. Worse still, he was in danger too, in danger of hurting her again. She was fragile. Perhaps he should end it now before... He had Jake to think of.

Once home, he threw the keys onto the table, strolled into the garden. The trees, shrubs and lawn were bathed in yellow light from the kitchen. Balmy air deepened the perfume of roses and night-scented stocks. He stood in front of the rabbit hutch he'd built so carefully after months of Jake's constant pleas for a pet. Under his son's watchful eye, every Saturday morning for weeks, he'd sawn and hammered the timber, nailed it into shape, weather-proofed the finished construction. Then Jake had dragged him along to the pet shop to buy this little grey Dutch Dwarf.

The rabbit hopped forward. Pavel poked his finger through the wire netting, tickled behind its whiskers, then he unrolled the sheeting over the front of the hutch, secured it with a brick. This was the attraction of pets, what made them so appealing: they didn't ask for much. Their uncomplicated lives were driven by the need for food, shelter and − if not separated from others of the same species − sex. Some women, maybe Cheryl, might scoff that a man's needs were not so different. They were wrong. Pavel tapped the roof of the hutch. Rabbits did not suffer from the conflicts of loyalty and responsibility. They may tremble at the sight of a skulking fox or a renegade pet terrier, but never fear being torn apart by love.

Chapter Twenty

Tracks

June 1984

London

Train wheels on sleepers clickety-clacked. Helen drummed her fingers on the table to the syncopated rhythm. Sitting opposite, Kath was flicking through the glossy pages of a magazine, ignoring recipes, horoscopes, problem pages and fashion shoots, until she found a crossword puzzle. 'Skipping around like a spring lamb on Tuesday, miserable three days later.'

'Is that a clue?' Helen said.

'It's you. You and Pavel. Don't deny it.' Kath tossed her pen on top of the magazine. 'If you need to talk, you can trust me, I won't tell Roly.' Since Peterborough there had been no other passengers at their table, unusual for a Friday evening. A group of women from the support group were chatting further down the carriage.

'What has Roly said?'

'Nothing. I haven't mentioned my suspicions.' Kath took Helen's hand. 'Pavel will always put Jake first, love. Cheryl's back tomorrow. Then what?'

Whatever Helen had thought she could handle when she'd fallen into Pavel's bed on Monday evening, now she longed for a future.

Kath picked up the crossword. 'And there's your job. You're Jake's teacher. Hardly professional is it: sleeping with his dad?'

244

Last night, Helen had left Pavel's house at midnight.

'When are you back?' he'd asked, watching her dress.

'Sunday afternoon, but I'll have preparation for next week's lessons so I won't see you.' Then she remembered that Cheryl and Jake would be back at the weekend anyway.

Hoped for promises, plans, a solution, had come to nothing. Just a kiss, then he'd walked her home in the dark, leaving her at Billy and Tibby's gate. Jake would return to Helen's class next week; Cheryl would take her place in her cosy kitchen.

Helen slid out of her seat, zig-zagged down the corridor to the buffet car, tripping over aisle bags and empty coffee cartons, through sliding doors and across the shifting join in the carriages which shook, creaked and threatened her feet. She stopped by the door, gazed through the window. The hurtling train was ripping the air apart between embankments and an endless border of Rose Bay Willow Herb swayed in its wake. She wondered how they held on. The train lurched and she ricocheted between walls. The doors to the buffet opened from the force and Helen darted through before they could close and trap her.

She placed a carton of coffee on Kath's crossword.

'Thanks.' Kath nodded towards a cool-bag on the luggage rack. 'What have you got in there?'

'Bread and butter puddings for my friend Isaac. And homemade jams, cakes. Stuff Tibby made for him. Don't look like that, Kath. He's an old man, not a lover.'

London teachers who supported the strike had offered accommodation to the women and met them at Kings Cross. Tomorrow delegates from various regions would present a petition to Downing Street and then gather at a number of locations for fund raising: Trafalgar Square, the Mall, Oxford Street, stations and market places across the city.

Once Helen had agreed where she would meet Kath the next morning, she took the overland train to Greenwich. Isaac expected her.

★ ★ ★

Dusk offered stillness, silence broken only by low voices from a neighbouring garden beyond Isaac's hedges. There was an enduring smell of barbecue smoke. Isaac lit a citron scented candle to keep away insects, but Helen was sceptical of its effectiveness, sure its sweetness would attract more than it deterred. They sat either side of a cane garden table, a bottle of red wine between them.

'Tell me then,' he said, 'what's happening in your world? I see the television news but would rather hear a firsthand account.'

Though glad to be reunited with Isaac, Helen had no stamina for a lengthy recount of recent weeks' events. 'It's not what it seems in the newspapers,' she said, flicking a midge away from her face. 'There are a few hotheads throwing stones. Mostly rebellious youth. But the majority are men like Pavel, fighting for jobs.'

'Monday's television was full of horrific scenes,' Isaac said. 'I suspect the event will lose the miners some support.'

She took a deep breath. She would have to defend Pavel. Isaac had only seen what the rest of the country had. Another television witness. 'You didn't see the results of men beaten by truncheons, Isaac.'

'The police say they were defending themselves.'

A white moth hovered above the candle, then fluttered across the lawn towards the light in the kitchen window.

'But what if the police charged first?' she said. 'What if the men were indirectly invited there, to be taken on, to be crushed? What if it was part of a Government plan to seize control, annihilate the unions and put down any opposition to their policies?'

Isaac frowned and leaned towards her, the yellowish veins in his temples throbbing in the candlelight. 'Then I would say we're in trouble, Helen. You're describing a conspiracy.'

She whispered, as if even the bushes and trees had ears. 'Weigh up the evidence. The police arrived in riot gear, with batons, shields, reinforcements on horseback. Prepared. But the pickets were dressed in jeans and tee shirts.'

Mention of Pavel seemed to stave off fatigue, strengthen her. She'd been called on to champion him. 'If some miners were less than political before the strike,' she said, 'they will certainly be political by the end of it. This is the same police force that protects the rights of the National Front to march.' Surely this would have resonance for Isaac.

'Yes,' he said. 'They can't win, can they? The police are damned if they do, damned if they don't. It's an unenviable job.'

'And what if there were men at Orgreave who were not police and not pickets?'

He shifted in the chair. 'Agents provocateurs? You're clearly convinced.'

Her recounts gained provenance as she spoke, her voice grew stronger, urgent. The stories she'd heard from Pavel, stories from men returning from picket lines across the region; stories passed on through networks and friendships formed among communities throughout the country. Recounted with belief: a picket smashed in the back with a fire extinguisher by a group of men in black unmarked boiler suits, for doing nothing more than being a spectator on a small picket line in the north east. Scurrilous slurs, goading, provocation. And her own experience of the wrecked pub.

'I know only too well what can happen,' Isaac said, 'when a uniformed group loses discipline, forgets its humanity and blames the job. Let's hope lessons will be learned before it's too late.'

She needed Isaac to believe, trust her accounts. If you were living in a battle zone you couldn't afford to be neutral. But this was London, and Isaac's impartiality forced her to reflect. While she needed him to understand the issues, she realised how embroiled she'd become. What had affected her more? Passion for the cause, or passion for Pavel? Could detachment from one undo the addiction to the other? 'On the other hand,' she said, 'Uncle Billy thinks the far left is using the strike for its own agenda and Pavel says some of the pickets would jump off Blackpool Tower if Scargill told them to.'

Isaac folded his hands on his lap. 'Mr Scargill is a powerful orator though I don't doubt his sincerity. I agree we should save mining communities but I'm naturally suspicious of orators. I've watched his gestures, listened to the tenure of his voice, its inflexions. The danger of the grand speech. The prime minister is a match for him.'

'Pavel says Scargill's right, that there's no other course of action than the strike.'

'It's a pity Mrs Thatcher has chosen to fight union power through the miners, though not surprising. A right wing government, a left wing union leadership, and the issue of pit closures sandwiched between the rhetoric.'

'She took on the steel workers first, let's not forget them,' Helen said. 'Destroyed communities are collateral damage for this government.'

Somewhere over the hedge a female voice – maybe that of a teenager – hummed the tune of the *Internationale*,' then giggled. A male voice laughed. Isaac cleared his throat. Chairs scraped on a patio. Dishes and glasses clinked, voices faded, a door closed.

'You mention Pavel frequently,' Isaac said. 'You've spoken of him before. An old friend if I remember?'

She had telephoned Isaac recently, spoken of her job and the support group but had not mentioned Pavel. 'His son's in my class,' she said. 'And I see him through my support work.'

Isaac looked bemused, quizzical. 'You don't have to tell me everything if you don't want to.'

Why should she lie? Isaac was a friend. 'It wasn't intentional but... we've become close.'

'In my experience affairs are rarely planned.' The furrows in his brow deepened in shadow. Weak flames flickered in the dregs of melting wax.

'Now I can't walk away,' she said, steeling herself for censure. None came.

'What will you do about Guy?'

'I'm meeting him tomorrow evening in the West End. He's taking me to dinner. We have a lot to discuss.'

'It will be an impossible situation if he hears you're sleeping with the enemy.'

'Do you mean *the enemy within*?'

Isaac pushed the cane chair away from the table, blew out the candle. 'I've made up the spare room for you. I'll say goodnight, Helen. Let's discuss this again before you leave.'

★ ★ ★

The women split into groups, their pitches chosen by the teachers' support group. Once equipped with buckets and signs Helen and Kath joined three London women and headed to a market in the East End where traders invited them into a clearing between stalls.

A man with a ruddy complexion dragged wooden crates from around the market, butting them edge to edge until he'd created a makeshift platform. Traders emerged from behind trestle tables, throwing handfuls of coins into the collection buckets. 'Let's start you off, girls.'

Helen had noticed a group of men chatting, sniggering, nodding towards them and now one of the men threw a tomato. 'Ask your fellers, girls: how would they like it?' Before the women could interpret the mood, they were covered in a hail of rotting fruit and vegetables. Smatterings of tomato skins and seeds ran down their hair and Helen reeled from the force of a lump of cucumber which hit her forehead, its slimy residue trickling down her nose.

Then a young man in a suit ran out from a nearby supermarket. 'You better come with me.' Eager to escape the growing mockery and missiles, the women followed him through a staff entrance and into a store room. At first, Helen was worried that this might be another ambush, but was reassured when he handed them paper towels and commandeered a girl unpacking boxes to organise a tray of tea. Once they were cleaned up and refreshed, the manager invited the women to place their buckets beyond the checkouts. 'You should be safer here.'

The collection was slow until an old lady, having paid for her shopping, pushed a trolley of cans towards Helen. 'My offering, dear,' she said. Then, as if to follow the woman's generosity, other customers tossed coins and notes into the buckets. Humbled, Helen recalled the tramp in Sheffield and her own naivety.

Having showered and changed in Greenwich and left her market clothes with Isaac and his washing machine, Helen caught a train into central London to meet Guy in Leicester Square. She was early. Another warm June evening unfolded. They had become the norm. She sat on a bench watching the bustle of theatre and cinema goers, tourists and lovers, listening to a busker entertaining with a squeeze box and a dancing puppet operated by his foot. Warmed by this cosmopolitan throng she realised how much she missed London.

A low sun dazzled and she shaded her eyes with her hand, but was startled by Guy looming above her, casting a shadow. 'You were miles away, darling,' he said. He pulled her to her feet, kissed her on both cheeks. She recoiled slightly. He smiled. 'I thought we'd go into China Town, like old times,' he said. 'Give market places a miss. At least you enjoy Chinese food.'

She cringed at the memory of their meal in the market place restaurant in Bickley, though she wondered if his reference was a pun. Did he know what had happened today? He seemed relaxed, looked handsome, younger in pale blue denim, a cream sweater slung across his shoulders. No one would have guessed his occupation. He hooked his arm through hers, leading her into China Town, past windows decked with red and gold lanterns, to a restaurant she didn't remember. Inside, the scarlet wallpaper was peeling at the edges, curling with age, a riot of fading golden dragons. The owner welcomed Guy, addressed him by name. Helen wondered if Guy had brought other women here since she'd left.

The heat intensified the smell of fried rice, chicken and plum sauce. They ordered sizzling beef, gingered pork and chop-suey; agreed to eat with chopsticks, chatted through amiable trivia. Safe ground. She remembered their early days in London when eating out in cheap restaurants was a common Saturday night jaunt, often after a theatre trip, and when she was thrilled by the prospect of a baby. Happier days.

Guy talked briefly about his committee work, told her how empty the apartment was without her. 'And Celia and Jack send their love. Did I mention Celia's pregnant?'

The news startled Helen. Guy's tone was goading, like a boast to heighten her pain, her sense of failure. She swallowed, smiled. 'That's great news,' she said. 'They must be delighted.'

'They might ask us to be Godparents.'

'They do know we're separated, don't they?' she said. 'You have told them?'

He poured the mineral water. 'So, when will you be coming home?'

'I might be expected to stay at school till the end of September. The teacher with the back problem may need more time than the Head first thought.'

'Will you be here for the summer holidays at least? I've had the apartment decorated. I think you'll like it.' It was difficult not to lose resolve under Guy's gaze. Why had she not told him she wouldn't be coming back at all? His eyes sparkled, his pupils were dilated. He seemed energised, yet on edge. 'You're not sure what you want are you, Helen?'

She put down the chopsticks, struggling to keep to her prepared speech. 'There's something you should know.'

Guy leaned back in his seat, folded his arms. 'I know all about Pavel Kowaleski if that's what you're about to tell me. Spare yourself the embarrassment of sordid details. I already have them documented.'

She felt sick. Her mouth was dry. She stood up. He grabbed her hand but she freed herself, told him she needed the bathroom. Before she could pick up her handbag she'd propped on the end of the table, he snatched it.

She leaned on the sink, gazed in the mirror. Her face had paled. What did he mean *documented*? If he hadn't kept her bag she could have escaped. She took a deep breath then opened the door to the dining room.

He held the chair for her as she sat down, smiled, nodded to the proprietor. The handbag was in place on the table; she dropped it by her feet. 'Disregard Pavel,' she said. 'We should be discussing our own relationship. I don't blame you for what's happened.'

'Don't patronise me, Helen.'

'When you and I met, we were both escaping. You wanted somebody you could mould. And I wanted to be protected, maybe reinvented. We deserved each other.'

His eyes flashed. He mimed slow applause. 'How long have you been rehearsing this?' His lip curled. 'Brave, I'll grant you.'

'You asked me here to discuss our situation. You said –'

'I found a poetry book lying around the apartment. You'd marked a page, bent one corner. An irritating habit. But let me quote. *"Then she pulled off her silk finished gown and put on hose of leather-O! The ragged, ragged rags about our door, she's gone with the wraggle taggle gypsies,O!"* That sums it up, doesn't it?'

'What do you mean? Don't be obscure.'

'You like poetry, don't you? It's anonymous verse, but clearly composed by a cuckold, betrayed by a wife attracted to a bit of rough. You want to resume a relationship with a low life. And what was Mr Kowaleski up to last week? Lobbing boulders I shouldn't wonder.'

'That's not true.'

'You told me he had a son. He's married. This whole debacle is about the excitement of forbidden sex.'

'You'd know all about that, not me. I didn't say I had a future with Pavel. I'm trying to be honest.'

He laughed. 'Honest? Stealing another woman's husband? Hypocrite.' His eyes softened, his voice took on a conciliatory tone. 'But you're right. I'm no example to be lecturing about fidelity.'

If she stood, she'd be off balance. He was ever the chameleon. 'Maybe I am a hypocrite,' she said. 'But I don't want to come back, regardless of Pavel. Can't you accept this is an opportunity? You could start again too.'

'How considerate,' he said. 'For God's sake be angry. That, I can cope with.'

'I lost my identity with you, Guy. Now I'm involved with the women's group, making my own decisions.'

'And a fine mess you're making of independence,' he said, tapping a chopstick on a glass.

'I don't want to cause you political embarrassment'.

'Generous. If your sordid affair becomes common knowledge, it will be too late. You're stabbing me in the back and twisting the knife.'

'It's not spite, believe me.'

'Doesn't your fling even things up? Let the man keep his wife and we can start afresh. Don't throw away ten years.'

She took the chopstick from him, laid it on the table. 'Pavel will probably never leave his wife. But that's no reason for you and me to stay together.'

He took her hand, ran a forefinger over her wedding ring. 'I'll never divorce you. I've finished with booze. There's no one else.'

'I'm glad. I'm sorry.'

'You can't be both.' He dropped her hand. 'Don't write us off, darling.' He crumpled his napkin.

Guy nodded to the waiter, called for the bill and paid in cash, tipping generously. 'Finish this senseless affair, Helen. When term ends I want you here in London. I need you. I refuse to give you up for a bloody miner!'

Come back. Prevent complications for Pavel. Slip back into Guy's life as if the strike hadn't awakened her sensibilities to injustice, her roots, the consequences of her husband's politics and her own hypocrisy.

He insisted on driving Helen to Greenwich. Pure Guy. Hauling her in, nothing too much trouble. The car's momentum pinned her to the seat as he accelerated from the car park. His hands trembled on the steering wheel, the muscles in his forearms flexed below the short sleeves of his summer shirt. He had tossed his sweater onto her lap as if to claim her, and she folded it, clutched it to her.

'I've had the second bedroom painted cream,' he said, 'stripped off the wallpaper clowns. We can always add a border of pink or blue rabbits or something, when the time comes. And it will come, Helen.' He turned, smiled. Was he serious? Or was it a sick joke? A wallpaper border of fluffy bunnies would make all the difference? Did he expect her to laugh? Was he unhinged? Her stomach churned as she thought of William. Her rehearsed speech had been useless, neutralised and now she was even more worried about Guy.

By the time she climbed into Isaac's spare bed, the memory of dripping tomatoes, the possibility of Guy losing his promotion prospects and the decreasing chances of Pavel offering her a future, rendered her sleepless for some time.

In the night she woke, remembering she had not told Guy about the false reporting of Orgreave or of the raid made by police in white shirts.

Chapter Twenty One

Sports Day

July 1984

Lundby South Yorkshire

Jake had been practising scales on his trumpet. His heavy school shoes thumped on the stairs. 'Is my kit ready, Dad? And my lunch box?'

The steam iron hissed. Pavel rubbed the metal sole with the dish cloth, removing the splashes of watery dirt that had spluttered through the holes in the base plate and threatened to soil his son's white polo shirt. He'd prepared the packed lunch, adding an extra carton of juice and the salt and vinegar crisps Jake had requested.

The strike had been a gift on three counts. It had given Pavel a taste of freedom above ground, returned Helen to Lundby and, since Pavel had spent more time at home, Jake had grown to depend on him. He folded the ironing board trying to ignore the nagging thought that he could not keep all three indefinitely.

It must have been midnight when Cheryl had crept into his bedroom. He'd been awake, mulling over possibilities, wondering when he'd find another opportunity to meet Helen. As Cheryl had drawn back the sheets, she'd whispered his name, kissed his shoulder. Pavel had feigned sleep. She'd shaken him gently and he'd turned, rubbing his eyes, offering a barely-awake, pained expression. 'Is something wrong with Jake?'

She knelt on the edge of the bed. 'Nothing's wrong, love. Move over.'

He turned his back on her, but undeterred, Cheryl slipped into bed beside him, wrapping her arm around his waist, one leg around his knees. He squirmed. She was intruding on Helen's space.

'I hate this deep freeze,' she said, nuzzling his neck.

He tensed. Things might have been different months ago, but not now. He couldn't fake desire for her when he had none. 'I'm sorry, Cheryl,' he said. 'I was asleep. Go back to bed. It's too late.' She would wonder if he meant too late tonight or too late forever. The mixed message was despicable, cowardly.

Buying time with ambiguity.

She'd backed off, flicking the sheet in his face, snatched up the spare pillow, using it to beat him around the head. 'Pig.' He could tolerate a truncheon of feathers. It was worth it for a night's sleep.

When had this cruel streak arisen? Since Orgreave? Was he trying to drive Cheryl away by making her hate him? If so it was self-defeating: if she left she would take Jake with her.

'I hate you,' she said, slamming the door.

'Shh. You'll wake Jake.'

He poured tea. Cheryl's eyes were red.

'Would you like a cup before you leave?' he said. She had refused breakfast.

'No. I'll get one at work.'

He wouldn't allow her to spoil his mood, even if he deserved her contempt. It was Jake's sports' day. A double pleasure: watch Jake, see Helen again. And tomorrow? He was a volunteer on Jake's class trip to the sea-side.

He congratulated himself. A single investment of his time would allow him to be with the two people he loved most.

Cheryl collected her cardigan from the kitchen chair. Jake was in the hall, packing his school bag. 'I'll try and leave work early, Jake, to watch the sports. Can't promise,' she said.

'It's okay, Mum, Dad will be there.'

'Of course. Good old Dad,' she muttered so that only Pavel heard. 'By the way, I'm taking Jake away again for two weeks in August. So you can rot here on your own.' Pavel stood at the sink, gazing out of the window. She hadn't noticed the roses. He'd cut five, added them to the one Helen had left on his pillow and popped them in a jug on the window sill. The single stem would have been conspicuous.

Nothing could dampen his optimism for long. Now that he knew her school holiday intentions, a plan took shape.

★ ★ ★

The school field thronged with spectators: more fathers this year, the crowd topped up by striking miners and their families. School sports were free and the weather glorious.

Struggle. Friendships. Loyalties. Helen. Jake. Pavel would always remember this summer's weather: blue skies unfolding like an album of picture postcards, page after page of picnic perfect days that belied strike bleak hardships. His son grew taller almost weekly: ever lengthening legs, sunshine in his freckles and playing in his hair.

Jake was warming up at the end of the track, waiting to start the sprint final. On the other side of the field, but still in his eye line, Pavel spotted Kath sharing a joke with the Headmaster. Helen was ready to blow the starting whistle, Roly was setting out drinks in plastic cups, and even

Coker was arm in arm with his wife, Susan. An interlude, a ceasefire.

Pavel took his camera from its case, snapped the scene. He would like this photograph to look back on, to define a moment in time, a glimmer of summer optimism in the coal black gloom of a strike that seemed endless.

It was the last race of the afternoon and Jake set off, arms pumping, legs stretching long and straight with each powerful stride, finally thrusting his domed chest into the finishing tape, a fraction behind the winner. Pavel cheered with unashamed pride, punching the air like an Olympic athlete winning gold. Jake continued his run till he reached his father on the side lines and Pavel swung him around. Then Cheryl arrived. Pavel bit his lip, looked on as she hugged and kissed her son. Their son.

The headmaster concluded the afternoon's events by shouting his appreciation – through a megaphone – to parents and friends of the school; but the crowd chattered over his tin-can voice. The field cleared fast, a few fathers, including Pavel, staying behind to help collect chairs and equipment.

Cheryl called to him. 'I'll take Jake home.'

'Fine,' he said. 'I'll follow soon.'

He lingered, scooping up hoops, stacking cones, folding skipping ropes, until he was the last parent on the field. Then he headed for the school building. Inside Jake's classroom he found Helen stacking chairs onto desks and picking up sports kit, shorts and tee shirts discarded by careless children who'd hurried off to meet their parents.

The only way to grab her attention would be to help her with the tidying He'd had no chance to speak to her since her trip to London. Pavel picked up a chair in each hand, followed her around the room. 'Cheryl says she's taking Jake away again in August.'

'Perhaps you should go with them.'

'I thought you and me... maybe spend some time together.'

'Why?'

The classroom door opened and Roly appeared.

'Hear that, Roly? Helen says the coach will leave at nine prompt tomorrow. We'll be on time won't we?'

Roly patted Pavel's shoulder. 'I'm looking forward to it.'

'Your friend Coker's coming too,' Helen said. The men grunted.

'I'm walking your way, Pav.' Roly said.

Pavel hesitated. 'So we'll see you tomorrow Helen.' She called goodbye from the stock-cupboard, her voice vague, disinterested. What had he done wrong?

The two friends set off down the school drive.

'Don't say it, Roly.'

'Say what?'

'I know what you're about to say, so don't. I've already heard it.'

'I'm saying nothing.'

'Good. Keep it that way.'

They ambled along the street in companionable silence.

★ ★ ★

East Yorkshire Coast

The children were engrossed in building chalk sculptures on the beach, arranging the rocks like Inuit stacks or laying them flat, designing butterflies, pictures of spaceships and 2D fire engines. Pavel turned to face the sea, watching Roly and Kath paddling with four children. It was not easy to hold a conversation with Helen without eye contact. If he stretched out his hand he might just touch her. She stood a few yards to his left, supervising the children, making sure they didn't throw stones or trap fingers between the rocks.

'Second week in August,' he said, without looking at her. 'Cheryl's taking Jake to her mother's again.'

'Convenient.'

He moved closer. 'Do you remember the chalk I carried home for you from this beach?'

'I'm surprised you remember.'

'I still get back pain from it'.

At last. She laughed. 'I had that rock for years,' she said. 'Guy... dropped it. It smashed.'

'I'll find you another... if you'll come away with me.'

Mr. Read blew the whistle to mark the end of the sculpture competition, summoning Coker to help him judge the winners and present the bucket and spade prize. Coker protested he knew nothing about art and seemed so suddenly twitchy that Pavel almost felt sorry for him.

'Come on, Dad,' Jake shouted. 'Take your trainers off. Come and paddle.'

'We'll talk later, Helen,' Pavel said.

Trousers rolled up to his knees, Pavel stepped gingerly over the pebbles, dipping his toes into icy shallows, the water sludgy where Jake had kicked at worm casts beneath the puddles. On the day trip with Helen, so many years before, the water had been clear; everything had been clear. Pavel had been a naïve nineteen year old, totally unaware of the undercurrents, the tidal waves of a future that would knock him flat. And now that he'd picked himself up, steadied himself, he realised how much since then the waters had been muddied.

★ ★ ★

'The wind was howling like an injured wolf.' Pavel cupped his hand to his mouth, howled, then swept his arms from side to side. 'And coal was strewn all along this shoreline, as the colliers – the boats that carried the coal from Newcastle – were tossed around, smashed into pieces, even though sailors had always called this area, *The Bay of Safety.*'

He'd gathered the children into three rows on the sand and they gazed out to sea open mouthed at his tale of a local shipwreck. 'It was in February 1871 and every year since...' The school staff and helpers were sitting on the sea wall, listening to Pavel's story and drinking coffee from plastic cups which Roly had bought from a nearby kiosk

'Is he making it up?' Roly said.

'Of course not,' Helen said. 'He loves History.'

'How do you know he loves History?' Coker asked.

'He mentioned it. On Jake's open-night.'

Coker grinned. 'Of course he did.'

'He's certainly a natural,' Mr. Read said. 'An excellent story teller.'

'Anytime soon,' Kath whispered, 'he might need to be.'

★ ★ ★

Coker slid the bolt into place and pressed his ear to the cubicle door, closer to the conversation. Roly and Pavel had been asked to accompany the boys to the public toilets, presumably keep them safe from the possibility of lurking strangers, but the boys were now lining up outside and the two men were left standing side by side at the urinals. Coker smiled. They hadn't noticed him sneak in. Didn't know he was listening. So much for guardians of child safety, they couldn't even watch their own backs.

'So I'm going away for a few days.' Pavel's voice.

'Do you good to get away with Cheryl and Jake. I'll be happy to hold the fort.' Roly's voice.

Coker tried not to laugh. Lying to Roly? Easy to guess what Pavel had in mind.

A gush of water muffled the subsequent conversation but Coker heard the gist. Though the talk was garbled it became clearer as the two men neared the exit then faded amid seagull squawk and kids' blather. He waited a minute, slid the bolt. He washed his own hands before he left: you never knew who had touched what in a public convenience.

The last time he'd earned his forty quid, he'd been told his services were no longer required. Something had made Mrs Eagleton's *friendship* less of a priority. Coker didn't know why he was relieved duty, but was glad he was no longer under obligation to Volvo Man. Maybe Mrs Eagleton's husband was dumping her after all, or maybe Tory boy would put an end to his wife's frolics, drag her home at the end of term. Though, if Coker had guessed correctly about Kowaleski's present intentions, her departure didn't sound imminent. It didn't matter. He had other plans.

He'd thought of it months ago, even made a joke of it to Pavel. His memory of it was clear. It had been the final straw: the comment that had caused Pavel almost to break Coker's jaw. It would make good reading. He'd drop in at the phone box later.

★ ★ ★

Lundby

Emptied of children, plastic sacks and sick buckets, the coach drove off. Helen waited with Mr Read until every child had been collected by their parents. Cheryl had been first in the queue of anxious mothers and had taken Jake home, but Pavel had stayed behind as porter for bats and balls, left over coats and lunchboxes. Mr Read locked the school doors.

'I'll walk along with you, Mrs Eagleton, help you carry that bag,' Pavel said. 'Looks heavy.'

Mr Read took his leave, thanked them both for their help and drove away, signalling a last goodnight with a flash of headlights.

'So, where are you taking me, if I say yes?'Helen asked.

'Somewhere that nobody in Lundby would visit in August.'

'You can't pay for a hotel, so let me. I've got savings.'

'I can't even pay the gas bill. I'll owe you. Consider it a loan and I promise I'll pay off my debt as soon as the strike's over... along with the rest.'

'No need. Don't give me the old *I can't let a woman pay* routine.

Uncle Billy's house was a few hundred yards from the school. Pavel carried the bag with the rock he'd collected. 'Better take care of this better than the first. Consider this mark two.' He laughed. 'Cherish it. The only rock I can afford.'

'I'll try.' She remembered the night of their miners' trip to the beach, his boyish proposal, her childish teasing.

He kissed her once and walked away. She ran upstairs, positioned the chalk on a lacy doyley on her dressing table and watched from the window until Pavel was out of sight. Would he cherish her more than he had the first time?

She drew the curtains and undressed in the dark.

Chapter Twenty Two

Quick Sands

August 1984

The Northwest

The hotel was a stone inn dating back to the eighteenth century. Its inglenook fireplaces, mullion windows and paintings of sailing ships suggested smugglers, pirates, the press-gang era. But from a leaflet Helen found in reception she learned that its history was rooted in accommodation for cockle merchants and industrial magnates. The inn had offered a nineteenth century getaway from the smoke and disease addled cities of Manchester and Liverpool. Perhaps a hideaway for the occasional Victorian mistress?

A faint odour of shellfish and seaweed seeped through an open window. She took in the view: to the north mauve peaks punctured a band of cloud above the Lake District while to the west – at the end of the promenade – the river flowed into Morecambe bay. A train rattled across the nearby viaduct on its way up the coast to Barrow and Whitehaven. The tide was low, water trickling in narrow channels between trenches of mud and whorls of sand. There was no one on the beach, if you could call it a beach: a strip of faded turf, and nearer the path, sparse tufts of marram grass sprouting from dusty earth. A rowing boat was moored on the shingle and in the shallows a Labrador barked and splashed.

It was liberating to be in an unfamiliar village, a place where no-one knew her, where she had no history and there were no expectations. It dissolved guilt, shame, as if she'd lost her memory and with it all responsibility. Surely this was why Pavel had invited her here. Somewhere they didn't have to look over their shoulders, somewhere they could recapture the essence of their relationship, make plans for the future.

To discover a British seaside resort without neon-lit arcades, rock emporiums and fortune tellers, was refreshing. No candy floss or ice-cream kiosks here. Just a row of shops: a tearoom, a grocery store, an antique dealer's and a bakery. A rag-tag of fishermen dotted the promenade waiting for the tide to turn; car doors, boots and rear hatches left open allowing easy access to bait, sandwiches and flasks of tea. Across the road a concrete pier jutted into the river and an elderly couple on a bench shared binoculars, observing oystercatchers and herons on the far bank: birds waiting for a passing meal, patient and still as garden ornaments.

The oversized four-poster left little room for opening wardrobe doors. Built into one corner was a cramped bathroom with a sink, toilet and a shower cubicle which creaked from the footfall on the floor above. Pavel lay on top of the bedspread; his eyes were closed though Helen knew he was awake. Constantly checking the rear view mirror and with knuckles white on the steering wheel, he had raced up the M6 with hardly a word.

'How's the headache now?' she asked; his forehead had smoothed though his face was pale and drawn.

'Easing.'

After delivering Cheryl and Jake to Skegness, he'd driven back to Lundby to collect Helen then headed north without stopping. She imagined the feeling in the pit of his stomach as he waved goodbye to Jake.

'You look exhausted, love' she said. 'You sleep and I'll read for a while; I'll wake you when I can't wait any longer.'

He opened one eye. 'Wait for what?'

'Food. I'm starving. Aren't you?'

He joined her at the window, pointing across the river. 'Over there. See? Coniston Fells. If we climb the hill behind the village, we'll have a panoramic view.' His arms encircled her waist, his chin rested on her shoulder. 'Glad you agreed to come with me.'

'I didn't take too much persuading.'

'Look. I know things are difficult and we can't see each other much. But I've no intention of letting you go again. I promise to sort things with Cheryl. I'm sick of having to stand in the playground with the likes of Coker, watching you through the classroom window, and making fake pleasantries when I come to collect Jake, "Yes Mrs Eagleton, no Mrs Eagleton." When all I want is to burst in and...' He turned her around to face him. 'Take you there and then. Right there on the desk.'

'After everyone's left I hope. Which desk?'

'What?'

'Which desk? Only if it was mine I'd need prior notice. It's usually full of staplers, scissors, craft knives, glue guns, guillotines and –'

'Any bloody desk.' He raised her hands to his lips, kissed her fingertips. 'Glad you've taken that flashy rock off your finger.' The diamond engagement ring and wedding band she had left in the dressing table drawer in Lundby.

He fumbled in the back pocket of his jeans.' Look what I've brought with me.' It was the sapphire engagement ring she had jammed on his finger, the night of Orgreave, the night she had left him sleeping. 'Wear it.' He placed it on her third finger. 'So what do you think of this place, Mrs Strike?'

'What?'

'That's what I signed us in as: Mr and Mrs Strike.'

'You are joking.'

'Nice touch I thought.'

'You're bonkers.'

'So... what do you think? Of this place?'

'Love it. It's peaceful. How did you find it?'

'Scouts. Years ago, we camped in the Lakes. On the way back we called here to join a sponsored hike across the bay. There's a guide by Royal Appointment, the only one qualified to lead walking parties. Morecambe Bay's full of quick sands. Notorious.' He nuzzled her neck. 'One false step, you're sucked in.'

'I was hoping we'd be able to swim or at least lie on the beach, sunbathe for a couple of days.'

'Beach?' he laughed. 'Mudflats you mean. Sunsets are legendary though.'

'Shame. Fancied a spot of night swimming. Naked bodies in a warm ocean.'

He lifted her, carried her towards the bathroom. 'Actually, I think my headache's gone. Scout handbook: When a warm ocean is unavailable, you have to make do with a shower.'

'Just do one thing for me.'

'Anything.'

'Don't mention the strike, Mr Strike.'

The menu in the dining room boasted local delicacies: salt-marsh lamb and Morecambe Bay shrimp. Helen sat on an oak settle facing the bar where Pavel was ordering dinner and chatting with a stranger: a man in a green quilted waistcoat, khaki chinos, a round jowly face obscured by over-sized spectacles.

'Who's that?' she asked when Pavel returned with drinks.

'He was asking if we'd caught the sunset yet. Says it will be worth watching tonight. I heard him tell the barman that he's a photographer. From a nature magazine. I think that's what he said.'

'Really? He looks a bit shifty to me.'

'And you said I was uptight. Relax. He's only interested in the flora and fauna. There are deer in the woods and some rare species of wild flowers. The barman said to look out for giant marine fossils on the rocks.'

'Photographer or not, he keeps glancing at us.'

'Not surprised. You are a bit fossil faced yourself tonight, Helen.' He leaned in and kissed her.

She'd felt safe in the bedroom, cocooned by the four-poster drapes and Pavel's arms. The man's glances alarmed her; she remembered Guy's comment. He had Pavel documented, he'd said. But surely, Guy would have nothing to gain from having them trailed. Still, she felt uneasy. The man finished his beer and left the bar with a cursory nod in their direction.

'What else did he say?' she said.

'I was only talking to him for a minute.'

'I should have mentioned it to you before...' The waitress delivered plates of cod, sautéed potatoes, carrots and freshly picked samphire.

'What... you don't like carrots?'

'About Guy. When I met him in London... He knows about us.'

'You told him?'

'Someone else already had. He insisted I should forget you and come home at the end of the summer.'

'I hope you told him where to −'

'He wouldn't accept any notion of divorce; brushed it aside. Guy frightens me, Pavel. He's... not right.'

'Bloody arrogant you mean. Bloody cheek...' He stopped. 'Let's not talk about Guy. Let's eat.'

'So, you think the man's genuine then?' she said. 'No questions about us?'

Pavel rolled his eyes. 'Just chit-chat. He asked how long we were staying, but that's all.'

The sunset did not disappoint: bands of lilac and lavender, gold and crimson, reflected on the sea in perfect mirror symmetry.

'It's breathtaking,' Helen said. 'I'm touched. You organised this just for me.'

'I do my best,' Pavel straightened his tie. It was his token 'dressing for dinner' tie he'd said, packed just for her. He'd joked it was the only one he owned.

'I've never seen a sunset like this before. Like a picture postcard. Imagine night swimming beneath that.'

'Yeah. Perfect − if you're suicidal.'

He drew her towards the railings overlooking the beach. 'If I gave Jake a packet of felt tips and asked him to paint a sunset, this is what it would look like. Unreal.'

There it was: a small wrinkle of worry on his forehead. At the first opportunity Jake had appeared, his presence etched on Pavel's face in both thought and resemblance.

The bay was flooded though they'd missed the siren that the barman informed them warned of the tidal bore.

'He reckons the bore moves faster than a man can run,' Pavel said. 'Course, the barman's never been on a picket line.' He laughed. 'He should see Roly with a copper on his tail.'

Jake, Roly. Who next?

'You'd expect *nature man* to be out taking advantage of the view,' she said. 'He recommended it. Isn't that what he came for?'

Pavel looked over his shoulder, glanced along the promenade. The worry line vanished as quickly as it had appeared. He grinned. 'No. Definitely not here. Think we're safe, unless that fisherman has a lens hidden in the end of his rod.'

'Very funny.'

'Did you know Robert the Bruce crossed the sands in 1322, on his way to raid Lancaster?'

'How did you know that?' She suddenly remembered the books in his bedroom in Lundby.

'I read it in the leaflet we picked up in reception. You would have known, if you'd bothered to read beyond the first paragraph.'

'Your fault; you distracted me. I wonder if Robert the Bruce lost any men.'

It was difficult to imagine that beneath the bay's millpond surface and its nursery-rhyme-book sky someone could be drowned, dragged down to the sea bed by powerful currents, swallowed by liquid sands. 'The river seems to be flowing in both directions,' she said. 'As if in the middle the tide's coming in, but flowing out near the banks. Strange. Like an illusion.'

'Talking of illusions, watch.' And within a few seconds the sun sank below the horizon, so quickly that she almost expected to hear a hiss of steam.

After breakfast they climbed the steep hill behind the village until they reached a stone table etched with a map of the vista: the bay, the seaside town across the river, the fells and peaks, each named, each shape on the map matched to the landscape. Pavel had brought a small pair of binoculars which he looped over Helen's head.

'Pity we can't stay longer. We could have taken the ferry to the Isle of Man. Three days is not long enough to do justice to the area.'

Skirting a meadow they stopped to consult a ragged wildflower pocket book Pavel had uncovered at the back of the car's glove compartment: the purples of thistle, bellflowers and crane's-bill reared jewelled heads above the grass while above them buzzards circled. At the bottom of the hill a narrow lane led between a field of sheep and a farmyard, down curving steps to a deserted beach.

Pavel pulled a cagoule from his rucksack and spread it across the pebbles, took out two packs of sandwiches, cans of coke and a newspaper he had bought from a shop near the inn. While he skimmed the headlines, Helen set out paper serviettes she'd pilfered at breakfast.

'Would you believe it? The government's announced it's prepared to spend "unlimited amounts" to defeat the miners,' he said. 'They think it's, quote: "a worthwhile investment for the good of the nation."' He stuffed the newspaper back in the rucksack. 'When will people realise the uneconomic pits theory's a smokescreen? A complete lie.'

'I thought we'd agreed on no-strike conversation.'

'I know but... I feel rotten about leaving Roly in charge. Bad enough I've let him think I'm in Skegness with Cheryl and Jake. He assumed that's where I'd be and I didn't set him straight.'

Roly, Cheryl, Jake. Hat trick.

'I'm sure Roly can cope. Tibby and Uncle Billy believe I'm visiting Isaac. You're not the only one making sacrifices.

Perhaps we should keep notes on the weather forecasts for the East Coast and London, co-ordinate our lies.'

'I'm sorry, Helen, but I hate lying.'

'You think I like it?' She threw down her sandwich and jumped up. 'This was your idea remember. Nothing and nobody could intrude on us, you said.'

'Where are you going? Sit down. Eat your sandwich. Don't get huffy.'

'The sandwich is full of sand.'

The tide was out. The bay had drained and the mud flats stretched so far there was no sign of the sea except in muddy pools. A few feet ahead a piece of blue nylon rope, a buckled petrol can and a broken kitchen stool lay washed up on a sandbank. On the horizon a black speck appeared to be travelling south towards Lancaster. It was probably a coastguard vehicle. She didn't want to ask Pavel for the binoculars so she narrowed her eyes, imagining the silhouette of Robert the Bruce's army crossing the bay and wondering if, faced with quicksand and fear of drowning, any of the soldiers had been tempted to desert. But then wasn't it Robert the Bruce who'd watched the spider weaving its web? *Try, try, try again.*

Startled by a heavy splash, she turned, expecting to find an animal, maybe a large sea bird or a stray dog flopping into a puddle, but there was nothing but furrows, whole wedges of mud liable to break off and crash into trenches at any time. Like small glaciers calving in the Arctic Ocean, the sands collapsed without warning. She kicked off her sandals and walked out further, her feet making imprints, her toes squelching.

The moan of the siren was low at first then rose to a high pitch: a long haunting howl like an air raid siren she'd heard on war films set in the blitz, made all the more eerie as it echoed between river bank and headland. If they'd wandered any further down the coast, they might not have heard it at all.

'Hear the siren?' Pavel shouted. 'You'd better come back.' Behind her, tiny streams had converged forming a channel, fast flowing northwards towards the mouth of the river, already separating her from Pavel. 'There's plenty of time, surely,' she said.

'No there isn't. You'll be stranded. The sea floods the perimeter of the bay before the bore rushes in over the flats behind you. Come on. You can paddle across. It's still shallow. I promise I won't mention the strike again.'

'*Don't mention the war,*' she muttered, reclaiming her sandals.

Ashamed of her petulance and keen to avoid a row she rolled up her jeans and paddled into the stream but, half-way across, the sand beneath gave way so that she lost her footing and fell onto her side, soaking her shirt. Pavel took off his trainers and waded in, offering his hand in rescue. She gripped it, dragged him down beside her. He rolled onto his back, gasping from the shock of cold water.

'Now look what you've done,' he said, sitting up and wiping salt water from his eyes. When he leant over to kiss her, his face slid along her cheek, as it had last night in the shower, warm water cascading over their heads. No space between them, wet skin on wet skin, so close he stole her breath.

They splashed each other for a few minutes, laughing, then snatching up their belongings they stumbled across the shingle to a patch of dry grass where they lay hand in hand for a few moments, backs soaking up the sun.

'If I wasn't so wet I'd fall asleep,' she said. She couldn't remember enjoying reckless fun with Guy. Even when they were first married, they had never abandoned common sense, behaved like teenagers, paid no heed to decorum or laughed each other into bed.

'Think we'd better go back,' Pavel said. 'Don't know how we'll explain the state we're in to the landlady.'

'Who cares?'

They clambered over a limestone pavement, slimy from lichen the colour of ochre and from green weed which clung to its clinks and grikes, then scrambled up the cliffs to join the coastal path that would lead them to the village. Mid-climb they paused to look back at the incoming tide. They could see the crest of the bore gaining momentum, sweeping the sands. Perhaps they had been in more danger than she'd thought.

At the top of the shallow cliff they came across an elderly man who was sitting on a bench, stroking an ancient-looking springer spaniel. The dog gazed at his owner with adoration, panting in the heat. From this position the man must have seen everything. He smiled then shuffled to the end of the bench to make space for them.

'Here. Sit down in the sun. Dry off a bit. You pair were having a fine old time down there, weren't you?' He nudged the dog with his knee. 'Budge up, Rory. Let the young lady sit down.'

'Better not. We have to get back to our hotel,' she said, holding the cagoule across her chest in case the water had made her shirt transparent. 'We fell over.'

'I saw you, you daft beggars.' The old man laughed. 'Your friend captured it all on his camera.'

Pavel took Helen's hand. 'Friend?'

The man took a bottle of water and a plastic bowl from a bag and set them on the ground. 'Too hot for my old lad today,' he said, pouring the dog a drink.

'You were saying – our friend,' Pavel said.

'I don't let him loose on the sands now. I can't chase him like I used to and he won't always come back if he's on a scent.'

'What friend?'

'Loyal through to his bones though, aren't you old feller?'

'What did our friend look like?'

'Aye. The chap with the big specs. Helluva piece of equipment he's got. Zoom an' all.'

'Sure he wasn't photographing the bore?' Pavel said.

'Well that as well, I suppose. I asked him what he was doing like, and he said you'd laugh when you saw yourselves.'

'We'd better catch up with him then,' Helen said. 'Nice to meet you.'

They set off, half running, half walking, Helen following Pavel on the narrow path, reflecting how everything could change in a heartbeat, how a promised three night idyll could shrink to a few snatched hours as furtive and illicit as any previous tryst.

The spaniel barked and the old man shouted, 'Be careful now. You don't want to be slipping onto them rocks. A hiker was killed down there a few year ago.'

'Okay,' Pavel shouted, showing no signs of slowing.

'Don't run too fast,' Helen said. 'He's right. This path's dangerous.'

'I'm a dead man already.'

By the time Pavel returned from settling their bill, Helen had packed.

'Our *friend* checked out half an hour ago; been *called back to London unexpectedly* he told the staff. Landlord thinks he's a journalist. Spotted a union card when the man opened his wallet to pay – in cash, of course. And how's this for imagination? A comedian. He registered as Arthur Thatcher.'

'I can't think Guy's responsible,' Helen said. 'If news of us leaks it could ruin his promotion chances.'

'Then who else?'

She zipped up Pavel's holdall and shut the lid on her suitcase. 'Who could be so malicious and vindictive? What would they have to gain?'

Pavel flitted about the room checking they'd left nothing in the bathroom, the chest of drawers, the wardrobe. 'Who's been sniffing around us recently with his special brand of caustic wit?' He picked up their luggage, flung the rucksack across his shoulder. 'Who causes mayhem whenever he so much as breathes?'

'I'm not following.'

'Who's behind this? I think I could hazard a guess.'

Chapter Twenty Three

Deserters

September 1984

Lundby Edge Colliery South Yorkshire

What was real, what was illusion? Drifting in and out of sleep had left Pavel confused. He couldn't shake bad dreams off easily, memories would plague him, haunt and distract for the rest of the day. He sat up in bed, exhausted, an image lingering of Helen floating across the sea, to the horizon. In his nightmare he'd tried to call out, swim after her, but fingers strangling him had robbed him of speech, sucked the breath from him while a shadowy presence – some beast he couldn't visualise – kneeled on his chest. Though he had no mental picture of the monster, he could still taste the fear.

It was a common nightmare: trying to reach a destination but getting nowhere. You didn't need to be a shrink to analyse it. But then Jakub had appeared. Pavel had hugged him, felt the bones of him, solid and real and the leather jacket as smooth and pliable as Pavel's own which he could see hanging from the back of a bedroom chair. The beast-like shadow had wrapped tendrils around Pavel and imprisoned him and Pavel had watched helpless as Jakub screeched off into the fog. The throb of a motorbike engine, his brother's voice. Then a thumping headache and cramp in his legs as he woke, well before the five a.m. alarm on his bedside clock.

He rolled back the sheet, reached for his jacket, rubbed the leather against his bristly cheek. Nightmares depressed him. And today was a picketing day. Bad enough, without an infestation of ghostly creatures crawling through his brain like cockroaches across an ash tip. He decided to wear his leather jacket, hoping to remember how holding Jakub and feeling his warmth had brought his brother back – if only for a second. Maybe Jakub could help him shake off the mood.

And there was the argument he'd had with Cheryl to consider. She'd reminded him that she'd had to buy Jake's new school uniform for the autumn term and that there were gas and electricity bills outstanding; the telephone had been cut off for non-payment. The *final humiliation* she called it. Despite hiding behind a Sunday newspaper, he couldn't avoid the issue. She had a point.

'What's more important, providing for your son or this stupid strike? Go back to work for God's sake. Other men are.'

The Sunday paper – his regular check. Each week he'd scrutinised the gossip columns, loitering in the newsagents, flicking through an assortment of tabloids.

'I'm no scab, Cheryl. I'm not weakening.' The word weakening inflamed the patch on his neck. Roly should have been voted picket coordinator. Roly had more balls for the job.

If she thought having her telephone conversations cut was humiliating, how would she react when she found out about Helen? If he told her now, Cheryl would leave. She'd already announced Lundby was *a godforsaken village*. Who could blame her if she took Jake from him? The way Pavel had behaved towards her – his indifference, his cold-blooded plotting to be with Helen – shamed him.

He lifted the jacket from the chair, ran his hands down the sleeves. Scabs would be arriving at work at six. A mass picket was expected. Home match this time. Confronting scabs and police, or Cheryl? Aggravation either way. He examined his face in the mirror as he shaved, avoiding looking into his own eyes.

There'd be a few miserable buggers on the green battle bus, shrinking behind the wire over the windows. The papers reported there'd been more since Thatcher's Hatchet-Man Macgregor had offered them a five per cent pay rise to return to work. What would her next move be?

He rinsed the soap from his face, held the towel against his cheeks for a few seconds.

Pavel detested scabbing. Was it cowardice, nagging wives or fear of debt that drove these men back to work? The brass neck of it. Turning their backs on their mates. How did they expect a settlement when they were weakening the cause? And when the men who'd sacrificed their families — all of them blokes knee-deep in debt — when they'd secured the pits and jobs, what would the scabs do then? Take the benefits? The word *scab* tripped off the tongue more easily these days. He'd sacrificed too much to let cowards beat him into submission.

He breathed into the towel, sniffed. His morning breath was stale and sour.

He harboured a secret notion that the strike could already be lost. Since Orgreave bitterness had escalated. He cleaned his teeth with extra vigour. Both pickets and the bloody police had declared a war that had little to do with the original cause. He pulled on a tee shirt and jeans ran downstairs.

Defeatist talk, Roly would say. He zipped up his jacket and stepped out into an empty street.

As usual pickets had arrived from all over the region but the mood was different. Banter was absent. Local picketing had been fairly good-humoured so far, apart from Orgreave. Bad feeling had been aimed mainly at the Nottinghamshire men for forming their own union and defying the strike. But there was the issue of the police road blocks. (So much for freedom. Barriers worthy of East Berlin on the Nottinghamshire border.) Coker had his success stories of conning his way through – but these mainly involved scumbag tales of sex with sympathetic women rather than strategic victories.

'They know how to look after their visitors, show proper hospitality,' he'd said with his usual brand of lying sleaze.

Coker fed on weakness – evil bastard – and had soon recognised Pavel's weakness was Helen.

Pavel raised the collar on his jacket. He hadn't spoken to her since their return to Lundby, his only acknowledgement of her was a brief nod, a hint of a smile through a classroom window. 'Keep a low profile,' he'd told her, though any difference it would make now was negligible. He should have made a decision sooner. She'd seemed more worried about humiliating Billy and Tibby than consequences for herself.

There'd be familiar faces on the work's bus and he knew some of them well. Names were whispered, passed around with a handful of chocolate bars and a few bittersweet cigarettes. The nights were darker earlier, September mornings sharper, and the men felt the chill keenly, especially after the recent hot summer. Someone had lit a brazier by the pit entrance and Pavel stood by it, knowing it would be a focal meeting point for his own men, though there were too many pickets to share the heat.

Younger lads — he spotted Gus and Swannie among them — had been collecting firewood from the woods lining the lane and a pile of logs was stacked at the edge of the path into the pit yard. As autumn approached strikers would need to heat their homes, light their fires, and with no coal to burn they'd be forced to switch off the central heating. And there'd be no money to run the second hand portable heaters that some of them had bought, hoping it might be cheaper if they kept the heat to one room. The bottled gas still had to be paid for. Pavel had warned Cheryl he'd have to chop down the wooden fence in the back garden and burn it, before somebody else did. He'd better keep an eye on the rabbit hutch.

Men were hauling branches across the lane to form a barrier against the inevitable convoy of police vans. Before long this ancient woodland he'd loved as a child would be decimated by winter's necessity. He scanned the crowd for familiar faces. He'd made a few friends over the last six months, meeting on various picket lines. Good mates.

Chipper as ever Roly arrived, rubbing his hands together as he tried to muscle into the group around the brazier. Roly's daughter Jen was leaving for university soon and Roly was rightly proud of her but he wouldn't be proud of his trusted picket coordinator when he found out about Helen. Pavel would have to tell him soon, before a Sunday paper did. And he really did intend to tell Cheryl. As soon as —

'Didn't expect this, Pav,' Roly said, abandoning any attempt at warming his hands when he noticed Pavel. 'How many do you reckon?'

There were already hundreds of police and pickets packed in the narrow road that was little more than a country lane.

'More than we estimated. Roly, I know this might not be the right time but I need to tell you something before anybody else does. It's important.'

A roar and a crowd surge took Pavel by surprise, drowning hopes of confession. 'Here we go,' Roly shouted. 'Watch yourself, lad.'

Police in riot gear advanced as two transit vans, each with wings fashioned from perspex shields, swept the men from the edges of the lane, making way for the battle bus to deliver the scab contractors to the pit. The brushwood barricade proved flimsy and police vehicles crossed it without hindrance, branches splintering beneath tyres.

The chanting rose to a crescendo. 'Scabs, scabs!'

Foot soldiers from the riot squad marched around the pickets until the men were outflanked, as if sandwiched between two armies. Pavel teetered on the front line, straining against the crush. Almost face to face with shield and helmet he feared he'd be swallowed, suffocated.

'Pavel, Pavel.' The shouting came from in front of him, not from his own men. He slipped, slithered to within an inch of a uniform.

'Pavel. Over here.'

He scanned visors seeking recognition but the faces were indistinguishable. A blur of scowls and grimaces. Then a blow to his neck propelled him forward and a sharp pain coursed through the back of his skull. Marbles were dropping like giant hail stones. A disembodied voice called through a megaphone. A plea for reason, calm, 'a ceasefire of all missiles.'

Swannie shouted at a few lads who were brandishing catapults. 'The gentleman means, "leave it out, you bleedin' idiots."' But Swannie's was one voice among a thousand and a ripple of laughter was lost above a sea of bobble hats and helmets.

Behind uniformed lines, a television crew had unloaded equipment from an outside broadcast truck. Lundby had never been of interest to the world before, apart from a murder in the sixties. But didn't the nation love death and tragedy? This would be titillation for growing prejudice, prejudice the government was fuelling skilfully, thanks to the media. And thanks to the lunatics at the back of the lines, the news teams would have their shots of catapults and marbles. Just what the union needed.

A truncheon brandished in his face forced Pavel to recoil, collide with pickets behind. Sucked into a swelter of heaving bodies and kicking feet and pressed from all sides, he reeled and spun, smacking his head against chins, chests and shoulders. He ducked and elbowed his way through the scrum until he reached the grass verge.

Pickets were leaping over a dry stone wall into the woods and on impulse Pavel followed. He ran along a path familiar from his childhood, a well-worn route towards the colliery railway line. The track would lead out of the chaos. But unlike the other men Pavel veered off, sprinting towards denser woodland, in the direction of the fishing lake, hoping Roly had not spotted him.

A few officers followed the fleeing pickets but as they were not locals, Pavel was certain they'd turn back.

Surely, no one else would run this far.

He stopped to catch his breath. Dew had drenched the grass. It soaked the bottoms of his jeans as he inched between bramble and thorn, tripped over exposed roots. The trees grew close together, the last leaves of late summer forming a brooding canopy. His tee shirt, damp with sweat, clung to his chest.

A rustling of branches startled him. He sensed movement in the bushes a few yards to his right. He inched forward. Twigs cracked. He froze, held his breath. One cautious foot in front of the other, each step matched with a creaking echo. Then a dark shape loomed, like the presence in his dream. He shivered. He'd seen his role as a negotiator, not aggressor. But he remembered his father, his life destroyed by events which followed the incursion of Nazi Jack boots. Were these not Jack boots in another guise? The rage of Orgreave was upon him and as the figure shot in front of him, Pavel screamed and dived at the man's legs, bringing him down and rolling him onto his back. He yanked the torso towards him, tugging the silver buttons on the black tunic. Buttons that boasted the Queen's crown in shining relief. He spat onto the grass. Perhaps the Queen should know how it felt to be hounded out of your job and attacked in your own village.

'Got you, you bastard.'

'Pavel, stop, for God's sake.'

Pavel flicked up the visor, rocked onto his haunches. 'Christ. What the – ?'

'It's me... Robbie.'

'Why the hell didn't you say so?'

The young policeman scrambled to his feet, dragged off his helmet, slammed it onto the ground. 'I've had enough.' He wiped his face with his leather gauntlets then cast them beside the helmet and tossed the truncheon under a bush.

Pavel stood motionless, open mouthed. Then he laughed, scooped Robbie into a bear hug. 'Bloody hell, Robbie. What are you doing here?'

'I'm supposed to beat the shit out of you, Pavel. God Almighty, I swear this is not what I joined the force for. '

All Pavel could see in the close-shaven cheeks was the boy he'd once cared for when it seemed no-one else did. He looked Robbie up and down, the dark uniform a contrast against his own jeans and the leather jacket he'd thought too good for picketing. He'd already muddied it. They sat down on a tree trunk.

'This is rich. I thought you were in Birmingham,' Pavel said.

'I am. I was. West Midlands Force. They deploy us all over the place. I should have told them I grew up here but I wanted to come back, see for myself. I thought I could hack it. Like you do when you join the force and have to. Sudden death, traffic accident, a dead child. But when I spotted you in the crowd, I couldn't do it. So when you ran, I ran after you.'

'Deployed? The woman's set the bloody army on us but denies it. Squaddies in bobby uniforms that don't fit? It's a farce. Then there's the Mets. And we're not sure you lot are much better. She may as well send tanks in. '

Robbie shrugged. 'Who understands anybody or anything anymore? This is crazy. Of all the public enemies I should be chasing, it has to be you!'

Pavel glanced over his shoulder. 'Better keep our voices down.'

'Sounds trite but I joined to make a difference.'

Pavel rolled his eyes. 'Hark at The Caped Crusader!'

'I was naïve.'

'We were all naïve before this, mate. I hate this crap as much as you do but I won't go back to work until I've tried everything I can to stop this bloody government closing pits. And I won't let men down.'

Pavel picked at a clod of mud on his trainers. Wasn't he letting everybody down? Hadn't he just run away? Robbie unfastened his coat, wiped his brow with his sleeve.

Pavel squeezed Robbie's shoulder. 'So where are you camping out then?'

'Army barracks six miles away.'

'Liars and crafty bastards aren't they? They know it's a bad idea to have local cops on their home picket lines. Too many from mining families. You poor sods are manipulated as much as we are.'

Robbie rolled up his trouser leg; one finger circled a mass of bruises. 'Pit boots. At the last picket line. They bloody hurt. And it's no fun being called a pig either.'

Pavel nodded. It was easier to face your enemy if you thought they were less than human, another thing when you recognised the boy in the man.

'A few of us played cards at one pit,' Robbie said. 'It seemed quiet. No trouble. Not many pickets. Bit of banter that's all. We kept an orange box in the van, a couple of camping stools, so we set them up, ate our sandwiches and played gin rummy. Next thing the bloke beside me is rolling on the ground, screaming. Ball bearing from a catapult, straight through both cheeks.'

Pavel rubbed the back of his neck. 'Bloody hell. Poor bugger. I can't deny we've a few idiots on our side. Nearly had a marble through *my* skull this morning.'

They waited, silent, listening for a few minutes. Until Pawel squinted at the sky. 'Looks like rain,' he said. The clouds seemed more threatening than they had at dawn. 'When I was a kid, I used to look for pictures in clouds. Once I saw a silver rabbit: long ears, haunches, the lot. So clear, I thought it was a sign that my dad was going to buy me one.'

'And did he?'

'No. Said I had to make do with my goldfish.'

Robbie laughed. 'And what do you see now?'

'Nowt but bleedin' clouds.'

'Just felt a drop.'

The drop was soon a downpour which ran down Pavel's face and neck. He could no longer hear voices. 'Reckon the scabs will be in work by now.'

'How do you think all this will end?' Robbie asked.

'God only knows. Do you ever feel you're a pawn? You try to do the right thing, make responsible decisions, but some force — and I don't mean you lot — takes hold and steers you into a situation you can't handle, you didn't ask for and you can't change.'

'Destiny? You always said you made your own luck. I know things were bad when your brother died but I thought you were okay now. Married with a son an' all. Settled. Strike can't last much longer can it?'

Where was tabloid man now? This would make a much better story than a love affair. The picket and the bobby, old mates sitting out the aggravation in wet grass. Like stories of football matches between German and British soldiers in the First World War. Except, he and Robbie had no intention of shooting each other after the final whistle.

He pulled Robbie to his feet, picked up the helmet and gloves, retrieved the truncheon from beneath the bush.

'I can't face another bloodbath, Pavel.'

'You'll go back, Robbie. Neither of us are quitters. But I want to show you something first.'

They trudged between trees, dipping beneath low branches, trampling through brambles until they reached a clearing by the Earl's lake. The rain pocked the surface of the water.

'It's all managed now,' Pavel said. 'Fish stocks carefully monitored. Licences hard to come by. Serious stuff is fishing. The warden's akin to Margaret Thatcher. New laws in place. Rules is rules. They've built this wall around and pulled out the bulrushes.'

'Shame. I liked it here when I was a kid,' Robbie said. 'I remember we once had a swimming race. You won.'

Pavel remembered their arms and legs slicing through the lake, propelling them quickly to the other side where they crawled out, shivering, onto a bank of jelly-like mud.

'I shouldn't have encouraged you,' Pavel said. 'The weeds could have snagged your ankles, the mud sucked you under.'

Many a young lad in a summer heat wave had been drowned diving into tempting waters and Pavel had warned Jake never to do it. God knows what might have been thrown in the lake. They weren't far from the *Dog Broth*: a stagnant pond where, when Pavel was a child, many an unwanted puppy had been drowned by a callous owner. Once, twelve years ago, he'd considered casting himself on its mercy. Not now.

A flock of geese landed with frenzied wings, ruffling the water. The rain stopped as suddenly as it had started. The friends watched, listened as quiet descended and the turbulence in the lake settled to a lick-lapping at their feet.

'They were good times,' Robbie said. 'Nothing wrong with taking risks when you're a kid.'

'No worries when you're a kid.' Pavel picked up a pebble and skimmed it across the lake. 'Helen's come back, Robbie. I've been... seeing her.'

'I should have known a woman was behind your philosophising. Seeing her? Is that code for...?'

'It gets worse. She's married to a Tory MP.'

Robbie laughed. 'You have to be joking.' Two mallards were squabbling in the reeds. 'So... you're a picket who's absconded into a wood with a bobby and you're sleeping with a Tory MPs wife. Nice one.'

Pavel scratched his chin. 'It's been a strange year so far.'

'I had a serious girlfriend till she ditched me. Too much overtime on picket lines.'

'There are compensations. You must be raking it in.'

'And nobody to spend it on.'

A fish leapt from the lake and plunged into the depths leaving behind a ripple of concentric circles.

'Roach,' Pavel said. 'Probably chased by a pike.'

Robbie grinned. 'Lot of it about. If it's any consolation, I never really liked your wife. Preferred Helen.'

'That's a big help. Thanks.'

They picked their way around the lake.

'Could stay here all day, Robbie said. 'It's so peaceful.'

'Quiet over at the pit now an'all,' Pavel said. 'We'd better hurry up. It's well past seven. You've got to get back to barracks. Like I said: we're not deserters.'

The reunion had washed away Pavel's nightmares but he felt a pang of guilt at the word *deserter*. 'We've got to face up to duty.'

'The van won't leave till I'm accounted for,' Robbie said. 'I'll tell the sergeant I chased a picket and got lost. Get a bollocking, but so what?'

'Good man.'

'Look after yourself, Pavel, and remember me to Helen.'

They ran through the woods past the railway bridge and towards the pit lane, stopping to shake hands then hug before parting.

Chapter Twenty Four

Misdemeanours

September 1984

Lundby

Soft boiled egg with soldiers was Jake's favourite Sunday breakfast and he'd bestowed on Pavel the honour of cooking it. Jake said his dad made the yoke runny but not watery. Perfect. Father and son sat opposite at the table, with eggs in hen-shaped cups. They'd been discussing Saturday's football scores – Rotherham beat Burnley 3-2 – until the conversation changed to plans for a local air show and the prospect of the Red Arrows flying over the village next weekend. Pavel flew a finger of toast around the table, humming the Dam Busters theme, much to the delight of Jake who was laughing with his mouth full.

Cheryl was still in pyjamas. Her dressing gown hung loose, flapping open as she stumbled across the kitchen. She shot Pavel a look of disgust, opened a cupboard and took out a bottle of painkillers 'Trust you to teach good table manners,' she mumbled, filling a glass with orange juice from the jug on the table; she swallowed two tablets, kissed Jake's head lightly. 'Eat properly, love.'

'If you've got a headache,' Pavel said, 'why don't you go back to bed?' The doorbell rang before she could reply but her pained expression told him that she would be unlikely to answer it. 'I'll get it,' he said.

Roly stood on the doorstep waving a newspaper. Pavel stepped into the garden, allowing the door to close softly behind him.

'I suppose this is what you were trying to tell me about, on picket line a couple of weeks ago,' Roly said, thrusting the paper into Pavel's chest, 'before we were interrupted by seven hundred truncheons.'

The paper was open at the relevant section, just a half page feature, photographic evidence grainy yet undeniable. This was the first Sunday for weeks Pavel hadn't been first in the queue at the newsagents.

'Has Cheryl seen this?' Roly said, glowering.

'I'm still standing aren't I?'

'I told you to stay away from that girl. Now what will you do?'

'I did try. Sorry mate.' Pavel felt lightheaded, almost giddy. Everything was unravelling.

'Not bloody hard enough. I'm disappointed in you, Pavel. You lied to me. Do you realise what you've done?'

'You'll have to take over the job −'

'I did that weeks ago, remember?' Roly nodded at the newspaper. 'When you went on your jollies with Tory wife. You've been somewhere else for weeks.'

'How do you think the lads will take it?'

'Just bumped into Swannie on the way here. The bugger laughed. "Don't know where he gets the energy from," he says. You've given 'em summat to snigger about.'

Pavel blushed

'Best thing I can do is take Jake off your hands,' Roly said. 'Tell him to find his football; we'll go to park for a kick about.'

'I'll come with you.'

'No. You'll get back in there and tell Cheryl the truth, salvage what you can.'

What was there for Pavel to salvage? Other than his son?

He hesitated, taking a moment to rehearse his excuses. Roly pointed a finger. 'Stop buggering about, man. Sort it.'

The radio was playing: *Is There Something I Should Know?* Pavel switched it off.

'What are you doing?' Cheryl said. 'I like Duran Duran.'

'I thought you had a headache.'

'You could have turned it down. What's the matter with you? You're fidgety. Why didn't you go to the park with Roly and Jake? And why are you looking at me like that?'

She drew a stool to the table and shook cornflakes into her bowl. Pavel clutched the rolled newspaper.

'That paper won't be fit to read by the time you've finished,' she said. 'Will you stop wringing it like a wet towel and sit down?'

'There's something I've got to show you.'

She poured milk over the cereal. 'Pass me the sugar will you?'

He sat down beside her, passed the bowl. 'Shall I make fresh tea?'

'No thanks.'

'Coffee?'

'What do you want to show me?'

'I need to explain something first.'

'Explain?' She crunched on a spoonful of cornflakes.

He waited till she had swallowed. 'I'm sorry you have to find out this way,' he said.

'I don't think I can eat this. Maybe I should go back to bed. What did you say? Find out what?'

He shifted the plates and egg cups, unrolled the newspaper, smoothing it out. 'You'd better see this.'

'What are you rambling about? No wonder my head's throbbing.'

'Bottom half of the page on the left.' Thank God Guy Eagleton was not in the cabinet. It would have made front page. Not that it made any difference now. If Roly and Swannie had read it then so would everyone else in the village. He placed the sugar bowl and jug on the edges of the newspaper to prevent it from curling.

'You've made such a mess of it, Pavel. Do you mean this section?' She read the headline. *'MINER MISDEMEANORS WITH TORY WIFE.'*

Cheryl squinted at the pictures, confused, as if she couldn't focus or interpret their significance.

'I didn't lie to you in the beginning, I swear...' he said.

'You know... after the band concert... when you asked me about her?

I hadn't seen her for years.

Never had any intention...

There was a journalist —'

'Is that you?' Cheryl said at last.
'Yes.'
'Where is this?'
'Cumbria.'
'When?'
'While you were in Skegness.'
'Who the hell is that woman?'
'It's not a very good likeness.'

Cheryl pored over the text, dropping her spoon in the dish. Pavel's heart hammered in his ears.

She read aloud. "*Mrs Eagleton is the wife of Guy Eagleton, Conservative MP for...*" Fucking hell!'

The photographs showed Pavel laughing as he pulled Helen to her feet on the beach. There were others: a picture of the inn with the caption, *Lovenest*, Pavel with his arm around Helen on the promenade, and an old photo of Thatcher on the campaign trail with Guy in the background.

Cheryl's voice faltered. *"'The Eagletons are thought to have been estranged... for several months. Mr Eagleton denied a separation, insisting his wife",'* she stopped, finger tips over her lips, regained composure. *"'insisting his wife was on holiday with relatives.'"* She looked up, tears welling. 'What are you, her bloody cousin?'

'I'm sorry, Cheryl.'

'Sorry?'

Pavel winced. 'If I could have stopped him I –'

'Don't blame the photographer, you bastard. How long?'

He cringed. Cheryl didn't usually swear; it scared him. 'Just since June.'

'Just? Three months? That's okay then is it?' She continued to read aloud, *"Pavel Kowaleski is strike coordinator at Lundby Edge colliery in South Yorkshire, the scene of recent picket violence. He is married with a son."* Too sodding right he's married.'

She scanned the columns dedicated to Guy's career and the retrospective account of Orgreave, pictures of pickets slinging stones. Cheryl's face paled. She held the collar of her dressing gown to her neck then continued, each word laden with sarcasm. *"Considered a rising star of the back benches, Mr Eagleton is a fierce supporter of Margaret Thatcher and the government's energy policy.'"*

'I know it sounds bad.'

'She's married to a man who wants to shut down bleeding pits for God's sake! Tell me you didn't know.'

Pavel sighed, bit his lip. 'I'm waiting,' she said.

'I did know. Billy Farrimond told me.'

'Typical. Encourage the pair of you, did he? "*Do me a favour, Pavel. Entice my poor niece away from the opposition?*" Is that what he said? Interfering gobshite. Bet he kept this quiet from his Labour cronies.'

'Billy didn't know. I never intended to —'

'Bastard,' she said, lips trembling. Tears ran down her nose, dripped onto the photographs. 'I know what you intended. Right from the start you lied about that woman. Coker warned me. He said she was a tart.'

Cheryl picked up the orange juice, swished it twice around the jug then tossed it into Pavel's face. It dripped onto his shirt and pooled on the table. He licked his lips. 'I know you're angry and you have every right but —.' Robbed of an anchor the pages curled, obscuring the photographs. He felt a second's curious relief.

'Cheating bastard.'

'I wanted to tell you sooner but —'

'Liar. Hypocrite. Shagging that slut.'

'You're shaking.' He attempted to put his arm around her shoulders. 'I'm sorry. I am. Really sorry. But we need to be rational. Jake will be home soon.'

'Here's fucking rational for you,' she said, jabbing him in the mouth with her elbow. He recoiled, tasted blood. 'If you'd considered Jake you wouldn't have touched the bitch.'

'I did think about him. Honestly. That's why —'

'It's the bloody strike. Your brain's turned to mulch. You'll be telling me next you love —.'

'I do love her. I'm sorry.'

Her face paled. 'You can say goodbye to Jake.'

'Listen to me, will you?' Pavel said, though he had no idea what he'd say next if she listened.

'I'm going to be sick.' She ran upstairs into the bathroom. He heard an empty retch.

What had he done? He didn't want to destroy her. She was sobbing now. 'Christ,' he said.

Would Jake hate him? Everything she'd said was justified – except for the insults about Helen. It was his fault, not Helen's, not Cheryl's. The juice had soaked into the photographs. He dumped the newspaper in the bin.

★ ★ ★

Monday. 4.30. p.m. The children had gone home, the playground was empty. The first day of what should have been Helen's last week at school. She'd only called to collect a few personal belongings. Mr Read had phoned early that morning, told her that in view of yesterday's newspaper article, which he assumed she'd read, he thought it would be better if she left the school immediately. He didn't want to be judgemental – and besides he felt partly to blame for not acting on his instinct and voicing concerns weeks before – but he would teach the class himself for the remaining five days before the teacher on sick leave returned. He promised to give Helen a reference.

'The children and staff are sorry to lose you.'

A reference? She wondered if she would ever have the nerve to apply for a teaching job again.

Uncle Billy and Tibby had been surprisingly philosophical; they had no time for gutter press and since Billy's term of office on the board of school governors was due to end at Christmas, he didn't expect Helen's affair to cause him too much of a problem

'But I'm disappointed you didn't confide in us,' he said.

'Billy, you knew all along,' Tibby said.

As Helen was ready to leave, children began crowding into the cloakroom. A football match. Damn it, she'd forgotten. The victorious home team were stamping muddy boots against the doorstep. Several parents were waiting outside. Jake startled her. He had changed into school uniform already and was standing in the classroom doorway, football boots dangling from his hand by the laces.

'Jake.'

'Didn't think you'd be here today, Mrs Eagleton.'

'Just collecting my things.'

His unfastened rucksack slipped from his shoulder, soiled sports kit spilling. He gathered the items quickly, squashing them into his bag. Helen imagined Pavel packing shorts and shin pads that morning, offering advice on tactics. Why was he not here to support Jake at least?

'Mum's been crying. She didn't go to work today. She's collecting me in a minute.'

Helen nodded, not daring to ask where Pavel was. Jake tightened the strap on his rucksack. 'She says we might move.'

The door to the playground opened. It always had an eerie squeak.

'Jake, come outside. Now!'

Jake's worried expression exaggerated his likeness to Pavel.

'It's okay, Jake,' Helen said, 'Go with your mum.'

'He doesn't need your permission!' Cheryl marched into the classroom. 'Wait in the car, Jake. It's unlocked.'

Jake fled, dragging the boots behind him.

'I'm so sorry...'

'You're sorry I found out,' Cheryl said.

'Pavel promised he'd tell you.'

Cheryl stepped closer; she seemed taller. 'You're not fit to teach my son or anybody else's. What a cheek: to join the support group when all along you're married to one of Maggie Thatcher's henchmen. How many other miners have you screwed?'

Helen fiddled with the beads at her neck, aware of faces gathering at the window.

'What is it Coker called you?' Cheryl said. 'A hypocritical tart with a high opinion of herself?'

'Coker? How can you mention Coker when you've been –'

'Been what? You silly bitch. Coker fancies every woman he meets. Do you think Pavel would have stood for any dalliance with Coker? Do you think he's a fool? Perhaps you don't know my husband as well as you think you do.'

Helen's heart skipped a beat. 'People said –'

'Gossip. Coker's always been jealous of Pavel. You're not very bright for a teacher.'

'Your marriage was over –.'

'Says who? We have a child. We're a family. I've never been unfaithful. Pavel prefers a quiet life. He enjoys the house and the garden. I like to go out with friends, have fun. He's okay with that. At least he was till you wrecked our lives. He knows I've never slept with another man since I married him. But why the hell should I explain our marriage to you?'

'I'm leaving today. I've just called to collect –'

'School chucking you out? Good riddance. What does Uncle Billy Farrimond think of his precious niece now?'

Helen backed away towards the teacher's desk. 'There's nothing more to say. I've apologised for the way –'

Cheryl grabbed Helen's blouse. 'Don't walk away. Is that all you've got to say? You think that's enough? "*Sorry*

300

I stole your husband and now if you'll excuse me?" Stuck up bitch. Who rescued Pavel when he'd been ill? Me. I've heard all about you. You chose money, status, before Pavel.' Helen felt Cheryl's warm breath, inhaled her perfume: *Anais Anais*. She'd always found it sickly sweet, cloying. She licked her lips; her palms were sweaty, her mouth dry.

'And where is he now?' Cheryl said, releasing her hold. 'Hardly on a white charger in the playground is he? Do you know what the support group women say about you?'

'You're not in the support group.'

'No, but I have friends who are. They say you're a fake. You're a joke. *All cashmere and collection bucket*. You don't fool anybody.'

'Stop that!' Mr. Read was at the door. 'I think you should leave, Mrs Kowaleski. You've had your say. This is not an appropriate time or place.' Hearing Cheryl addressed by her rightful title stung Helen.

Cheryl faced Mr Read. 'Appropriate? You should report this woman for gross misconduct.' She marched to the door. The cloakroom had emptied; the faces at the window had disappeared. Perhaps Mr Read had shooed them away. 'Unless of course you think it's acceptable for your staff to sleep with their pupils' fathers?' Cheryl left, leaving a whiff of perfume and a poignant silence.

'Maybe she'll feel better after that,' he said eventually, his sympathy failing to stem Helen's shame and humiliation.

She mopped her eyes. 'I'm so sorry, Mr Read.'

'Go home, Helen.'

Where was home?

★ ★ ★

By the time Tibby came into the bedroom, Helen had packed and was snatching tissues from a box on the dressing table. Tibby sat on the bed. 'You don't have to leave.'

'I'm the classic other woman, aren't I? A fool. Cheryl loves him.'

Tibby scoffed. 'You've humiliated her – everybody gossiping. You've hardly destroyed a great love-match. You let her browbeat you because you were feeling guilty. Pavel will tell you –'

'Pavel? Where is he now? Skulking, trying not to offend his wife again. I'm the discarded mistress.'

'You know that's not true. I've seen the way he looks at you.'

'And did you know that it's Pavel who tends the garden and the house? I thought possessions and domestic trappings were all Cheryl wanted from him, a kitchen full of white goods, a garden full of floribunda. I bet it's bloody Pavel who polishes the letterbox.'

Tibby frowned. 'What letterbox?'

'I needed him today.'

Tibby tapped the bed. 'Come and sit here.'

Helen blew her nose.

'I can't say I approve of what's happened,' Tibby said, 'but I do understand.'

'Please don't be reasonable. I can't cope with any more sympathy.'

'During the war,' Tibby said, 'nobody knew how long they had left for anything. They snatched at life. Affairs were commonplace. Because Billy was a miner he had a reserved occupation so he stayed in the village. The country needed coal then – ironic isn't it, given what Mrs Thatcher is doing? Anyway, we met at a Saturday night dance. I married him but... I'm ashamed to admit it. I was unfaithful.'

'I can't believe that,' Helen said. How many more shocks could she stomach? 'You've always been loyal.'

'It's true. It was just once, but that doesn't excuse me. A soldier I'd once been sweet on came home on leave. I was unfaithful with a man in uniform – an insult to a man like Billy, not able to enlist, yet up to his neck in just as much sweat and muck for the war effort. He was devastated when I confessed but he did forgive me eventually.'

Helen had never imagined her aunt either young or in love. She remembered Billy's look when he'd told her to sort out her marriage, said that no man deserved to be messed about. She'd thought he was taking Guy's side. It made sense now. 'Are you suggesting I save my marriage?'

'No. We certainly don't want you to go back to Guy. It's just that... when war begins, things jog along pretty much as they always have for the first few weeks, fool you into a false sense of security. After a while, when madness is an everyday occurrence, what was unacceptable or outrageous before the war becomes almost normal behaviour. People act out of character.'

'The strike's not a war.'

'Tell that to Scargill and Margaret Thatcher. Or Pavel for that matter.'

'So you think Pavel has behaved out of character because of the strike?'

'Not exactly. I'm sure he loves you. You shouldn't have parted twelve years ago. But he might not have embarked on an affair, if he'd still been working down a mine forty hours a week. The strike has thrown you together. It's been... intense, sudden.'

'The strike has nothing to do with it.'

'You did get a bit carried away, love. You can't just pick up where you left off when you were nineteen. He has responsibilities. I tried to warn you.'

'You also implied Cheryl was unfaithful.'

'Did I? I don't remember saying that exactly. She's certainly a flirt.'

'Well she's not giving up on Pavel.'

'And you are?'

Tibby gathered Helen's nightdress, tucked it beneath her pillow. 'We aren't judging you, Helen. I'm the last person to do that under the circumstances. We can withstand a bit of gossip. We want you to stay. With or without Pavel. Give him time. Maybe that's where you went wrong before. You'd not known Guy long before you were engaged.'

'I'll have to leave. It will only fuel resentment if I stay in the village. I'd hate for Jake to be the butt of jokes at school and if I hang around that's more likely. You needn't worry. I'll never go back to Guy.'

Tibby stroked Helen's hair. 'Well that's something! I'll make tea.'

A gin and tonic would be more effective. Tibby left. Helen slid the nightdress from beneath the pillow and packed it.

As she shut her suitcase, she heard hushed voices in the hall. Billy. Pavel. She listened from the landing, deciphering only that Pavel had rushed here as soon as he could. She imagined Uncle Billy nodding, accepting his excuses. Maybe everybody fell under Pavel's spell – except Coker. She hauled the suitcase downstairs and deposited it by the front door.

Pavel followed her into the sitting room. 'Jake told me Cheryl came to see you. I was at a meeting. There were a few jibes and smutty jokes but that's all. We'll survive this, Helen. Are you okay, love? You've been crying.'

'Jibes? Expect you've risen in the lads' estimation. Scored a goal against the government, have you? You let Cheryl attack me. I feel cheap.'

'I didn't think she'd –.'

'What did you think she'd do, send flowers? You let her find out in the worst possible way. You're a coward.'

He flopped into an arm chair. 'I've made a mess of things.'

'That's an understatement.'

'I was waiting for the right time.'

A car horn sounded. 'My taxi's arrived. Your time's run out.'

'You don't have to leave. Please don't.'

'I'm going to London. Isaac's to begin with until I find a place of my own. You'll be polishing your letterbox, I expect. At home with Cheryl.'

'What's the letterbox got to do with anything?'

'I should never have come back.'

Uncle Billy hefted her suitcase into the boot of the taxi and Helen climbed into the back seat. She waved to Tibby. Teapot still in her hands, Tibby nodded, lingered at the front door, biting her lip.

Pavel didn't appear.

★ ★ ★

It was midnight by the time Helen arrived in Greenwich. Isaac had left the light on over the front door. Wearing dressing gown and slippers he answered the bell on her first ring.

'I'm sorry to keep you up so late, Isaac.' He seemed smaller, frailer than when she had last visited. She wished she could have caught an earlier train.

'It's no problem. I wondered if you would make it here at all tonight. I've been sleeping in a chair. You look tired. But come in, come in. Leave the suitcase. I have a surprise for you.'

She detected the smell of fresh paint and sawdust above the customary beeswax. The kitchen had been refurbished with grey cupboards, a split-level electric cooker and a bench table.

'My sons were convinced I would blow myself up with the old gas oven. Solly called me a *mud-stick*.'

'A stick in the – ah. You can't catch me out so easily.'

'Yes you've come a long way in many respects, Helen. Rather like my kitchen. New cupboards, but the same old man rattling round in it.'

'It's a great improvement. Very trendy.'

'That's the word Solly used. I think *trendy* is a euphemism for expensive but I suppose it adds value to the house. I fear it will belong to my grandsons before long.'

'Isaac. Please don't make me more depressed than I am already.' She longed to curl up beneath a duvet, sob into a pillow. How long could she maintain cheerful conversation?

The new automatic kettle cut out as it boiled and he made tea. They sat at the table with a plate of biscuits between them. The bench seats were upholstered in a tartan fabric.

'This your family tartan, Isaac?'

He laughed. 'A joke. All is not lost then? So what will you do now, assuming you don't intend to return to Guy?'

'Find a flat to rent until we reach a settlement? I've not spoken to him yet.'

'It will be difficult for Guy. He'll be hurt and angry. The sooner you meet the better. I read the article. I've been buying the cheaper Sunday newspapers ever since you wrote to warn me. Much to the consternation of my sons. They were concerned by my sudden interest in salacious gossip. "Who reads this rubbish?" I asked them. "Apparently you do, Dad," they said. So I had to tell the truth. I hope you don't mind. Now Solly is keen to meet Grandpa's friend, the celebrity.'

'That's not what Pavel's wife called me. Among other things I won't repeat, she called me *a fake*. She's right. But not in the way she meant. I was a phoney wife for ten years. Guy deserved better.'

'You lived in two worlds and had settled in neither.'

'I was happy in the school in Lundby. Reconnected. Part of a community. Working at last.'

'And Pavel?'

'When I was with him — you'll think I'm stupid — I felt whole somehow. In spite of the subterfuge I felt justified. I'm ashamed to admit I thought I was reclaiming what had always been mine.'

'Two halves. The soul mate theory. I warned you. It doesn't always work.'

'You're right about two worlds. I don't know where I belong, as if I'm permanently displaced.'

Isaac laughed, patted her hand. 'You'll get used to it. I read, write and speak English; I mumble and curse in German; I pray in Hebrew. We're cultural mongrels you and I. Mongrel is healthy.'

'I shall have to go to the apartment sometime, sort out the paperwork, collect the rest of my belongings.'

'On the subject of accommodation — the kitchen is not the only room to have been refurbished. The boys set the decorators on me. The bedrooms have new wallpaper and have been repainted. You'll find a difference in the guest room. Max and Solly have cleared their old toys, sold them to raise money for computer games.'

Her eyelids were closing.

'Now listen. Before you fall asleep.' he said. 'I shall understand if you prefer to search for a flat, but the guest room is yours if you want it. You can pay me a nominal rent if you're happier with a business arrangement.'

'Deal,' she said, perhaps too quickly. 'You're very kind, Isaac.' She stacked the cups and plates into Isaac's new dishwasher. 'Though it doesn't ease my guilt. I'm seeking refuge with you, taking advantage of your hospitality yet again.'

'Refuge? Now *refuge* is a word I understand.'

Chapter Twenty Five

Conciliation Services

October 11th 1984

Lundby South Yorkshire

The window was open. Pavel heard a sail-like flapping from the garden: the wind lifting the plastic sheeting he had rolled over the rabbit hutch before he went to bed. A neighbouring family had recently discovered their rabbit half eaten, decapitated by a fox which had chewed through the wire netting. A fox would kill for pleasure and Pavel wanted to protect not merely the rabbit from a ruthless predator but his son from the horror of finding a dead pet, its blood spattered across the lawn.

The curtains billowed. When the door creaked Jake was silhouetted against the landing light. 'Dad. I can't sleep.'

Pavel threw back the covers. 'Come on then.' Jake climbed into bed beside him. 'What's the matter?'

'I can hear the wind... I'm worried.'

'Worried about the wind?'

'Worried about you.'

Pavel kissed Jake's head. 'There's no need.'

'I don't want you to leave.'

Pavel's heart sank. He squeezed Jake. 'I'm not leaving.'

Jake wriggled. 'But you're going to London tomorrow.'

'Yes, with Uncle Roly and some of the other pickets. There's a meeting to find a way to end the strike.'

'Will you be making a speech?'

Pavel smiled in the dark, nuzzled Jake's neck. 'No. Union officials far more important than me will do the talking. We'll be outside – like supporters.'

'So you'll be coming back?'

'Of course I will.'

'A boy at school said Mrs Eagleton lives in London.'

Was Jake suffering from taunts? 'I'm coming back, Jake. I'll be gone no more than one night. I promise.'

'Phew,' Jake said. 'Will you bring me a present then?'

★ ★ ★

October 12th 1984

London

Much of the conversation had focused on the Brighton bomb blast in the early hours rather than union talk. Someone had brought a radio. A reporter said that the Tory conference would carry on in spite of the carnage. 'Thatcher will see to that,' Pavel said. 'And to think the woman's after our blood. We're pussy cats compared to that set of murdering bastards.'

'And she calls us "the enemy within",' Swannie said. 'Makes you sick to think she labels us like terrorists.'

'Wonder how they did it?' Gus said. 'With all that security.'

'Probably planted somebody in the hotel weeks ago,' Roly said. 'A sleeper leaving a timing device.'

'I wonder how many sleepers we've got on the picket line,' Pavel said. 'Might not plant bombs but just as explosive.'

'A bomb won't change a thing,' Roly said. 'The IRA won't get concessions by blowing up the government. Thatcher feeds on the moral high ground. That's why she's out to discredit us, make us out to be traitors.'

'Isn't it time we heard something from this lot,' Swannie said. 'My feet are cold.'

Roly, Pavel, Gus and Swannie had joined the crowd of NUM members waiting for news outside the ACAS building in Euston Road. Pavel rolled the words of the acronym around his tongue. *'Advisory, Conciliation and Arbitration Service.* Do you think MacGregor understands what the words stand for?'

Rumour had spread that MacGregor had said of the office building, 'This place stinks'.

'A man like him thinks negotiation stinks,' Roly said. 'That's why Thatcher gave him the job.'

Earlier an official had emerged to inform them an agreement was hopeful, but the men had heard nothing since.

'What did I tell you?' Roly said. 'A waste of time.'

Roly had a point. With funds threatened, the union could ill-afford transport costs on hopeless missions, though Pavel was glad to offer support to the delegates, even if he did have ulterior motives in coming to London.

It was late afternoon. Men were drifting away. Office workers headed for buses and the Underground. The coach that had carried the men south would pick them up later, near King's Cross, but Swannie suggested they walk into Soho first, take a look around China Town, find a cheap meal. Gus had never been to London and Swannie was keen to show his younger friend the sights, namely sex shops and strip joints.

'We can't stay too long,' Roly told them. 'And we can't afford London beer prices either. Two hours maximum then we make our way back to the station.' Pavel would need more than two hours.

He'd met Billy Farrimond in the High Street in Lundby. According to Billy, Guy had suggested Helen spend a couple of nights at their apartment, sorting out her belongings while he was in Brighton. But Billy didn't trust Guy and it had taken little to persuade him to hand over Helen's address.

It was six o'clock when Pavel left his friends. Scrutinising the map he reckoned on a hike of about four miles to find her. With little chance of meeting the deadline for the bus he told Roly he'd hitch-hike up the M1 later. It was a relief to be honest with Roly about his intended destination.

If London was a collection of villages as Pavel had once read, then his walk through Bloomsbury confirmed it: elegant town houses, gardens in Georgian squares, wrought iron fences, antique shops and corner cafes. Quiet, sleepy. Leaves swirled about his feet. His trainers wouldn't last the winter. He turned up the collar on his jacket.

He wished he had time to browse, money to spend. He would like to have visited the British Museum, the National Gallery. He stopped to look in the window of a book shop. Everything here from historical tomes to glossy coffee-table volumes. He used the local library in Lundby, hadn't bought books since the beginning of the strike, but he would like to replace the art book Cheryl had trashed. He'd left it by his bed after reading about the Expressionists. He loved the vibrant paintings. There was so much Pavel had missed by leaving school at sixteen. The longer the strike went on the less he looked forward to working underground. A world without colour. While the right to work was sacrosanct, the reality jarred. He checked his wallet, found three pound notes and went into the bookshop where he bought *I Spy at the Seaside* as Jake's present.

The image of books plummeting into the garden was one he'd never forget. It was two days after Helen returned to London, the day he spurned Cheryl's final offer of reconciliation. When she believed Helen had left for good.

He had just finished washing up. Water from the sink gushed and gurgled from the outside pipe as the first books fell past the kitchen window and into the open drain. Thud. Thud. Pavel ran out into the garden, mystified. Assuming Jake had knocked something from the window ledge he'd called out. 'Jake? Are you up there? What's going on?' But Jake was preparing to clean out the rabbit hutch and emerged from the garden shed carrying a bag of straw. By this time at least ten books had tumbled from the window, pages flapping, some landing open on the path, some face down; some smaller paperbacks standing spine upwards like miniature tents on the lawn. Those that Cheryl had aimed across the garden hung from branches, unlikely blooms in the rose bushes, or had hit the hutch dispatching the frightened rabbit into his sleeping quarters. They were Pavel's books from the spare room. Ten books became twenty. Twenty became fifty.

It was too late to stop her. He'd heard of wives throwing out their husband's clothes, or taking scissors to their shirts, but never this. Jake was crying, scrabbling beneath the kitchen window trying to retrieve what he could.

'Mum, stop. These books are Dad's.'

Pavel pulled him away. 'Leave them Jake. I'll collect them later. It's okay.' Jake leaned into him, sobbing.

Pavel made his way across New Oxford Street, down to the Strand and onto the Embankment, feeling the throb of the city: the rumble of trains across the bridge, the distinctive chug of black cabs. The energy intrigued him, though he could never live here. It was hectic. Where would he find peace? He'd miss the woods, the stillness, the walks to the lake, the smell of leaf mould beneath trees, a white flash of a badger at dusk. The parks here were too manicured for his tastes. Even so, liberated from strike talk for a few hours, he could think clearly in spite of the traffic. One day he'd expose Jake to art, music, literature, take him to the science museum, to concerts. He wondered at Cheryl's motives. Had she intended to pour scorn on his ambitions or were his books the first things to hand?

It was dark by the time he found the apartment block. Would Helen turn him away?

He heard music, a recording he recognised. *The Police* singing *Walking on the Moon:* the twang of a chord; the three note follow-up of a bass guitar. He understood that song. It described how he'd felt when he was nineteen, walking her home, lightheaded, as if he were losing his gravity

He rang the bell. The intercom clicked. 'Who's there?'

'Helen, it's me. Pavel.' There was a buzz then the lock released. He jumped the stairs to the apartment, two by two.

★ ★ ★

October 13th 1984

Brighton

The glare from a patrol car panned the walls like a searchlight. Guy drew the sheet to his neck. The curtains were open. The glow from street lamps shone through the lace panels over the windows striking the wardrobe and casting a long shadow across the carpet. It was 3 am. Guy lay awake with a searing headache.

Yesterday, dust and debris had floated on the waves. Furnishings and the personal belongings of The Grand Hotel's guests were embedded in promenade benches. He reached for the whisky bottle and the packet of aspirin he'd left on the bedside table.

He'd managed to be alcohol free for five months and the promise of promotion had sealed his new deal with his conscience: no booze, no whores, and a promise to control his temper. But he needed Helen's return to keep the bargain and she'd ruined everything, destroyed it all with her flagrant abuse of trust, making a fool of him.

He lifted the pillow, thumped it.

Now his promised job would go to Jack; Jack who had everything: a wife, a house in Richmond, a new-born son. The party chairman had said that Guy's promotion prospects were damaged in the short term, but a couple of years would be ample time for the public and the changing face of the cabinet to forget his wife's transgression. But he would need to rein her in. Alternatively find another one! An unfaithful wife was a liability.

She was back in London, must have ditched the lover. She'd have found no solace in her village where they would hate her, now they knew she was the enemy. She was cornered. He threw back the quilt, made his way to the bathroom, dropped the empty whisky bottle in the bin, cleaned his teeth.

How had the Irish bastards done it? Where had they planted it?

He'd been in the bar at The Grand Hotel only two hours before the explosion, with backbench colleagues, celebrating Jack's promotion. How else could he have mourned the loss of the job that should have been his, but with whisky? He'd only just fallen into bed when he'd heard the blast, and his hotel which was only yards

315

away from The Grand, had rocked, trembled; the glass and bottle by his bed had rattled.

The police would drive along the sea front around the clock until the conference ended, though it was too late. There might be another hundred pound bomb here, now, waiting to explode, ticking below him. He looked under the bed.

He paced the patterned carpet, running his hands through his hair and patting the walls for signs of loose panels. Dust had crept in, settled in a film on everything he touched. There could be a device behind the bath, in the ceiling, under the floor boards. Impossible to tell. Guy forced his hand into the gap beneath the wardrobe. Finding nothing, he dressed.

The heart of the Grand Hotel had been ripped out. Its façade had crumbled, though the newspapers said that its sound Victorian fabric had saved it from complete destruction. The Victorians were cock-sure with their solid buildings, their empires, corporations, city fathers and foundations. And their enduring marriages and acquiescent wives. Guy envied their vision, their ordered view of the world.

Eight floors had collapsed into the basement and two ministers were dead. He'd watched the report on the television in this room: the Trade and Industry Secretary stretchered from the rubble. Norman Tebbit, poor man. In bloody pyjamas. And everything illuminated, exposed by the arc lights of a television crew who just happened to be close at hand. Cameras were always there to capture the moment, no respecters of privacy or position. At least Helen had learned that lesson. He boiled the kettle, emptied a sachet of instant coffee into a mug.

Margaret Thatcher, there was a woman! Not one you'd want to sleep with, but to be revered. She'd emerged invincible, commanding the opening of Marks and Spencer at four in the morning for the delegates who couldn't retrieve their clothes from their bedrooms. And she'd insisted the conference continued at 9.30. a.m. giving a rousing, defiant speech that had moved Guy to tears. Everything moved him to tears. The standing ovation had lasted an hour.

A letter opener lay on a leather writing pad on the desk. He tapped the blade on his palm. His careless wife and her subversive boyfriend had been a time bomb. They'd shaken Guy's foundations, torn apart his career.

If he ever met the miner... he'd like to cut out his heart.

Helen had phoned Guy, explained she was renting a room at a friend's house in Greenwich. Hadn't he given her a lift there once? Guy had no intention of allowing his wife to have the last word on their marriage.

A police siren startled him.

He dragged clothes from drawers and hangers, packed his bags. One white shirt sleeve stuck in the zip of his holdall, the cuff hanging over the edge like a luggage label. He left it. He drank the dregs of the coffee, locked the room and, bypassing the lift – lifts were fatal in fires and bomb blasts – he took four flights of stairs down to the deserted reception area. He rattled the front doors of the hotel. They were locked. Thank God there was some security. Someone tapped his shoulder. He spun round. It was a night porter he hadn't noticed, offering help. Guy thought he detected an Irish accent and wondered if the man's credentials had been subjected to adequate scrutiny.

'Could you check the time of the earliest train to London?' Guy said.

He'd leave at first light, forgo breakfast.

Guy perched on the edge of an armchair by the window, flicking through the pages of country magazines and yesterday's newspapers, one eye on the activities of the porter.

On the promenade police radios crackled.

★ ★ ★

October 13th 1984

London

Last night he'd held Jake close; Pavel had not forgotten the promises. His arm tightened around Helen's waist. 'Are you awake?' he said.

'Yes. Thinking.'

He kissed her. 'I don't want to leave you. I don't trust Guy.'

'He won't be home till after the conference and I'll be at Isaac's by then.'

'What are you thinking about?'

'Guy told me he'd redecorated this bedroom, got rid of the clown frieze.'

'Why would he lie?'

Helen climbed out of bed, took a small photograph from her purse on the dressing table. Pavel watched, admiring her naked silhouette in the grey pre-dawn half-light.

'Perhaps he intended to redecorate but events overtook him,' she said. 'I expect he thought fresh paint could mask the pain.'

'Tell me. About William.'

She switched on the bedside lamp, handed Pavel a photograph and slipped back into bed. William lay in a transparent crib, a hospital crib like Jake's. But unlike Jake, an eight pound baby, William was the tiniest scrap Pavel had ever seen, his size contrasted against an adult hand in the corner of the snapshot. Helen's hand. Pavel recognised the distinctive facets of her wedding ring. The baby had tubes attached to his nose, wires taped across his chest above his heart. A lump rose in Pavel's throat. He remembered the rush of emotion when he first held Jake. 'He's so tiny, he'd fit on my hand,' he said.

'I only held him after he'd... We were never able to bring him home. I blamed our problems on losing William but I was wrong.' She took the photograph from Pavel. 'There were gaping holes in our marriage from the start. A relationship has to be strong to survive the loss of a child. He couldn't discuss it.'

Pavel imagined Guy's cloistered grief, his guilt at moving a heavily pregnant wife to London against advice. Sympathy for Guy heightened the shame he felt about deceiving Cheryl.

'I've only spoken to him on the phone,' Helen said, 'but I think he needs professional support. I can't help him. I expected him to scream and shout about the newspaper story but he's... distant, vague.'

'Cheryl's keeping Jake in school till half term, then moving to Lincolnshire. Come back to Lundby with me.'

'What? Remind you of how you lost your son? Until the strike's over, you won't even be able to visit him.'

'At least I'd have you.'

★ ★ ★

Guy caught the earliest train to London and let himself into the apartment. He kicked his luggage aside in the hall.

There was music playing. Popular rubbish he couldn't name. He could hear laughter, a man's voice. He crept into the kitchen, stood in the archway into the dining room.

They were barefoot, dressed in jeans and tee shirts. It was the bare feet, the cosiness of the scene that enraged him: bare cosy feet, her toenails painted pink. The man was holding her close; they were swaying to the music.

There were plates on the table, mugs, a French loaf, a bread knife. This moron had screwed Helen before Guy had even met her and again in this apartment. *His apartment.* He had never seen that look on her face before. He captured it, processed it. She'd never looked at Guy like that.

They'd spotted him. She stepped away. Guy drew in his breath, held it. He must stay in control. She said she was sorry, hadn't realised that Pavel − now Guy remembered the name − would be in London; Guy mustn't think it had been planned.

'Guy. This is −'

'Get out!'

The yob said he had to leave anyway, return to Yorkshire.

'You're a low life,' Guy said. 'You are not taking my wife!'

The yob took a step back before Guy could swing a punch so his fist made no contact. He must try to predict the man's next move. Accuracy was everything. His father had taught him that.

'Stop this, Guy,' she said. 'Pavel has to leave. His son is waiting for him.'

A son? Jack had a son. Jack had his job. Once Guy had a son.

Pain seized Guy's chest, his left arm. He slumped on a chair. He was hot; he yanked at the knot in his tie. Helen had her hands on his shoulders now, her voice soothing.

'Breathe Guy. It's okay. We'll phone for an ambulance.'

Guy sank to his knees, gripping her ankles. He needed to anchor her. 'Don't leave me,' he said. He felt sick. His tears dripped onto her toes.

★ ★ ★

The ambulance drove away, blue lights flashing, the siren drawing neighbours to windows. The paramedic had diagnosed a possible heart attack. 'Don't worry, he'll undergo a full assessment,' he'd said when Helen had told him of Guy's erratic moods.

Helen had to be safe. Last night she'd supplied a full account of Guy's behaviour. Pavel's initial reaction was an urge to beat the man to a pulp, but then today, watching Guy disintegrate, reminded him of his own unravelling years after Jakub. 'I'm not leaving you here, Helen. Come back to Lundby.'

'Go home. Make the most of your time with Jake. I can't leave now. I'll have to stay in London at least until Guy comes out of hospital.'

'Then he'll never let you go.'

'What else can I do? He has no family here. I'm his next of kin, remember. I promise I'll stay with Isaac in the meantime.'

She cleared the table, loading the breakfast crockery onto a tray. 'You'll have more chance of access to Jake without me.'

'You'll be home with Billy and Tibby at Christmas surely?'

'I don't think I can face Lundby just yet. I might spend Christmas with Isaac.'

'You said he was Jewish.'

She pulled on a sweater. 'If there's such a thing as a kosher Christmas pudding, Isaac will buy one.' She laughed, carried the tray into the kitchen.

Dejected, Pavel collected the rest of his belongings from the bedroom and made for the front door. But before he could leave, Helen rushed from the kitchen, a coat on her arm. 'Wait for me,' she said. 'You're not hitching; I've ordered a taxi. I'm buying you a train ticket.'

Chapter Twenty Six

Disconnected

December 1984

Lundby South Yorkshire

The basket in the hearth brimmed with logs hewn from fencing posts; the sawn-up panels were stacked in the porch. Pavel pulled off his gloves, struck a match, lit balls of newspaper. The sticks which he'd chopped earlier, he dropped onto the flames. He'd waited until dark, donning two sweaters and finally an old fleece he kept for gardening, before he surrendered to shivering and raked out last night's ashes. The only consolation of Jake's absence was that he didn't have to worry about keeping his son warm.

While he waited for air to be drawn through the vents in the grate, he held a sheet of newspaper across the fireplace, staring at a photograph of warring police and pickets, until the paper scorched and burst into flames.

Newspapers were a luxury; his mother's stockpile saved him the expense of firelighters. Without Cheryl's wages Pavel couldn't pay the mortgage and had agreed to move in with his mother after Christmas, advertise the house for sale in the New Year – though he was unlikely to find a buyer.

The flames licked the sticks. Pavel rubbed his arms, standing as close to the hearth as he could to warm his legs, until his breath no longer made vapour trails.

Since the phone was still disconnected, Cheryl had arranged for Jake to telephone Pavel at Grandma

Kowaleski's house once a week, but the agreed date was days away. He sensed that Jake was unhappy at his new school and missed his friends, but Pavel had no money to visit.

From a box on the kitchen table he took a tin of corned beef, baked beans and a can of coke. He hadn't eaten today. Earlier Kath Beresford had delivered a food parcel.

'Heard from Helen?' she'd said.

'A letter today. Guy's out of hospital. She's taking him to his parents in Cheshire for Christmas, then going back to London. I won't see her.'

'Come to us for Christmas dinner, Pavel. And bring your mum. We still have my wage, remember.'

The radio churned out a collection of irritating Christmas pop, and a garrulous DJ announced the number one hit: *Feed the World. Let them know its Christmastime.* 'Tell that to the government,' he said, cutting his finger on the lid of the corned beef tin. Blood dripped into the pan as he stirred the beans on the gas ring until they bubbled. He poured them over the meat and carried his plate through to the sitting room, switched on the television. The electronic *Doctor Who* theme invaded the room. It was a preview for a series starting in the New Year but it screamed of Jake's absence. *Dr Who* was Jake's favourite programme, mostly viewed from behind a cushion. He had always watched from the sofa curled up beside his dad. Appetite waning, Pavel threw down the knife and fork. There was only a week until Christmas. Maybe if his mother loaned him the train fare, Cheryl might allow him to visit.

He washed the dishes, tidied the kitchen. Restless, he ran upstairs into Jake's bedroom, as if trying to recapture his son. The room was emptied of toys, books and posters and the bed had been stripped of sheets and duvet. Bare, lifeless. He stumbled to the window, looked down onto the garden. Cheryl had insisted Jake leave the rabbit behind and Pavel had dragged the hutch into the shed for the winter. The grass had yellowed where it had once stood.

He opened the wardrobe door. All that was left hanging was Jake's cub uniform, like a ghoulish effigy, the neckerchief still attached to the green jumper, the sleeves dotted with badges Pavel had sewn on: camper, cook, collector. He buried his face in the woollen fabric hoping to retrieve Jake's scent but smelled only soap powder. He remembered washing the uniform before Cheryl left, hoping Jake would pack it and join a cub troop in Lincolnshire. In the bottom of the wardrobe, Pavel spotted an instrument case. He took out the trumpet, pursed his lips to the mouthpiece, intending to play the first line of *Men of Harlech* which Jake had taught him, but he gave up at the first rasping note and shower of spittle.

Jake had left behind half his life.

Downstairs, the fire had reduced to a pile of glowing ashes and a chill had refurnished the room. Unable to settle to watch television or to read, Pavel found a bobble hat and scarf and prepared to cross the village to his mother's house. He was certain she'd allow him to phone Jake. He'd ask her if he could move in immediately. When a house was empty, devoid of warmth and family, when there was no music playing or cooking on the hob or baking in the oven, a house reverted to its own smell. In the past, when he'd returned from a family holiday, it was the first thing he'd noticed on opening the door. A new house smelled of sawdust and fresh plaster, an old house of damp and the history of its owners embedded in peeling wallpaper. Maybe this house had always smelled of loneliness.

★ ★ ★

The phone rested on a small table beneath the stairs. To avoid banging his head on the sloping ceiling Pavel knelt, hunching his shoulders.

'Jake? It's Dad. Did you see the preview for the Dr Who series?'

'No. Grandma says it's unsuitable and I won't be able to watch it. Granddad's taking me to the cinema. Mum wants to speak so I'll hand you over. '

Pavel sank to the floor. Not even a goodbye. Did Jake hate him already? Had Cheryl's father taken his place? Were they poisoning Jake against him?

Pavel told Cheryl of his immediate plans to sell the house. 'If we pay off the mortgage there should be enough for a deposit on a small property for you and Jake.'

She seemed to appreciate this, at least she thanked him. He heard Jake's whispered goodbye to his mother. The door shut.

'I hate to admit it but Jake's missing you,' Cheryl said. 'He's miserable, Pavel. If you're moving out, maybe we could stay in the house over Christmas? That's assuming your fancy woman hasn't moved in.'

'Helen's living in London.'

'Dumped you?'

He bit his lip, ignored her provocation. He couldn't risk Cheryl changing her mind.

'He's not settling at school and not eating,' she said. 'However much I hate you for what you've done, he'll hate me more if I prevent him from seeing you. None of this is Jake's fault.'

She couldn't see Pavel's smile, hear his heartbeat.

'Are you still there? I'll ask Mum and Dad to come with me,' she said. 'You can visit, maybe take Jake out. But that's all. Make sure the house is clean and tidy.'

'Don't I always?'

'I've consulted a solicitor. We may as well start proceedings.'

'Fine. Tell Jake I tried to play his trumpet but it won't work for me.'

When he'd replaced the receiver he punched the air then hugged his mother. 'Jake's coming home for Christmas.'

★ ★ ★

Cheshire December 24th 1984

Woods flanked the country lanes, trees like sentinels for several miles. When a fallow deer emerged and stood motionless in the headlights, Helen braked, skidded. The seat belt dug into her chest as the deer shot across the lane, disappearing between oaks. 'Watch out, Rudolph.' She laughed, brittle, a little shaken, embarrassed by Guy's continued silence. 'That was close,' she said. 'Are you okay?'

He nodded, 'Fine. Don't worry about me.' She detected a note of sarcasm but at least he'd responded.

The journey seemed interminable. It had taken longer than expected owing to holiday traffic jams and patchy fog on the M6. This was the final leg of the journey to Cheshire, Guy a glowering presence beside her. She'd turned on the radio, tuning into classical music to fill the space between them. A second hand Mini was not ideal motorway transport but it had got them this far without problem. The vehicle had cost her a hefty chunk of her savings from her term's teaching and though there was little use for a car in central London, she'd recognised it could facilitate a quick escape if necessary. She couldn't have contemplated sitting opposite Guy on a long train journey. Z bends unnerved her. Tendrils of mist slowed their progress. Slow, accelerate, slow.

Eventually she pulled onto the Eagleton's drive, crunching gravel. Lights blazed welcome from every window. If Helen left lights on Tibby switched them off, scolded her for extravagance.

Inside, the house was filled with the scent of fresh evergreen. A spruce studded with white lights embellished one corner of the hall and from the kitchen the smell of mulled wine beckoned.

'How are you, darling?' his mother asked, pecking Guy's cheek. 'How hungry are you?' Guy shrugged. Helen told her they'd stopped at a service station for coffee but hadn't eaten. His father gave Helen a cursory nod then supported by a walking stick he hobbled into the sitting room. Mrs Eagleton explained that her husband had had a mild stroke recently and was undergoing physiotherapy. 'You'll find him less ebullient than you remember.'

'Guy didn't mention it,' Helen said. Poor Guy. He had more than an errant wife and a damaged career to worry about.

'Motorway services, you say? Ghastly places.' His mother winced. 'I wasn't sure what time you'd arrive. We heard on the radio that there were delays so I've set out a buffet. Come through.' She ushered Guy and Helen into the dining room. The linen napkins were printed with poinsettias. A porcelain nativity scene and fat red candles in silver holders graced the windowsill. By the fireplace, boxes wrapped in gold tissue and tied with tartan ribbons had been stacked at angles beneath a second Christmas tree. Not a string of cheap tinsel in sight. Were the boxes empty adornments or real gifts? Nothing would be left to last minute forages in the loft for decorations.

Every year Billy hung crepe paper garlands across his sitting room, pinned a balloon in each corner. And a snowman scene with plastic sleighs on a bed of cotton wool always decorated the mantelpiece, regardless of fire hazard or good taste. Tibby's serviettes were paper, remnants of festive teas, patterned with holly wreathes, Santas, or gold coloured words from well-known carols. Like the artificial tree, they emerged from a battered cardboard box with the tinsel, lacy doilies and a sad-faced plastic fairy Helen had always loved.

Back in Lundby the strikers were probably blowing dust from tinsel trees right now – as Helen bit into a mince pie, the pastry rich with ground almonds, the mincemeat laced in brandy. A sprinkling of sugar stuck to her lips.

When Guy and his father had gone to bed Helen joined her mother-in-law in the sitting room. Holly garlands draped the mantelpiece. There had always been an air of formality between Helen and Guy's parents; she had never been invited to address them by their forenames.

'Guy should live here until he's well,' Mrs Eagleton said, pouring herself a glass of wine. 'Are you sure you don't want a drink?' Helen shook her head. 'I need help with his father and taking care of someone else can be therapeutic in the case of depression. One thing is certain, my son must not return to politics. A heart attack at such a young age is a warning. I knew he'd never withstand the pressure. It's destroyed him. But he won't be without a job when he recovers. His father still has connections.'

'I was afraid you'd blame me,' Helen said.

Mrs Eagleton gave an acid smile. 'I blamed you wholly at first. You failed Guy. But he must have given you provocation. I'm not blind. It's not easy living with a womaniser. I should know. Perhaps if William had lived...'

'Guy couldn't express his grief.'

'He always found emotion difficult. He was a lonely boy and his father bullied him. Sometimes when a woman is torn between husband and child, she attempts to pander to each of them and fails both.'

Was this an apology? Had Helen been the sacrifice on the altar of Guy's fragility? 'I always knew Guy's father thought I was unsuitable,' she said.

'We both did, I'm afraid. You were the last of a series of unsuitable girlfriends. I think in you Guy saw someone he could dominate. That worried me. And your backgrounds were so different – are you sure you wouldn't like a glass of something? Whisky perhaps? Brandy?'

It was late and the central heating had switched off. A draught from the French windows reached Helen's legs and a soft swoosh of pine needles landed on the carpet. 'The problem we have with real trees,' Guy's mother said. 'I doubt this one will last till Boxing Day. I'm forever vacuuming. Hate the artificial things though, don't you?' She stood up. 'Let me at least make you a cup of tea.'

'No, really. I should go to bed. Look. I'm sorry about... Guy losing the promotion. I take full responsibility for that.'

'Losing the job may have saved his life.' Mrs Eagleton threw a log on the fire and sat down.

'We did have happy times once,' Helen said. 'At least in the beginning.' Her eyes were drawn to the sideboard. Something was missing. The photograph of Guy and Helen on their wedding day had disappeared.

'Beginnings are easy, Helen. Once Guy became an MP it was clear any cracks in the marriage would become cavernous. Politicians need wives who embrace their beliefs. In the circumstances that was never likely. Still... he needed you.'

'Need? Need is not love though, is it? Guy's obsessed by Mrs Thatcher. Almost a religious convert to her policies. He worships her.'

'The vulnerable are needy. They look to the strong. He admires that Margaret Thatcher doesn't tolerate weakness, and now he believes he's become a fool and an old fashioned cuckold. I don't mean to be too harsh on you. You could stay, you know... if you have no other plans. It might help.'

'I wouldn't want to give Guy false hope.'

Interrupted by the clock in the hall striking midnight, Helen found the excuse she needed to retire, leaving Mrs Eagleton, empty glass in hand, staring into the embers.

Once undressed, Helen stood naked in front of the dressing table. Her nipples had darkened. It was ten weeks since her last period and yet, in spite of the grim weeks spent visiting Guy in hospital, helping to take care of Isaac and missing Pavel, she felt a weird content. She had experienced this state of well-being before, when she was pregnant with William. Her body would do all it could to nurture and protect a new life.

Pavel's surprise visit in October had overtaken caution. She'd remembered too late that she'd discarded the pack of contraceptive pills in a bin on Doncaster station when she'd left Lundby. She couldn't tell Pavel yet. Certainly not over a telephone. It was bad timing. She needed to gauge his reaction by looking into his eyes. He was a terrible liar. That red patch on his neck. She would know. She'd rather be a single mother than a burden. Besides it was early days. Experience demanded restraint.

The old wardrobe with its demon face reminded her of the evening of the harvest ball, the night of Guy's seduction, the consequences of a reckless lapse of resolve, of her own weakness. She curled up, hugging a pillow.

After a breakfast of dry toast which no one questioned, she packed her bag, wished the family a happy Christmas and made her farewells.

Guy followed her to the car. 'I wish you'd stay,' he said.

'I can't, Guy. I'm sorry. I'll put the apartment up for sale in January. And don't worry, I'll organise everything. Just get well.'

'Where will you go now?'

'I'll visit Tibby and Billy... then back to London.'

Guy kicked gravel against the tyres. 'I suppose you'll see him then. The Pole?'

She hoped so but said nothing, merely kissed Guy's cheek lightly and climbed behind the steering wheel. The family waved her off. When she glanced through the rear view mirror, she noticed Guy held his father's arm and was steering him towards the house.

As it was Christmas Eve, the service station was teeming with families – visiting relatives for the holiday or en route to airports seeking winter sun? Children queued at Santa's grotto and even the washrooms echoed with hackneyed Christmas pop.

From an open kiosk she phoned Uncle Billy, one finger in her ear masking the constant jingling surrounding her. Despite turning down the Eagleton invitation to stay for Christmas, the thought of being alone in London held no appeal. Isaac's sons had arranged a surprise holiday to Israel and the whole family had flown out from Heathrow yesterday. Helen had helped Isaac with last minute packing. He'd become frailer during autumn and confided he'd prefer to stay at home. His initial expressions of delight and gratitude had been for Max and Solly's benefit only.

'I know I said I'd go straight back to London but I can't face it, Uncle Billy. Is it too late to change my mind?'

'We might be out of fatted calves,' Billy said. 'But Tibby's bought a turkey big enough to feed the village.'

In the background Tibby shouted. 'You can help at the children's party this afternoon if you get a move on.'

★ ★ ★

Lundby South Yorkshire

It was more than Pavel could have hoped for. Cheryl's parents' trial retirement to the seaside had not proved the idyll they'd hoped for. They missed their friends and extended family and were keen to return to Lundby as soon as possible. Last night when Pavel had called to see Jake, Cheryl's father had invited him in.

'I should give you a bloody good thrashing, Pavel, but I dare say it's too late for that. Jake comes first. I have a proposition.' Pavel had hovered by the front door, a nervous hand on the handle. 'I want to buy this house. We would live here with Cheryl and Jake but you'd have to give up all rights to equity. That will be my daughter's nest egg. You owe her that much. If we're amicable we might save on solicitors' fees and heartache.'

Pavel would have agreed to anything. Hadn't he already decided to give Cheryl the equity? No loss then.

Jake was practising a Christmas carol on his trumpet, safely back in his bedroom.

The mile long walk to the Institute seemed shorter with Jake by his side. Pavel had been charged with delivering Jake to the children's party.

'There is no Father Christmas, Dad, so don't try to con me.'

'If you say so. Personally I like Father Christmas.'

'I think it will be Mr Farrimond dressed up, don't you? You can always tell.'

'Can you?'

'Yeah. Fake Santas forget the boots. They either wear a pair of wellingtons or their own shoes, or worse still, trainers. And cotton wool beards. What do they take us for?'

This was Jake's last year in primary school. In a few years he might leave home for university. Thank God Pavel could be a part of his son's life again. He felt a pang of hope, a glimmer of Christmas cheer. He left Jake at the door of the Institute reminding him that Cheryl would collect him after the party. 'I'll see you in the morning, help you open your presents.'

★ ★ ★

The concert room smelled of smoke. Tibby had organised a rota of helpers but the woman due to make sandwiches had succumbed to flu. Though happy to be substitute Helen had little recent experience of potted beef and chocolate spread, and the smell of hard boiled eggs turned her stomach. She wouldn't tell Tibby. Not yet. Tibby was unrolling crepe paper runners along trestle tables and Uncle Billy had taken his Santa outfit into a store room where he could change.

There'd been no time to let Pavel know of her arrival, though she'd hoped to find him helping at the party, maybe inflating balloons or wrapping up prizes. There was no sign of him; perhaps it was too painful to watch children having fun when his own son was so far away. When she'd arrived she'd noticed Coker on hands on knees in a corner of the room, fixing fairy lights. Hearing her heels crossing the dance floor he'd looked up.

'Not you again. You've made more come-backs than a bloody boomerang.'

She'd cocooned herself in the kitchen. If she retched it was better to have no witness.

The counters were cluttered with tins of donated buns, jumbo-sized packets of crisps, trays of pizza slices and sausage rolls. Clearing a space big enough to butter bread, she uncovered a tape of Christmas carols and remembered from her breakfast duties that there was a cassette player in a cupboard above the sink.

In the bleak mid-winter was interrupted by a tap on her shoulder. 'Coker. What do you want?'

He swaggered, waved mistletoe above her head, singing. 'What can I give him poor as I am... A little bit of what Pavel gets, maybe?' His breath smelled of beer.

She pushed him towards the door. 'Get away. You're drunk.'

'Just one Christmas kiss for old times' sake.'

'There are no old times, Coker. Now leave before –'

'I was never good enough for you, was I? Eh? Good enough to do your maths homework though, carry your bloody satchel around school. Lap dog Coker. Down boy. Don't you remember? Selective memory?'

'I remember you helped me with my maths and I was grateful,' she said, edging away, sliding against the cupboards.

'Helped you? Gave up playing footie with my mates at lunchtimes to explain quadratic equations to you. Trigonometry? You were hopeless with cosines. Extra tuition you got for free. Got you through the bloody O level I did. Grateful you call it? Telling me to drop dead? You knew how I felt about you.' Coker slumped onto a kitchen stool, picking white berries from the mistletoe, flicking them at her feet.

'I was only fifteen, I didn't know any better,' she said, cringing. 'I'm amazed you took it so much to heart. I knew... I was scared... I could see... you had a crush on me. It was embarrassment I suppose. I'm sorry if I hurt you. I didn't mean to.'

'Bollocks. Dumped me when I were no more use to you, exams looming and maths paper sorted.'

'I said I was sorry. It was crass.' How could she have been so cruel? 'Why did you leave before your exams?'

'Don't think that was down to a broken heart, *Miss up-your- own-arse*. That was my dad's idea. No choice.'

'That's a shame. You could have done well.'

'Patronising cow. You're a User. Used a well-connected husband to climb the social ladder didn't you? Now you've done for him an' all. The poor bugger's cracked up, I've heard. Don't look at me like that. Blame *Billy-Big-Mouth's* spouting. Snooker rooms have ears.'

'There's no more I can say. You've made up your mind about me. You should leave. Now.'

'What, before Pavel arrives to defend your honour? Don't make me laugh. He couldn't knock the skin off a —'

'He managed to knock the skin off your jaw.'

'He took me by surprise. That's all.' His eyes welled. 'I could still forgive you... for one kiss. You've gone pink. It suits you. Come back here.' He got to his feet waving the denuded stalk of mistletoe then sat down again, head bowed, gazing at his feet. The laces of one trainer were unfastened. He looked so dejected, helpless that she was almost moved to touch his shoulder.

'Helen stuck-up Farrimond,' he said. 'To think... I loved you once.'

The door opened. Billy walked in. 'Helen, do you think you could make me a cuppa before — ? Everything okay in here?'

Coker laughed. 'Christ. If it's not Saint Kowaleski to the rescue, then it's bleedin' Father Christmas. Great timing, Santa. Don't worry, I'm off.' He staggered to the door, stuffing the scrap of mistletoe into Billy's cotton wool beard before he left.

By the time Helen had finished the sandwiches, Santa had distributed his gifts and party games were underway: a hectic programme of musical bumps, musical chairs, statues and sleeping lions; the snatch and rip of pass the parcel. It was only after the scramble and sprint following Tibby's announcement that party food was ready, and the children had found their seats at the tables that Helen spotted Jake.

Amid screeching foil trumpets, a sea of streamers and garish paper hats, she delivered a platter of sandwiches and savouries to his rowdy table. Someone nudged her. Sausage rolls tumbled from the plate and were caught or snaffled by greedy hands.

'Hello Mrs Eagleton. Have you come back as well?' Helen had to crouch by his chair to hear Jake above the music. Crackers snapped. Sparks flew. The odour of sulphur and aroma of cheese and onion crisps did nothing to calm her queasiness.

'Jake. I'm surprised to see you.'

'Have you heard the news? We've come home. I'm going back to school here in January.'

'No. I hadn't heard. That's great. Will your dad be collecting you after the party?'

'No. He brought me. Mum's picking me up.'

'I see. Well have a wonderful Christmas. You deserve it.'

She dashed into the kitchen insisting on washing up. 'I've got a headache,' she told Tibby. 'Will you take over out there?'

Men were stacking chairs; sweeping crumbs, torn streamers and blobs of jelly from the floor. The last of the children, including Jake, waited in the hall to be collected. Since Billy had to stay behind to lock up, Tibby encouraged Helen to go on home without them.

It was on her way out that Helen met Cheryl in the porch. Hoping not to be recognised, Helen had wrapped a scarf around her mouth and tipped her brimmed hat over her forehead.

'I'm surprised to see you here, Mrs Eagleton. It is you hiding under that hat?'

'Jake told me you were home,' Helen said.

Cheryl grinned. 'Didn't Pavel let you know? Tsk. That's men for you. He's thrilled we're back. You're living in London now aren't you?'

'Yes. Only here for a couple of days.' Helen slipped off the porch step and strode out into the night.

'Well don't let me keep you,' Cheryl called, her voice sugar-sweet with sarcasm. 'And be careful you don't fall. It's icy out there.'

★ ★ ★

Christmas morning had proved beyond anything he could have wished for. Pavel emptied his glass of the last of the cheap wine his mother had won in the support group raffle.

'Fantastic,' Pavel said. 'Best Christmas dinner I've had this year.'

'Are you sure he's Polish, Mrs Kowaleski,' Kath said. 'I detect a touch of blarney.'

He sat back in his chair, blowing cigar smoke upwards so that his party hat fluttered. The cigars were part of the prize. He couldn't remember the last time he'd smoked.

'We're going to need more than blarney to stop men from strike breaking,' Roly said, returning Pavel to reality. 'I reckon after Christmas we should visit them individually. Face to face. It'll take time but could be worth it.'

'£650 pounds bonus to anyone back to work by the end of November,' Pavel explained to his mother. 'That started the avalanche.'

Kath groaned. 'Can't we talk about something else?'

'Hard for single lads not to waver,' Pavel said.

Roly nodded. 'They've done well when you consider they don't receive a penny in benefit. P'raps we should get Billy Farrimond to give a pep talk at the Institute. He can't stand Thatcher or Macgregor.'

Kath brought in the Christmas pudding and Pavel rubbed his hands. 'True,' he said. 'But he's not much fonder of Scargill is he?'

'Talking of Billy,' Roly said. 'There was a red Mini outside his house when I passed last night. You don't think Santa's bought himself a little car for Christmas to match his outfit do you?'

'Red Mini?' Pavel said. 'Helen has a red mini. Bought it weeks ago to...' He jumped up. 'Why didn't you say so? I'll see you later. Sorry can't stay to wash up, Kath.'

'If it was Helen wouldn't she have phoned?' his mother said. He kissed her, grabbed his coat. 'Thanks for a lovely dinner. Be back later, Mum.'

The streets were empty as Pavel raced through the village, over pavements twinkling with hoar frost. It was three forty-five. The Queen's speech had ended and the afternoon light was fading. Children sporting new cycles and skateboards had long since gone inside and were probably curled up on sofas watching *The Sound of Music*.

The red Mini outside Billy Farrimond's house had also disappeared, along with Billy's fickle niece.

Chapter Twenty Seven

A Plea and a Prank

January 1985

Ice crystals shimmered beneath street lamps, pretty yet bleak; cars parked by the roadside were covered in snow like curious igloos. No one had cleared drives or pavements; doors had been bolted, curtains closed, as if shutting out not just the weather but neighbours, friends, suspicion.

Pavel and Roly had agreed to call on the vulnerable: strikers most likely to be considering returning to work. As they approached this particular house – the tenth tonight – Pavel noticed the gate was missing. He lost his footing on the garden path but managed to stay upright, clutching Roly's sleeve then finding purchase for his fingers in the pointing between frosted bricks. On the inside of the front door a piece of cardboard secured a panel of splintered glass while on the outside, cracks like wheel spokes fanned from a hole the size of a pebble. Pavel tapped on the window. A gap between the curtains provided a glimpse of flickering shadows and an orange glow from a small fire. A toddler appeared, squashed a stub nose against the pane then shied away into the sitting room.

When a shrill voice yelled, 'Round the back,' the two men tripped and skated to the back door, holding onto each other as if they were school boys on blades for the first time. A light came on in the kitchen, a key turned and a woman's pale face appeared behind a door chain.

'Is he in, love?' Roly said. 'Just a quick word.'

'Who is it?' A man's voice. 'If it's Roly Beresford tell him to sod off.'

'Torville and Dean doing a triple salchow,' she said. 'Come and see for yourself.'

The door closed, the chain unhooked, the door opened. The woman had disappeared and a tall unshaven man stood on the threshold, holding a baby in a pink pyjama suit. Pavel held out his hand; the baby gurgled and clasped his fingers.

'Now then, little one, what's your – '

'What do you want?' The man drew his daughter to his chest. 'I've told you. It's too late.'

'Late in the day admittedly,' Roly said, 'but not too late to change your mind, mate.'

The baby whined and the man popped a dummy into her dribbling mouth.

'Expect she's teething is she?' Pavel said. 'Jake was just the same.' Roly nudged him. Pavel hoped to be invited inside. His lips were chapped, his fingers throbbed; he couldn't remember where he'd left his gloves: probably at the first house they'd called at, where they'd at least been offered mugs of tea. He buried his raw hands in his pockets, shivered.

The man scowled. 'My wife doesn't work like yours do. We can't eat in a poxy soup kitchen forever and I can't feed my kids on fresh air – or on donations of Russian bloody meat loaf.' He glanced over his shoulder, lowered his voice then looked at Pavel. 'She's threatening to leave and take kids with her if I don't start bringing in a wage.'

Pavel nodded. 'I'm sorry.' He felt an elbow in his ribs. Roly had warned him they'd have to be tough. 'But if you go back to work now you'll waste everything we've achieved,' he said.

The man shook his head. 'Come off it, Pav. We've achieved bugger all.'

Pavel swallowed hard. 'We knew winter would be tough. Don't pack it in now. There's bound to be some concession from the Board soon.'

The baby coughed, her dad rolled his eyes. 'With this Government behind 'em? Who are you kidding?'

'Pavel might be soft on you,' Roly said, 'but when it's over, the men who stay out won't be so forgiving.'

The baby grizzled, butted her head against her father's neck. He winced. 'Don't threaten me, Roly. And you of all people, Pavel – you know damn well I've done my best. Been at every picket line. Got the boot prints in my back to prove it.' He sniffed, wiped his nose on the cuff of his sweater. 'I don't want to choose between mates and my missus.'

The child whimpered, spat out the dummy. The man rocked her. His wife's shouts echoed as if the house were empty or carpets removed. 'For God's sake shut the door. You're letting the heat out. She'll catch her death.'

'We'll all catch our death. I'm going back on Monday and that's my final word, Roly. So bugger off.' The baby's face crumpled.

The chain slid back into place, a bolt clunked. Raised voices and the baby's howling followed the men down the garden path. 'Well that told him,' Roly said.

A fall of snow had covered their footprints and was drifting, obscuring the gutter. Pavel steadied himself on the gatepost and the branches of a neighbour's privet hedge which shed a canopy of snow over his work boots. His trainers were finally done for.

'Right,' Roly said. 'We've time to call on a couple more dissenters.'

Pavel stamped, kicked his toes against the post, wondering how much of it would be left for the family to burn tomorrow. He couldn't call a man a scab who'd given ten months of his life to the strike. But there'd be plenty who would.

★ ★ ★

There were only six of them on the picket line. Pavel warmed his hands on the brazier. Burning logs were the only light at five thirty in the morning, save for a hurricane lamp Roly said he'd found in his garage. Another shift to come, another battle bus, another stream of once loyal men falling prey to Coal Board promises, threats of sackings and the Government's smearing of the union's name.

Two pickets stood at the roadside, sharing a thermos, watching for the arrival of police and scabs, listening for the warning rattle of the metal mesh over the works' bus windows. Swannie and Gus were aiming snowballs at each other – and at Roly who was wearing a child-size police helmet his daughter Jen had given him as a joke Christmas present. Perched at an angle on the top of his balaclava it was fixed in place by a chin strap across his nostrils. Bombarded by snowballs it toppled to the ground.

'Glad somebody's finding summat to laugh about,' Pavel said, picking up the helmet and drying it on his jacket.

'I've had an idea,' Roly said. 'Government orders, remember? No more than six pickets. So make yourselves useful, lads. Build a snowman. Let's make it seven.'

Gus and Swannie scooped up handfuls of snow and patted them around a bollard which had recently been erected at the entrance to the pit yard. Roly stamped his feet. 'Lend you my helmet when you've done.' He turned to Pavel. 'Cheer up. Have you heard from Helen yet?'

'She phoned yesterday. She's staying with the old man I told you about. He's been ill since he flew home from a holiday abroad, so she's helping the family out. He's frail but they don't want to send him into a nursing home.'

'He must mean a lot to her,' Roly said. 'Did you sort out the Christmas fiasco?'

'Took her till New Year's Eve to answer the phone.'

'Will she come back?'

Pavel nodded. 'Says she will, eventually.'

'Then I expect she will.'

'Wish I had your confidence.' Pavel didn't understand how Helen could let Cheryl's mischief fool her, or why she hadn't trusted him. Hopefully Cheryl would back off now that she had a boyfriend. The haulage company she'd worked for had quickly reinstated her and she was dating the lately divorced owner. It hadn't taken her long to get over the supposed heartbreak. It irked Pavel that another man should play dad to Jake. A complete stranger.

The bollard snowman finished, Gus dug beneath the snow finding gravel for eyes, mouth and buttons, and a twig for its nose.

'Cops coming.' At a shout from the two roadside pickets, the men shuffled to attention, lining up either side of the snowman, the bollard camouflaged.

Down to six pickets and a snowman. Was this what they'd been reduced to?

A police van pulled in. The doors opened and a sergeant and five young constables jumped out. Gus hummed the theme from *The Good, the Bad and the Ugly*.

'Very funny,' the sergeant said, eyeing the snow picket. 'Knock that bloody thing down, idiots.'

'This is a law abiding citizen,' Swannie said, patting Roly's police helmet on the snowman's head.

'The only one of you silly buggers who is then.'

The sergeant nodded to one of his men – the one grinning. 'And since you think it's so funny, you can get back in the van and run it over.'

Pavel stepped forward. 'Hang on, Sergeant – '

'You! Keep your gob shut. Won't take much to rile me this morning. I'll have your arse in the back of that van before you can pick a bloody *scab* off the end of your nose.'

The constable climbed into the driver's seat, reversed, then crunching gears and revving the engine, he drove at the snow picket. At the sound of buckling metal, Pavel covered his ears. Swannie inspected the vehicle, examining the mangled bumper. 'Nasty prang, Sergeant.'

The snow head and helmet lay on the ground. Swannie lit a cigarette, nodded at the remains of the seventh picket. 'Sergeant, may I inquire if your driver is insured for personal injury?'

When the workers arrived, laughter turned to half-hearted shouts, insults and threats as the sergeant lowered the bollard and the bus slipped past the pickets and into the pit yard. Another victory for Margaret Thatcher. Another day-shift nearer defeat.

It was typical of Roly to rally his men with a prank. But the ugly scenes Pavel had witnessed: arguments, fights in the high street and outside shops – even at the Institute – were sickening. There seemed little hope. The issue of who stayed out on strike and who returned to work was splitting families, marriages. Already there were brothers dead to each other, swearing never to speak again. If you worked in a death-trap, humour was the only way to survive. Roly had taught him that. Banter and jokes cemented friendships, created bonds; miners watched out for each other. There would be little to laugh about before long. In the future Lundby Edge miners would watch over their shoulders, mind their backs.

'May as well go home,' Roly said. 'Have a kip.'

★ ★ ★

Trees were weighted with snow, branches bowed and snowflakes were spiralling onto the lawn like thousands of feathers. Helen had made it back from her hospital appointment just in time. Roads were gridlocked, Greenwich was frozen.

Isaac's eyes were closed. 'I'm not asleep,' he said. 'There's a peculiar light that seeps through eye lids. An anomaly. In the same way that silence can often deafen. Both woke me.'

'Snow muffles everything. The traffic's at a standstill.'

'Could you help me to sit up, Helen? I'd like to see through the window.' She lifted his shoulders, plumped his pillows. 'How was your dental appointment? My cousin was a dentist. As far as I remember he didn't deliver babies.'

Helen blushed. 'I'm sorry, Isaac. I didn't want to lie. Just wanted to be certain.'

Keen to reassure her, the obstetrician had attached electrodes to her belly, allowing her to listen to the baby's heartbeat. On the way home she had even dared to think of names. 'I didn't want tell you until I was past the three month marker. And certainly not while your daughter-in-law was covering for me. I don't want your family to think I'm not up to looking after you.'

Isaac smiled. 'My daughter-in-law worked until she was eight months pregnant with Max. She would understand.

Besides you won't be able to keep the secret for much longer.'

'I know. I can't fasten my jeans.' A long blouse covered an open zip.

'And when do you propose to tell the father?'

'Soon. I speak to him each week.'

'About what? The weather? You should tell him soon.'

Isaac had returned from Israel with a cold which had deteriorated into a chest infection. He seemed to be past crisis point but Helen had spent anxious afternoons watching the slow rise and fall of his chest and listening to his laboured breathing. In the city she'd bought a few tapes of his favourite classical music and rescued the cassette player from the apartment. 'Now we can listen to Rachmaninov upstairs,' she said.

'I read somewhere that it's good for babies to listen to music before they're born,' he said.

'So many children at school only recognised music as themes to advertisements. I call it *Beethoven's butter syndrome.*'

'At least your child will know that Rachmaninov was more than a film score.' He chuckled, coughed. 'You should go home, Helen. Home to Pavel.'

★ ★ ★

'It's for you, Pavel. It's Cheryl.'

His mother shrugged, handed over the receiver. 'She sounds agitated, says it's urgent.'

There was always a moment's dread when Cheryl phoned, a jangling of nerve endings, even when the urgent matter she needed to discuss was nothing more than a forthcoming school open night or a request for Pavel to babysit.

'It's mayhem out here,' Cheryl said. 'Neighbour's gone back to work and they're waiting for him. A mob. Police outside. I can't leave the house to meet Jake.'

Jake had insisted that being collected from school by a parent guaranteed teasing so would only allow his mother to meet him half way home.

'He'll be scared, Pavel, when he realises what's going on. Can you head him off?'

With no chance of sprinting in the snow and too late to meet Jake at the school gate, Pavel tramped towards his old home, but finding the street blocked by a police van and a crowd surrounding a scab shift bus, he waited on a nearby corner where he might spot Jake approaching. It seemed a safer option to distance himself from this particular row. But the officers were clearing the pavements of onlookers, sweeping the area in a thirty yard radius. At first it was a polite plea, then a shove, a push supported by threatening barks from a German shepherd.

In the midst of the crowd stood a hapless school crossing patrol man, his STOP lollipop held aloft. An angry woman emerged from a house waving a yard brush but Pavel couldn't fathom whether her curses were aimed at the police, pickets or terrified scab.

'Move on.'

Pavel stumbled from a shove to his shoulder. 'I'm just waiting for my son.'

The copper's face was in Pavel's. 'And I said, move on.'

'He'll be scared when – .'

'So will you if you don't shift.'

'I promised to meet him. I'm not here for trouble.'

'Then scram and you'll get none. If you don't move...'

Pavel could see Jake approaching. He elbowed the officer, dodged around him. 'Go to Grandma's, Jake,' he shouted as he was knocked to the ground, a hand inside his shirt collar, a kick to his heels. Handcuffed Pavel landed on the floor of the police van. When he looked up he saw Coker already on the side bench.

Pavel groaned. 'Not you.' The officer closed the door. 'But my son is – '

'Going inside the house with your wife,' the policeman shouted. 'Stop whinging. You're nicked.'

The cell stank of piss, vomit, fish and musty grey blankets that were folded on the end of a narrow bunk. The walls were a sickly cream. There was a sink and a cracked lavatory missing a seat. A metal door, a grille. Pavel leaned against the wall; Coker sat in the middle of a bare mattress, head between his knees. Neither spoke. Jangling keys reminded Pavel of a film. *The man in the Iron Mask,* maybe? Or *a Tale of Two Cities?* A *heads dropping into baskets* scenario either way.

A uniform at the door. A new prisoner: the elderly crossing patrol man, stripped of his lollipop but still in his waxed jacket. 'Here we are. See if you can help these two chumps across to the other side,' the gaoler said.

Coker made room on the mattress. 'We'll have grandmas and school kids in here next.' The man dropped onto the end of the bed, complaining about innocence and injustice. Pavel and Coker laughed, the patrol man cried.

Coker tapped his foot in an unrecognisable rhythm, presumably to some tune in his head. He stopped, fixed his eyes on the ceiling.

'I'm sorry, mate,' he said. 'You know, for 'owt I shouldn't have said or done. Your girlfriend. I was out of order.'

Pavel nodded. What did he mean? What had he done? *Girlfriend?* The word made him smile.

Coker sank his head further between his knees. 'Did you know I asked her out once? She turned me down.'

'She never mentioned it.'

Coker looked shrivelled slouching on the mattress, his head sunken into his shoulders.

The crossing patrol man said his wife would wonder where he was. She'd be furious. 'I'm scared I'll lose my job.'

'Aren't we all?' Pavel said.

The grille panel slid. 'Ready lads? You're going home.'

Coker straightened and, regaining stature, he raised a salute and nudged the patrol man's shoulder. 'Don't worry, mate. It'll probably cost you no more than seventy-five quid and an earful from your old lady.'

Swamped by his oversized coat, the man waddled to the door. 'Alright for you to talk. Union pays your fines.'

Coker looked at Pavel and shrugged. There was no money left in union coffers. Pavel hoped the desk sergeant would release them without charge, so they wouldn't be sacked. The police were as jaded as miners.

Coker winked and bustled the patrol man through the open cell door. 'Tell you what, my old mate. I'll have your job. You have mine.

Chapter Twenty Eight

Returns

March 5th 1985

London

The apartment was sold, emptied of furniture and Helen had banked the proceeds from the sale of the Mini intending to spend it on baby equipment. There was nothing much she'd wanted to keep from joint belongings. Guy's mother had visited in February, reported her son's improvement. She'd gathered his clothes, albums of jazz, unused golf clubs, books and his collection of antique watches. Helen had given her the silver and crockery. The guilt gifts and jewellery Guy had brought back from business trips abroad and her wedding ring and solitaire diamond, were sold off to raise funds for the premature baby unit which had cared for William.

'I'll take the suitcases then,' Billy said. 'Meanwhile make us a cup of tea if you've still got a kettle and a pot.' These were the only items remaining apart from two mugs and a couple of boxes. She hadn't seen her uncle since Christmas but his shock at the news of the pregnancy had been softened by her announcement that he would be called Granddad.

They sat on the last boxes, drinking tea. 'Tomorrow will be a grim day for the lads having to march back to work,' Billy said. 'Having their noses rubbed in it.' He squeezed her hand. 'But at least I'm taking my girl home.'

When they finished, Billy hefted a box onto his hip and took it out to the car. The kettle and mugs she would leave for new occupants.

The strike was lost. A tragedy the miners had not foreseen a year ago. They'd suffered a humiliating defeat; she could only imagine how Pavel and Roly felt. Starved back to work by cut benefits, letters of bribery and intimidation and there'd be more hardship to come with mounting debts and pits still to be closed. A few empty bank balances, a few ruptured hearts, a few broken marriages, a few fractured limbs, a few severed families. A picket and a taxi driver dead. The latest price of coal?

She cradled the growing bump in her belly. Strike Baby.

She dragged the last box closer, hauling it by a flap. There were photographs of William in here, and some of the clothes he never wore. She opened a small black velvet jewellery box. The night before Isaac died, when he'd been at his most lucid and when his family had gathered around him, he had given her a diamond pendant which had belonged to Miriam. His family had insisted she accept. She would treasure it. She slipped it into her handbag.

It had been a privilege to have cared for Isaac and although it had kept her from Pavel, she would always remember the days since Christmas. Isaac's stories, his common sense when she floundered, his humanity, his ability to listen rather than pass judgement. The music of Rachmaninov would always be his.

She sat on the bare floor, resting a hand where she felt a tiny limb thumping.

As Uncle Billy had reminded her, the equity alone on the apartment would buy a terraced house in Lundby. She would miss only the river and Greenwich.

Uncle Billy was nothing if not parochial. 'Strike Baby will be born in God's Own County,' he said when he returned from the car. 'Just a thought: he'll be able to play cricket for Yorkshire.'

Jack and Celia had called to say their goodbyes earlier, brought their little son. He'd crawled around the apartment with Celia in exhausted pursuit.

'We knew you and Guy weren't happy,' Celia said, always the master of the understatement.

'You'll be crossing the house then, Helen?' Jack said with a cheeky grin.

'I'm going home, Jack.'

No mention of a miners' strike or the outcome. Jack talked about the by-election in Guy's constituency; said there was no surprise at his friend's breakdown, seen it coming for months. Had Guy ever had true friends? Maybe Jack had tried his best.

She sealed the last box with sticky tape. Everything packed.

★ ★ ★

March 6th 1985

Lundby South Yorkshire

It was over apart from a mile of boot scuffing marching. Heads held high. And the band would lead them. What worried Pavel most were those men who'd been sacked for nothing more than standing on a picket line and looking the wrong way at a policeman. What chance of other jobs? What hope of paying off debts? He'd been lucky not to have lost his own job after the incident collecting Jake. Of late, sacking had become the norm but on this occasion he'd been let off with a caution.

Jake was coming for tea. What pleasure simple family routines brought. There had to be something to look forward to. Whatever bills were left owing, he was damned sure his first wage packet would go on a trip to London. Sort out this ridiculous situation with Helen. He'd have collected her sooner if he hadn't had to sell his car. She had to finalise the sale and pack up the flat, but how much longer would she need?

He stamped his feet, cleared his throat. In the pocket of his anorak he found two foil-wrapped toffees left over from Jake's Christmas stocking and handed one to Roly. A mixture of breath trails and wisps of smoke hung over the assembling procession, the conversation around them a mumble of resentment with occasional pockets of bravado and bursts of brittle laughter; some men silent, others coughed. Only the Colliery brass band tuning up at the front of the crowd provided distraction.

Roly zipped his coat to his chin. 'Can't believe it's a whole year.'

'I'd do it again, Roly,' Pavel said. 'Wouldn't you?'

Roly ground the heel of his boot, stubbing out a cigarette. 'Yes, but don't ask me to just yet. I've a few bills to pay first.'

Hadn't they all? And the anxiety for jobs that had sparked the dispute was far worse. All they could do was wait.

A few yards to his right, Pavel spotted his mother chatting with Billy and Tibby Farrimond. Billy was a stubborn old goat, just like his niece. If Pavel had been a praying man, he'd beseech God to grant him another chance with Helen, but he reckoned even God would have a problem telling a girl like her what to do.

Pity he'd never met Isaac. A man with a history would have understood the plight.

He noticed, a few rows in front, a miner jabbing a finger across the crowd. Pavel nudged Roly, sighing in the face of likely confrontation.

'His brother's watching outside the newsagents,' Roly said. 'Went back after Christmas. They've already had one punch up.' Some men would be marked as scabs for life. How many would leave the village?

Stories, stories. There would always be stories... and humour: cat and mouse games with police; the Russian cans of food that nobody could identify; the man from the Electricity board whose appearance prompted residents of a local housing estate to build a barricade believing he was on its way to cut off their power when he'd only come to read the meters.

Roly lit another cigarette and drew on it deeply. 'And the most ironic thing, Pav, is that there wasn't a plan to shut Lundby Edge colliery.'

'These families will never forgive. The priority has to be to get the sacked lads their jobs back.'

Billy Farrimond waved. Pavel wondered why the old man looked so cheerful.

★ ★ ★

Tired from the four hour journey on the M1 and from helping Billy and Tibby to empty her belongings from the car, Helen had been left to sleep late. Her aunt had told her they would be supporting the men in the march back to the pit but advised her to stay away.

Helen showered, washed her hair and dressed in a maternity pinafore she'd bought from *Mothercare*. Her size belied more than the confirmed twenty-one weeks. The dress was voluminous and added to her bulk, but nothing else would fit. She put on her winter coat and with no hope of fastening the belt, left it open. She could still run when she had to. And she had to, if she wanted to be there in time. Perhaps it would be wiser to do the Scouts' pace Pavel had once taught her. Twenty runs, twenty walks, heart pounding.

★ ★ ★

'I wish they'd get going,' Roly said. 'I'm glad Kath's at school and not here to watch. Break her heart.'

Pavel waved to two women from the Support Group who were joining the line. Wives hugging each other, women stronger than they were before the strike. They may have been oblivious to the women's movement in the seventies, but now they were emancipated by their men's struggle. Bloodied, but not broken.

'It's hard for them today, Roly,' he said. 'They've given everything.'

A raw wind bit into Pavel's cheeks and he rubbed them. Roly flapped his arms around his chest, jumped up and down. 'I hope it works out for you and Helen, Pavel, even if I did warn you off.'

Pavel laughed. 'If I ever see her again.'

Several young women with pushchairs joined the line.

Here we go, here we go, here we go. Applause.

Pavel thought of Jake. At least he had his son. The worst thing would be the march down the lane where many a midnight frenzy for fuel had thinned out the trees.

The woods and the lake were the only places he'd found any sense of peace in his darker days. When he forged a path through autumn leaves or discovered a flush of wild flowers in summer, even a once-confirmed atheist like

Pavel found it difficult to ignore the possibility of some grand design beyond his comprehension. He'd abandoned atheism and was sitting on the religious fence. He'd burned plenty of fences recently.

The band started in earnest, though he couldn't make out the tune. Someone ahead joined the procession with a placard: 'Our day will come!' He straightened, held his head up, determined to be strong. He could hear Roly beside him, sniffing. Best not look at him. Boots scuffed the tarmac. There were a few final attempts at humour, but then for Pavel, just a sick feeling in his belly. The procession set off; his eyes were on his feet. He recalled how after Jakub died, to put one foot in front of the other was all he could do to proceed down the tunnel at the bottom of the shaft.

He heard his name. It was Gus behind him. 'Hey, Pavel. Summatt you've not told us?'

Pavel glanced over his shoulder, frowned. 'What are you on about?'

Gus nodded across the road. 'Looks like Pav's been doing a bit more than picketing.'

Pavel squinted, made a visor of his hand to obscure a pale sun. What was it the lads could see? Helen. He stopped and the two men behind bumped into him. Roly kneed Pavel out of the line. 'Better sort it.'

Helen ran to him. He kissed her, swung her around.

'Perfect timing, don't you think?' she said.

'Not before time,' Pavel said, holding her close.

Wolf whistles, cheers, laughter. 'Put her down you don't know where she's been, Pav.'

'Think it's obvious where she's been,' Swannie shouted. 'Look at him. He's speechless. Reckon he's blubbing.'

Here we go, here we go, here we go.

As the procession passed, the strains of the band and the chants grew fainter until Helen and Pavel were alone in the middle of the road, holding onto each other.

'Come on. Think you'd better walk with me or I'll be late for work,' he said.

Here we go, here we go, here we go.

They followed the procession towards the pit lane, passing the last few women still watching: women who picked up empty shopping bags, wiped away tears on fringed knotted headscarves, headed for the supermarket or just went home.

Epilogue

April 2014

East Yorkshire Coast

After a winter of storms has ravaged the coastline, fractured railway lines and turned lowlands into lakes, Pavel is surprised by an unexpected lull in the weather – a warm spring day. The family has walked the length of the promenade, around two bays, Pavel telling his twin grandsons the story of a Victorian shipwreck.

He is resting on a bench, his daughter Luiza beside him. On the beach below, the four year old boys are etching stick figures in the sand, watched by their father, Jake.

'Mum loved this seaside stuff, didn't she?' Luiza says. 'Candyfloss and sand castles, picnics and funfairs. She made us excited about day trips.'

'This was her favourite beach,' Pavel says. 'It's where she taught me to waltz,'

Luiza laughs. 'No wonder you can't dance.'

'Your mother thought that once you reached sixty you could be taken captive by nostalgia if you weren't careful. I'm surrounded by memories here.'

'That's why she insisted you had a smart phone and an iPad. Keep you up to date with the movers and shakers.'

Pavel smiles. 'Not sure about the shakers but I'm certainly kept busy with lecturing and local party work. You have to stay positive with students... and voters.'

His grandsons ride by on plodding donkeys; reins jingle. 'Those boys don't allow me time to mope.'

Gulls circle, caw, glide and swoop; beaks snatch at discarded ice-cream cones, a half-eaten sandwich tossed from a pushchair, a fragment of sugared doughnut on the seawall. A young couple stroll barefoot, stop, kiss.

Pavel swallows. 'And getting involved with your documentary helped me, Lu. Gave me focus. It's good to meet up with old mates.'

Robbie, Gus, Swannie. Roly has always been there: a hand on the shoulder.

'The camaraderie we had in the pits... well, friendship like that doesn't come along often.'

History. Memories. Raw grief. Gut wrenching loss. Irrevocability. Emotions reel with the gulls and kittiwakes.

'All lost to history,' Pavel says.

'Nothing's lost, Dad. No experience is wasted Mum said. Almost everyone we interviewed about the strike agreed they'd do it again.'

'I suppose we have to stand up and be counted at some time in our lives.'

'And, unlike some miners, you were lucky. You had a second chance.'

'I was lucky: I married Helen Farrimond.' He laughs, bites his lip.

Luiza squeezes his hand. 'We have to do this,' she says. 'It's over a year. You've waited too long already.'

'I know. I owe her some bravery at least. I promised. It's helped having you home while you've been filming.' He's touched that Luiza used a little of his testimony as voice over to the final credits – a plea for all governments to respect community – and proud to see her work televised to mark thirty years since the strike.

He stands, leans against the promenade railings, watching white horses wash over the shingle. Luiza joins him. 'When your uncle Jakub died I could see no future,' Pavel says, 'no shape to anything. Now wherever I look I see...' He hesitates, searches for words... 'pattern? Purpose?... Maybe. Some days I feel her around me. You'll think I'm mad: I find myself reading snippets from the newspaper to her over the breakfast table as if...'

Luiza rubs her father's shoulder. 'Mum will appreciate it.'

They watch as a sleek gannet from a nearby cliff-sanctuary dips, folds its wings and arrow-like dives into the sea in a flash of yellow.

Luiza glances at her watch. 'Come on. We'd better go. And don't tell me I should wait here.' She retrieves the canvas bag she earlier stowed beneath the bench.

'I wouldn't dare.'

'Granddad.' The boys are calling. The donkey ride has ended. 'Come and help us build a sand-car.'

'I'll be there soon,' Pavel shouts. 'Get started on a Ferrari.'

Jake laughs and looks up to the promenade. 'Great. Thanks for that, Dad. Nothing like ambition, is there? In that case I'll wait for you before I start digging.'

Pavel takes the bag from Luiza and they make their way south for a half-mile, through a cacophony of amusement park pop-music and down to the harbour, where a man with a speed boat is waiting. The man nods, tugs a denim cap over his forehead, dons sunglasses. He steadies the boat with one foot, helping them aboard as the boat rocks in flotsam and patches of oil. The engine splutters and chugs, filling their nostrils with diesel fumes, snagging their throats.

As soon as they've rounded the harbour beacon, they speed north past deck chairs, wind-breaks, donkeys and kiosks, past Ferris wheel and dodgems; bouncing across the bay, spray in their faces. When the boat is opposite the chalky beach – where Jake and the twins have embarked on a game of skimming pebbles – Pavel shouts. 'Okay. Stop here.' The man cuts the engine and the boat bobs in blue-jade swell.

'Let me help,' Luiza says.

Pavel lifts a box from the bag, scoops out a handful of ash and allows it to flow between his fingers over the edge of the boat. Luiza takes the box from him, empties it swiftly as if to cut short his pain. The boat man, who has until now averted his eyes, turns. 'You okay, mate?'

Pavel smiles. 'I'll be fine. Just give me a minute.'

The boat rocks, circles, drifts through a panorama of lazing day trippers, luminous white cliffs and pastel-painted huts. Pavel trails a hand through the water, watching the ash as it floats on the choppy surface then sinks. The horizon blurs. He wipes his eyes with the cuff of his shirt.

'Let's go,' he says. 'My grandsons are waiting.'